The Race for Second

Chase Potter

CHASE POTTER BOOKS
www.chasepotter.com

The Race for Second
Copyright © 2014 Chase Potter

ISBN-10: 0615982603
ISBN-13: 978-0615982601

Für Josh und Tim,
ohne die mein Austauschjahr
nicht dasselbe gewesen wäre.

ACKNOWLEDGEMENTS

It was a little over fourteen months from the Saturday afternoon in late November 2012 when I began writing to the day I finally made the last changes to this story. But this novel has been much longer in the making. Every life lesson accumulated over my twenty-five years has contributed in one way or another. In my mind, these experiences are stacked together like books on a shelf, each telling a different story that helped me to create this one.

The great number of friends and family who stuck with me along the way have helped *The Race for Second* become more than I ever hoped it could be, I'd like to wish a sincere thank you:

To my husband, Mitchell, for so many things, but above all his patience, without which I would never have finished the first draft. I love you, always.

To my friends, Josh Tebbutt, Darrin Rahn, Russell Dahlke, Kathryn Lawson, and Lauren Piper, all who suffered through early drafts and offered encouragement and suggestions. I'd like to specifically credit Russell for helping develop Ethan's Diagono into so much more than just a timepiece.

To my sixth grade English teacher, Gary Johnson, who taught me more about writing than I learned in four years of college, and whose boundless faith in my abilities gave me the courage to do this.

To my parents, Norman and Jeanne Ellig, for their unwavering support through the years, even when my path has taken me to places that are hard for them to understand.

To my grandma Deloris, who was always so excited to hear updates as this book progressed but didn't live long enough to see it in print. And lastly, to my grandpa Bill, who has always been a role model to me, and who I hope can find merit in this story.

Chapter 1

"No one gives a shit about history, Ethan." The words sting even though I've heard them a dozen times from him. "And I definitely don't get why you need to go to some foreign university to learn more about it."

"It's important to me, okay?" It was a bad idea to let him come over while I packed, but he insisted.

"Whatever," he says, throwing himself onto my bed in momentary defeat.

"Corey, you're lying on clean clothes." He rolls onto his side and throws a wad of white cotton socks at me. They fan out in flight, so I have to pick them up off the floor. Stuffing them into the large traveling backpack at my feet, I turn back to my dresser to get the rest of the socks.

His brooding eyes bore into the back of my head. "You could go for a May or summer term instead, then you'd only be gone for a month or two."

"Why are you still trying to talk me out of going?" I snap. "I'm leaving *tomorrow*."

I expect Corey to get pissed, but his expression is filled only with resignation. His tone softens. "I just don't want you to go. We've been together three months, and it's like you don't even care." Like an iceberg hidden beneath the surface, there's a whole lot more behind his words. Things we should have gotten out a long time ago but never did.

Sighing, I slump to a seat on the edge of the bed. How do I tell him that those three months haven't meant to me what they do to him? We were each other's firsts. First boyfriends, and first time being *with* another guy—for both of us. Except I never felt like Corey did, and in the back of my mind, I always knew it was going to end.

"I do care," I say. It's not a lie, but it's also not entirely the truth. "I just need to do this." I'm not leaving the country to get away from him, but it sure makes it a lot easier.

"Why do you have to go for so long, though? It's going to be a pain in the ass to do the long distance thing for a whole year. I don't even know if I can afford a plane ticket to visit you." He sounds pensive, even vulnerable.

We should have discussed this before now, but after so many fights that always ended the same way—at an impasse with me emotionally exhausted—I've been purposely avoiding it. "I think a year is too long for us," I say quietly.

"What are you saying?" His voice wavers nervously.

No way to sugarcoat this now. "I think we should break up."

Tears well up in his eyes. "You are not breaking up with me right now." He jumps up from the bed. "Screw you, Ethan," the words catch in his throat, and a sorrowful glare cuts into me.

For all the arguments that ended with me kicking him out, this time he leaves without a fight. A pang of regret hits me in the chest as he walks out of my room and my life. Not because we should stay together, but because I feel bad for hurting him. We had some good times—a lot actually—but I won't miss his testiness and short temper. No, it's time to move on.

Outside the tiny oval window, the sun creeps above the sea of clouds on which we're sailing. The speakers crackle as the pilot picks up the cockpit microphone. "*Guten Morgen, meine Damen und Herren. In ungefähr drei Stunden erreichen wir Frankfurt Flughafen . . .*" I understand a lot of it, mostly because pilot announcements are pretty predictable. Once he's done in German, he repeats in accented English, "Good Morning, ladies and gentleman. In approximately three hours we will arrive at Frankfurt International Airport, at twelve-thirty local time."

I push away the memory of the previous day breaking up with Corey. My adventure is about to begin. Until then, a few more hours in this cramped flying machine remain, so I curl into the gray plastic cabin lining as it curves around the window. The cold at thirty thousand feet pierces through the fuselage wall, and I tug my white hoodie closer around me to ward it away.

When my eyes flutter open, the sun is out of sight high above, bathing both the plane's wings and the land below with brilliant daylight. We're still several thousand feet up, but the descent must have already begun, because my stomach is tingling.

The patchwork of farms and fields below has turned the land into a sprawling quilt, stitched by roads and punctuated at irregular intervals by little towns. There's something strange about the towns, but it takes me a minute to realize what it is. It's almost too far to see, but not a single one is built on a grid. Streets and alleys roam in random directions with no right angles and no rectangular blocks.

Soon we've descended even farther, and I can see cars moving on the roads. Even lower now and the larger branches of the trees become visible, lower yet and the runway is below us. A brief wave of nausea catches me off guard as the rear of the plane dips downward, reaching out to touch the earth. The wheels make contact and our smooth flight turns gravelly. Fingers tightening around the armrest, I close my eyes and force myself to take steady, even breaths until the plane's rumble on the runway quiets to the soft sound of taxiing.

I'm just about to start my sophomore year in college, and I've never been to another country. Not before today, anyway. I've always wanted to study abroad, but now that it's finally here, I'm not sure how to feel. Will I think back on this as the moment my year overseas officially started?

I'm also not sure if I'm ready to live here for a whole year, but I hope so. Mom kept telling me not to forget that "it's not America," which is possibly the worst advice she's ever given me. Of course it isn't America. If it were, it wouldn't be studying abroad.

Mom would never say it, but she doubts that I've got what it takes to do this. I'm not worried. I've been waiting too long for this chance to let this place beat me. But really it doesn't matter whether she's right or not, because my return flight is eleven months from now, and there's nothing extra to buy a new ticket with.

I have a scholarship from my school back home, the University of Minnesota, but it only covers tuition. Somehow I managed to convince Mom that I needed to do this, so together we saved for the last year to afford it.

My stomach is still upset from the landing, but we're almost to the gate now. Eyes glued to the window, I absorb every detail I can of this new place, hovering between excitement and trepidation for what's waiting for me beyond the airport. Somewhere out there is the place that will become my home.

The straps of my traveling backpack are digging into my shoulders, and the muscles in my calves burn from hauling its weight all day. With the sun glinting over the treetops, I finally breathe a sigh of relief. I've just gotten my key from the *Hausmeister*, the caretaker of the student dorms.

Around me the buildings of the student colony stretch toward the sky, every one bearing the same pale tan color of the little stones embedded in their concrete façades. Every structure is rectangular and of varying heights, making me feel like an ant skittering through a child's set of wooden blocks. The air is warm but as a breeze brushes against my neck, a shiver slides down my back.

As I cross the colony, following the map given to me by the Hausmeister, the sun dips just behind the trees dotted between the various buildings. My eyes jump from one example of brutalist architecture to the next. They seem out of place, forced to find an ungainly spot for themselves between modernity and the pristinely authentic wooden homes and cobblestone streets of the villages my train passed through on the way here.

The front door of building 52 is wide and painted dark red. The key clutched against my sweaty palm, my eyes aim upward to appraise the building. It's only three stories, and balconies protrude from the second and third floors, with long tables and chairs packed onto both of them. I turn the key over in my hand, noticing that just like the door it goes to, it's unusually wide.

Despite its odd appearance, the key slides into the weathered lock with ease. A long hall stretches out before me with late afternoon light drifting in at the far end. It's cool down here. Stone floor tiles and white concrete walls lead to a staircase made of steel and stone that's solid as hell. Whenever they built this place, probably in the '70s, they certainly weren't lacking sturdy building materials.

The Hausmeister assigned me to room number one on the second story. At least I think that's what he said, but it was hard to understand his rural dialect. In any case, in German, "second story" really refers to the third floor.

My room is right at the top of the stairs. Curiosity tiptoes through me. This is where I'll spend the next year of my life. Everything is still unfamiliar, but I will eventually walk these stairs hundreds of times over. What will this place feel like then? Dropping my backpack in front of the door, I wander down the hallway.

Another three doors with room numbers just like mine are on the left, while a door on the opposite wall opens to the shared bathroom. Every bedroom door except mine has a mat with shoes in front, so they must all be occupied. At the far end of the hall is another closed door. I bite my lip, debating whether to just go in. It has to be the kitchen.

Easing the door open, I peek inside. It's quiet and the room is empty, but it's the kitchen all right—two small refrigerators stand across from each other like they're keeping watch over whatever happens here. Between them is a stove built into a center kitchen island, and at the end of the room is an impressively stacked mound of dirty dishes beside a single sink likewise filled to the brim.

An itching feeling in the back of my mind makes me glance over my shoulder toward the balcony. On the couch is a guy staring at me. He's wearing a blue v-neck tee and khaki shorts riding up above his knees a few inches. His face is clean-shaven with a defined jawline.

With light olive skin and thick, short brown hair, he doesn't look very German. He's stretched out on the couch with a textbook in his lap, but his dark eyes, a mixture of blue and gray, are looking right back at me. He's wearing a curious expression like he's not sure what he's seeing.

"Hi." I venture an awkward smile.

"*Was tust du hier?*"

The initial shock of finding him staring at me hasn't quite worn off. My mind rushes to translate after the fact. *What are you doing here?* "Um," I say, mentally switching into German. I pause, struggling to find the words to explain. "I . . . um, just moved in. I mean, I'm about to."

His expression seems to harden as I stumble over the language. "You're American," he says bluntly. "Are you sure you have the right place? Let me see your papers."

Swallowing my apprehension, I take a step toward him and hold out the lease document with the map from my back pocket. "This is the paper from the Hausmeister." I'm pretty damn sure this is my building. The key worked on the door, so it has to be, right?

Sitting up, he balances his book on the armrest and takes the paper. His eyes travel quickly over the page. "You're in room number one," he says, flicking his gaze back to me.

"Yeah, I know."

The muscles in his forehead tighten as he stares at me. They must not get new roommates very often here. "I'm Ethan," I introduce myself, holding my hand out. Germans are big on shaking hands I think. Instead of taking it, he places the paper in my outstretched hand. I stare at him.

"Do you need something else?" His book is still precariously balanced on the edge of the couch.

I swallow, my face growing hot. "Um, no." I knew living here was going to be an adjustment, there was never any question about that. The hard part was supposed to be the language though, not getting along with my roommates. Taking a deep breath, I leave him alone in the kitchen to take my first look at where I'm going to be living.

The door to number one is heavy like the kitchen door and shuts with a solid click behind me. The room is small and the bed looks like a barracks cot, but the window is huge and square and even now light is pouring into the room. I drop the backpack by the wall and sit down on the bed. I've met rocks that were softer than this. With only the bed and a wooden desk and chair, it feels barren. A rug and a plant or something might give it some life.

A full-length mirror spans the height of the door. If I lean forward from the bed I can just see myself in it. Standing up, I set myself in front of the mirror. I look like hell from all the traveling. My light brown hair is matted and there are dark circles under my eyes. Sometimes I break out when going on trips, but at least my skin is clear.

I've always wished I were taller. One more inch and I'd be five foot ten. That would be okay. Mom used to joke that if she'd fed me more as a toddler, then I would have ended up a little taller. I never thought that was funny. Especially because it might actually be true. We never had much money, even before my dad left.

I haven't changed clothes since I left the States, so my shirt is starting to smell a little sour. I peel it off and toss it into the corner. Running a hand across my chest, I pause at a few stray hairs in the middle. I'll take the razor to them later. If there's any reason to be glad about my height, it's that I'm proportionally well built. There are those skinny tall kids who are all arms and legs, but I'm not like that.

After digging through my backpack for a pair of shorts and a t-shirt, I change into clean clothes. I still don't smell that great, but at least it's covered up for now. A sound from the hall makes me stop and listen. Footsteps, followed by low voices talking, and finally light laughter. Another door shuts and then there's only silence. Straining to hear anything else, I'm abruptly mauled by hunger.

My heart thrums as I walk down the hall toward the kitchen for a second time. All of my roommates can't be like that first guy I met. At least I hope not. Through the door I can hear someone moving around and the sputtering of hot oil. Steeling myself, I open the door. A young woman who looks just a few years older than me is at the stove. She stops mid-stir when she sees me. "Hi," she says, her thin face and sharp eyes focused on me.

"Hey."

She looks like she's not sure what to make of me. Then in a moment of realization, her expression brightens. "Oh my goodness, did you just move in?"

"Yeah," I say, giving her a tentative smile.

"Welcome to floor two. You're going to love it here. What's your name? My name's Paula."

"Um," I say, "I'm Ethan."

"This is my third year here, but I love it. That makes me sound kind of old, doesn't it?" She pauses to take a breath. "I guess I kind of am. I'm twenty-five. Is that old?"

I have to force down a grin. "No, not old at all."

"How old are you?" Her enthusiasm must be settling down a bit because she's started stirring the ground beef in the pan again.

"Nineteen." I don't know what she's cooking, but my stomach rumbles noisily.

"Oh you're so young! American exchange students always are, it seems," she muses.

Is it really so easy to tell I'm American? I hope not.

"Well," she says, "Are you going to help out? You look hungry."

"That sounds like an . . . uh," I struggle to remember the right German word, "invitation to dinner."

"It is if you help me shred cheese and cut up veggies." She winks at me and nods her head toward a block of cheese and three tomatoes on the counter. "We're making tacos, if you hadn't guessed."

Eager to make a good impression with at least one of my room-mates, I oblige and start in on the tomatoes. I've just sliced through the last one when a guy I don't recognize comes in off the balcony.

"Food almost ready?" Gesturing casually at me with an empty beer bottle, he asks, "And who's this?"

"He's our new roommate," she beams. "His name is Ethan."

"Hi Ethan, I'm Florian." He's got a thin beard and light curly hair that's just starting to touch his ears.

I quickly wipe my hands on my shorts and shake his outstretched hand. "Nice to meet you."

"Likewise," he says, opening the door to the fridge. "Ethan, you want a beer?"

Actually that sounds great. "Sure." It's weird to think that yesterday I was two years away from being old enough to drink; now I've been legal for three years.

"Aren't those Daniel's?" Paula chides playfully.

"He won't care." Handing me a beer, he takes two more out and heads back to the balcony.

I take a long swig. "Who's Daniel?"

Paula looks up from the pan where she's warming tortilla shells. "He's our other roommate. He's nice, you'll like him." *Oh really?*

"Do you guys always cook together?"

"Just once a week on Thursday. It's just kind of a fun thing we do."

Laughter drifts in from the balcony. "You're all pretty good friends then?"

"More so some days than others," she jokes. Turning more serious as she dumps the ground beef into a serving bowl, she explains, "Yeah, we're all friends. Florian and Daniel are closer though. Must be a guy thing." Surveying the counter, she claps her hands together. "Alright, ready to eat?"

"Definitely." I carry the plate of tortillas and my beer while Paula somehow manages to get everything else balanced on her hands and forearms.

A narrow table runs down the center of the balcony, with benches on either side. Sitting beside Florian is the guy I met earlier on the couch. I can feel his gaze on me from the moment I set the plate of tortillas on the table.

"Daniel, this is Ethan. He's our new roommate," Paula introduces us. His eyes snap to the beer in my hand, and I feel my ears get hot.

"Actually," I say, "we kind of already met."

"Really?" Florian asks. "Why didn't you mention anything?" He directs this question at Daniel.

"Must have slipped my mind," he responds, eyeing the table.

Florian glances from Daniel to me. "Ah, I see. Well, let's eat."

The tacos are amazing, and both Paula and Florian keep the conversation going, including me wherever they can. Daniel though, remains mostly silent except when asked a direct question.

Eating with my new roommates, beer in hand, I realize this is exactly how I hoped my first night in Germany would be. Well, almost anyway.

Cupping both hands under my crumbling taco, I lean over my plate so I don't make a mess. Liquid from the meat is dribbling out the end of the tortilla and down my fingers when an itch of intuition makes me glance up. Daniel's dark blue eyes shift away the second we make contact, but not before I detect the threads of curiosity laced through his gaze.

We've only just finished eating when Daniel stands up.

"Leaving already?" Paula sets down her fork and gives him an accusatory glance.

"I've got homework to do. See you guys later." He stares at us for an awkward moment before he leaves.

After a long minute, Florian suggests, "Paula and I can clean up. I'm sure you're tired after all that traveling today."

He doesn't need to tell me twice. "Yeah, I am actually. Thanks for dinner."

"Have a good night," Paula calls after me. "Sleep tight and sweet dreams, Ethan!"

I'm tired, but it still takes me a long time to fall asleep. I like Paula, and Florian is nice enough too. He and Daniel were definitely laughing and having a good time before I went out on the balcony, so he's clearly not so distant with everyone. Maybe it just takes a while for him to warm up to new roommates.

Chapter 2

The next day I head into town before any of my roommates wake up. Normally I'm not a morning person, but jet lag has had me up since 5 A.M. I tried to fall back asleep for a while but eventually gave in and got up to shower.

Nestled in a star shaped valley, the university town of Freiburg and its sprawling offshoots are connected by the *Strassenbahn* network of trams. Luckily there's a stop right outside the dorms.

Most of the seats are full, so instead of squeezing in next to someone, I find a spot to stand by the door. The brushed metal handhold is warm under my sweaty palm. As the tram takes off, my grip tightens. Greenery flies past, gradually transforming into infrastructure as we enter the city. My eyes keep darting to the map to make sure I don't miss my stop.

Armed with my passport, I hop off right at the center of town and follow the signs toward the university office. I was too stressed yesterday to pay attention, so today, under the full southern German sun, is my first chance to see what Freiburg is really like. Roughly hewn square cobblestones cover every square foot of the university and the *Altstadt*, the old town, which has been the heart of the city since medieval times. At least that's what I read on a plaque. It's easy to believe though. The buildings here are far older than anything back in Minnesota, and the streets are narrower.

On the ride in, I saw plenty of cars, but here in the Altstadt there isn't a single one. Without them, the morning is quiet apart from the occasional Strassenbahn rumbling past and the bustle of people heading to work.

Stepping to the side of the stream of pedestrians moving through the university square, I take a moment to appreciate that I'm finally here. All the planning, the hours spent convincing my mom, and the fights with Corey—it was all worth it, because now I'm here, and it's real. The sun is warm on my face, so I have to squint to see the last sign for the university office just ahead. Taking a deep breath, I step inside.

Four hours later and I've just gotten everything sorted out. I was halfway done with my paperwork for enrolling at the university when they realized I didn't have my visa yet. So I had to go to the *Ausländeramt* on the other side of town to finish my visa application and have it pasted into my passport. After that, I trekked back to the university to finish the paperwork. Long lines in both places drew out the hours. The scary thing is, I have the feeling I only got a taste of German bureaucracy today.

While I wait for the Strassenbahn to take me home, the sound of shouting drifts down the track, only audible when a lull in the noise of the city permits me to catch a few seconds of raised voices. Staring down the street toward the south, I can just make out a group of people walking in a circle. They're shouting and holding big yellow signs with an image of a shopping cart on them. I have no idea what their placards are supposed to mean, and it's too far to hear what they're saying. Probably nothing interesting anyway. Welcome to Europe, the land of endless protests.

After finishing the sandwich I made myself for lunch, I set my plate at the top of the stack of dirty dishes in the sink. As it turns out, when Florian and Paula offered to clean up last night, they just meant carrying everything to the sink.

I'm staring at the sprawl of dishes that must stretch back at least a week when the door from the hallway opens. "Hey Ethan."

I turn to see Florian. "Oh, hey. What are you up to today?"

"Working on my thesis," he sighs, extracting a bottle of water from the refrigerator and taking a seat on the couch with a laptop.

I wonder if it's a master's thesis. He seems too old to be an undergrad. I'm pretty sure that all of my roommates are older than me. If I had done my year abroad during my junior year, I would be a year older, but even then I'd only be twenty.

When I ask Florian why that is, he speaks to me in English for the first time. "You know, Ethan, we have thirteen years of school, and after that we make a year of *Zivildienst* . . . civil, uh, service." He must be proud of his English, because his grin is so wide it practically touches the tips of his ears.

"What kind of civil service?" I reply in German, lifting the faucet handle and turning it toward hot.

He follows me back into his native language. "You can either do six months of *Militärdienst*, military service, or a full year of Zivildienst. For Zivildienst, it's things like volunteering in a hospital or working at a youth center." He leans back into the couch and watches me flick my finger under the water. It's not quite hot yet.

"What did you do for your service?" I can't imagine the chipper Florian serving in the military. Heaving stacks of dishes out of the sink and onto the counter, I plug the drain and the water level begins to rise.

Florian glances away, mumbling his answer just as Paula comes into the kitchen, followed by her mop of mousy hair. "Well boys, what are you up to?"

Squirting a line of soap into the water, I say, "Dishes."

She flits around the center island and peers into the sink. "Dishes?" Her voice soars in pitch. "Why would you do dishes?"

I shrug and submerge a stack of bowls, separating them first to toss a splash of soapy water over each. "I don't mind actually. It's kind of relaxing."

She raises an eyebrow but shifts her attention to Florian. "And you Flori, what about you?"

"We're discussing . . . Germany."

Not letting him off the hook that easily, I explain, "He was about to say what he did for Zivildienst."

Paula leans over the island on her elbows toward Florian, "Oooh," she croons. "Well?" she stares pointedly at him. "*Zugeben*."

"What does that mean?"

I turn back to the dishes but feel her gaze on me. From the corner of my eye, I can just see her put a finger to her chin. "Mmm," she pauses, "*Admit*, that's the English word for it."

"Admit what?" I repeat the word I've just learned to help me remember it.

"He doesn't like to say what he did for Zivildienst."

"What was it?" I don't turn to face them, because I'm scouring a bit of granola cemented to a bowl with dried out milk.

Florian mumbles something that again I don't catch.

"Louder, Florian, louder," Paula laughs, slapping her hand on the stove in emphasis.

"Alright, alright. I was an ambulance driver."

I'm about to ask what's wrong with that when an image of him behind the wheel, hair bouncing and a goofy expression on his face pops into my mind, and I burst out laughing.

"Yeah, I get that a lot."

From behind, I hear the sound of the door opening yet again. Since three of us are already here, there's only one possibility of who it is, but I turn to look anyway.

"Afternoon, Daniel," Florian says, risking a quick look at me. "How's it going?"

"Fine. I just got back from the grocery store." He's hard to understand, because he talks so fast that his words run together. Slipping the backpack from his shoulder, he sets it on the counter next to me and begins to unload it into his cupboard. I steal the opportunity to give him an up-down glance. A few inches taller than me, he has muscle tone too. He's wearing a white t-shirt that looks a little small for him.

There's no use in letting myself be intimidated by him. "Hey," I venture.

He stops what he's doing, his fingers tight around the box of pasta in his hand. Turning his head ever so slightly toward me, he eyes me. "Hey," he says, stuffing the pasta into the cupboard.

I stare at the tiled backsplash, waiting to see if he'll say anything else. He empties out the rest of his bag and slings it back over his shoulder.

"Why don't you stick around?" Paula says. "We're getting to know Ethan."

"No, thanks, I've got things to do," he responds from the doorway. Then he speaks again, but it's so fast that I can't be sure what he says. The only words I can make out are "at least" and "cleans."

My hands hover motionless above the soapy water, and my heart pounds. I venture a look behind me, the three of them staring at one another. Florian looks confused. Paula is giving Daniel a dirty look and holding the door open for him. "Out," she says. Her voice isn't angry, but there's no doubt she's serious.

"See you later," Daniel says. I have the distinct impression he's only referring to Florian and Paula.

Once he's gone, I ask, "What did he say?"

The two of them exchange another look, but Paula speaks first. "He just said he was glad that you like to clean, since none of us do."

"It didn't sound like that."

She smiles halfheartedly. "He can be a bit prickly sometimes."

Sometimes? I haven't finished with the dishes, but I pull out the stopper and the water drains, gurgling as it disappears. "I think I'm done." Drying my hands on my jeans, I walk out the open door, leaving Paula and Florian staring after me.

It's almost 10 P.M., and jet lag is starting to kick my ass again. I'm in the bathroom that's barely bigger than a phone booth, brushing my teeth with my free arm braced on the pedestal sink. I examine my eyes in the mirror, trying to see if I can find the source of those hazy shapes that occasionally float across my vision. They're like pieces of dust on my corneas, but trying to focus on them just sends them darting away.

That's when the reflection of Daniel appears out of nowhere, heading straight for me. "Whoa, sorry!" he shouts, catching himself on the doorframe at the last possible moment before he would actually barrel into me. "I didn't think anyone was in here."

I try to tell him it's no problem, but toothpaste in my mouth reduces the words to muffled noises.

"Huh?" he says, his hands fumbling at his waist. My eyes snap down to the open fly that he's quickly trying to close up, his boxers showing briefly. He must really have to piss if he already had his zipper open by the time he plowed in here. At the same moment he notices me staring at his crotch; I nearly choke on the frothy ball of spit and toothpaste in my mouth. Spinning around, I spit into the sink before I end up sputtering toothpaste all over both of us.

Rinsing my mouth out, I turn and say, "Don't worry about it." But he's not standing behind me. Leaning into the hallway, I scan its length, but he isn't there either. Damn. Now he's caught me staring at his crotch. I'm sure *that's* going to improve his opinion of me. I slog back to my room and throw myself onto the bed with a groan.

*   *   *

On Monday, the *Sprachkurs*, a month-long intensive language course, begins for all of the exchange students. They make us take a test first to split us into different classes based on the results. Most of the questions are pretty easy, but they become progressively harder, and by the end the questions about conditional tense and subjunctive "mood" start to trip me up. I'm in the middle of butchering question 113—*Translate the following sentence into German: The patient's life could have been saved, had he been immediately operated upon.*—when the buzzer goes off.

The first real day of class begins on Tuesday, and we're each assigned to our own group of twelve to fifteen students. Despite the difficulty of the test, I must not have done too badly, because I get placed in one of the advanced classes. I thought my German wasn't that great, but apparently it's pretty good, at least compared to the other exchange students. Our teacher, Frau Schmidt, is an imposing woman built like a tank, but she's actually pretty nice. Class starts at nine every morning and gets done by two, so I can't complain about the hours.

Everyone is pretty quiet, but I'm getting to know two French students who sit at my table, Bastien and Corinne. Bastien is tall with thick black hair. He's good looking, I guess, but he's just so *big*. He must be six foot five. Corinne on the other hand, is petite and blonde. She's quiet, so we haven't talked much, but I'm working on her.

At the end of our first week, Frau Schmidt gives me the perfect excuse to make a connection with Daniel and smooth out our rocky start. She explains that we all need to find a *Tandempartner* to practice German with. Basically, we find someone who is interested in learning our native language and is fluent in German. Meeting weekly, we spend a half hour speaking one language, and then switch to the other for the second half of the time. So we learn each other's languages in tandem. Tandempartner. Makes sense.

Frau Schmidt told us that we could either find a Tandempartner or go to the language lab for three hours a week. It might not sound bad, but the same day she also gave us a tour of the language lab, and I'll be damned if I'm going to fool around on some ancient computer for hours and pretend to learn German from audio disks straight out of East Germany. Besides, the idea of a Tandempartner actually sounds like fun.

*   *   *

As soon as I hop off the Strassenbahn, I march to my dorm and straight up to Daniel's room without stopping to drop off my bag. I know Paula and Florian are both busy working on their thesis papers, but I'm pretty sure Daniel doesn't have class right now. I knock three quick times on his door. It's kind of a long shot, but since we live together, I feel like I should make a legitimate effort to find a connection with him. Who knows, maybe this will even be the thing that lets us become friends.

"Hey," he says, pulling on a t-shirt as he opens the door. "Do you need something?" Between the cool greeting and his partial state of undress a moment ago, I lose all track of the words I rehearsed to say. "I . . . um . . . in our *Sprachkurs*, we are supposed to . . . to get a Tandempartner." God, he must think I can't speak German to save my life. "To . . . uh, get more practice speaking German, and we can then speak English afterward, if you want," I finish with a flourish. Finally I managed to get something to come out right.

He's eyeing me with that same look, like he's not sure what he's actually seeing. Then something shifts in his expression and before he even starts to speak, I know he's going to say no. "I don't really have time for a tandem, and," he pauses, still examining me. "And I don't speak enough English for that to work."

I nod, staring at the ground and struggling to conceal my frustration. "Oh . . . okay. I just thought I'd ask." My voice is flat. "Thanks anyway." One last time I raise my eyes to meet his. Apparently I didn't do a very good job at hiding my reaction, because a muscle in his jaw clenches and he's got this rueful look like he's just hit a puppy. Whoops.

I walk slowly back to my room after he shuts his door. Whatever, I hope he feels bad about it. He's a jerk. And as for his English, it's obviously not a requirement that we spend time speaking English. Frau Schmidt couldn't care less about that. It's more of an incentive for the German speaker to do the tandem, because they all love to practice their English. But he said no, which means three hours a week in the language lab for me, damn it.

Chapter 3

The Sprachkurs trundles along through the first week, and it turns out it's not so easy to turn my in-class friendships into connections outside. Bastien and Corinne, the pair of Frenchies, are nice, but they have an irritating habit of switching into French for clarification whenever they aren't sure about something. They do agree to get a beer after class on Friday afternoon. The moment they say yes, a warm elation blooms in my chest. It will be good to spend a few extra hours away from my room.

We're at one of Freiburg's many *Kneipe*, tiny bars that dot the city and often have patios or just tables and chairs out on the sidewalk. The air is warm, but the cars passing are too loud. Most of the Altstadt had cars banned from it thirty years ago, but we're on the edge where they're still allowed. I shift in my chair to position a tree between myself and the afternoon sun.

"Danke," Bastien tells the waiter as he delivers our beers. His accent makes it sound like he's trying to smooth out the German, but of course German doesn't go that way. Corinne thanks the waiter too, though her accent is more staccato and sounds less like she's trying to force the words into a silky French box.

The second day of class, I asked Bastien about her accent. They're both French, but hers is definitely different. He laughed, surprised that I'd noticed. "She's from Alsace," he explained, indicating the province just over the French border to the west of Freiburg. Leaning in conspiratorially, he whispered, "Alsace isn't really France. Even their French sounds like German. Very different from Parisian French, *trés différent*," he finished.

I'm not about to tell Corinne what Bastien said about Alsace, but I'm curious to know more about her, so I ask, "You're from Strasbourg, right?"

She nods, setting down her beer and quickly swallowing so she can speak. "Yes, well, I go to university there. I'm actually from Colmar."

I have no idea where that is, so I nod politely. "Cool. Why did you decide to learn German?"

"Ohhh," she draws out the word, accentuating her Frenchness. "My grandparents spoke German."

Bastien gives me a knowing look. "Alsace was traded between France and Germany like three or five times in the last hundred years. Most people have both nationalities in their family." He finishes with a grin, proud of himself for being so knowledgeable. By Parisian standards, he probably is.

Corinne fires back at him in French, apparently irritated about what he said. Or maybe how he said it. While they bicker in French, I shift my gaze to the River Dreisam gurgling along on the other side of the street. The sun has slid a little lower in the sky, and its rays, cut by the trees above into slivers of shadow and light, flicker over my face. I scoot my chair over a little farther to put the tree trunk back in between me and the sun.

We finish our beers and they want to go, but I tell them I'm going to stay in town for a while longer. They just live on the other side of the little lake behind my dorm, so I could go with them, but I'm not ready to leave yet. I watch them walk toward the Strassenbahn stop, but as they disappear around the corner, I turn toward the river. Waiting for a break in the cars, I skip across the street and step up to the stone balustrade railing running along the sidewalk. Swinging my legs over the wide ledge, I plant my butt on the stone and let my legs dangle in the air. Late afternoon light plays off the water as it jostles down the river.

Even though I was just with friends, I can't shake a feeling of loneliness. At the end of every day, I really am alone here. No family, no old friends. It's as though the time I do spend with acquaintances and new friends here serves only to fill the hours between the moments when I return to being by myself, an ocean away from everything familiar.

I stare into the water, letting the minutes slip past. There isn't anything waiting for me at my dorm room except my laptop and a few hours until bed, so I might as well spend my time here. Occasionally my eyes wander to the street and the German university students still enjoying their summer break, walking in bunches and chatting. I think I see Daniel, but when I look back, it's not him. The guy notices me staring and gives me a confused look, so I drop my gaze.

Pressing my open palms against the gritty ledge, I allow my breathing to slow. Behind me, the sounds of the cars grow more distant. In turn, the mild summer air and the rippling water and the light filtering through my closed eyelids fill my senses. The stone beneath me is my anchor, without which I might drift away.

I stay until the alcohol tingling in my fingertips has faded, and my mouth feels dry. Hopping off the balustrade, I walk toward my Strassenbahn stop. The evening hasn't yet begun to cool, and the smells of food and sounds of summer carry through the narrow pedestrian streets of the Altstadt. If I were with another person, I don't know if I could appreciate the evening atmosphere like I am right now. For a few minutes, I don't mind being alone in this city. Maybe I could even get used to this.

By the time the Strassenbahn glides to a stop, that feeling has dissipated, replaced by the somber isolation that's been impossible to truly escape since I arrived. Inhaling deeply, I let Freiburg's valley air fill my chest as I board the train.

I pass Daniel in the hallway when I get home. Looking back over my shoulder, I catch him staring after me with that same indecipherable, searching look. He has a bit of a despondent expression, like he's watched too many sad movies recently. The moment our eyes meet, he turns and walks away. Feet unmoving from the spot, I roll my shoulders, trying to work a kink out of them. What thoughts are hidden behind those blue-gray eyes? Something inside is warning me to be cautious, but mostly I'm just curious.

I should probably just give up already, but something about the way he arbitrarily brushes me off whenever I talk to him makes me wonder if this isn't really about me at all. Yet there's no question that he's purposely trying to keep a distance from me specifically. Why would he do that?

Instead of returning to my room, I knock on Florian's door.

"Hi there," he says, holding open the door for me.

I take a seat on the corner of his bed. "Can I ask you something?"

"Sure." He looks a little uneasy.

"Why does Daniel dislike me so much?"

Florian gives me an apologetic look. "I've been trying to figure that out myself. We've been friends for a few years, and I've never seen him act like this around anyone."

Massaging my forehead with one hand, I stare at the floor. "I just don't get it."

"Did anything happen when you two met that first night?"

"No, I just walked in and said that I was just about to move in. Then he asked to see the paperwork."

"He made you show that to him?"

"Yeah, I thought it was kind of strange."

"Huh . . . I honestly have no idea what's making him go off on you," Florian admits.

This conversation is only making me feel worse about everything. I was secretly hoping to find out I'd inadvertently offended him somehow. "Any ideas on how to get on his good side? I'd rather we get along." Considering how that might sound, I quickly add, "Since we're roommates and all." And for no other reason, I reassure myself.

"Well, I've always thought that the way to Daniel's heart is a case of Rothaus."

"Beer?"

"Yep. It's a special beer only brewed right here in the Black Forest."

"Huh, okay. I'll try that then I guess." I open the door to leave.

"Ethan," Florian calls after me. "I'm sorry about all this. I'm sure it sucks."

"Yeah, thanks."

The following night, armed with a six-pack of Rothaus, I find Daniel in the kitchen. I'm determined to have a proper conversation with him—one that doesn't begin with me asking him for anything and doesn't end with him walking away or shutting a door in my face. If I show an interest, ask him a few questions about himself, things might straighten out.

He's cooking, stirring chopped-up pieces of something like ravioli along with onions and bits of bacon. It smells really good, but I can't let myself get distracted. "Hey, Daniel."

Glancing up from his cooking endeavor, he meets my eyes for less than a second, his eyebrows narrowing almost imperceptibly before flicking his gaze downward. "Hi Ethan," he says flatly, his interest fixed on the frying pan. A pang of redness hits my cheeks. He won't even *look* at me. This was a mistake. I don't know why I even bothered trying to talk to him again.

There's a weight in my chest that's getting unbearably heavy. He mechanically stirs the ravioli in slow circles, all but ignoring me.

"I . . . um, wanted to . . ." My concentration, absolutely necessary to formulate the German grammar, begins to unravel. The cardboard handle of the six-pack digs into my fingers.

"Spit it out, Ethan. What is it you want?"

I can feel my face turning even brighter red. I can't do this anymore. "Actually, never mind," I tell him, switching into English. "This is for you, by the way," I snap, setting the beer hard on the counter. I turn and leave before he can be any more of a dick.

In my room, I switch off the light and lie on the bed in darkness, taking deep breaths. For years I've wanted nothing more than to study abroad, dreaming about how much fun it would be. Except nothing is turning out like I imagined.

The language is coming too slowly, it's hard as hell to meet anyone, and the people I do meet aren't looking for new friends. To be fair, that's not entirely true. Bastien and Corinne will hang out sometimes, but I know they've got a group of Frenchies that they spend most of their time with. Don't even get me started on the Germans. Florian is nice, sure, but we could never be friends. He's too eccentric. And Daniel . . . well, roommate or not, I won't keep wasting my time on someone like him. If we didn't live together, I would have given up a long time ago. Tonight was his last chance. He can go to hell.

The giant square window above my bed is open, and the cricket chorus drifts in from the cool night outside. I can hope that things will get better, that I'll find more friends and the language will start making more sense, but the summer's days of warmth are going to draw to a close soon. Already the coolness of the night rolling in through the open window is a sobering reminder of the impending change of season. With it comes an unspoken conviction that the rest of my year will be more of the same nights spent alone, longing for how this year should have been.

Chapter 4

My dad split when I was three, but I've gotten over it. I was too young to really understand what it meant. He was there one day and then the next he just . . . wasn't. He probably talked to me and squeezed my shoulder before he left. Or maybe not. It doesn't matter, because in the end he left anyway, and I haven't seen him since. Mom's official story is that she never heard from him, but I wonder if she only said that to make it easier on me.

Growing up, sometimes I told people my dad was just out of town on a business trip. For a while, I tried saying that he died when I was little, but my mom overheard once and gave me a talk about making up stories. I think she wished she could fabricate a story about him too. Anything was better than him just leaving us.

I turned out fine, more or less. I really can't remember much about him, so deep down if some small part of me is still hung up about it, it's because I feel like I should be, and not because there's a gaping emotional hole somewhere inside. To me, it was normal to grow up with just Mom and myself. Some people have two parents. I have one.

I'll tell you what really got to me though. When I was fifteen, Mom had the guts to ask if the reason I was different was because I was missing a father figure. I would have reamed her out for pulling that psychology horseshit, but an hour earlier she'd walked in on her teenage son kissing another boy. I figured I'd cut her a break. What bothered me most was the premise that there must be something wrong with me, that she needed a reason to explain why that had happened, or something to blame it on I guess.

She couldn't really afford it, but she sent me to a therapist anyway. I think she was hoping he would somehow fix me and I'd be interested in girls like I was supposed to be. The whole thing backfired on her though, because the shrink—Albert, but he let me call him Al—told me that being gay wasn't a bad thing, just different.

It all would have been over just then, but I'd also told him I was afraid sometimes that Mom might leave me too. He insisted on meeting several more times to talk about my fear of losing people close to me. At first I thought he was full of it, but eventually I realized that other kids my age didn't lie awake at night wondering whether their parent was still going to be there in the morning. How should I have known that wasn't normal?

Anyway, Mom still isn't that okay with the whole gay thing, but about a year ago I told her that I wasn't mad anymore about her freaking out and sending me to the shrink. I'm sure it's scary to discover that your kid has turned out, in some way at least, completely different from what you thought. I reminded her about when she had caught me with the other boy and how her outburst had scared the shit out of him. Mom and I had a laugh about that. His name was Ryan.

Chapter 5

The second week into the Sprachkurs, the weather turns unseasonably hot for early September at 28 degrees Celsius, which is almost 85 degrees Fahrenheit. Corinne and Bastien, possibly sensing the last hot day of the season, invite me after class to go swimming in the tiny lake behind our dorms. I walked around it a single time last week. It's basically an elongated pond, but the water is clear, and a well-maintained path ropes around it, so it seems safe enough to swim in.

Taking the Strassenbahn home together, we split up for our respective dorms across the lake to get changed. After tugging on my swim shorts, which feel like they've shrunk a little since last year, I start down toward the lake. It's probably good to get some swimming in, if my tight shorts are any indication. I make a mental note to start exercising more.

The heat was unbearable in class, but outside it's not as bad. Even so, a line of sweat is collecting on my forehead. I stop swinging my keys around on their Universität Freiburg lanyard long enough to reach up and wipe the moisture away. It's then I notice I've forgotten my towel. Brushing my hand on my shorts instead, I pause for a moment, debating if I should go back. *Ah, screw it.* I'll just air dry after we're done. I also left my sandals behind, but that was on purpose, because I love feeling the grass between my toes as I walk.

I wave to Corinne and Bastien, who are already in the water when

I arrive, and swim out to join them.

"Hey Ethan." Bastien nods to me and his hand climbs out of the water to give a little wave.

We're far enough out that we can't touch the bottom, so we tool around, treading water. Even the lake has already started to cool for the season, but the day is so warm that it feels good. Amid labored breaths from treading water so long, I ask Bastien, "So what do you think of the Germans?"

Horizontal arm strokes keeping him afloat, he says, "They're fine, but I don't know many. It's hard to make friends, I think."

"You too, huh?" Nice to know I'm not alone at least.

"Are you talking about someone in particular?" Corinne chimes in, swimming closer so that we're positioned in a tight circle.

There's no one around, but Bastien leans in, grinning. "*Jemand . . . besonderes?" Someone special?*

"Not like that," I say. Corinne gives me a pointed look, but I glance away, shrugging so my shoulders rise out of the water a few inches.

"Whooo?" Corinne drags out the word, which sounds so silly with her accent that I can't help but smile.

The way she's staring at me, she's clearly waiting for an answer. I swallow nervously, pretending to be catching my breath before talking more. "Uh, his name is Daniel. He lives in my building."

Confusion flits over Corinne's face, and she switches into rapid French, directing her question to Bastien.

I stare as Bastien shoots back at her, and I know my face has that blank look that everyone gets when they're watching someone speak another language.

Whatever he says must answer her question, because she makes a non-committal noise and looks embarrassed. In contrast, Bastien doesn't appear even slightly fazed.

Recovering, she asks, "What's he like?"

I could tell her about those storm gray eyes that always seem to linger a moment too long, or the turbulent depth of emotion I'm convinced lies just beneath the surface, but the overriding emotion for the whole situation is anger. "He's a dick," I say.

Corinne waits until it's clear I'm not going to elaborate before changing the subject. They keep talking but my heart isn't in it anymore. My arms sway under the water and my legs occasionally produce a kick, but it's only the bare minimum required to keep me afloat.

When my friends announce they're heading home, I tell them I want to stay a while longer to swim. I watch them clamber out of the water and dry off. Once they begin to walk away, I set off toward the opposite shore. The water is calming and the afternoon sun feels good on my face and shoulders. Something about slicing through water lets me channel everything I feel into my muscles. Anger, disappointment, frustration, embarrassment, they're all fair game, fuel to propel me forward. Burning through every muscle fiber, those emotions always lend me their strength when my own falters.

Daniel can't actually hate me. The number and nature of our interactions make it impossible to develop such a polarized feeling. Whatever his problem with me is, there has to be more to it. It can't be just about me. That should be a relief, but actually it just pisses me off more.

My arms churn the water ahead, switching from my own energy to the new fuel. It wasn't about me when my dad left either. Which should have made it easier, right? It wasn't my fault, so I shouldn't feel guilty or blame myself. For the most part, I didn't. What made me feel the worst was that my dad simply didn't care enough to stay. God, if only I had mattered enough to him to have been the reason he left, or at least part of it. A contributing factor or even a distant afterthought on his way out would have been preferable to being invisible.

It's been too long since I've swum like this, because my strength is flagging before I've had the chance to ignite every drop of emotional hydrocarbon. In high school, I could have crossed this narrow section of the lake and back again without missing a beat. I'm only halfway when I have to stop to catch my breath. Limbs burning, I tread in place and wait for a second wind. If I stay here treading water until the verge of muscle failure, maybe these old swim shorts will fit better tomorrow. It's tempting, but then I might not make it back at all.

Exhaustion has reduced the frequency of my strokes keeping me afloat, and my nose and mouth slip briefly under the surface before a solitary kick propels me sputtering up again. Ready or not, it's time to head back to shore. It feels so much farther than the way out, probably because the fear of not making it is nagging in the back of mind.

Pressing on, I ignore the worry inside. I'll make it because I have to. My muscles seethe with rage, but they have a bit of fight left in them. Just a little farther.

By the time my feet can finally touch bottom again, I'm panting and my heart is pumping acid instead of blood. My legs are shaky taking the last few steps out of the water when a sharp, deep pain erupts into my foot. "FUCK!" I scream and fall over sideways into the shallows, gripping my ankle. As my foot breaks the surface, the transparent curve of a chunk of glass settles back into the sand, dark trails of red clinging to its edges before dissolving away. I'm on my back in about six inches of water, warm wetness flowing down over the bottom of the foot I'm holding up. Fat drops of blood plink into the lake, clouding the water around me. The pain is a sharp knife, biting deep into my foot.

I frantically glance around, but there's no one nearby. There are eighty million people in a country a thirtieth the size of the United States, so where the hell are they? I'm still on my back, holding my foot in the air like a dumbass and gritting my teeth in something like the worst pain of my life, but it's obviously getting me nowhere. I let go of my foot but keep it held above the water, using my hands and other foot to push myself over the small bank and out of the lake.

Alright Ethan, breathe. In: my chest expands. Out: it sinks back down. With the familiar action, the pain backs off a bit, but not much. *Now, think.* All I wore down to the lake is my swim shorts, and there's no way I'm taking them off to try and staunch the bleeding from my foot. Goddamn it. I need to get back to my room. My keys are zipped into my shorts pocket, so if I don't run into anyone by then, I can at least call 911. Actually, is that even the emergency number here? I'll have to deal with that later.

I bend my knee and pull my foot close, hoping to get a better look at the damage. There's blood everywhere, and now holding my foot at this angle, it's dribbling onto my other leg as well. It's such a mess that it's hard to tell visually, but it *feels* deep. I try to wipe off the red globs that are sinking into my white swim shorts, but I only succeed in smearing them around. Swallowing to fight the pain, I push myself up onto my other foot.

The exhaustion from the swim slows me down as I begin a limping hop toward home. The quarter mile between me and my dorm will take me back down the path, up a hill and through a cluster of bushes. I must be out of my mind, but pain and adrenaline continue to force consciousness on me. Blood flows out of my foot all the while, leaving a bloody trail behind me. If Hansel and Gretel had thought of this one, they never would have gotten lost in those woods.

My arms and legs already stiff, now my uninjured leg is beginning to shake from exhaustion. I almost lose my balance twice on the hill, so when I reach the steepest part, I give up trying to hop and lie on my back, using my good foot and arms to push myself up the last few feet to the top. Dirt and rocks scratch and dig into my back, but it's barely noticeable compared to the stabbing pain in my foot, growing sharper now that the adrenaline is wearing off.

I'm just behind my building now, less than a hundred feet left. One of my hopping footfalls lands partially on a rock, and with a yelp I topple over into the bushes. The hurt and horribleness of the situation force tears out of my eyes. I wipe the first wave of them away with a part of my wrist that isn't covered in blood or dirt. *Get up, Ethan. You can do this.*

I push myself to my feet and round the corner to the front of my building with a rush of relief, because there's someone on the balcony, their back turned to me. I think it's Florian. "Help," I croak. The person turns and my heart sinks. *Why does it have to be him?* Daniel's expression changes in the matter of an instant from curious concern to recognition and finally gruesome surprise.

"My God," he gasps, dropping his textbook on the table. "Hold on!" he yells, jumping up and running into our building. I can hear him shouting for Florian.

It can't be more than ten minutes since I stepped on the broken glass, but it feels like it's been a lot longer. What should have been relief at not being alone anymore in this ordeal is quashed by the knowledge that it's Daniel coming to my rescue.

The ground sways under me. I'm surprised he's even willing to help. I half expected him to give me one look and say he'd love to lend a hand but was just too darn busy with homework at the moment. A feeling of lightness is spreading through me and fog begins to roll across my vision.

It's only another second and Daniel bursts through the front door. It feels like I'm weightless, falling, but that can't be. The fog turns dark.

"Come on, Ethan, wake up." The voice is so close I can feel breath on my cheek. I'm being carried. One arm supports my back and another my knees. He seems to be carrying me effortlessly, the muscles of his forearms pressed against my wet skin. My eyes ease open as my head lolls to the side. The stair railing moves across my vision. We're just inside our building. I must have only been out for a few seconds.

Turning my head just enough to see him, I shut my eyes the moment I do. He speaks again, this time in a whisper. "You're going to be okay, buddy. Just hang in there."

I'm a bloody, dirty, wet mess that's shirtless and shoeless, wearing only a pair of blood-soaked board shorts. Why couldn't it have been Florian on the balcony? Or a random stranger. Anyone but him. I don't want him feeling obligated to help me. And I sure as hell don't want to owe him anything.

"Put me down," I wheeze. My throat is scratchy.

"We're almost there, just another minute." His voice is quiet, reassuring, and . . . caring. It's not what I expect.

Opening my eyes again, I turn them toward him. "Put me down," I repeat as firmly as I can. "I'll wait until Florian gets here."

Chest contracting, Daniel sighs, glancing away as he carries me up the last set of stairs sideways so my foot doesn't hit the railing or the wall. Why won't he listen to me? All the while, drops of blood fall from my heel. When he looks down, there's concern in his expression, but there's also something new that I've never noticed before. Whatever it is, his gaze has become softer.

He doesn't say anything more until he pops open the door to his room with his elbow and lays me down on the bed so my foot hangs off the end. It's soft, and I sink a few inches into the comforter. A scent, which must be his, rises around me musky and masculine, latent in the softness of the down.

I bring my gaze to a reluctant rest on my rescuer. His shirt and shorts are covered in splotches and streaks of my blood. His hands too. He traces a line with his finger across my forehead, brushing the bangs out of my eyes. "Everything will be ok," he says quietly, glancing surreptitiously down to my foot, and, no doubt, at the blood already collecting on the floor.

Where did this person come from? The guy I've interacted with over the last two weeks has been replaced by an imposter who's actually nice. And just because a hunk of glass sliced the shit out of my foot? It doesn't seem real, but here I am, lying on his bed while he fusses over me.

Darting out to the hallway, he yells again. "Florian!"

"Coming!" his voice calls back, echoing down the hall.

Florian appears a moment later with a roll of gauze, a bowl of steaming water, a washcloth, and opaque latex gloves. Kneeling at the edge of the bed, he examines my foot.

"Ethan, you're going to be fine," he says after a minute with a reassuringly medical conviction. It takes a moment for me to remember that he used to work with an ambulance crew.

He begins to clean the wound while speaking to Daniel in rapid-fire German. What Florian's doing stings, and I can only catch a few words in their conversation like blood, ambulance, and hospital. After a minute, Florian says, "It's pretty deep. He definitely needs *Stiche*." I've never heard that word before, but I assume it means stitches. It still hurts after he binds the wound with gauze, but at least the incessant hot drip down my foot has stopped.

"Do we call an ambulance or drive him?" Daniel asks.

"It's probably faster to drive at this point. Want me to handle it?"

"No, I'll take him."

Florian glances up from my foot and holds Daniel's eyes for a moment. "Alright," he finally says with a nod and leaves the room before I can say a word.

Daniel appraises me, concern still lining his face. "Does it hurt much?"

It feels awkward to shrug while lying on my back, but I try anyway. "Yeah, still quite a bit, but it feels better since he . . ." I'm not sure of the right word.

"Bandaged?" Daniel offers.

"Yeah, since he bandaged my foot."

"You need to go to the hospital to get Stiche."

"I thought I heard Florian mention that." I sigh weakly. "You'll drive me there?"

Standing in the doorway, he nods. "I'll take you, yes. Will you be alright while I bring my car over?"

I didn't know he had a car. No one our age really does. It's an unnecessary luxury in a country with unparalleled mass transit. "I'll be fine." I swallow my apprehension at being left alone again. *What if he doesn't come back?*

While he's gone, I take in what I can of his room from my vantage point. A computer desk with a laptop and a small potted plant beside it are across from the bed. I can't see behind me, but birds' voices are drifting in, so the window must be open. A tall bookcase stands stoically in the corner, overlooking the entire room. Textbooks fill a large portion of it, but there are a good many other books as well. Lying on one of the shelves is an imposing leather-bound book that looks suspiciously like a Bible. It would be strange, since hardly any young Germans are religious.

A minute later he reappears in the doorway, panting from exertion. Crossing the room, he tosses me a white shirt from the top of his dresser. "You can wear this."

"It's going to get blood on it," I point out, even though he's already gotten my blood on everything he's wearing.

"Don't worry about it. We can't have you walking shirtless into the emergency room."

I pull it over my head, half-dried blood from my hands smearing across the fabric.

"Ready?" he asks.

I sit up on the side of the bed and put tentative weight on my foot. Pain jets up my leg. Forcing it away, I push myself up onto my good foot. "I think I can walk," I venture, glancing up at him. I don't want him carrying me again.

He looks skeptical. "Are you sure?"

Favoring my injured side as I stand, I immediately realize it can barely take any weight at all. In an instant, Daniel is at my side. He drapes my arm over his shoulder, and we make our way down the hall.

We get to the stairs, and I'm considering that it might be easier to hop down on my right foot step by step when he kneels, slips his arms under my back and knees, and picks me up again.

"Hey," I protest, "Put me down, damn it. I don't need your help." He doesn't meet my eyes, and he doesn't let go either. What he's doing is emasculating, and it pisses me off. Locking me to his chest with a firm grip, he carries me all the way to the first floor before setting me down.

Scowling at him, I adjust my shirt. His shirt, I correct myself.

Down the hall and through the glass doors at the front of our building, I can see a silver car. It looks out of place, because the paths that go between the buildings are only for pedestrians and bicycles. "You drove up to the front door?"

Looking sheepish, he says, "An ambulance would have driven up to the door too, and my car isn't nearly as big." I shake my head but don't press it. After all, it saves me from having to walk so far.

I stop just as we're getting close. "Um, that's an M3." It's the ultra-fast sport edition of the BMW 3 series.

"Yeah, that's right," he says, holding open the passenger side door.

I'm still staring at the car. From the outside it's unassuming, but this machine has over four hundred horses under the hood. I wouldn't have guessed that he comes from money, considering his spartan room in the budget student dorms—the same student dorms Mom and I had to scrounge and save to afford this year.

I'm acutely aware of the mostly dried blood covering my hands and shorts as I lean into the black leather seat. "Sorry about all the blood," I murmur as he slides the manual transmission into first and we zip away down the paths normally reserved for pedestrians.

"It's fine," he says dismissively without taking his eyes off the path ahead. The muscles in his face tense with concentration as he guides us down the narrow walkways. His jawline is strong, defining his chin and complementing high cheekbones. He glances at me, and I look away, embarrassed. I'm completely at a loss as to why his attitude toward me has changed so dramatically. Rounding the last bend, he swerves around a guy on a bicycle who gives us a dirty look.

Finally he pulls off the paths onto the street and presses hard on the gas. The engine rises eagerly to meet the challenge and hums with power, though it feels like the car could go much faster if he desired. Nevertheless, the acceleration pulls me into the leather. This car and its seats were built to hold their passengers securely though, so it's not unpleasant, and it doesn't force me to adjust my injured foot.

It's early evening by the time we get home. Armed with crutches and Daniel still at my side, I make the way from his car back to our dorm. We arrived at the hospital in just minutes thanks to his driving, and the emergency room admitted me right away without any questions about insurance or payment.

Daniel insisted on staying with me the entire time. At first the nurse wasn't going to allow it, but he explained his presence away by saying that I might need a translator for the medical terms. Since he never had to translate anything for the doctor who spoke perfect English, and he outright told me the week before that he didn't speak much English, I'm a little suspicious about his explanation.

After we get to my room, he lingers in the doorway. I lean my crutches against the wall and flop onto my bed, noticing how hard it is compared to lying on his earlier. He's still eyeing me, a note of sternness filtering into his voice as he speaks. "You should really be more careful. Swimming alone isn't safe, even if you're a good swimmer."

A flutter of embarrassment flares in my chest at being called out and my skin prickles. I wonder if his kindness has run out and he's going to start being a jerk again. I level my eyes to his, determined to discover if his words are out of irritation at having spent his afternoon carting me to the hospital, or whether he's driven by genuine concern. There is no trace of impatience or annoyance in his expression, but it's impossible to forget how he treated me the last couple weeks. "Whatever," I say, "It was just bad luck."

"I'm serious, Ethan."

"Screw you. You've ignored me since I moved in, so don't pretend like you suddenly care." The words are out before I even have a chance to think. The anger I've been holding in surprises me.

Daniel takes a step back. "I'm sorry," he says, staring at his feet. "Let me make it up to you." His tone is hopeful, but I don't respond. After a moment, he glances up, daring to meet my eyes. "Are you still looking for a Tandempartner?"

We were supposed to have our partners picked out last week, but Frau Schmidt might make an exception. It would save me hours in the language lab, which is worth it, even if it means spending an hour with Daniel every week.

"Are you really volunteering?"

"Yeah," he says quietly, turning to go. He's pulling the door shut when he adds as an afterthought, "But we're only doing German, no English."

Once I'm alone, I lie back on the bed. Today ran away from me. Daniel's change of heart, change of attitude, or whatever the hell happened, doesn't make a lick of sense. But I'll take it over him ignoring me or being an asshole. Somehow I got a Tandempartner out of the whole affair as well.

Chapter 6

Cars were another reason that it would have been great to have a dad—one that stuck around until middle school at least. I love them. In high school, before making dinner so Mom could eat when she got home from work, I'd go out to the road and watch the cars. The speed limit was only forty-five, and I'd sit where I could see every vehicle that passed. It let me see the make and model names inscribed on the back. We didn't have a computer then, so it was how I learned what was out there.

It was rare that anything cool came along. No one with money had any reason to go near Twin Meadows trailer park. Except one time, the last week of class before the end of tenth grade. It was almost time to go inside and start the spaghetti and meatballs I was planning. But there were still a few more minutes. Maybe a Corvette or Mustang would zoom past, and the wait would be worth it. Wind blasting last year's dead grass as it rolled up to the road, I lay back, crossing my legs at the ankles and staring up into the clouds. I was kidding myself. That night was just like all the others in that damn place. I stood up to head inside, and then I heard it. A deep purr with a rich timbre, coming up fast.

My head snapped to the point in the road where it would emerge from behind the trees. In a rush of gray and chrome, the enormous sedan erupted around the corner. Its flat nose and massive grille spoke of earlier times, but the flowing lines proclaimed it to be modern. It was easily the largest car I'd ever seen, both in length and girth. The rumble of its engine struck a reserved note that belied its current speed far over the limit. Then it was gone.

I didn't have any idea what the heck it was at the time, other than a really expensive car. In retrospect, it was probably a Rolls Royce or a Bentley. All I knew is that it was beautiful, every part of it. Even the sound felt like the engine was singing to my soul. Okay, sometimes I'm full of shit, but it really was awesome.

Chapter 7

I duck under the awning of a bookshop to escape the fat raindrops plopping down all around. I've been meaning to get a German book for a while now, though the sudden downpour is what actually drove me in here. The door is heavy, and it takes some negotiating with my crutches to get it open. A bell chimes cheerily as the door shuts behind me. Inside it's quiet, almost deserted, and it smells like dust and old books. Wooden shelves stained dark red rise up almost eight feet, brimming with literature, non-fiction, travel guides, textbooks, and more. I drag my finger along the spines of the books, skimming the titles and hoping to get a feel for the sections I'm passing.

"Kann ich Ihnen helfen?" asks an older woman with square framed glasses that disappear into a permed ball of gray hair. Lines form creases around her eyes and mouth, and her cheeks are sagging.

Can I help you? I'm surprised by the use of the formal "you." I'm used to people using the informal with me.

"Um," I stall, formulating my next words. "I'm looking for a book that's . . . easy to read." Before I make myself look like an idiot, I quickly clarify. "I don't mean for kids. I want to improve my German, but it can't be too difficult."

Her gray hair bobs as she nods. "Yes, I understand. Follow me please." The shop is small, but it's a miniature labyrinth in here. After a series of turns and sliding a rolling shelf aside, we're standing in front of what looks like juvenile fiction. Adjusting her glasses, she bends over to get a closer look. Making alternatively pensive and dismissive noises as she scans the rows of books, she eventually pauses. Straightening, she gives me another look before carefully extracting a book from the packed shelf. Her face impassive, she hands it to me.

On the cover is a guy lying on a dock, propping himself up on his elbows. Beside him, a white rowboat is tied to one of the posts. Flipping the book over, I try to skim the back cover, but I keep losing my place. The saleswoman hasn't moved, apparently content to simply watch me. Moisture wicks onto my palms and when I turn the book over to see the cover again, it almost slips from my fingers. She's probably thinking that there's no way I'll ever get through this book if this is how fast I read.

I've read through the first part of the synopsis twice now, but something is bothering me. "Excuse me," I say. "Can you make sure I'm reading this right?"

"Of course," she smiles sweetly, no doubt thinking I have the German capability of a preschooler.

I point to the fifth sentence, describing the main character Phil. "This says that he's . . . uh . . ." Redness starts to smolder in my face. I force the words out, hoping I haven't misunderstood. "That he's in love with another guy, Nicholas?"

"That's right." Her face is still inscrutable, as if we were discussing the weather.

A tingling feeling fills my chest. I've never read a book like this before, and definitely never in German. A part of me wants to take it home and lock myself in my room until it's finished.

But why would she pick out this book in particular? Did she guess that I'm . . . no, that wouldn't make sense. People don't usually know until I tell them. She's still looking at me, so without anywhere else to direct my gaze, I stare dumbly at the book held in my sweaty hands.

If I buy it, that would confirm her suspicion that I'm into guys. I don't want to support that sort of guesswork. It doesn't matter that she'd be right. Though who knows, she might try to peddle this particular story on every confused foreigner that wanders in here. If their German isn't good enough to decipher the back cover, they probably buy it. Otherwise she just gets a kick watching them squirm. Watching *me* squirm.

Another thought occurs to me that scares me more than rewarding her guesswork. What if—after asking for the clarification on the synopsis—I then decide to *not* buy the gay book. Then she'll think I'm a homophobe who doesn't want to read about dudes getting it on. What a clever saleswoman. There's really no way out of this one. She's either going to think I'm an American gay boy or an American bigot.

"Actually," I say, stumbling over my words, "I have to go. Thanks, anyway." I hand her back the book, my blood running hot. I get out of there as quick as I can. Representing your country is hard sometimes.

Inexplicably, the rain has stopped. The clouds are already breaking apart and fleeing from the valley, and as I crutch along the cobblestone-paved streets, glimmers of sun cast thermal swaths across my feet. Back home, the weather is slow to change and irritable. It will rain for three days straight or snow on and off for a week in the middle of April. Everyone says they get used to it, but they never really do. Freiburg is different. The temperatures aren't as extreme, but no one leaves the house without an umbrella, even if the sky is perfectly clear.

It's a pain having to use crutches, but after staying in my room all weekend, I'm willing to endure the discomfort and inconvenience as long as it gets me out of the stupid dorms.

Before I've even reached the heart of the Altstadt, the sun bursts completely free and wisps of steam begin to rise off the street. I step off the sidewalk but have to wait for a Strassenbahn to rumble past before crossing. Down another narrow alley and I enter into an expansive square. I've seen the *Münster* cathedral at the center of Freiburg in passing, but never up close. It's clear now that seeing it poking above the rows of old buildings from several blocks away doesn't do it justice.

The spire rises so high that I have to tilt my head all the way back to see the top. Stretching away from the tower, the main part of the church is massive. Covering the entire structure are exquisite ornamentations of gargoyles, cherubs, and animals. Everything is carved from reddish ocher stone of varying shades.

Eyes fixed skyward, I circle around to the front where an information sign for visitors has been set up. I read through as quickly as my German will allow, and when I'm finished, I can't help but feel small in comparison. Construction began in the year 1200; the spire and nave were completed in 1330, but the rest of the cathedral—namely the choir room and a few other extensions—wasn't completed until 1512.

Ancient history classes are always hard for me to pay attention in, because the events they deal with are so far removed from present day.

In contrast, medieval history isn't as distant, but since the oldest buildings back home are less than two hundred years old, it's always been difficult for me to appreciate what it's like to live in tangible proximity to the last thousand years.

My stomach is tingling in realization, in transformation of my perspective. I'm standing in front of an edifice, built of stone, that is eight hundred years old. The time it took to construct it alone is longer than the entire span of U.S. history. I struggle to process what that means.

On the edge of the square is a row of food trucks selling French fries and curry bratwurst. Lines have formed in front of each stand as foreigners and Germans alike wait for their turn to order. Meanwhile, a steady stream of photo snapping tourists files in and out of the cathedral.

It doesn't seem right to live in or even visit a place like this and be oblivious—or worse, apathetic—to its rich layers of history. I should really pay more attention to the old buildings and their stories scattered around the city. If anything, it might do something to fill my days. Finishing my gimping journey around the back of the Münster, I turn to leave the square. The interior will have to wait for another day, when I can actually walk without help.

Crossing the university's red sandstone courtyard on my way to the Strassenbahn stop, I hear the electronic buzz of a megaphone sounding across the cobblestone square. Nestled among the cluster of university buildings, all built with the same colored stone as the Münster, the square is filled by a crowd of students facing a man standing on a bench, his words spewing out of the bullhorn.

Rocking back and forth on the heel of my good foot, I give in to curiosity and approach the assembly. His voice is clear and his German is easy to understand except when occasionally punctuated by a hiccup of feedback from the megaphone. ". . . the German State is trying remove one of your fundamental rights. The change may not be great, but with the newly introduced *Studiengebühren* of five hundred Euro, the State has declared that education is no longer a human right." I'm not sure what *Studiengebühren* means. Something to do with studying, that's obvious at least.

Most of the other people gathered here seem to be like me—students passing through the square who stopped to see what the guy was going on about. My gaze skips around the group. A pair of young women arrive and start whispering to each other, while a guy in his late twenties must have decided he's heard enough, because he adjusts the backpack hanging by a single strap from his shoulder and walks away.

The man continues to speak, but I'm more interested in the yellow and black plastic banners hung up on lampposts around the square. They're the same ones I saw when I first arrived in Freiburg. In the middle is a shopping cart with what is unmistakably a brain sitting in it. I definitely didn't notice *that* when I saw these banners from afar. Around the image is a circle with a slash through it. The Studiengebühren must be some sort of student fee that was just added.

Five hundred Euro doesn't sound like very much. Europeans seem to complain about everything, but if their tuition is already expensive, it might actually be a tipping point. Wracking my memory, I try to recall if anyone has mentioned how much tuition costs here, but I'm forced to conclude that I'm honestly not sure how much the German students pay.

When I leave the demonstration, the guy on the bench is still talking, proclaiming that education is soon going to be a privilege of the rich. Like in the United States, he must mean. Before the scholarship, there wasn't much hope for me to go anywhere but community college, and even that seemed like a stretch. Mom always said I would go to college of course, but she sure didn't have a plan in mind to pay for it. My stomach growling, the question of tuition and student fees disappears from my mind. Time to head home.

Just having finished dinner, I set my plate and fork by the sink next to a new pile of dirty dishes, most of which aren't mine. Since cutting my foot, I haven't felt up to standing one-legged for an hour to wash them. If none of my roommates do them soon, we're going to run out of clean dishes.

Sprawling out on the couch, I take out my homework and prop my leg up on one of the dilapidated pillows that must have originally come with the aging piece of furniture. All I have to do tonight is a worksheet on indirect speech. Apparently a different tense is used when paraphrasing someone else. Twirling my pencil around my finger, I read the first example. The whole assignment is a little pointless, because it's so rare for Germans to even use the tense that no one in our class could ever remember hearing it. Reading the sentence again, I slide the tip of the eraser into my mouth and hold it between my canines. It still doesn't make sense to me.

I'm on question three when Daniel comes into the kitchen. We haven't talked since he brought me back from the hospital, but I'm pretty sure that's only because he was gone all weekend.

"What are you working on?" he asks, opening the fridge.

Glancing up, I toss the notebook onto my lap. "Indirect speech. I hate it."

He takes a swig from a liter milk carton before stashing it back in its place. "That bad, huh?"

For a second I bristle, but his expression is free of sarcasm. "Worse."

"Want some help?" He closes the fridge and takes a seat next to me on the armrest. "Since we're Tandempartners and all."

I show him the notebook. "Hmm," he muses, appraising the page. "You're doing this wrong." I try to snatch the notebook back. "Hey, settle down," he says, tightening his grip. "Stop being stubborn and let me help you."

I glare at him, but I let go anyway. "I don't get how the conjugation works. It sounds all wrong."

"It's kind of supposed to. Use the first person conjugation for everything you're paraphrasing in third person." He points to the first example where I've scribbled out and rewritten so many times that it's almost impossible to read the original question. "'*He says that he has never seen the movie.*' Alright, now use indirect speech instead."

"Uh," I stall, gnawing on the end of the pencil. "He says he *have* never seen the movie?"

Daniel smiles widely, revealing white teeth. "Perfect."

"It sounds like crap."

"Yeah that's why we don't really use it. Let me know if you need any help with the rest of it," he says, getting up. "Oh and Ethan?"

"Yeah?"

"Take it easy on that pencil."

Grunting, I spit out a chunk of eraser onto the floor.

Chapter 8

At the end of my first week on crutches, a Polish guy who's been trying to catch my eye approaches me after class. Over the last few days, he's been staring whenever I look up, and somehow we always end up next to each other when leaving class. Despite my efforts to show disinterest, today he walks right up to me. His blonde hair covers his ears and meets the top of his cheekbones, thin and soft as they slope toward his pointed chin. "You're Ethan, right?" His Polish accent makes his German sound clipped and choppy.

I relax into my crutches to let them hold me up. Glancing at the ground, I say, "Yeah." A second ticks past, then another. "Sorry, I didn't catch your name."

His smile falls. No doubt he's aware that if I paid any attention to him in class, I would know his name. "I'm Nikolai. You can call me Niko." Oh yeah, I remember now. "So what happened to your foot?" he says.

I hold it out like we're having show and tell, even though it's bandaged so he can't see anything. "I cut it on a piece of glass in the lake behind the dorms."

He grimaces. "Sorry. That sucks."

"Yeah," I chuckle halfheartedly, "I'd say that's pretty accurate." We start toward the Strassenbahn stop and he tells me about himself, that he's studying German and political science.

I nod politely and ask, "What do you want to do with your degree?"

He seems to cheer up at my question, apparently pleased I'm showing interest. "I want to work for the European Union."

"Like diplomacy?"

"Maybe," he says, stepping around a plastic grocery bag being blown across the sidewalk like a tumbleweed. "I guess I'm more interested in policy work."

"Specifically?"

"Human rights if I can."

We're almost to my stop. "Do you take the *Landwasser* line?" I gesture to the glowing sign with arrival times.

"Nah," he says, but he doesn't move. He's staring at the ground, digging the tip of his shoe into a crack in the cobblestone. My fingers squeeze into the foam handles of my crutches. This is beginning to get a little awkward. Finally he says, "Maybe we could get coffee sometime?"

I give him a noncommittal nod. "Sure." I hope that satisfies him. I have a sneaking suspicion that "coffee" means a date. He asks for my cell number. I'm sighing in exasperation on the inside, but I give it to him anyway. He says goodbye casually, but I can tell he's trying hard to control his enthusiasm. Yeah, this is going to come back to bite me.

He walks away down the block toward a different Strassenbahn stop. He's interesting enough and a good mix—outgoing, friendly, foreign, cute even—and back in the States I probably would have jumped on him, maybe literally. But getting involved would add a new complication to my life, and I already have my hands full keeping up in class. It's not just that, though. Breaking up with Corey felt messy and wrong the way it ended. It makes me nervous to get into another relationship just for fun.

I'm overdue for catching up with Mom, so I call her on Skype when I get home. "Ethan!" she exclaims when the live feed from my camera pops up. "I'm so glad you're okay."

That's weird. I never told her about my foot. How could she have found out? "Uh . . . yeah," I try to stall. "I'm sorry for not calling you sooner, but my foot is fine, really."

"Your foot? What happened to your foot?"

Oh crap. "I cut it open. What were you talking about if you didn't know about my foot?"

"Oh my God, you cut yourself?" her voice rises an octave, pressing the boundary toward hysteria.

Groaning in frustration, I ask again, "Why did you say you were glad I was okay, if you didn't know I'd gotten hurt?"

She waves my question away. "I just meant I hadn't heard from you in two weeks. I was worried about you. Never mind that though, tell me what happened to your foot."

"Damn, Mom, you could say please." She doesn't look impressed, so I give up and tell her anyway. "I cut it open on a piece of glass."

"Why weren't you wearing shoes?"

"I was swimming."

"Who were you with when it happened?"

She's worse than the Spanish Inquisition. "Well, I um . . ." I should have anticipated this question. Before I can lie that Corinne and Bastien were there, she infers the truth.

"You were *alone*! Ethan, you have to be smarter than that. You could have died!"

"Oh please, don't be so dramatic." I decide I'm going to have to be a little more forthcoming if I want the interrogation to stop. So I tell her about Daniel and the hospital and getting stitches. She lights up a cigarette.

"Jesus, Mom, you said you quit."

Blowing the smoke downward, she ignores my last statement. "So who is this guy again?"

I swallow, hoping she doesn't notice my unease. "He's uh, one of my roommates." Before she reads into that, I correct myself. "Floor-mate, rather. We don't live in the same room."

"Hmm." She only says that when she doesn't buy what I'm telling her.

"Seriously, Mom. He just happened to be around and helped me out. Really."

"Fine," she says, flicking a cone of ash from the end of her cigarette. It takes all my will power not to tell her that smoking is the stupidest habit in the world. It would be a waste to get her going again though, since she's only just settled down. Instead I direct the conversation on to other topics. I skirt around how lonely I've been, but she can probably tell anyway. At least Daniel's not being a dick anymore, so I don't have to hide that particular challenge.

She fills me in about the latest on Ms. Dickens, the crotchety old woman who's lived in the trailer next to ours as long as I can remember.

"You mean she hasn't died yet?"

Mom's hoarse laugh comes through the speakers. Despite its gruffness, her face comes alive when she laughs. The sound ends almost as soon as it began, and she turns serious to scold me. "Ethan, I will not have you speak about her that way. She has been a good neighbor for many years."

"But?" I prompt. There's a juicy tidbit of information buried here or Mom wouldn't have brought her up.

The corner of her mouth pulls up in a hint of a smile. "Well, since you insist. George has been spending an awful lot of time at her place lately." George is an older guy, maybe sixty, who manages the Twin Meadows park. He's in decent shape for his age other than a huge curve in his back that shouldn't be there for another decade.

My eyes widen. "They're hooking up?"

A snicker escapes her. "That's what I think. It's really the only explanation, especially considering that Ms. Dickens had to be taken to the hospital last week for a fractured hip." Another gale of laughter comes through the computer speakers as she finishes.

"No way, I don't believe that old fart still had it going on."

"George or Ms. Dickens?"

I grin, mentally picturing the two of them. "Either of them," I say, and we both laugh.

Mom wants me to promise to email or call at least once a week. At first I won't agree to her terms, but she refuses to let me go until I do ("And don't you dare hang up on me, mister.") So I tell her I swear I'll call and email more often. The things I do for her.

The following weekend the weather turns cool, especially in the mornings when the mountains surrounding Freiburg release their frigid air to let it roll down into the city. I haven't done much lately, since I've been laid up for the last week. Getting around is kind of a pain, even just going to the kitchen or the bathroom.

Today is the first tandem meeting with Daniel. Part of me has been looking forward to this, but mostly I'm just nervous. He did help me with my homework a few days ago, but I'm still wary of him. He was either a dick or flat out ignored me for almost two weeks. Without any idea of what caused the change or whether it's just temporary, why should I trust him?

It's early afternoon and the sun shines in my eyes as I crutch through the sliding door. He's leaning back in one of the lawn chairs, sun on his face and eyes closed. We're both wearing long sleeved shirts. His is forest green and contrasts with his lighter blue jeans. He must hear me lean the crutches up against the wall and take a seat across from him, because his eyelids open reluctantly and he sits up. His chin is defined by a couple days worth of stubble that extends down toward his Adam's apple.

"Were you sleeping?"

"Only a little," he says, grinning lazily in a way that makes it impossible for me not to smile back.

His tone is friendly, just like it's been since the day I sliced myself open, but I'm afraid I might say the wrong thing. What if something sets him off and he suddenly hates me like before? Okay, I doubt he actually hated me, but he sure didn't want anything to do with me.

"So, Ethan, tell me about yourself."

"Um," I say, searching for somewhere to put my hands. *On the table or off?* Daniel is staring at me expectantly. "I . . . uh, what do you want to know?"

Even when Corey and I were getting to know each other, I never cared that much about accidentally making a bad impression. I've never felt the need to censor myself or apologize for being the way I am, so it's stupid for me to be anxious about this. If he wants to start being a jerk again, that's fine. We'll just go back to ignoring each other. But I hope that's not how this all turns out.

He must have a mental list prepared, because he begins to pepper me with questions—where I'm from, where I go to school, my hobbies, and more. Dutifully I answer them all. It's an easy way to drive the conversation forward, but it's odd because he actually seems interested in the answers.

"How old are you, actually?" he finally asks.

"Nineteen, why?"

He shrugs like it doesn't matter that much. "You just look kind of young."

It's irritating how he always makes me feel like a kid around him. "I'm a sophomore," I say, defensiveness creeping into my voice.

"I didn't mean anything bad by it." I don't respond, and silence threatens to fill the space between us. Finally he speaks again, straying a bit from the bread and butter questions he's exhausted. "Do you have German roots?"

"Like were my great grandparents German or something?"

"Yeah," he says, leaning forward. "Is there any German blood in your family?"

"Why do you want to know all this stuff?"

"I just want to get to know you."

Huh, really. "I don't know, maybe there's German somewhere in my family. Mom is English I think."

"And your father?"

I swallow, sliding my hands under my knees. "I don't really know much about him."

"I'm sorry, I didn't mean to—"

"It's okay," I interrupt. Usually I hate talking about my dad, or lack thereof, but something makes me want to share. "He left when I was little."

Daniel glances up from the wooden planks of the table. "That's hard."

I want him to say more, but I don't know what he could say that would change anything. Apparently he doesn't either.

"What about you? You haven't said anything about your family."

"Not much to say. I grew up near Stuttgart. My parents still live there."

"Shouldn't you have a strong accent if you're from Stuttgart?"

"At home, yeah," he pauses. "But here in Freiburg I only speak standard German."

"Isn't it uncomfortable having to change the way you talk?"

"Maybe a little, but no one would understand me otherwise."

"Not even other Germans?"

His shoulders bobbing up and down, he replies, "People from the area would, but the ones from the North would have trouble. And there are a lot of exchange students like yourself who would struggle to understand it too."

Before I can stop myself, I say, "Like when you came into the kitchen a few weeks ago, you said something I didn't quite understand." Cringing at my impulsiveness, I swallow anxiously. In case he's forgotten what he used to think about me or if he was unsure whether we should really be doing these tandems, now is his opportunity to tell me off and get away.

His face seems to gain a reddish hue, but I can't tell if it's just from the sun or if he's actually blushing. "Yeah, like that," he says. He doesn't get up to leave. For a second it even looks like he's going to say something more. Instead he shifts his gaze, staring out across the dormitory complex. A full minute passes.

We watch as a pair of girls pass under the balcony. They're only wearing shorts and tank tops, and they look cold. A falling leaf caught in the wind gets blown toward the girl on the right and taps her on the forehead before sliding aside and sailing off again.

"Do you have any brothers or sisters?" I ask.

Without turning back to face me, he says, "No, it's just me and my parents." He finishes with a finality that makes me wonder if he already wants to be done. My suspicion is almost immediately confirmed, because he stands up. "Your German is good, Ethan, you just need to learn to relax while you're speaking. I think you get nervous and overthink what you're trying to say."

Of course he would think that. If he had spent the last thirty minutes paranoid about saying something that might put an early end to these tandems, he might have had trouble concentrating too. "Thanks," I say.

"Stop by my room and let me know when you want to meet next," he calls over his shoulder as he steps through the sliding door.

I stay on the balcony for a few more minutes, soaking up the autumn sun. I suppose it was a little presumptuous to hope that he would suddenly drop the evasiveness and share openly about himself, but he's still being civil at least.

Chapter 9

Another week of the Sprachkurs has just finished, and the material we're covering is getting progressively more difficult. I'm learning a lot, but it's hard to keep up and I often leave class discouraged.

Once home, I head into the kitchen to make myself a sandwich, setting my crutches against the cupboard. Soon I won't need them to get around anymore. The stitches haven't been removed yet, but it doesn't hurt as much to put weight on my foot. I can't wait to be rid of the stupid crutches and walk freely again. Not being able to run to catch the Strassenbahn means I've been missing them a lot, and every time it happens I sink into a foul mood.

While I'm taking cheese and meat out of the refrigerator, Florian enters the kitchen with some homework, sitting down at the long table next to the door. Hurriedly stacking my sandwich, I take a seat at the table with him before he can become engrossed in his work. "Hey, Florian."

"Hi Ethan," he says, looking up. "How's your foot doing?"

"It's good. I've been wanting to thank you for, uh," I take a second to remember the word Daniel taught me, "bandaging my foot."

Florian nods and his curly brown hair bounces. "No problem. Lucky that I had the supplies to patch it up, or you would have bled all over on your way to the hospital."

"Daniel would have loved that." I take a bite of my sandwich. Florian doesn't say anything more, instead turning back to his homework. Sensing he's trying to end the conversation, I swallow the bite half chewed. "I've been meaning to ask you something."

"Oh yes, what's that?"

"That day I cut myself in the lake, you seemed surprised when he offered to take me to the hospital."

Florian looks hesitant, and he shifts in his seat. "Well . . ."

"Yes?" I prod him.

He leans back in his chair, folding his arms across his chest. "Daniel has always kept to himself, but the last year or so, he seems to have been even more distant. He used to hang out with me and some of the others sometimes—go out for drinks, to the movies, even a day trip into the mountains once. But not anymore."

I've long since set down my sandwich. "Did something happen?"

"No idea. He never said anything, and I've never asked. I don't think he would tell me something like that anyway."

"And why were you so surprised that he'd take me to the hospital? Because he keeps to himself?"

"Yes, partly that, but also because it seemed like he just didn't like you." Florian assumes a pensive expression. "Honestly, I'm surprised he didn't just leave you bleeding in front of the building and have me handle everything."

He's not the only one surprised that didn't happen. "You really have no idea why he helped me, then?"

"Nope, honest. For some reason though, he's taken a liking to you now, and how you got him to agree to be your Tandempartner, I have no idea."

"He asked *me*."

Florian glances up. "You're serious?"

"Yeah. How do you know about that anyway?"

He chuckles. "This is too small of a dorm for secrets." I give him my sternest I'm-not-impressed look. "Okay, Paula told me," he confesses.

"I didn't tell her either!" I throw my hands up in exasperation, almost toppling what's left of my sandwich.

Now he's really laughing. "I think she overheard from the bathroom when you guys were talking."

I stand up, grabbing my sandwich. "You guys are ridiculous." Florian is still laughing as I hobble out to the balcony to finish my snack.

The new information rolls through me like a dump truck. Daniel wasn't always this way. From Florian's explanation, I definitely got the worst that he had to offer. There has to be more to the story than I'm getting. The way his gaze lingered all those times, even before the incident in the lake.

What was it about the moment he saw me bleeding that caused the sudden change in his manner? And what's buried inside him that I'm only now getting a glimpse of? Of course, it could be *that*. It doesn't make sense though. I always pegged Daniel for straight. Then again, most people assume I am too.

When I get back to my room, I have a text from Niko. *hey Ethan, wanna grab coffee at Aspekt?*

Crap. I knew this was coming. I've passed the place before. It's a café in the Altstadt, pretty close to the university. For a moment I debate whether to say yes or no. My eyes wander to the window. A breeze picks up, batting around a tree's last leaves until one finally lets go and is carried away in the wind.

I text him back that I'm sure sorry but there's just so much laundry to do I can't make it. After a few minutes I still haven't heard back, so he must have gotten the message.

Craning my neck forward, I peel back the bandage on my foot and examine the wound. The dried blood has flaked off, giving way to new skin, melted together in a pink line through the stitches. In another day or so I can probably get away with ditching the crutches completely.

Replacing the bandage, I shift my attention to the project for my Sprachkurs, a ten-minute presentation on something unique or interesting about the city of Freiburg. I went back and forth for the last week trying to pick a topic, but in the end I chose one of Frau Schmidt's suggestions—Freiburg's environmental friendliness. I have an outline with most of what I want to say, but the sentences are jagged and untamed.

My gaze hovers on the door. Daniel might be willing to look it over. We're Tandempartners after all, so it's kind of like his job to help me with German things.

Laptop slung under my arm, I hop without my crutches over to his room, holding my right foot in front of me like a lance. The twilight of early evening has already settled over the valley, and the hall is lined with shadows. At his door, I let my hand roll as it strikes the wood, creating a distinct note as each knuckle makes contact. The sound leaps down the hallway before returning as an echo. The moment stretches out until long after the sounds have faded.

I'm just turning away when I hear the slippery metal snick of a deadbolt retracting before the door opens. Behind him, the warm light of a floor lamp casts a yellow hue over the room. Ear-covering headphones lie next to his laptop, tinny music spilling out onto his desk.

"Hey Ethan." He's staring at the foot I'm holding off the ground. "You aren't supposed to be walking on that yet."

"I know. I'm not really walking on it anyway, it hurts too much."

He snorts. "I bet it does."

"Are you done playing parent?" It comes out harsher than I wanted.

His eyes narrow, but after a second, the creases in his forehead relax. "Okay," he concedes, "I'll shut up."

I press on with my original intention, gesturing to my laptop. "I'm wondering if you could look over this presentation I'm supposed to give?"

"I do have homework myself," he says, nibbling the corner of his lip. He shifts his eyes between me and his room. "I suppose I can spare a few minutes. Why don't you come in and sit down." I'm acutely aware this is only the second time I've been in his room, the first being when I was hemorrhaging blood all over the floor.

Minutes skip past as he pores over my laptop and what has to be the worst presentation script he's ever seen. He keeps muttering, changing words around, and occasionally stopping to say things like "What are you actually trying to communicate here?" and "I'm sorry but this sentence just doesn't make sense."

We're sitting on his bed and our knees are touching. He's so close that I can hear when he exhales, his breath smelling like fresh mint.

With his attention riveted on the glowing screen, I take the opportunity to watch him work, taking in a myriad of details that I've never noticed before. The way the grain of his hair curves abruptly before ending at the top of his neck, how his shoulder blades protrude when he's leaning forward, or how he stretches out and points his feet while he reads.

Ever so casually, he turns to look over his shoulder, effectively catching me staring at him. He holds me in his gaze for just a moment before returning to the laptop. For whatever reason, he doesn't seem bothered that I'm watching him, almost as though he expects it.

I'm glad he's gone back to correcting, because my face feels hot. I've never met anyone like him before. It still feels like he's holding me at arm's length, but his ice is melting. Whenever we interact, there's still something else beneath the surface that I can't quite identify. It's there and it's close, but invisible like air swelling with humidity before a thunderstorm. And just like a storm, there's a sense of impending change. Not quite yet, but eventually though, conditions will change and the rain will surge forth in a torrential onslaught.

"There," he finally says, "It's perfect."

"Really?"

"Well, it's as good as it's going to get." Only now seeming to realize how close we're sitting, he scoots over a couple inches before handing me the computer and moving to his desk chair. He looks like he's about to ask me to leave, so out of courtesy, I thank him for the help and stand up from the bed.

"Anytime," he says, jumping up to get the door for me. "See you around, Ethan."

Laptop in hand, I hobble back to my room and open the window. It's chilly, but outdoor air helps me think, especially in the fall. Staring at the branches swaying eerily in the wind, my eyes venture to the shoes by the door, and a thrum of impulsiveness courses through me. Tentatively I put weight on my foot. It's really not so bad. Another gust of air sweeps through the window, and I've made my decision. Pulling on a second and third sock over my injured foot, I ease the laces of my shoe so that it will fit comfortably with the extra bulk.

Once outside, I follow the worn dirt footpath around the back of our building and through the bushes, stepping gingerly to minimize the pain. It's slow going, favoring my foot as much as I am, but I press on, and soon enough the little trail joins the paved path that snakes its way around the lake. Ironically, this is the same route I took after slicing myself open on the glass almost three weeks ago. No lights shine on the path, but the half moon overhead and a smattering of stars light the way over the slate gray pavement.

With the air verging on being too cold for the sweatshirt I'm wearing, I thrust my hands into the pockets but otherwise ignore the chill. The water is still, and an almost perfect copy of the moon reflects from the surface. The image wavers, the mirror disturbed, and a moment later a cool breeze runs its hand across my face.

A hill of grapevines slopes up from the shore, and at the top a wooden watchtower overlooks the inky water. I've seen this place from across the lake several times, but it's my first time actually out here. Weathered boards creak under my feet as I navigate the spiral walkway to the top, but they hold firm.

Far from any roads, the only sounds are the groaning trees and the whistle of the wind, more fierce up here, as it whips through the watchtower. Curling up cross-legged, I lean against the wooden center of the tower, the lake and lights of the dorms still visible through the guardrail's vertical slats. Surrounded only by the solemn sounds of fall, I exhale a low breath and allow myself the chance to admit what I've been afraid to.

My year abroad sucks. It was supposed to be the top of my college experience. Every moment was going to be a memory worthy of reminiscing. I would master the German language and make friends I would keep for life. Instead, I'm living in a room smaller than I did my freshman year, the Sprachkurs gives me a headache, I've only met a handful of friends, and all too often I find myself alone. Like I am now.

And there's Daniel. Why is he so hard to figure out?

Eyes sliding involuntarily to the side, my vision slips out of focus. I blink rapidly, bringing the world back to clarity, and pull my knees up to my chest. The closer we get to actually being friends, the more important it seems to spend time with him. When we're together, it's like there's someone else in the driver's seat. I don't like feeling as if I'm not in control.

I shouldn't compare the two of them, because Daniel is most likely straight, but I never felt this way with Corey. The experiences I had with him were completely new, but I always called the shots. Call it selfishness, but I was just watching out for myself. I didn't want to get hurt.

With Daniel, it's different. After just a handful of weeks, my thoughts are starting to revolve ever more closely around him. It's like I'm caught in his gravity, and by the time I realize the danger, it will be too late to escape. The thought scares the hell out of me.

Chapter 10

Daniel and I are wandering through the Altstadt for our second tandem meeting. We met after my Sprachkurs finished for the day—his suggestion, not mine. He'd given me his phone number just in case, but as soon as I rounded the last corner to the university courtyard, I spotted him right away waiting on a bench.

The day is just warm enough that we're comfortable in t-shirts and jeans, and we take our time as we pass the shops. He's been pointing out quirks and hidden bits of Freiburg's past, like the designs set into the cobblestone near shop entrances that are supposed to reflect the nature of the businesses. A mosaic representing a diamond ring is outside the jeweler, and another showing a five-foot pair of glasses laid into the sidewalk is in front of the optometrist. I love getting to know this hidden side of Freiburg. It's the part tourists never see.

"What about these little, uh . . . rivers running everywhere?" Knowing I've used the wrong word for them, I point to what I mean. About a foot wide, a network of tiny canals, the water an inch deep, passes down almost every street in the Altstadt. Through the university and around the cathedral square too, they're nearly everywhere.

He kicks a rock out of his way, and it bounces across the cobblestone street past a woman and her toddler. It catches the boy's attention and he stares at Daniel with wide eyes. "They're called *Bächle*. It means like . . . little stream, I guess."

"What are they for?"

"They used to be for fighting fires, but now they're just a part of the city. Plus they look cool."

At first I think it sounds silly, but I remember in one of my American history classes, we talked about the Great Chicago Fire and how a substantial portion of the city was destroyed. They might have been better off with some Bächle of their own. "Fighting fires? How old are they?"

"Almost as old as the city itself. Maybe seven hundred years, give or take."

"Damn." I try to imagine what this city and its "little streams" were like seven centuries ago. The history latent in every corner of Freiburg is astounding. In my hometown, the oldest building is the Carnegie library, which isn't even that impressive. In contrast, the narrow street we're walking down has a distinct age and authenticity to it. Vines creep up the brick and stucco of the shop fronts and the apartments overhead, adding splashes of green to the alley. The leafy masses have even sent tendrils snaking across an overhead cable suspended between the two sides of the street.

"Want to grab a beer?" Daniel asks.

There's a cafe at the end of the street with tables out front in full sun that must have given him the idea. "Isn't it a little early?"

He shakes his head. "No, it's the perfect time. Just look."

Almost every table is filled, and as we get closer it becomes clear no one is eating, except for one woman with a piece of pie. Most patrons have tall glasses of wheat beer in front of them. *Alright, I'm convinced.* I peer through the collection of tables, chairs and chattering Germans, looking for a place to sit. Trying to see around a street lamp, I take a step back. As I do, I expect to find solid stone under my heel, but there's only air and the electric shock of losing my balance jolts through my chest.

Before I've pitched backward more than a few inches, Daniel's arm is around me in an instant, pulling me back upright. A rope of muscle in his arm presses against my back.

"Thanks," I say, angrily looking to see what sort of vindictive hole in the ground just tried to upend me. I'm hoping to see some egregiously missing cobblestones but instead it's a Bächle, the water flowing cheerily along.

"Didn't we just talk about this?" He's trying not to smile, but there's no meanness in his voice.

I ignore him and the embarrassment swelling in my chest. Pointing to an open table nearest to the street, I suggest, "What about there?"

As we take our seats, he pulls the drink menu from the holder in the center of the table. "You know, if you accidentally step—or fall," he interrupts himself, "into one of the Bächle, legend says you'll end up marrying someone from Freiburg."

"Is that true?" I ask. He glances up from the menu card, giving me a look. I sigh. "That was a joke. You must think I'm kind of an idiot, huh?"

He studies me for several seconds. Passing the menu across the table, he says, "That's not true at all. Why would you say that?"

Before I can answer, the waitress arrives at our table. We both order half-liter glasses of *Hefeweizen*, the wheat beer that comes in the tall curved glasses. After she leaves, he looks at me expectantly.

"I don't know," I stall, trying to find the right words.

His eyebrows lifting upward, he leans back in his wooden folding chair. "You've got to give me more than that."

A bit of dirt on the edge of the brown painted table catches my attention, and I scratch it off with my fingernail. The coat of paint on the table gleams in the sunlight as if it were still wet. Maybe he'll forget what we're talking about if I wait long enough.

The waitress returns with our beers. Waves of bubbles materialize at the bottom of the glass and rise through the golden orange liquid to join the half-inch head. What a weird name for the foam on top of a beer.

"Prost," Daniel says, lifting his glass. Making eye contact with him as we clink our glasses together, I take a long pull. He takes a drink from his too before setting it down. I think it's impolite to take the first drink any other way.

"Well?" he prompts.

So much for burying the topic. Without looking up from my glass, I say, "The first couple weeks here, you either ignored me or made snide comments." This is the second time I've brought this up. It's probably something better avoided, but damn it I deserve to know why he acted the way he did. "You treated me like shit, Daniel."

He purses his lips into an even line, and there's a look in his eyes that's almost sad. "I'm sorry I made you feel that way."

Now that I've broken the seal on this, I might as well press him for an answer. "Why though? Why did you try so hard to push me away?"

Taking another long drink from the glass, he sets it down. It's just over half full. "I . . . I'm just bad at meeting people and making friends." It's a bullshit explanation, but some part of me knows it's all I'm going to get for now. In either case, I like spending time with him too much to press him further and endanger our friendship any more than I already have.

He finishes his beer before me, so I start to drink faster. The waitress comes again to ask if we want another, but Daniel tells her no and pays for both of us. If he'd asked permission I would have said no, but I'm kind of glad he didn't. I don't have much set aside for spending money this year.

After the waitress leaves, Daniel leans back in his chair, stretching his arms out behind him. As he does, his shirt rides up a few inches above his belt, revealing a smooth stomach and grooves angling downward from his hips.

There's a pulling sensation in the back of my throat and for some reason I can't drag my eyes away from that swath of exposed skin. I swallow to make the feeling go away, but it doesn't. It seems like forever, but finally he leans forward and the moment passes.

On our way back to the Strassenbahn stop, he has more to say about the city, explaining this statue and that fact as we pass through Freiburg's streets, but mostly I just nod, occasionally asking him carefully-timed questions so he'll think I'm still listening. As much as I try to ignore it, the image of him leaning back in that chair is stuck in my head.

Chapter 11

I'm downstairs loading the washing machine when I get another text from Niko. I stare at the phone, unsure if I want to bother with this right now. Setting down the laundry basket, I open the message. *hey Ethan, a bunch of us from the sprachkurs are going to the KGB bar tonight for drinks. you should come too*

It's Friday and the Sprachkurs just ended today, so I wouldn't mind going out, especially now that I can walk without those damn crutches. Florian volunteered to take out the stitches himself earlier in the week, to which I heartily agreed. Anything to save me a trip back to the hospital.

Going out with Niko would be risky though. He could be trying for the friend tack now, which would be a welcome change, or he could just be very determined to get me on a date with him. I tap out a reply. *not sure if i'm going out tonight. i'll let you know*

My annoyance at his unwanted advances fades as I consider what Daniel would think if he knew about my own errant thoughts. In a way, it isn't so different than Niko coming on to me. Except I've never actually made a pass at Daniel, and I don't intend to. Tossing the rest of my clothes into the machine, I make a guess which wash mode is right for my mixed colors. For what it's worth, Daniel is probably straight anyway.

* * *

Without any specific command from me, my feet lead me down the hall just after nine o'clock, coming to a stop in front of the door two down from my own. I should leave him alone, because he must have better things to do, but I just can't. I knock and hold my breath, my fingers drumming out a made-up rhythm on my thigh. Part of me is hoping he isn't here.

He opens the door. "Hey, what's up?"

An involuntary grin takes over. "I, uh, was wondering if you wanted to get a drink at the KGB? Some friends from my Sprachkurs are going there."

I dart a glance downward. Aside from his white t-shirt, he's wearing only a pair of basketball shorts. He doesn't even have socks on. His eyes flick to the side, then back to me. I'm sure he's going to say no. Hanging out with a bunch of exchange students he's never met before? No way. He scratches the side of his chin. "Sure. Give me a minute to get changed."

Ten minutes later, we're at the Strassenbahn stop. The air is still while we wait, but finally the tram rolls up. It's mostly empty, but we take seats next to each other anyway. Daniel is quiet as the train glides through the night.

We're almost to the edge of the city when he asks, "How many people will be there, you think?"

"Maybe five or ten. I'm not really sure. Why?"

"Just curious." His thumb and forefinger are kneading the knuckles of his other hand, but his gaze is directed out the window. *Is he nervous?* Maybe I shouldn't have asked him to come out tonight. I have no idea how he'll react to meeting half of the students from my Sprachkurs. I want him to have a good time.

At the center of the Altstadt, we alight from the tram and make our way through cobblestone alleys, which although dark now, are actually perfectly respectable pedestrian walkways filled with shops. From the outside, the KGB bar doesn't look much brighter than the darkened glass of the shops it's nestled between.

"Have you been to this bar before?" I ask.

"A few years ago, but I haven't gone out in quite a while."

"Why's that?"

He shoves his hands in his pockets as we step through the door and are greeted by music. "No reason."

Niko catches my attention and waves us over. I recognize Corinne and Bastien right away, but there are a few others from my class that I never got to know that well. After introductions, I pull another table up to make room for us.

"The KGB bar is named for its Soviet theme," Niko quickly explains in his clipped German accent. "It's famous for having the widest selection of vodka in Freiburg, over three hundred different kinds."

When the waitress comes, we decide as a group to start out with a platter of fruity vodkas ranging from banana to boysenberry. Daniel orders a beer. I give him a look that says *come on*. He has the good humor to appear apologetic but doesn't change his order. He looks comfortable enough though, despite the fact he's never met any of these people before.

Taking our first round of shots while Daniel sips dutifully on his beer, we order another round. We joke about Frau Schmidt, our Sprachkurs teacher, and how serious she sometimes was when we made simple grammatical mistakes. "*Deutsche Sprache, Schwere Sprache*," I imitate her voice—*German language, difficult language*, she would always say. This drags a smile even out of Daniel, the only German among us.

Normally, there aren't any native German speakers along when we exchange students get together, so disputes about grammar or the finer points of word meaning often drag on without resolution. Taking advantage of his presence, Corinne asks him a question about past perfect versus preterit passive constructions that we were debating after class today.

Daniel blushes, admitting, "I don't actually know what you're talking about. Can you give me an example?"

Niko nudges me from the side while Corinne gives Daniel two examples of sentences with the passive construction. "You ever notice," Niko says, "how Germans don't know anything about their own grammar? They just know if it's right or wrong when they hear it."

"Yeah, they're all like that."

After Daniel answers Corinne, the others take more interest in him and begin showering him with questions. Ironically, since we're all exchange students, it's refreshing to meet someone who *isn't* doing their year abroad, learning German, and studying something like international relations or global studies.

With Daniel fully engaged and the center of attention, I get up to find the restroom. He's fitting in surprising well, but I'm certain that questions about his family or background will be deflected in favor of talking about Freiburg and the university.

The bar is so dark I decide to just walk up to the bartender to ask. He has a messy faux hawk and looks maybe a year or two older than me. He points to a hallway that disappears away from the bar, and then he winks at me.

"Thanks," I say and follow his directions. Why would he wink like that? No one has ever winked at me since I got to Germany, so it's not just a *thing* here.

Back at the table, I quietly whisper to Niko, "Guess what just happened."

"Spill it," he whispers back.

I'm peripherally aware that Daniel is watching us while I quietly explain about the wink, but he's in the middle of responding to a question about the history of Freiburg's cathedral. He may or may not actually know the answer, but we all like to assume that Germans know everything about all parts of their country, regardless of where they're from. I return my attention to Niko. "Do you think bartenders just wink at everyone here?" I ask him.

He leans back to see around a structural column between the bartender and us. He shakes his head slowly. "No, I don't think so. He's cute though."

"Yeah, I noticed. Do you think he's gay?" I wasn't checking him out exactly, but I definitely noticed he was good looking—built well enough that his arms were threatening to stretch the sleeves of his polo.

Niko is still leaning back, staring at the bartender with a scheming expression. "No idea. I think we should go talk to him."

"No way," I exclaim. "Are you serious?" I can feel Daniel's gaze on me again, but there's no way to include him in our conversation without making a big production of it.

"Sure, why not?"

I glance between Niko, the bartender, and Daniel, who meets my eyes for a moment before looking down at his beer.

We toss back the second round of shots, and Niko gets up. Should I leave Daniel here by himself? Wiping the sweat off my palms, I follow Niko as he marches toward the bartender. The establishment is getting fuller now, but since no one is ordering anything besides vodka, he doesn't have much to do.

With forwardness I can't imagine myself mustering, Niko sidles right up to the bar. "How's your night going?" His accent seems to come through stronger than normal. Is he doing that on purpose?

The poor guy must be pretty bored, because his face brightens and he abandons the rag he's been wiping the bar with. "It's pretty good." He's talking loudly so we can hear him over the music. "And you guys?"

"We're great." Niko pauses before continuing, directing his eyes downward as he speaks. "So do you have anything behind that counter that's not on the menu?" He's grinning like a cat eyeing a bird out the window. I have to stop myself from rolling my eyes at his double meaning, but I hold it together and keep a straight face.

The bartender has a subtle smile and a look in his eye like he knows what's going on here, but he plays along anyway. "Actually, we do. It's a free shot as long as you drink it all at once and don't smell or taste it first."

Bolstered by the guy's friendly challenge, I match Niko's enthusiasm. "We'll do it."

Niko looks surprised at my declaration, but it's too late to back out. Now the bartender is the one with a mile-wide grin as he pulls an unmarked, clear glass bottle from a mini-fridge under the bar. If it hadn't been for the shots we'd already taken, I would be chickening out right now. Maybe this is the special bottle laced with ipecac syrup for patrons that hit on the bartender. I give Niko a nervous look and he responds with jokingly worried eyes, but we don't say anything as the two shots are poured.

"Alright," the bartender says, "Both drink on three. *Eins, zwei, drei—los!*"

We toss back our shots. At first, I feel only the mildly unpleasant burn of the alcohol and, in relief, think he's just been messing with us. Then a second, nastier feeling comes. A spicy, earthy burning races down my throat and through my nostrils as I explode with a cough. Niko is likewise seized by a fit of coughing while the bartender chuckles mischievously.

"Damn," I sputter, "What was that?"

Quelling his laugh, he explains, "Pepper vodka. It has a bit of a kick. Like you wanted, it's not on the menu," he says with a smirk. I'm about to conclude that he's an ass when he pours two mixed drinks. "Here," he pushes them toward us, "This will help clear the taste out."

As we drink, it's easy to see that Niko is smitten by him, because he heartily drives the conversation forward. We learn that the guy's name is Alex, and he goes to school at the Universität Freiburg too. Of course, he could tell immediately we're foreign by our accents, but when he learns I'm American, he wants to speak only English. Apparently, Niko doesn't mind either, since he doesn't often get to speak it. Something about the presence of a native speaker makes everyone want to practice. It's always irritating when this happens, but both Niko and Alex want to, so I decide not to push it.

It's with relief that I watch the two of them flirt. The last thing I need right now is someone crushing on me. Despite my initial reservations about coming tonight, I'm starting to genuinely enjoy spending time with Niko. He's fun to be around, and it's a good distraction from other things that have been on my mind.

We finish our first drinks and wait while Alex pours a trio of beers for some vodka-haters. When he returns, he has another pair of shots for us. "Not more pepper, I hope!" I say.

"No, I think this is raspberry or something," he says to me off-handedly, keeping his eyes on my friend. I smile to myself. Niko's forwardness might actually be rewarded.

The conversation increasingly revolves between Niko and Alex, who continues pouring drinks for us as soon as we finish them, alternating between shots and cocktails. I'm not used to having alcohol supplied so readily, and it's catching up with me. With a year of college behind me, I've been to plenty of parties, but this is definitely different. The drinks just don't seem to slow down here. The room is beginning to tilt back and forth as I pull my wallet out of my back pocket. There's thirty euro inside, which isn't enough to pay for all the drinks we've had by half.

The music has grown louder, and Alex and Niko are both leaning forward to hear each other, their elbows perched on the bar. From this angle, the silhouette of Alex's face is crisp against the dim lighting behind the bar. He's thin, which is reflected in his face, but his features are all well defined. I wait until they both laugh about something to sneak my hand around Niko's bicep. Pulling him toward me, I yell over that music that I can't pay for all my drinks.

I thought I kept my voice hushed, but Alex must have overheard me, because he speaks before Niko does. It's a bit of a struggle to discern his accented English over the noise, but after a second I put it together. "No problem, it's on the house."

"Thanks," I mumble, feeling my face flushing, even though it's probably indistinguishable over the heat of the alcohol.

Alex waves dismissively. "No problem."

Under my feet, the floor is starting to sway as well. My thoughts drift back to Daniel. *Shit! I forgot all about him.*

Niko will be just fine by himself, but I want to at least tip our new friend. There's a five-dollar bill that has been tucked away in my wallet since I left the States. I slide it across the counter to Alex, who looks at me quizzically, but I push it farther forward until he takes it. It would be a big tip if it were in Euro and I'd actually paid for my drinks. Being U.S. dollars, though, it's more of a novelty tip. In either case, it's the last American money in my possession until I fly home next year.

Making my way through the crowd back to the table, I see Daniel still sitting with the others from my Sprachkurs. He's nursing the dregs of a beer and isn't involved in their conversation anymore. His eyebrows are scrunched together and his gaze doesn't leave the table.

When he finally glances up to see me approaching, I can tell he's mad about being left here for so long. I pull out my phone—it's past midnight already. I kind of have to pee, but I know he wants to leave. "Are ya ready to go?" I ask, slurring the German words together.

"Yeah, sure." He's already paid his tab, so he starts to fight his way to the exit. The crowd is so thick that it would be problematic squeezing through if I weren't following in his wake.

The outside air strains to pull me back to sobriety, but it's not working very well. The ground is swaying and my shoes keep catching on the cobblestones. Daniel watches me stumbling, and frustration permeates his voice when he speaks. "We missed the last Strassenbahn, so now we have to walk home."

"I'm sorry," I say, articulating carefully and concentrating harder on not tripping. "The bartender kept giving us free drinks."

"Yeah, okay." He still sounds pissed.

I stop and put my hand on his shoulder so he turns to look me in the eye. "I'm sorry, alright?" I wouldn't let myself touch him like this if I were sober, but he gives me a weak smile, so I'm glad I did.

He exhales a long breath, and with it his irritation seems to subside. "It's alright, but we do have a long way home." He's still upset I think, but not as much as before. We walk in silence, passing only a handful of other late night revelers on our way out of the city.

Soon we're crossing the arching bridge that connects the Altstadt to the west side of the city while spanning a dozen long-distance rail-road tracks. The pressure below my waist is becoming harder to ignore, especially since there is a good forty-five minute walk ahead. I glance back toward the Altstadt. No one is in sight. It's just the two of us on the path alongside the Strassenbahn tracks that run over the bridge.

"I have to piss," I say, moving to the edge of the bridge and planting myself in front of the balustrade. About twenty feet below is the ground, the green grass of a city park. Positioning myself between a pair of stone pillars, I unzip my fly. The night air is cool against me, and then, ah, sweet relief. I sway forward while the pattering of liquid striking dirt rises up from below. Then the sound doubles. My eyes snap open.

A few feet to my right, Daniel is likewise pressed up between a pair of the miniature stone columns. Noticing me looking at him, he says, "What?" His eyes shift away into the darkness ahead. Mine drift toward his waist, but there's nothing to see but denim and carved stone. He finishes peeing before me, even though I started first. After zipping up, we continue on our way.

The lamps illuminating the path are farther apart now, and only the trees occur at regular intervals. Pulling his jacket closer as the wind picks up, Daniel says, "Thanks. For bringing me out tonight."

"I thought you hated it."

"Yeah, I kind of did," he chuckles. Turning serious, he says, "It's been so long since I went out. Tonight reminded me what it's like to have a good time with people close to you."

The last shots I took at the bar are beginning to take effect, and my stomach is giving me a warning, but I'm determined to stay lucid for this conversation. If I pick exactly the right words, maybe he'll open up. "What changed, that you don't go out anymore?"

A momentary wince fills his face before he looks away. After a pause, he inhales sharply, but I'm not sure if it's from the cold or if he's really trying not to cry. When he speaks again, his voice is clear. "It's like you said, things changed."

A painful roil in my stomach indicates there's no more time to take another shot at discovering a part of Daniel's past. Bile is rising in my throat. I *hate* puking. Sprinting off the path, I don't make it ten feet into the trees before dropping to my knees and throwing up. I'm careful to keep my hands and everything else out of the way while I heave several times.

An embarrassed glance over my shoulder confirms Daniel is wait-ing under the orange halo of a streetlamp as I fight through the worst of it. My knees are planted in the grass, and I'm still spitting to clear the acid from my mouth when I feel his hand come to a rest between my shoulder blades. His touch is warm, and I'm glad for his presence next to me. "Come on, Ethan, let's go home," he says quietly.

I force my eyes open, and the ceiling comes slowly into focus in the dim light. I blink a few more times to clear the sleep from my vi-sion. My throat is dry and I'm terribly thirsty. Reaching for the glass of water always on my nightstand, I turn and realize that this is all wrong. "What the hell . . ." My groggy brain struggles to process the situation as I sit up. My nightstand isn't here, and neither is my desk. I'm on a mattress, but it's on the floor. Then in a split second of understanding, everything becomes familiar. This is Daniel's room. Which leaves me with my original thought—what the hell? I don't remember a damn thing after throwing up.

I give the room a once-over and conclude that Daniel isn't here. I'm lying on the pullout mattress that's normally concealed under his bed. It's actually comfortable, not that a hard mattress would have kept me from sleep last night. Shifting my position, it becomes immediately apparent I'm not wearing the jeans I had on yesterday. Shooting a look under the covers, I'm relieved. At least my boxers are still on. Nothing else though.

At that moment, the door opens and I drop the blanket. It's Daniel, wearing only flip flops and shorts, his silhouette framed by light pour-ing in from the hallway. I take in the etched lines around his biceps, pectorals, and the toned edges of his stomach before dropping my gaze like I did the blanket.

"Morning," he says, sitting down at the swivel chair in front of his desk. Taking a sip from a glass of orange juice, he watches me casually. He looks like a model. The words almost pop out of my mouth, but luckily something stops them. My face flushes.

When I finally manage to speak, my voice comes out as a croak. "I'm not wearing any pants."

He raises his hands as if to declare his innocence. "You took them off yourself." He points to a pile of clothes by the door that contains my jeans, shirt, and socks, with my shoes perched on top.

"How did I end up sleeping here?"

He's opening the shades now, and bright light cascades in, spilling over his olive skin still bronze from summer. The warm taste of longing spreads in the back of my throat. I grit my teeth. This is impossible. If only he would put a shirt on, I could at least think clearly. I direct my eyes at the floor.

"You don't remember anything, huh?" he asks rhetorically. "Well, we got home, you let us in the front door, and then I went to my room. But somehow you managed to lose your keys between downstairs and your room. I helped you look for a while, but we couldn't find them. You could hardly put a full sentence together, so I pulled out the spare mattress and let you sleep here."

"Oh." I can't think of anything else to say. I think there must still be some alcohol upstairs mucking up my brain. "That means I've lost my keys."

"I promise you they're in the building. I watched you use them to get in."

"Unless I flushed them down the toilet or something stupid like that," I mutter.

He sits back down and takes another swig of orange juice. "Actually, I didn't think to look in the bathroom. You might have just dropped them on the floor."

I should head back to my room now, but I haven't been good about keeping my eyes off him. At the moment, a traitorous part of me has decided it likes seeing him shirtless, so I'm not exactly at liberty to toss the covers off and get dressed with him watching. "Um, thanks for letting me sleep here," I say, hoping he'll get the hint.

"No problem." He looks unsure what to do. "Do you want me to go out?"

I probably stripped down to my boxers right in front of him last night, but I obviously can't do that now. I'd prefer to let him think I'm comfortable with dressing in front of him, sober or not, but I don't really have a choice. "Could you like, turn around?" I try to make it sound like I don't care that much.

He spins in his chair so he's facing his computer. Good enough for me. Without another moment's hesitation, I tug on my jeans with lightning speed and snatch up my shirt and shoes, letting myself steal one last look at him before slipping out the door.

While taking a piss, I spot my keys lying in the corner of the bathroom by the shower. Go figure. Back in my room, I crack open a bottle of carbonated water and drink until I can't hold anymore. Bodily needs satisfied, I hop up on the bed with my back against the wall. Pulling my legs into my chest, I wrap my arms around myself. Something about this position always makes me feel safe. When my dad left, I spent a lot of time curled up like this.

Chapter 12

Bastien and Corinne from the Sprachkurs have been planning a trip to Colmar all week. It's supposed to be a cute little French town just on the other side of the French-German border. Corinne's from there, so all week in class she's been going on about how beautiful it is. She's talked it up so much that I decide it might actually be a good time, and I stop by Daniel's room after class on Friday to invite him.

"You don't have to do the tandems anymore now that your class is done," he says, a hint of confusion in his tone.

"I know, but I thought maybe we could just . . . I dunno, hang out?"

I can see the battle going on inside that always plays out whenever I ask him things like this, but it seems to be resolved faster than usual. "Yeah, okay, that sounds like fun I guess. I haven't been to France in a while."

"Awesome," I say, fighting to keep my voice level. "We're leaving from the main train station at ten tomorrow, so we can catch the Strassenbahn into town a little before that."

"Sure, just stop by."

I practically skip back to my room. Daniel and I are going to France! Sure it's only fifteen miles to the border, and probably just another ten or twenty to Colmar, but still. It's France.

Come Saturday morning though, there's a text waiting on my phone from Bastien. *sorry man, Corinne and I were out real late last night. we're totally not up to a bus ride*

My fingers tighten around the phone as my mood darkens. They've been planning this for a week, and now they cancel the morning of? They knew we were going today, so why did they drink so much last night?

There's a sinking feeling in my chest at realizing that Daniel and I won't be spending the day together after all. Who knows if he'll agree to go the next time I ask? Maybe this was a one-shot deal, my one chance to redeem myself after what happened last week at the KGB bar.

After showering, I check the clock on my laptop. It's almost nine. At the very least, I have to let Daniel know we're not going. After that, I can while away my free hours in whatever miserably boring way I want. Dragging myself down the hall, I knock on his door. It opens a half-second before my fist would have hit the wood for a third time. Daniel's bright expression changes when he sees my face. "What's wrong?"

Letting out a sigh that doesn't hide my disappointment in the slightest, I admit, "My friends from the Sprachkurs cancelled. They're not going anymore." I look away, but I can feel his gaze still on me.

"Hey," he says, brushing a knuckle against my shirt right over my sternum. My skin tingles at the contact. This brief touch is able to lift my eyes to his more effectively than words ever could. "Why don't we ask just Florian and Paula if they want to go with us? Just because your friends aren't going doesn't mean we can't. It's going to be a beautiful day, so we might as well enjoy it."

"Really?" I doubt that either of our other roommates will be free. They've been holed away in their rooms every weekend working on their thesis papers since I moved in.

"Sure, why not?"

My concerns turn out to be justified, because both Florian and Paula turn us down, albeit apologetically. After the second door closes in front of us, Daniel turns to me, apparently undeterred. "So do you want to still go?"

"Oh, yeah! You really want to go since it's just the two of us, though? Not that you wouldn't, but I thought that—" I stop mid-sentence before I make more a fool of myself.

He's trying not to smile. "Yeah, I'd still like to."

"Should we head to the Strassenbahn then? I'm not sure of the bus schedule, but I know they leave from the main train station."

"You mind if we just take my car?"

Of course, why hadn't I thought of that? "Hell yeah."

"You have a thing for Beamers or what?"

"Something like that. Any nice car, really." And nice guys who drive nice cars. He doesn't need to know that though. "Your car is kinda sweet," I concede.

"Oh that old thing?" He grins over his shoulder at me.

"Shut up," I say laughing, shoving him as we pound down the stairs.

Once the engine growls to life, Daniel cranks the radio to some German song with a solid beat and peels out of the parking garage and into the street, throwing us back into the seats. *What a show off.* But I like it. Even the sound system is good in this car. Like, *really* good. It's crisp and clear, and when the bass hits, it massages my back through the seat. Trees and other cars whiz past as he leads us out of Freiburg, following the green signs marked "Colmar." He taps a button in front of the rear view mirror, and the sunroof opens up, bringing a fresh current of fall air into the cabin.

The singer on the radio is going on about monkeys in the city or something, but it's kind of hard to understand. The song is a bit weird, but it's catchy. Dialing back the volume knob on the head unit, I raise my voice over the noise of the road and the wind and the music. "Who is this?"

"Peter Fox. Ever heard of him?" When I shake my head, he explains loudly so I can hear. "He's also the singer for Seeed. You've heard of *them*, right?"

I shake my head again. "Sorry."

"Come on," he complains, "You've got to listen to the radio more. You're missing out, man."

Stretching my hand out over the armrest, I look away out the window. The music abruptly goes quiet, and without any other warning, he starts belting out some German song. "*Ooh ooh, du hübsches Ding, ich versteck' meinen Ehering, klingelingeling wir könntens bring, doch wir nuckeln nur am Drink . . .*" He doesn't continue even though it's clear he knows more of the lyrics. His voice isn't going to win him American Idol, but it's cute to hear him sing. I raise my eyebrows and smile.

It's as though he only now realizes what he's just done, because he turns red and looks away. "So you haven't heard that song either?"

"Nope." I'm still smiling. "I think you need to sing some more and see if there are any other German songs I know."

"Whatever." He turns the radio back up.

Just a few minutes more and we're pulling into Colmar. I didn't even realize we'd left Germany. Thinking back, the big river we crossed must have been the border. Daniel parks the car and tosses some money into the machine.

I want to ask him where we're going as I follow him away from the car, but it seems like he knows the way, so I make myself stop worrying about our destination and simply enjoy the town instead.

It's picturesque like the Altstadt of Freiburg, but more . . . fairytale. Freiburg's old buildings all look like they're three hundred years old because they *are*, but the multistory houses towering over us now with their red, yellow, and blue tinted façades almost feel contrived. I'm sure they're authentic, but there's something strangely Candyland mixed with Disney that seems to permeate these cobblestone streets.

"Does all of France look like this?" I ask Daniel, gesturing vaguely around us.

"Nah, at least not in the cities." We pass a salesman in front of a cart filled with freshly cut flowers.

"It's just all so . . ."

"French?" Daniel offers, hanging a right to take us deeper into the old part of town.

"Yeah. It feels weird." It really is pretty here, but the streets are quiet. Probably because it's still early. Having taken Daniel's car, it took half the time it would have with the bus.

Letting the sun's warmth soak into me, I take a moment to be thankful that he was still up for coming here. Beside us is a canal, maybe ten feet wide. Unlike Freiburg's Bächle, this is a real waterway, with occasional bridges spanning its width.

Stepping out of the way of a group of kids yammering in French, Daniel asks, "You want to get something to eat? I didn't have anything for breakfast." In answer to his suggestion, my stomach rumbles. He smirks. "So that's a yes?"

I nod, looking around at the shops. Most are either closed or selling crap for tourists. "You know a place?"

"Not really," he says, shrugging with a nonchalance you'd only expect in a country with a thirty-five hour workweek. Quite aptly, that's exactly where we are. "But we'll spot a *patisserie* soon, I'm sure. They're everywhere."

I give him a look. "Patiss-what?"

"A bakery," he translates the word into German and points up ahead. "Voila."

The smell inside is amazing, but even that doesn't do justice to the array of baked goods spread behind the glass cases. Everything from donuts to loaves of bread to premade cold sandwiches. There's even a row of those big pretzels they sell at baseball games in the States, except these have a golden-colored cheese melted all over them. And bits of ham. They look good, but I'm in the mood for something sweet.

Beside me, Daniel is gazing into the gleaming cases as well. An old lady in front of us has just paid and leaves the shop, clutching her bag of rolls. Behind the counter, a young woman with blond hair about our age announces, "*Bonjour.*" She almost sounds bored. Daniel repeats her greeting, but continues looking through the glass. I ignore them both, my attention drifting to a display of a thin pancake covered in chocolate.

"*Tu vois quelque chose qui te plaît?*" she says to Daniel, a coy smile playing across her red lips.

To my surprise, he points to one of the sandwiches and answers her in French. "*Eh, oui, je prends celui-ci.*"

"*Et pour lui?*" She gestures to me but doesn't take her eyes off him.

"What would you like, Ethan?" Daniel switches into German as he addresses me.

I swallow, feeling awkwardly left out of their conversation. "Could I get one of these pancake things with the chocolate?"

"*Il prend une crêpe au chocolat,*" he says with a nod toward the pancake display.

"*Bien sûr,*" The girl pours out a dollop of batter onto a circular hot plate behind her, spreading it into a thin circle with a little stick contraption. It cooks fast, so after just a minute she's already ladling liquid chocolate all over it. Folding it into quarters, she sets it in a paper cone and hands it to me.

Before Daniel can get his wallet out, I set a five Euro bill on the counter. The girl gives him the bagged-up sandwich and takes the bill, dropping the change into a curved plastic tray. "*Merci,*" I say, pocketing the coins.

Our loot in hand, Daniel and I emerge onto the street. "Is that the only French word you know?"

"Maybe."

Whatever he thinks about that, he doesn't say. Instead he nods toward a bridge that arcs over the canal. "Let's sit down."

We hoist ourselves up onto the wide stone ledge that guards the sunward side of the bridge, letting our legs dangle over the water. It's still a while before noon, and the sun shines into my eyes, forcing me to stare into the canal. "Was that girl hitting on you?" I ask.

Waiting until having swallowed the first bite of his sandwich, he makes a noncommittal noise. "Maybe, I don't know for sure. I'm not that great at French."

He could have fooled me. "Uh huh." I dig into the pancake. It's light and practically melts in my mouth. Chocolate oozes out the end onto my fingers. "So what did she say to you?"

"Just asked if I saw anything I liked."

"And did you?"

He hesitates for a moment, and then looks pointedly at his sandwich. "Sure did."

Before I have a chance to decide if I should read into that, he grins and says, "You look like you're enjoying that crêpe."

I wave what's left of the pancake in the air with my chocolate fingers. "Did you just call this thing a 'crap?'"

He chuckles, shaking his head. "A *crêpe*, Ethan. It's a French *Pfannekuchen*."

Oh for Christ's sake. "Is that German for *pancake*?" I say the last word in English.

"Yeah, I guess. But your American pancakes are giant and oddly thick. A Pfannekuchen is like what you have there."

"I don't care what it's called, it's tasty." I pop the last piece into my mouth, swinging my feet back and forth over the water. Holding my sticky, chocolate-covered fingers in front of me, I look around for something to wipe them on, but we didn't get any napkins. Then I notice Daniel's gaze on me. "What?" I ask, licking my fingers clean.

He's got a crooked smile on his face. Reaching out a hand, he ruffles up my hair. It makes me feel like a little kid, and I glare at him from under my bangs. "Hey, cut that out," I snap. A dislodged hair floats in front of me for a moment before a breeze carries it away. Daniel doesn't say a thing, instead turning to face into the sun.

Corey used to do shit like that all the time to me, and I hated it.

Unbidden, a memory surfaces in my mind. We'd been together for about a month, and we were in line at the movie theater waiting to buy tickets. The place was packed, and we'd been waiting forever already. Just as we were almost to the ticket counter, he announced in an unnecessarily loud voice, "Dude, your fly is open."

Of course everyone within earshot looked, myself included, to check on what was sure to be a gaping zipper. The moment I looked down though, he started tickling the shit out of me. I could have fucking killed him. Instead, I stormed out of the theater with everyone's eyes on me. We almost broke up right there in the parking lot. Not that we were really dating, not then anyway.

Daniel is still staring off into the morning, his eyelashes catching the sunlight. From this angle, his cleanly shaven face is crisply defined, the lines and curves of his features so smooth they could have been carved from stone.

He shifts to meet my stare. "What is it?"

"Um, nothing." Turning to hide my face, I carefully hop onto the walkway of the bridge. "Come on, let's see the rest of this town."

Hours later, we start the trip home. The ride goes fast, with the soothing quiet of late afternoon carrying us back across the German border. It was fun to see the charming buildings and shops of Colmar, but I'm glad to be heading home. Spending the day there was like eating too much cake. It was colorful and sweet and covered in French frosting, but it wasn't substantial. Freiburg is solid and practical. It certainly has its own charm, but it's tempered with a down-home sort of humility.

Yawning, I crack my neck to the left, then to the right, before sneaking a glance at Daniel. His eyes are tied to the road, and he guides the vehicle with his usual precision, not once straying outside the lines. It was cool of him to agree to spend the day together. I'm not sure if any of my other friends here would do that. Does that mean something about Daniel and me as friends?

"Thanks for inviting me along," he says as we pull into the parking garage. "I had a good time today."

"Yeah, me too." I'm glad to know that we won't stop spending time together, just because our tandems have ended. Once we're back inside our dorm, I wait at my door and watch him move away down the hall. His arms sway as he walks, like his biceps get in the way of regular movement. Not wanting to let him catch me staring again, I push open the door to my room before he gets to his.

A feeling of unease has begun to smolder inside me whenever Daniel and I are apart. It's like a piece of me has disappeared, and I can't seem to find it. I guess it doesn't take a psychologist to figure out why that is, but it's more than that too. Our friendship is the best thing that's happened to me so far this year. When I'm with him, it feels like I actually *belong* here. Not to mention that my German has improved tremendously.

But I don't want to feel this way. It makes me feel so . . . exposed. It wasn't really an accident that I ended up with someone like Corey who was attractive and fun—while occasionally an asshole—but from whom I never wanted much more. It was safer that way, and always so easy.

When we first started seeing each other, he'd come over, we'd goof around, play video games, occasionally do something useful but usually not, and then we'd get off. And when he left, that was it. I didn't think much about him until the next weekend rolled around. That was the way I liked it.

As last summer wore on, though, things started to change. I remember it was just after we'd started having real sex. Actually, we were having sex when it happened. The day was one of hottest of the summer, and my cheap student apartment didn't have air conditioning, so we were dripping even before we ran to the bedroom. Already shirtless, we didn't have much more to go before winding up naked on my bed.

Hips pumping with an inexhaustible stamina, his body loomed over me like the thunderheads outside on the horizon. Maybe it was the thick humidity or maybe just because we started without any preamble, but it was taking longer than normal. It was good though. Really good. And I knew from the way Corey's jaw was clenching every few seconds that he thought so too.

We were both getting really close when he leaned down on top of me so our stomachs touched. Still thrusting and his breath coming in hot gulps, he growled in my ear, "I fucking love you, Ethan."

The ensuing look of shock and bewilderment on my face made him recoil so much that he ended up pulling out, so fast that I winced in pain. Kneeling back, his expression shifted in a way I instantly recognized. Already having hit the point of no return and unable to stop himself, he came, ejaculating on the sheets between us.

His face was bright red, but it could have been from the heat. "What the fuck, Ethan?" Hurt and anger rebelled against each other in his voice like curdling milk in citrus tea, unwilling to mix together.

The words we exchanged that day roll around in my head. It was the moment everything changed. From then on, our interactions were always strained. We didn't break up, but our time together was always tainted by fear. His was that he'd lose me, and mine was that I wouldn't have the strength to push him away. At least that's what I thought at the time, but what was I afraid of really? Yeah, Corey could be super irritating at times, but we weren't that bad for each other. We always had a good time, even when we were fighting.

I grit my teeth in frustration. How is it that I moved across an ocean but I still can't get away from him? Maybe it's because for the first time I can imagine myself being on the other side of that fear. I've never considered it before, because until recently, I'd never met anyone I could feel that way about, but the thought kind of scares me. What happens when the person you're with, like really *with*—body and heart and soul, or whatever—what happens when they leave you?

Chapter 13

Regular classes are now in full swing at the university. After the fun I had with Niko at the KGB bar, I decided to ask if he wanted to hang out after our classes got done for the day. We're meandering along the Strassenbahn tracks that carve their way through the heart of Freiburg's old quarter. The sun is shining in typical Freiburg fashion, making today feel warmer than it really is.

"What do you think these gold-colored bricks were put here for?" I ask, leaning down to examine a small square of metal inserted snuggly into the web of cobblestone. It's a dull gold color, maybe brass, and has years of wear visible in the scratches and scuffs on its surface. A name and address are engraved into it, as well as a pair of dates.

Cocking his head slightly, Niko says, "They're called *Stolpersteine.*" *Stumble stones.* They mark where the Jews used to live that were taken from Freiburg by the Nazis."

Even though I'm warm inside my jacket, a shiver grips me. "Oh." It's never pleasant to get slapped in the face by Nazi history. I know Niko isn't Jewish, but the Poles weren't exactly spared by the Nazis either. We continue moving along the street, and as we walk, I see several other Stolpersteine. It's strange I've never noticed them before. In my four months in Germany, World War II has been mentioned barely a handful of times. Even though it's rarely voiced, the history here is so close it's almost tangible, like an invisible current running through everything. Even under our feet apparently.

It's as if Niko can read my thoughts, because as we start down one of the central streets that cuts through the Altstadt, he says, "You know, this street used to be Adolf Hitler Strasse before they renamed it after the war."

"You're kidding."

"Nope," he chuckles darkly, "Named after the bastard himself."

We don't say anything more, because there's nothing else to say. I try to imagine the street as it looked seventy years ago. The buildings in this part of town are all far older than that, so they wouldn't have changed. Closing my eyes, the banners that now proclaim the upcoming Freiburg Wine Festival are gone, replaced by rows of red, white, and black Swastika banners. I shudder.

A shop that sells only things made from honey snags our attention. A gust of cool air follows us in and a bell at the top of the door jingles. The shopkeeper must be in the back. "Take a look at this," I say, gesturing to the display of honey spirits.

"You actually like mead?" Niko asks.

"I've never had it before. I really like honey though."

"Buy a bottle then. I'll bet you the guy makes it himself."

"I wonder if Daniel likes mead," I muse.

"Is he the roommate you brought to KGB?"

"Uh, yeah."

Niko gives me a look. I pretend to ignore him. We pick out a bottle, and the owner of the shop appears from the back in time for us to make the purchase.

Back in the alley with the bottle wrapped securely in my backpack, we return to the transfer stop in the center of the Altstadt. Even though it's cooler today, the sun is bright and makes me reluctant to go home already. "You want to, like, stick around in town a little longer?"

Niko pauses, examining me. Unlike when Daniel mentally debates things—an odd battle of indecision always waging inside—Niko seems to be won over quickly. "Sure, what did you have in mind?" A moment after I give him a clueless look, his eyes grow bright. "Oh I know, let's go to *Augustiner Platz!*"

"What's that?" I think I've heard the name before, but I can't put my finger on it.

"Oh, you know," he says, already starting down the street. "It's that square next to the museum where everyone hangs out on the steps."

Ah, right. I remember now. "Sure, why not."

Despite my initial skepticism, a lot of other students are sitting on the steps of the Augustiner Platz simply enjoying the afternoon. We grab a spot near the center that was just vacated by a group of girls. It only takes a minute to notice that everyone around us is drinking. Mostly beer, but other stuff too. It's like a BYOB bar in the middle of the square.

The sun still far above the tops of the buildings, Niko squints as he turns to me. "Too bad we didn't bring anything to drink."

"Yeah, seriously." And then I remember.

"What are you doing?"

"The mead, it's a twist off," I explain, taking the bottle out of my bag. "I remember specifically because I thought it was kind of trashy." Handing it to Niko, I zip up the backpack.

He opens the bottle and takes a small drink, making a face. "That's . . . interesting."

"What?"

"It's . . . oddly sweet, but still tastes like alcohol."

"Here let me try." I take the bottle from him and tip it back. I grimace. He's right, actually, but it's not *that* bad.

Niko laughs, shaking his head. "I told you so."

"You're not going to drink anymore then?"

"Of course I am. Hand it over."

I oblige him, watching as he takes a long drink and stares off across the square once he's finished. It's always so easy being with Niko. We've never even discussed that we're both gay, because there's no need to.

He holds the bottle out for me. "What?"

"Nothing." I look away. I don't want him to get the wrong idea, because that's not what I'm after at all. I feel a tug inside, but it's not one of attraction. It's the warm, bubbly feeling of realizing that I've made a real friend.

Another pass of the bottle between us and I'm telling him about Corey. Niko listens patiently as I explain how we met and started dating. About what he meant to me but more importantly what he didn't, and lastly how I ended it the day before flying to Germany.

When I finally finish, he stays quiet. I feel like it should bother me that I'm buzzed already and have just confessed to being an asshole to my now ex-boyfriend, but for some reason it doesn't. Being honest with Niko feels . . . natural, and just because it took a little alcohol to get me there doesn't diminish how comfortable I feel around him. "Well," I prompt. "What do you think? Am I terrible person?"

Taking a sip from the bottle, he sets it down on the stone step beside our feet. Only about a quarter of the mead remains, so by unspoken agreement we've slowed down to make it last. "No," he says, giving me a long look. "You're not a bad person Ethan. You're just . . . a person. We all make decisions we're not happy about. Whether or not it was the right thing to do, it doesn't really matter, because it's done and you can't change anything now."

"Yeah, I guess." Even if I don't feel that much better right now, I have the sense that getting it off my chest was what I needed to do.

Niko squeezes my shoulder, giving me a supportive smile. "Don't worry about it, buddy. Shit happens. This Corey guy will get over it, and so will you."

I nod weakly and try to swallow away my guilt over the breakup. I'm emotionally torn but glad that we decided to hang out today for a lot of reasons. Not only am I convinced he's no longer interested in me as more than a friend, I'm also starting to believe he's actually a really good guy.

Niko's tram is already waiting when we get back to the stop, so we say a hurried goodbye and he sprints across the square through the waiting doors.

Leaning against one of the stone columns that line the square, I watch him scamper up the steps and take a seat by the window. The dirty glass obscures all his features except his blond hair, which is clearly visible even at this distance. Niko and I might have actually made a good match. We enjoy spending time together, have similar interests, and he's certainly good looking. But somewhere inside, I know that dating him would have been too much like dating Corey. He's friendly and fun and we get along, but I've never felt that telltale pull, the attraction, the chemistry, whatever it's called. In a way, I think that the absence of a strong attraction is the very thing that drew me to Corey, because I never had to worry about getting hurt. I don't think I could do that to someone again, especially not someone like Niko.

My Strassenbahn doesn't come for another five minutes, and I remember that the lockbox in my room is running low on cash. I should really make a withdrawal from the cash machine on the other side of the square.

The ATM pulls in my card slowly like it's having problems, but I brush the worry aside and put in my code, requesting two hundred euro. This money will have to last me longer than the last two hundred did. There isn't enough in my account to burn through spending money like the rest of the exchange students do. Most of them go out four or five nights a week and take trips on the weekends to other cities.

The machine makes some noises before giving me an error message and spitting out my card. "Stupid piece of shit," I say in English and kick the base. An older woman hobbling past glares at me, but I'm not sure if it's because she's a German purist or because she actually understood what I said. I jam the card back into the machine, and this time it slides in smoothly. Finally, the ATM spits out the cash in time for me to dash across the square and hop on the train home.

Chapter 14

Later in the week, Daniel and I arrive home from grocery shopping, fully laden with our plunder. He at least has one hand free, so he opens the door to our building for us, stopping to check his mail. "You go on up," he says, "I'll be right behind you."

"Sure," I grunt, overloaded with a backpack about to burst, a pack of carbonated water in one hand and a case of beer in the other. The walk back from the grocery store never seemed so far. It's going to be well worth it though, because with as much as I bought, my cupboard will be stocked for a solid week. With only a backpack to get everything home, grocery shopping three times a week is common around here.

I trudge up the stairs, fingers burning from where the water pack's plastic handle digs into them. I'm starting up the last flight to our floor when I hear the front door to the building shut, signaling that Daniel has finished getting his mail.

Three steps from the top, my foot catches on the edge of the stair and I trip, falling forward toward my right side. With both hands full, there's nothing I can do to stop myself. Time slows down as I realize in horror what's about to happen. If only I had tripped with the other foot, the plastic water bottles would have taken the impact and bounced harmlessly off the stairs. Instead it's the case of beer bottles being driven toward the stone steps as I topple forward, the overloaded backpack throwing off my balance even further.

The high pitch of breaking glass is immediately muffled as foamy liquid erupts from the cardboard pack. It's all I can do to prevent myself from falling on top of the disaster. Beer flows liberally from every opening in the cardboard and onto the black stone, cascading both forward over the steps just beneath and backward onto the second floor staircase eight feet below.

Daniel's voice echoes up from downstairs, "Woah, dude!"

I'm not sure whether to be angry or laugh. First I set the beer-logged cardboard case aside amid the slick clinking of wet broken glass. Ripping the top open, I can see an inch of beer still in the bottom, gradually seeping out. Only one of the beers didn't break, meaning nearly three liters dumped onto a stone ledge ten inches wide.

I can't help but stare in shock as it continues to drain off the steps, pouring onto the staircase a floor below. Daniel calls up, sounding excited. "Ethan, come down here quick, you have to see this."

Careful to avoid stepping in the worst of the flooding, I tiptoe down the two flights to the first floor. Thumbs looped through the straps of his backpack, Daniel is staring, his eyes wide. The deluge of liquid didn't stop at the second floor stairs but continued to cascade down to the first, finally dripping onto the ground floor. It's essentially raining beer at the rate of a cloudburst, and because the drops keep hitting new surfaces every eight or ten feet, a fine beer mist is rolling off the stairs in waves. It smells of caramel and older times, and it engulfs us where we stand, covering us in micro droplets.

"It's like we're in a rainforest."

"It's amazing," Daniel says. His red tongue sticks out to catch the beer mist wafting down.

"You say that now, but once we're done cleaning this shit up, we won't even have any left to drink." I shudder at the thought. "Actually," I correct myself, "one didn't break."

"Who said I was going to help you clean this up?"

I give his shoulder a hard shove. "You wouldn't dare."

Two rolls of paper towels and half an hour later, we've finished cleaning the stairs (all three flights of them) and have just settled down on the balcony to absorb the afternoon warmth of the autumn sun. The air smells woodsy and fresh, hinting like always at the changing seasons. The only bottle to survive unbroken sits on the table between us. Daniel takes it and snaps off the bottle cap on the edge of the table.

I haven't yet learned the trick to getting the tops off using random objects.

He takes a long pull before handing it to me. I don't wipe off the top, even though there's moisture around the lip of the bottle that's sure to contain a bit of his saliva. We didn't discuss grabbing glasses for it either. Sometimes you just need to drink a beer from the bottle, and there was only one, so here we are.

"I can't believe that happened," I say, shaking my head and handing him the beer. It's already a third gone.

"That's got to be the coolest thing I've seen in a long time. That mist . . . it smelled like a caramel factory." Daniel laughs warmly. He has a good laugh too, kind of like Mom's. Except his is richer, more masculine. Buried in it though are chords of regret. He's too young to have a laugh like that.

"It's gross that you tried to catch the mist on your tongue," I say. "It poured all over the stairs, you know."

"Yeah, that was a little disgusting, huh?" He takes another drink. I smile but don't say anything. No need to ruin a perfect afternoon with a lot of talk. There's no wind, and it's the perfect temperature in the sun to be comfortable without a jacket.

As the minutes slip by, we pass the beer back and forth until it's gone, and neither of us ever wipes off the top.

An email from Mom is waiting for me when I sit down at my laptop. She's upset that I haven't called or emailed in over two weeks. I haven't bothered to give her an update since before my stitches were taken out, so it's kind of understandable. But as it's been over a year since my high school graduation, she should be used to having less contact with me by now. I think she's just paranoid because I'm in a different country. She's never left the Midwest, not even on vacation.

I decide to humor her and call on Skype. It rings forever but finally her face appears, mixed up with the look of confusion that adults use on technology they don't understand. "Hello?"

"Yeah, Mom, I can hear you."

"Oh good," she says. "I can see you now too." I resist making a smart-ass comment that that's how Skype works.

Reluctantly, I tell her about my foot's progress. "Why haven't you called sooner?" she questions me.

"Um..." I stall, "I just got busy with stuff."

She doesn't look very happy. "Do you have anyone helping you out while you're laid up?"

"My foot is fine, really. I can walk on it and everything now. And yeah, Daniel was helping when I needed it, remember?"

"He's the one who took you to the hospital, right?" She asks, sounding like she's trying to sniff out a murder. "I'd like to hear more about him."

"Maybe another time." I bite my lip in indecision but can't resist. I blurt out, "He asked me to be my . . ." But I have to stop to think of a good English equivalent to *Tandempartner* before she can jump to conclusions. "My language practice partner." With a twinge of regret, I remember that our tandems are technically over now.

"Don't you already speak German with everyone?"

"Yeah, but most of my friends aren't native German speakers. And this way he knows that it's okay to correct me. Otherwise it can be rude if you get corrected mid-conversation." That seems to appease her, but I can still see the gears spinning.

"Alright, but one last thing." *Oh hell, what's next?* "You got a letter in the mail from the credit union. I think it's about life insurance."

"Is that seriously what you wanted to ask me about?"

"Do you mind if I open it?" She sounds excited.

"I don't care." She is so weird sometimes. "I have to go, okay?"

She tells me she was glad we could talk and wants me to call again soon. I tell her I will. But not that soon. We hang up and I flop down on my bed. She drives me nuts sometimes. A lot of the time, actually.

Chapter 15

Rapping my knuckles on Daniel's door, I hold my breath as the sound echoes down the empty hallway. Earlier this week, the teacher for my local history class, Herr Werner, provided details for the term paper we're all expected to write. As the other students and I wallowed in collective dread, he explained that we would have to pick our own topics—anything from Freiburg's colorful nine hundred year history.

When the door opens, Daniel wedges himself between it and the wall, effectively blocking his room from view. "Hey," he says, sounding slightly out of breath. A pair of basketball shorts ends just above his knees and his gray t-shirt stretches across his chest, small dark patches under his arms revealing that he's sweating. "What's up?" he prompts, since I still haven't responded to him.

"Uh," I say, tripping over my thoughts. His biceps are really defined, more than usual it seems, and the veins in his forearms are sticking out. I have to force my brain into drive, because it seems stuck in park. Why did I come to his door again? Oh yeah, the paper. "For my history class we have to write a paper on something in Freiburg's past, but I don't know what to write about and Herr Werner didn't give us any topics, so I was wondering if you had any ideas?" I finish all in one breath.

Whatever he's thinking is hidden behind an inscrutable mask. The roots of his short brown hair are mingled with moisture. What was he doing in there to work up such a sweat? I transfer weight from one foot to the other, shifting my position to see around him, but his torso is pressed firmly against the door.

"Yeah, sure," he finally says. "Can you give me a few minutes though? I'll meet you in the kitchen."

The bench is hard underneath me, and it feels like I've been waiting forever. The couch on the other side of the room is enticing, but Daniel will be here any minute. When he enters the kitchen, he's wearing the same t-shirt and shorts. His feet are laced into white and red running shoes. "Do you mind if we go for a run while we talk?" Rocking back and forth on the balls of his feet, he looks at me expectantly.

My Adam's apple bobs up and down as I swallow. Working out together wasn't what I had in mind. I haven't done any real cardio since the day I tried to swim across the lake and practically eviscerated myself, and that was weeks ago. At the thought, a lance of phantom pain shoots from the scar up through my leg, and I wince.

He must have noticed the pained look on my face, because he says, "We can do it another time."

As he turns to leave, something inside makes my mouth move of its own accord. "No, wait." I'm trying to remember where my gym shorts and running shoes are buried in my closet, forgotten since the beginning of the year. "Just give me two minutes to change." Giving me a half nod, he tells me to hurry up, and I scamper out of the kitchen.

Our feet strike the ground in unison, propelling us along the path that meanders around the lake behind our building. Today was warm, but the temperature has dropped, so I'm glad we're moving at a decent pace. It's been a long time since I've run, but it feels good. Other than our shoes on the pavement, the only sound is our breathing. Daniel's chest puffs out when he inhales, and his breaths are regular and measured. Mine are shorter and more erratic, but at least I can hold my own against his pace, if only barely.

The path curves around the southern tip of the lake and I have to speed up to compensate for the longer distance at the outside of the turn. Our footfalls are opposite one another for a few moments until he shortens a stride and we fall back into sync.

"So what do you want to write about?" he asks, fitting his words neatly into an exhaling breath.

I'd nearly forgotten about the paper again. I shrug, but he doesn't seem to notice. "I'm not sure. Werner didn't give us a list of suggested of topics or anything."

"That makes it harder."

"I know," I say, feeling constriction in my chest as we round a tiny hill with a bench perched at the top. This time Daniel is on the outside of the curve and effortlessly increases his speed to keep our pace matched.

We continue in silence, accompanied only by the sounds of our movement. At last, when it feels like a noose is tightening around my airway and my legs are burning, he says, "Race to the end?"

He's got to be kidding. "Sure," I huff.

Shadows lengthening across the path, Daniel breaks into a sprint around the last bend, leaving me a distant second.

When I finally catch up to him, he directs us to another bench positioned invitingly off the trail. Doubling over, hands on my knees, I fight to catch my breath. Daniel simply rolls his shoulders, continuing his steady breathing as he starts cool down stretches.

When he's finished and I don't feel like throwing up anymore, he sits down next to me. The circles of light cast by the lampposts scattered around the lake don't quite reach this far. I'm hot from the exertion, but the cool darkness helps. I wonder what it would feel like to reach out and touch him, to see if his skin is hot as well. Does it burn like mine whenever we're close, or is it just after a run that he feels the heat?

His voice breaks the stillness. "What period of Freiburg's history interests you the most?"

The dark water of the lake mingles with the glowing reflections of the lamps alongside the path. Staring ahead, I consider his question. Medieval Europe is certainly interesting with its castles and battles, deception and coercion, and even bitter feudal wars.

The long past history of Freiburg isn't what really draws me in, though. The walk with Niko when we talked about the deported Jews and the Nazi influence over the city comes to mind. Germans are sensitive about it, but if I'm going to write a whole paper on something, it might as well be on a subject that fascinates me.

After holding my breath for a moment, I tell him, "World War II, I suppose. I'm really interested in that."

"The Third Reich? It's a theme that has been studied at length, but for good reason."

"Did anything interesting happen during that time in Freiburg?"

He laughs. "Of course. Plenty of things happened."

"Anything that would make for a good paper?"

We've both kept our gaze on the lake, but now he turns to face me, searching, appraising. "Have you heard of the White Rose?"

"It was some kind of resistance, right? I didn't know it happened in Freiburg."

Shifting his eyes away, he's quiet for a moment. "It didn't. Not really anyway. Most historians would tell you it had nothing to do with Freiburg."

He stands to leave, and I'm forced to follow him to continue our conversation. "So," I prompt, "I guess that's not a good topic then, since it doesn't have anything to do with Freiburg."

Smiling wryly, he says, "Before you discount it as a possibility, look up Magdalena Ernst." My eyebrows pull together. Getting rid of jerk Daniel took forever. Now I have to deal with cryptic Daniel. Absolutely *wunderbar*. Burying my irritation, I promise I will, and we begin the walk home. As we pass under one of the lamps, we're bathed in orange light, revealing that the dark areas under his arms have grown. His shirt is sticking to him and the fabric is mottled with moisture, especially in the middle of his lower back nearest to the waistband of his shorts. I swallow and direct my gaze elsewhere.

His hair is likewise wet with perspiration that has drawn the individual strands together into a field of short spikes. Passing from the circle of illumination, we're surrounded by darkness once more.

We're walking close, and every now and then the backs of our hands brush. Still a few hundred feet from our dorm, he says, "Thanks for the run."

"Sure."

He's quiet, but the tension in his bearing electrifies the air between us. The hairs on my arm rise to attention. There's something more he wants to say. "I . . . uh . . . I had a good time. It's good to run with a partner again." There's a vulnerability in his voice that was never there before.

I want to reach out and touch him. And I want to run away as fast as I can. Instead I nod, even though he can't see the gesture in the darkness. "Let's go again sometime."

* * *

I close my eyes, but my mind won't slow down enough for me to fall asleep. What is it about him that takes me by storm whenever I see him? Running with him tonight felt so . . . good. Almost enough to convince me to abandon my restraint and give in to what I feel. A shiver snakes down my back even though I'm warm in bed. What would it be like to actually be intimate with him? Physically, I always thought what I had with Corey was as good as it got, but I never felt for him the way I've started to about Daniel.

A memory from the end of our run surfaces in my mind. The one of his sweat-soaked t-shirt curving down his lower back and over his butt. Goddamn he has a nice ass.

What would it be like to touch him? To run my hands over his arms, his chest, and elsewhere too? I can sense myself getting hard, but I ignore the feeling. Being with him isn't worth thinking about it, because it will probably never happen. Even if he's into guys, which I don't really know, I'd be afraid of where things might go. I can't trust myself around him.

Ignoring what's going on down south isn't helping. I softly bite my lower lip, my gaze drifting to the door. I know it's locked. Exhaling a quiet breath, I slide my hand across my stomach and under the elastic waistband of my boxers. My eyelids close slowly as I adjust my position and push the covers aside, my hand starting to move up and down.

The image of Daniel shirtless in his desk chair dominates everything. Glass of orange juice in hand, sporting his innocent grin. The muscles of his shoulders rolling down into his arms. I want to touch every square inch of him.

My chest rises and falls more quickly now. Euphoric warmth spreads away from my center, coursing through every muscle and nerve, getting stronger until I can't take it anymore. Clenching my teeth, my muscles tense as I come on my stomach.

My breathing slows as I savor the fleeting feeling. After a few seconds, my eyes open, and I expel the air held in my chest. *Christ, Ethan, what are you doing?*

Chapter 16

It's a quiet Saturday afternoon. Leaves carpet the ground in a calico of orange and brown, and the air is laced with that autumn scent that's a promise of the real cold to come, even though it hasn't yet arrived. Daniel is reclining in a wooden chair balanced on its rear legs, his feet propped up on the narrow table that runs along the edge of the balcony.

"Do you think anyone will ever take me for a native German speaker?"

Teetering forward, he glances up from his textbook. The sun is shining on his face, making his blue-gray eyes shimmer. "Maybe one day." He pushes back off the table, leaning precariously far back.

I sigh and rest my chin on my hands.

"Give yourself more credit. You're doing really well for how long you've been here. A lot of people never learn to speak without an accent."

"Yeah, I guess." My foot is tapping out a hurried cadence under the table. Taking a pull from the green bottle of Beck's I'm drinking, I swish the beer back and forth over my tongue, savoring the light carbonation and semi-bitter flavor. I set the bottle back down on the table, watching how the sunlight twists as it hits the towers of bubbles rising from the bottom, casting miniature shadows across the wood.

"How much longer do we have before winter?" I ask. Back home, we would have already been under threat of snow.

Daniel looks up from his book again. "A few more weeks at least. It usually stays warm in Freiburg longer than anywhere else in Germany." Instead of resuming reading, he continues to watch me. "You don't like the cold?"

"No, it's not that." I prop myself up on my elbows. Flecks of peeling paint from the table are stuck to my arm. I try to brush them off, but they cling to my fingers and refuse to let go. When I look up, Daniel is watching me with an amused smile. I wipe my hands on my pants. "I just feel like the best part of my year is already over, and all I have to show for it are a few bad hangovers and a stupid scar."

"That sounds like a better summer than most people have," he says, playfully prodding me in the ribs.

I squirm away and take another sip of the beer. "I just wanted something more, you know?" Digging my thumbnail into the foil band around the neck of the bottle, I gouge away a silver strip to reveal green glass beneath.

"What do you mean?"

"Oh you know, the *summer* stuff that everyone does. Grilling out, riding roller coasters and motorcycles, going skinny dipping, that kind of thing."

He stares at me for a full minute. "It's a little late for skinny dipping." Sliding his feet off the table, his chair drops to all fours with a clunk. He takes my Beck's from the table and rotates the bottle in his hand, running his thumb over the dozen or so scratches in the foil. "There might be time yet to take a spin on a motorcycle though."

"You mean like rent one or something? I've never even ridden one before."

"Don't any of your friends back home have one?"

"Uh, no." Nor four wheelers, or snowmobiles, or jet skis. The kids whose parents had those toys lived on the other side of town.

He hands back the bottle without having drunk any. "You do know *someone* who has one."

At first I'm not sure what he means, but then I put it together. "Are you serious?" I try to suppress the excitement in my voice in case he's messing with me, but it doesn't really work. Tossing his textbook onto the table, he stands up to leave. "Where are you going?" I ask.

He's halfway through the door to the kitchen when he looks back. "What are you waiting for? Go put some jeans on," he says, gesturing to my plaid shorts.

My fingers twitch in anticipation as Daniel rummages through his closet. "Here, try this." He hands me a matte black helmet. It's heavier than I expect. He watches me lift it over my head and attempt to pull it down.

"I think it's too small."

"No, it looks perfect." Putting his hands over mine on either side of the helmet, he pulls down, hard. The firm padding on the inside slides over my face, dragging my ears down with it. As soon as it comes to a stop around my jaw, my ears flip back into the upright position.

"Now move your head from side to side." I do as he says. "It looks good and snug. It doesn't hurt does it?" I shake my head, and the helmet follows my movement without any slack or sliding. "Good," he says.

I start to work the straps hanging below my chin. The clip is similar to a belt buckle, but it just doesn't want to go together right. Daniel is digging in the closet for more gear, disentangling a jacket and another helmet from a pile of dirty towels. I'm still fighting to secure the metal clasp when he says, "Here," holding open his hands in an offer to help.

Releasing the straps, I drop my hands and raise my chin. His fingers brush against my neck as they deftly slip the strap through one side of the loop and out the other, pulling it tight until the cool metal touches the underside of my chin. His eyes hold mine for a second as he finishes. "Thanks," I say. He nods and turns back to the gear he's fished out of the closet.

"Your helmet looks bigger," I say as he tugs it down over his head. "Why do you have this one?" I rap my knuckles on the side of mine.

He pulls on a neon green and black riding jacket, and his eyes shift behind the plastic visor. "It's just extra."

I follow him out to the long garage that houses the vehicles for all the students living in the dorms. The building looks like it could hold maybe fifty cars, even though there must be at least a thousand students living in the dorm complex. It goes to show how few of them have cars.

Daniel pulls the metal grate aside, and there beside his silver M3 is a green and black sport bike. I noticed it when we got back from Colmar, but I didn't know it was his. Swinging his leg over the seat and turning the key, he presses the engine start switch and gives it some throttle. The resulting rumble echoes through the entire structure. Sweeping his foot back, the kickstand clicks into place against the fairings, and he backs the bike out of the garage.

With his heels, he snaps the passenger foot pegs down one at a time. Lifting his visor, he asks, "Ready?"

I nod and struggle up onto the passenger seat. It's higher than where he's sitting and angled downward, so I squeeze the seat with my legs and grab the tail with my hands to keep from sliding into him.

Looking over his shoulder to check on my progress, he chuckles. "You're going to fall off sitting like that."

"There's nothing else to hold on to," I protest.

"Hold on to me."

I swallow past the reservation in my throat and reposition myself a few inches closer to him. Sliding an arm under his, I ball my hand into a fist at the center of his chest and use his position to steady myself. The other hand I leave on the tail.

An interaction I don't quite understand between his hands and feet takes place and we're off. He pulls into the street and we accelerate, the wind grabbing at my helmet and shoulders. It's so freeing with nothing between us and the road ahead. Everything is so close—other cars, the road, the curb. It's exhilarating. With a shiver, I realize that if I let go even briefly, I would get to see the pavement even closer yet.

He takes us around the edge of Freiburg at a relaxed pace. As we continue around the city, the rhythm of riding begins to feel more natural, even though it's still strange to look down and see the ground right there.

Whenever he speeds up from a stop, I hold tight to him and the tail. By the tenth stoplight, my fingers are becoming sore, but I don't change my position. There aren't many cars out, but inside the ones that are, I see people staring back at us. It's unclear whether it's just because we're on a flashy motorcycle or because we're two guys riding together. I want to ask Daniel, but even if it weren't for the wind, it would be impossible for us to communicate with our visors clamped shut.

While we're passing a BMW wagon, the driver, a guy about our age, glances over and seems to get a kick out of what he sees. Daniel must not notice, because he continues to pass the car at a regular pace. Either that or he doesn't care what anyone thinks of us. Tightening my grip on the tail, I slide my butt farther up the seat to put another couple inches between us.

With the city almost at an end, we pull up to the last stoplight in sight before open road. Waiting for the light to turn, he cracks his visor and twists in his seat so I can hear him. "I'm going to go faster now that we're out of the city. Make sure you hold on, okay?"

"I will," I say, but my voice gets reflected back at me. I'm about to reach up to open my own visor when he confirms with a quick nod that he's already understood.

The light turns green and his wrist snaps down on the throttle. In less than a second, I start sliding backward off the seat, and I have to wrap my other arm around his chest to keep from falling off the back of the bike. My fingers interlock to form a stronger bond, the knuckles of my left hand pressing into the muscles of his chest.

He keeps accelerating until we come to a wide curve in the road. As he turns to follow the road, the whole bike angles to the side like in the movies. *Shit, we're going to fall.*

But we don't. Somehow the bike stays up as we move through the curve. I first try to keep my torso perpendicular to the road, but it doesn't feel right, so I adjust my position to match Daniel's. With the movement, the bike's center of gravity shifts. He cocks his head to side, but nothing else happens.

Coming out of the curve, he opens the throttle again, the widest yet so far. The engine howls and we rocket forward. Inertia fights to drag me off the back of the bike, but my arms are locked around Daniel's chest, keeping us bound firmly together. The warmth from his back penetrates through both his riding jacket and my hoodie, while the roar of air rushing past melds with the sound of the engine, its pitch rising in intervals as he shifts through the gears.

Numerous curves and coastings and accelerations pass, and eventually I stop holding my head up to see around his shoulder. Instead I just lean into his back. Whenever our speed changes, our helmets tap lightly together, but I don't think Daniel minds. Trees sail past in a perpetual blur of fall colors, and suddenly I realize that all along we've been climbing upward, out of the valley where Freiburg rests.

In failing daylight, we pull over a final hill and into a tree-encircled area with several parking spaces. Dropping the kickstand, he turns the key, and the engine quits with a cough from the exhaust. Loosening my arms, I slide off the bike, grateful for solid earth beneath me. "Where are we?"

"Near the top of the Schlossberg. Freiburg is a few kilometers that way," he points off into the trees. We unbuckle our helmets, and he locks them to the motorcycle using a clip by the rear tire.

He grins expectantly. "What did you think?"

"It was great. Really."

"I'm glad you had fun," he says with an air of satisfaction.

"What now?" I ask, massaging the muscles in my hands, which are still sore from holding on so tightly.

Nodding toward the trees, he says, "I thought we could go for a walk through the woods. There's a place I want to show you."

Tilting my head slightly, I give him a long look. "I'd like that."

Daniel leads us off the road to a pathway that dives into the forest, only patches of amber light finding their way through the trees. The lush greenery seems to have diminished somewhat since the summer, but the undergrowth is still a tangle on either side. He plods along in front of me, since the trail is too narrow for us to walk side by side.

It's getting chillier, but exertion and burning curiosity keep me warm as we make our way through the up and down cadence of the hills. Eventually the ground levels out and he turns off the main path onto a smaller trail. It's almost dark now, and hardly any light filters down. The forest is quiet except for the crackle of twigs breaking under our feet.

Soon enough, the path widens out into a small clearing where the trail ends at a curved stone bench. Without the tree cover, the first stars of evening glimmer down. In their dim light, it's apparent the stone has been long worn by time. The nearest quarter of the bench has even crumbled and broken in its old age.

We didn't say much on the way here, and now sitting next to one another, the minutes tick past in silence. We've been friends for a couple months, but it's still so hard to read him, to know what he's after.

I pull my hoodie closer to ward off the cold. Everything about him draws me in, as much as I try to resist. Something has been kindled inside me that can't be ignored. Yet despite all my reluctance and hesitation, and the silent fears that he isn't into guys and it could never work, this moment feels right. I can see the progression of our interactions and the development of our friendship, all leading up to this point.

Has he just been too shy to share that part of himself? A few weeks ago I wouldn't have let myself think that, but here we are, alone in the woods with mere inches separating us.

Daniel speaks first, staring ahead into the forest. "I come up here sometimes, to think."

A humming energy fills the air, connecting us, binding us. I glance up, but he doesn't turn. "What are you thinking now?"

"I . . ." He hesitates, as though unable to find the right words. "I need to tell you something."

Can it really be? My fingertips tingle with anticipation of his confession, for the moment still unspoken. But now that the question is almost laid to rest, what should I do? Haven't I been preparing myself to turn him down if it actually came to this moment? He has too much power over me because of what I feel for him. I can't just surrender myself. What if he's just looking for a single night, and then he's done? Or worse, what if it lasts a whole month before he leaves? Can I risk that?

Another thought flares into existence. Can I risk *not* finding out? I've never felt about anyone the way I do about him. And I've never even touched him. Not like that, anyway.

As the battle is waged inside, a warm pressure rises in my throat, building like a wave. I never anticipated it all happening like this. It's so unexpected, so natural.

"You can tell me anything," I whisper.

His gaze drops to his lap, and his voice is reluctant, almost sad. "It's . . . hard to say. I . . ."

It's no longer a question in my mind what he's struggling with. He's dragging it out, but it doesn't have to be that way. It could be so much easier, spontaneous. The moment stretches on until I can't stand it any longer.

Before he can say another word, I reach out and touch his chin, turning his head toward me. Gazing into his eyes, I'm mesmerized by the shadow of longing buried in their whirlpool depths. I want him so bad, it's impossible to think clearly.

"I know," I breathe. Without pausing to reconsider, I advance with my other hand and draw him toward me. Against my own lips I feel the softness of his, his warm wetness, the rough texture of his facial stubble, the firmness of his jaw under my hands.

A second passes, and then another. Something is wrong. He hasn't moved his lips. The thrill in my fingers is replaced by adrenaline fear, paralyzing me with its iron grip. Another instant and his hands are pushing me away. The force of his movement catches me first in the chest and then on the underside of my chin. Against his strength, my head twists away to the side, the edge of my tongue getting clamped between my teeth as he shoves me back.

I leap away from the bench to put space between us, the metallic taste of blood spreading in my mouth. He's still on the bench, his eyes wide and his face screwed up like he's downed a bag of sour candy. His expression is frozen, and no words escape him. *God, what have I done?*

His eyebrows knit together, his shock fading to an emotion I can't bear to decipher. When I can't look at him any longer, I run. The adrenaline previously locking me in indecision now fuels my flight as I push my legs as hard as they will go.

"Ethan, wait!" he calls after me.

Wind whips around my face as I hurtle away from the clearing. If he says anything else, I don't hear it. My heart thunders, but I can't think about anything except being as far from him as possible. Pounding footfalls and labored breathing are the only sounds as I push myself further. I sprint along the path deeper into the forest until my lungs are about to burst.

Finally dropping to my knees, I let myself collapse onto my back at the edge of the path, dead leaves crunching under my weight. The mixture of blood and saliva in my mouth tastes hot and sticky. I turn my head and spit, but it doesn't make it far enough and a gooey trail lands on my cheek.

My breathing is a frantic panting, but the pain crushing my chest isn't from the exertion. Shame pours through me, filling me so completely I'm afraid I'll drown in it. Then it overflows, and one by one, tears drip from my eyes and sink into the earth.

I've never been so forward with someone like that. *Why now? What made me so sure?* Expelling another wad of blood and spit, I wipe the latest round of moisture from my eyes. This was always a possibility, that he was straight. It was a stupid impulse that took over. And I let it, because for a moment I wanted something to be true so badly that my heart tricked me into believing it.

Now those few seconds are going to change everything about our friendship, if it survives at all. I inhale through my nose to clear the wetness. I deserve every bit of this for being such a dumbass. But goddamn it hurts. It would have been so perfect, so right. Would have. Except it never *could* have.

When my eyes are all cried out, I force my breathing into regular intervals until my thoughts run clear again. How can I ever go back and face him? Just pretend that nothing happened? I tried to make out with my straight roommate. What was I thinking? It's the cardinal rule of roommates. Don't develop feelings for them. Ever.

Seeing a guy in his boxers and sharing a beer doesn't mean shit if he's your roommate. I was an idiot, and now I'm going to pay for that stupidity.

Lying in the woods, my tongue throbbing and a rock jabbing uncomfortably into my back, it's clear that my penance has already begun. The cold is biting my fingers and toes, so I pick myself up and start the walk home.

I get lost getting out of the woods, so when I finally find the road, it's still an hour walk before I reach the base of the Schlossberg. Another half hour wait for the Strassenbahn near the end of the line gives my tongue time to stop bleeding. When the tram finally arrives, I'm thankful there are only a handful of people on board, because I'm drenched in cold sweat, and my clothes and face and hands are covered in dirt and crap from the woods.

The tram rolls along through the night while those few seconds play over and over again in my mind. Touching him felt so right. He didn't pull away or even flinch when my fingers first made contact. Even that look in his eyes was exactly what I expected—a faint longing, a hint of regret. I can't believe I did what I did, but he could have stopped it before it ever got that far. Why the hell didn't he? I slam my fist against the glass and a thud reverberates across the pane.

It's almost eleven by the time I get back home. A blue sticky note is attached to my door. *Ethan, I waited an hour for you. Hope you're okay. —Daniel*

If I hadn't gotten lost for so long, we might have run into each other. I crumple the note in my fist and throw it in the trash. Staring at the ball of blue paper I've just thrown, it occurs to me that Daniel was about to tell me something important before I screwed it all up. Obviously he wasn't about to confess his attraction to me. So what was it then?

Chapter 17

Light streams in through the window, but I've lost the will to move. If only I could sink down into the blankets and disappear forever, letting my embarrassment and shame wink out of existence along with me.

I absolutely cannot handle the thought of seeing him right now, so I resolve to clear out for the day. Checking the hallway first, I slink away to the bathroom and shower with superhuman speed. Taking a moment to examine my tongue, I run my finger over the three dark red spots where my teeth sunk into it the night before. A burst of anger erupts within me, but there's no reason to be mad at him for what was clearly my own fault. He did what any straight guy would do.

My feet practically roll down the stairs on my way out, fingers tapping out a text to Niko as I go.

I'm halfway to the Strassenbahn stop when he calls me. "Hey," I answer.

"Ethan, are you okay? I wasn't sure what you meant in your message."

I let out a deep sigh. "I'm fine. Something bad happened last night is all. Can I come over to your place for breakfast?"

"Of course." As he gives me directions to his apartment, I realize I've never been there before.

"Alright, I'll see you in a half hour." I stuff my phone into my pocket and jump over the handrail onto the platform beside the tracks.

Going through my head are the memories of all the times Daniel and I stood here waiting.

Once I'm on the train and headed into the city, it's almost impossible to look at anything without thinking of him. The spot alongside the tracks where he put his hand on my back after I got sick walking home, or the street we strolled down during our first tandem. Everywhere I look, he's there. His presence in my memories is so strong I'm not sure I'll ever be able to see this city without him in it.

On the walk up to Niko's apartment, I see a guy who looks suspiciously like the bartender from KGB, but our eyes meet for only a second as we pass. When I arrive, Niko buzzes me inside. It almost cheers me up to find he's laid out a traditional German breakfast with rolls, cheese, and sliced meats. "You're the best," I say. "I'm totally starving."

"No problem," he says, sitting down. "I've been meaning to have a proper breakfast lately." While I butter a roll and stack meat and cheese on top, he asks, "So what happened last night?"

My mouth is so full I have to swallow before speaking. "You know my flatmate Daniel?"

"Yeah, yeah. The hot German guy who went to the KGB bar with us."

"That's the one. Anyway, we've been getting to know each other. We're Tandempartners and we've actually become pretty good friends, too."

"Okay, so what about him?"

"Last night, he took me up to the Schlossberg on his motorcycle, and we hiked to this bench in the middle of the woods."

"That's . . . weird." Niko gives me a confused look, and his eyes grow wide. "Wait, wait," he drops his hands to the table for emphasis, "He's not gay, is he?"

I shake my head. "No, he definitely isn't." I pause, biting my lip. "Except, I didn't figure that out until I kissed him."

"You what?" His voice becomes shrill right before he bursts into laughter. "Oh man, what did he do?"

"It is *not* funny." I throw the uneaten half of my roll at him in outrage, but he ducks and it sails over his head, which only makes him laugh harder.

He finally shuts up, but only because I'm refusing to say any more until he does. "Okay, I'm sorry. You have to admit it's pretty damn funny though. So what did he do?"

I drop my face into my hands with a groan. "He pushed me away, of course. Didn't say a thing, only looked at me like he'd just eaten a lemon."

"Definitely straight, then. And after that?"

"I . . . uh, well, I ran."

Niko's expression is thoughtful, and after a moment's reflection he says, "I probably would have too." I follow up by telling him about the note Daniel left me.

"At least you know he doesn't hate you, or he wouldn't have written the note. I wonder what he was about to tell you though."

"I know, it's killing me."

"You would know if you hadn't, you know . . ." he trails off, snickering.

"Shut up!" I yell, but I'm trying not to laugh too. For a moment I almost forget how lousy I feel.

It's with reluctance that I finally board the Strassenbahn home. We spent most of the day in the city, taking a few hours to look around Freiburg's tiny shops, including a gift shop next to the cathedral and a handmade shoe store. I was determined to stay away from my dorm as long as possible, so Niko let me come back home with him too. We watched movies until finally he said he had to go to bed.

Streetlights fly past in a blur, and a weight settles over me. Surrounded by a thousand lights, how can I feel so alone? The feeling sinks into me, dissolving and diffusing into every cell, and nothing seems to shake it.

I've only just gotten back to my room when I hear a quiet knock on the door. It's him, it has to be. I remain silent on the bed, clutching my knees to my chest. He knocks again. "Ethan." He's speaking quietly, but I can still hear him. "Ethan, can we please talk?" A minute passes, then a barely audible sigh and footsteps moving away.

I wish I could just block out his voice, his face, his touch. Tears slide down my cheeks and drip onto the bed. I switch off the light and wrap my arms around my feather pillow, burying my face in its softness. I want to touch him, to hold him, but that's impossible. There's no changing it, there's no reasoning with it. The impossibility just *is*. Talking can do nothing but delay the terrible truth that I've fallen for someone who could never feel the same way.

Chapter 18

Ordinarily it should be tremendously difficult to steer clear of some-one who lives down the hall, but Daniel must have understood that I need space, because I haven't had to duck into the bathroom or kitch-en to avoid him yet. Nor has he come knocking at my door again.

I'm so busy trying unsuccessfully not to think about him, that when a box arrives for me from the United States, I don't have the slightest idea what it could be. Of course once I see it's filled with boxes of stuffing mix and cans of pumpkin puree, I remember the Thanks-giving supplies I requested from Mom almost a month earlier. She complained about having to buy everything, and then she made even more of a fuss about the cost of shipping, but in the end she came through.

Enjoying the distraction, I throw myself into the preparations. I'm determined to show my flatmates and friends the true spirit of Thanksgiving—unabashed gluttony—by preparing more food than they imagine possible. I try not to think about the fact that cooking for everyone would also include Daniel.

Niko is over helping me pick out recipes, but he keeps suggesting traditional Polish dishes like kielbasa and pierogi. After he describes bigos, which apparently is a stew made from sauerkraut and meat, I finally tell him, "We're not going to have any Polish food, okay? It's

Thanksgiving. You can't just pick and choose whatever you want."

In response, he slumps into his chair.

Now I feel guilty for snapping at him. "How about we go to the store and get all the canned food? Since we can only carry home what can fit in our backpacks, we'll have to make another trip anyway."

"Yeah, alright," he says. That seems to cheer him up, so hopefully it won't be necessary to piece together an awkward apology for offending his Polishness. Niko is my anchor right now, and I can't afford to mess up this friendship too.

When we get back from the store, both of our backpacks are overflowing with cans of green beans and mushroom soup, onions and potatoes, spices, and anything else I thought we'd need. I'm lucky Mom sent the pumpkin puree and stuffing mix, because we couldn't find anything like that. Even cranberry sauce was impossible to locate. I was about to ask a worker if they had it, but in the end I didn't even bother, because German doesn't really have a word for cranberry. They use the word *Preiselbeere*, and a lot of people will tell you it's the same, but it's not. Why? Because it turns out it's a different plant and a different berry, and that means it's not the same. Sometimes this country drives me crazy.

My cupboard is overflowing, and we're trying to reorganize it without everything falling out onto the floor when Daniel comes into the kitchen. He freezes the moment he sees me, smiling tentatively and trying for a second to catch my eye. Niko stops mid-motion to watch the exchange, his arms buried in the cupboard. When I won't meet Daniel's gaze, he backs out the door, shutting it quietly behind him.

I don't understand him. There wasn't even a trace of disgust or the *"we can still be friends but just stay the hell away from me"* look. He shouldn't want to come near me with a ten-foot pole, and my attempts to stay clear of him should be a joke compared to how hard he should be trying to avoid me. It's almost as if he wasn't terribly bothered by what happened. Except that's impossible. I was there when he shoved me away.

Niko and I continue organizing and putting food away, but I'm dreading his impending questions. After ten minutes he still hasn't said anything about what just happened. He just keeps right on working, and it makes me that much happier to have him as my friend.

* * *

I drum my fingers over the keyboard, the clacking sound melding with the German techno song playing softly in the background. Niko left about an hour ago after we straightened up the cupboard. I have a few free hours before bed, but leaving my room isn't worth the risk of seeing Daniel again.

Hunting through the stack of papers beside my laptop, I find the yellow sticky note where I scrawled the name Magdalena Ernst—the place he suggested I start the research for my history paper. Pinching the yellow square of paper between my fingers, I try to convince myself that I'm just doing this because it might be a lead on a paper topic. It certainly doesn't have anything to do with needing to feel like he hasn't disappeared from my life. It's just about satisfying my curiosity over his cryptic suggestion, that's all.

Clicking on the Wikipedia link that appears at the top of the search results, I groan when I see the article is only in German. Day to day conversations have become easy for me now, but written German has a depth of vocabulary that can still prove challenging. It's also much faster to skim in English.

I buckle down and tromp through the article. It's not very long, and it has an acute lack of information. Magdalena was a student at the University of Freiburg from 1940–43, but there's only a vague sentence about reports that she was linked to the White Rose. The article has a little information about where she was from and what she studied in Freiburg, but overall it's completely devoid of any details about what exactly her connection to the White Rose was. I click on an underlined link for the White Rose. It might help to get a better idea of what the group was about.

This article begins explaining that the White Rose was an intellectual resistance group started by university students in Munich. In the face of almost certain death, they began secretly writing and printing anti-Nazi leaflets to distribute at the university. At the heart of the group were two siblings, Hans and Sophie Scholl. I skip the next sentence filled with words I don't know and pick up on the other side. The group continued producing and printing leaflets for months, receiving funding from a sympathizer in Stuttgart and guidance from their philosophy professor Kurt Huber, until while attempting to distribute a fifth leaflet, the brother and sister were caught.

Reading further, a subtle warning echoes in my chest before I get to the part that describes what happened to them. It's with a sinking feeling that my fears are confirmed. "On February 22nd, 1943, four days after they were discovered as members of the White Rose, Hans and Sophie were tried, sentenced to death, and executed later that same day by guillotine." My stomach turns. They were barely older than me, and the Nazis cut off their heads for disagreeing with them.

Chapter 19

I manage to wait another two days, but ultimately I find myself in front of Daniel's door. The shadows and coolness in the hallway cause me to shiver involuntarily. I haven't seen Daniel since the night in the kitchen, but a slit of golden light shining from underneath the door means he must be here. Not a single sound comes from his room. Maybe he's asleep. I almost change my mind, but I know that eventually, inexorably, like salmon hurling themselves upstream, I will be drawn back to this spot.

My knuckles tap softly on the wood, and I wait, my heart beating out rapid tempo to the following seconds. I'm half hoping he won't answer. But the door opens, and there he is, the same as always. He gives me a small, reassuring smile. "I wasn't sure if you were ever going to come by again," he says, holding the door wide for me to enter. I move past him and take a seat on the bed. He sits down in his computer chair, swiveling to face me. In his high-backed chair, his appearance, which has always been striking, is intimidating. It makes it seem as though I'm here to account for my actions.

Uncomfortable silence, quivering with instability, hovers between us until he says, "Say what you need to, Ethan." His words aren't angry, just direct, which isn't really a surprise. It's what I've gradually come to expect from Germans.

I swallow, burying my fear and apprehension. This might be the end of our friendship, but if that's what's meant to happen, I'm not going to struggle in vain trying to stop it. Steeling myself, I try to explain. "I'm really sorry about what happened in the woods, when I . . ." The words get caught somewhere in my throat and refuse to budge. It's impossible to finish the sentence, so I move on. "I like you, Daniel. A lot."

It's ever so slight, but he winces, as though he was expecting it while hoping all the same it wasn't true.

Refusing to lose my nerve before I've gotten everything out, I continue. "The way I feel about you, it's different than with anyone I've ever met or . . . been with," I finish halfheartedly, a thread of resignation woven through my words. There's something deeply personal about confessing my feelings to someone who can't reciprocate.

As if on cue, he says quietly, "You know I'm not . . ." He's about to say "gay" I think, but he seems to decide against it. "Attracted to guys, right?"

I nod slowly, my voice sinking to a rueful whisper. "Yeah, now I do." If only I'd just listened to the warning inside myself that night, this never would have happened. I'd still be wanting him right now, more than anything else in the world, but I wouldn't feel so shitty. And I wouldn't be thinking that tonight is the night our friendship will end.

He doesn't say anything else, so I repeat the words I've rehearsed. "I wanted to apologize for what happened. I made a mistake, and I'm sorry. If you never want to talk to me again, I understand, and I'll leave you alone."

There, I said it. Now he's going to act like he's thinking about it for a few seconds and tell me to get lost. The next few weeks will be terrible, but I'll get over him. My chest sinks, expelling the dead air in my lungs. It's taken me this long to come to terms with the idea that our friendship is over. Now we're here, and I've said what I came to say, and this whole ordeal will be ending soon.

A full minute passes before he answers. Holding my eyes firmly with his, he says quietly, "I don't want you to just leave me alone. I want us to be friends still, if we can."

My teeth clench but every other muscle is still. How can he possibly mean that? It wasn't supposed to happen like this. He had just one thing to do, and it would have gotten me out of his life forever. But he didn't. He still wants to be friends? Suddenly I'm mad. "What the fuck, man? I don't understand you." I've never sworn at him before.

His face fills with confusion. "What do you mean?"

I make a frustrated gesture. "First of all, if some girl kissed me—hell, if some *guy* kissed me who I wasn't interested in—I'd tell them to get lost. Which is sort of what you did, but only after you let me kiss you for a full five seconds." I take a quick breath and continue my rant before he can speak. "Jesus, Daniel, why did you even ask me to go for a walk with you on the Schlossberg that night, anyway? What kind of straight guy asks another guy to go for a hike into the woods in the dark and stops at some romantic little bench?" When I finish, I'm out of breath.

"Um," he fidgets, "I'm not exactly sure where to start."

I cross my arms. "Start with the bench and why you waited to push me away."

He has the nerve to grin sheepishly. "Well, you have a very firm grip."

I almost laugh, and for a moment it's as if that night never happened. Instead, I glare at him. How can he joke about this?

"Okay, okay," he puts his hands up in mock surrender. "You caught me by surprise, alright? It took me a bit to realize it wasn't going to stop unless I made it stop."

My face burns hot with embarrassment, but my anger at his initial response is melting, giving way to that ache in my chest. Tears spring at my eyes, but I wipe them away before they can fully form. I'm determined to actually get some answers out of him. "Why did you take me to that bench?"

"To be fair," he says, "I didn't know you were into guys. You've never mentioned it, if you recall."

Oh please. "You must have guessed."

He shrugs. "I suspected, yeah, but the only really good clue was when you got all those free drinks at the KGB bar. I figured maybe you were just good at scheming drinks off bartenders."

I can't help myself and a chuckle escapes me. He smiles in response. I'm not ready to give up the hunt yet. "You still haven't explained why you took me out into the woods in the first place, or what you wanted to talk about."

He sighs. He's been deliberately avoiding this. "I was about to tell you when we were up there. I suppose now is as good a time as any." He pausing, smirking. "As long as you don't try to make out with me again."

I roll my eyes but don't dignify his joke with a response. His grin disappears. "Do you remember our first tandem meeting when you asked if I had any siblings, and I told you no?"

I nod, unsure where he's going with this.

"Well, that wasn't exactly accurate. The truth is, I don't have any siblings *anymore*. I had a brother, Marc, but he passed away."

The news is so abrupt and unexpected that I don't know how to respond. My mouth moves mechanically. "I'm sorry." I want to reach out and touch him, comfort him, but of course I can't do that. Not after what happened the other night, anyway.

He nods. "It's been hard. We were . . ." his voice trails, like he's not sure which words properly describe their relationship. "Close." He's staring off into memory, but I catch his eye. He seems to retreat from his sad thoughts but apparently can't bring himself to smile back.

"Marc and I hiked up the Schlossberg once when he came to visit me during my first year. We found that bench and thought it was the coolest thing. I figured it would be a good place for you to hear about him."

That makes more sense. It also makes me look like a complete as-shole. He wanted to tell me about his dead brother; instead I came on to him. Looks like I've taken things to a whole new level. *Way to go, Ethan.* "What was he like?"

This time, the memories streaming through him seem less sad. "Marc was really bright, but he kept to himself a lot and didn't have many friends." Daniel's expression is pensive. "I was that way too actually, so I guess we were there for each other a lot. In a way, we were like best friends, though it might have been better if things were different."

"What do you mean?"

Leaning back in his chair, he drops his arms into his lap and stares at his hands. "It was hard for him when I left for university. He got pretty lonely sometimes."

"I'm really sorry." I know I shouldn't, but I reach over and take hold of his hand and squeeze. At first he looks surprised and starts to pull away, but he must see something in my expression that makes him relax. The moment passes and I release his hand.

"Thanks." A few seconds trickle past before he says, "I haven't shared that with anyone before."

"Does it feel better to talk about it?"

He glances up. "Yeah, I think it does."

"I'm glad." I let my words hang in the air and dissipate. When I'm sure he isn't going to say anything more about Marc, I stand up to leave. Daniel doesn't move from his seat. At the door, I look back. "Thanks."

"For what?"

"For not telling me to get lost."

In response he only nods. Shutting the door quietly behind me, I exhale in relief.

Chapter 20

A couple days later I catch Daniel on the way back from the bathroom. I've dutifully given him some space since our talk, but I can't wait any longer. "Hey," I call tentatively.

He turns, and I'm relieved that he doesn't look bothered to see me. "What's up?"

Emboldened, I ask him the question I've been holding inside for days. "Are you free this Thursday night?"

"I get done with class at six. Why, what's going on?"

"Six is perfect." The thought of sharing this part of my life with him ignites an excitement that crackles like static electricity through my chest. "I'm making Thanksgiving dinner for our floor and some other friends too. I'd love it if you came."

"Wouldn't miss it," he says, smiling. "I don't think I'll be there early enough to help cook or anything though."

"Don't worry about it. My friend Niko is coming to help. Maybe a few others too."

His brow furrows. "Niko . . . he's the guy from the KGB bar that you got all the free drinks with?"

"Yeah, that's him."

"Are you and he," he pauses like he's searching for the right words, "more than just friends?"

My mouth turns down into a frown. "You're as bad as my mom."

It's seems like a bad idea to tell Daniel that I don't have eyes for anyone but him, so I stick to the simple truth. "And no, we're just friends."

"Oh, okay." He sounds disappointed.

"Actually," I correct myself only half in jest, "You're worse than my mom."

Chapter 21

As it turns out, it's not so easy to find turkeys in Germany. Thanks-giving day has arrived, and I'm standing in front of the sink with my hands gripping a half-frozen chicken submersed in frigid water, while several other pale-skinned birds bob alongside. I don't have a god-damn clue what I'm doing. Niko thought it was hilarious when we bought four *Sonntagshähnchen*—*Sunday chickens* (the *big* ones)—and stuffed them into our backpacks to get them home. Now he's wear-ing an expression somewhere between confusion and disbelief as he watches me grapple with the bird and flop it onto the cutting board.

"Do I just put it in the oven like this?"

Niko shakes his head in resignation. "You don't know how to pre-pare these? Why did you buy them?"

I shrug my shoulders. "I thought it would be easy." Glancing at the spice rack, I add, "Maybe some pepper and . . ." I grab one of the jars to read the label. "*Muskatnuss?*"

Daniel walks in from the hall. Niko and I stare at him, our expres-sions frozen. His eyes bounce between us and the chickens. I can tell he's trying not to grin, so I try to divert him. "Is Muskatnuss good on chicken?"

Unable to restrain himself any longer, the rich timbre of his laugh fills the kitchen. As much as that pisses me off right now, I love the sound. Every time he lets it out, I love it more, because it's always a little different. Today it's a mixture of sunny afternoons and honey wheat beer, but always with that melancholy undertone. If only I could hear it more often.

He rounds the kitchen island and leans against the counter next to me. "Muskatnuss is like a holiday spice," he says, snapping his fingers impatiently like he's struggling for the right word. "*Nutmeg*," he translates. "That's what it is."

I give him a look. "I thought you said you didn't know any English?"

"Just a few words." He flashes me a wide smirk, revealing white teeth.

"Right. Just simple stuff, like *nutmeg* and *internal combustion engine*, right?"

He has a knowing look but refuses to reveal any secrets. I'd bet a kidney that he speaks far better English than he lets on.

"So what are you doing to those poor chickens? Unlike in the United States, we have laws regarding the treatment of animals, you know." He teases me with the same tone he uses when gently telling me off for doing something stupid. That sort of thing happens to me about once a week. It's way too easy to do things the not-German way.

"Very funny," I say. Niko snickers behind me. "We're cooking them," I tell Daniel firmly. "We don't need any help." I look to Niko for backup. His eyes are wide. I might as well have just declared the world flat.

Daniel glances at Niko, then back to me and the bird on the cutting board. Water tinted pink is puddling underneath, gradually sliding toward the edge of the counter. "Ethan," he speaks my name slowly, "Are you sure you don't want help? I could season a chicken blindfolded."

"Well . . ." I can't really afford to tell him no, but I'd rather prove to him I can prepare this meal by myself. With Niko's help too, of course.

"Great," Daniel says, as though my indecision is confirmation enough. "I'll handle the chickens, and you and Niko can work on everything else. I'm sure there's more than enough work for all of us."

I'm not about to let him take Thanksgiving for a joyride, but I remember his earlier assertion that he has an afternoon class today. "I suppose we could use your help, but you have to leave soon, right?" I'm pleased with myself. This way he can help us for a little while, and by the time we're on the right track, he'll have to go to class. There won't be any need to credit him with saving us from a culinary disaster.

He smiles widely. "I've decided not to go today."

Niko is waiting to see my reaction before fully revealing his pent-up amusement. I move aside, watching helplessly as Daniel plucks the chicken out of my hands. He flips the bird over and douses it with splashes of olive oil from the bottle on the counter. For a few minutes, Niko and I look on as he expertly grabs spice after spice from the rack, rubbing the savory flavors into the olive oil coating. I have to hand it to him, the guy can season a bird.

Reluctantly pulling my gaze away, I start on the green bean casserole while Niko cuts up potatoes. It's almost noon, and the goal is to have everything ready for dinner at six. With the help, it seems like we might actually finish on time. For a while we work in relative silence, accompanied only by the sounds of Niko's knife and the wet, muffled slapping noise of Daniel seasoning the meat. I grin to myself at my own private joke.

It's past two o'clock by the time everything is ready to bake. Laid out on the counter are four stuffed chickens, a green bean casserole, three kilos of mashed potatoes, cranberry and orange relish, and a pumpkin pie. "Now what?" asks Niko. His shirt and jeans are covered in bits of potato, and I'm pretty sure some pieces disappeared into his mop of blond hair too.

"Now we put everything in the ovens and hope it all finishes in time," I say. Niko helps me fill both levels of our two ovens with the chickens. The casserole, potatoes, and pie will have to go in later.

Handing both of us beers, Daniel says, "Good job, guys." I take a long drink, enjoying the acerbic sensation of carbonation traveling down my throat. He gets a beer for himself too, but aims for the door to the hallway.

"Where are you going?" I ask.

"I have to catch up on some homework before we eat. I'll be back out to check on the chickens though."

Niko peers after him as he leaves the room, only looking back after the door clicks shut. "He's really cute." He takes a swig of his beer and throws himself onto the couch.

"Yeah, I know." I take the chair next to the couch. It's stupid, but I don't like what he just said. "Don't hit on him or anything, okay?"

"We both know he's straight. What's wrong with a little *flirten*?"

I bristle but keep my tone steady, "I just don't want you to, alright?"

"Sure, sure," he nods, tilting his beer toward me in deference.

*   *   *

After a few hours of hectically swapping dishes and chickens in and out of the two ovens—first to cook and later bring back up to serving temperature—everything is ready to eat. I glance at my phone; it's only six twenty. Just twenty minutes later than planned, not bad at all.

The table is set with candles casting wavering shadows across the place settings. The candles are courtesy of Florian, who happened to have a full set of tapers in his room. Germans are weird like that. You never know what odd assortment of domestic items they'll have stashed away in a student apartment, but it can sure come in handy sometimes.

In addition to Florian, Paula, Niko, and Daniel, my friends Bastien and Corinne from the Sprachkurs are here. Daniel helps me carry the serving dishes to the table, where everyone is already sitting. After we take seats next to one another, Daniel watches me expectantly. Everyone else is looking at me too.

I stand up, accidentally bumping the edge of the table with my knee and causing all the glasses to wobble. I wipe the moisture from my hands on my jeans. I've never liked speaking in front of people, and monologues in German are even more stressful. "Thank you all for coming," I begin, proceeding to blabber on about the pilgrims and the Mayflower and the first Thanksgiving. At the edge of my vision, Daniel is smiling. It's not mean, but it's the smirk he gets when I'm speaking bad German.

Since everything but the mashed potatoes and chicken are things no one here has ever seen before, I decide to introduce the food as well. Pointing out the green bean casserole and stuffing goes smoothly, and I begin to think I'm in the clear.

"And this is—" I gesture to the orange peel and cranberry relish. I don't know the word for relish or orange peels, so I use the closest thing I can think of. "This jam is made of cranberries and orange skin." Half the table bursts out laughing. Noting the laughers, I identify that only the Germans are amused. Daniel at least is trying to suppress his grin, probably for my sake. "What did I say?" I ask him from the side of my mouth.

"Orange skin means—" he has to stop and hold his fist in front of his mouth so he doesn't laugh. "It's like . . . when a fat woman has lumpy skin on the back of her legs."

"Cellulite?" I exclaim. Bastien must have also just realized the

119

meaning from Daniel's explanation, because he's chuckling and speaking rapidly in French to Corinne.

Eventually everyone settles down, but my face is still bright red as I halfheartedly name the last dish—the pumpkin pie. I can tell everyone is eager to start, but I want to make this as much like home as possible. "Normally, we go around the table and say what we're thankful for. I can start us off," I say, wiping my palms once again on my jeans.

"I'm thankful for the good friends I've made here." I glance at Niko but not at Daniel. No eye contact is necessary for me to be acutely aware of his presence. It's like an invisible cord is always connecting us. "And for the opportunity to study in a country with amazing public transportation and beer." Florian and Daniel rap their knuckles on the table with approval.

As we move around the table, most of the thanks are directed toward friends and family. At last it's Daniel's turn. The flickering candlelight illuminates his face with intermittent clarity. "I'm thankful for . . ." He pauses, sending his gaze toward me, and then down at the table. "I'm thankful for second chances. And for my friends and family, of course."

The moment he finishes, everyone begins to dig in, and for the first time today, the tightness in my chest and shoulders dissipates. It was a quite feat to pull off, but somehow I did it. With help, but nonetheless an accomplishment. Daniel loads up his plate eagerly as I look on. Second chances for what? That seems like something more appropriate coming out of my mouth. He certainly gave me a second chance. What does he need one for?

Having already spent the day with me, Niko makes his exit just as we finish. Corinne and Bastien follow suit, citing plans with friends at a bar. At a pointed look from Daniel, Florian and Paula volunteer to clean up and put away what food is left. Which leaves Daniel and me.

We leave the kitchen and retire to familiar territory—his room. I'm stuffed, and he must be too, because he lies down on his bed with a groan. "No wonder Americans are all fat," he says with a yawn, raising his arms up and behind his head.

My eyes lingering on the underside of his biceps while he stretches, I recline in the computer chair. "I'm not fat."

"A few more of your holidays and I might be though."

"Yeah right, you're always running and working out."

120

He raises an eyebrow. "Oh I am, huh?"

"You're like zero percent body fat."

Sitting up, he lifts up the bottom of his t-shirt. Leaning forward, he pinches his stomach. "What do you call that?"

"Are you serious? That's skin. You couldn't even get a hold of it without practically doubling over."

Grinning, he drops his shirt. "You want a drink?"

"What do you have?"

He gestures to the bookcase. "On the bottom shelf is a bottle of apple schnapps. There should be some glasses next to it."

I grab two of the tiny glasses and pour the schnapps. Handing him one of the glasses, we toss them back. The liquid is appley sweet but smolders down my throat.

"Pour a second round."

I do as he says. After we take the second shot, he sets his glass on the nightstand, and I retake my seat at the desk.

"I looked up that girl, Magdalena, but I didn't find anything."

He levels his gaze on me, questioning me with his eyes and tone. "You didn't find *anything*?"

"Well, no," I concede, "I did find some information, but I couldn't figure out what she actually did."

"That just means you weren't looking in the right place." He stands, moving to the bookcase where the apple schnapps is still on the shelf. Taking the bottle in one hand and a leather-bound book in the other, he returns to his spot on the bed. "Here," he holds out the book to me.

The leather cover is dark brown, worn smooth through either age or use, maybe both. As soon as I open it, the pages cleaving apart under my thumb, I recognize the feather light paper. It's a Bible. My muscles tense. "What am I supposed to do with this?"

"Settle down, Ethan." His voice is calm but the words catch me off guard. I remain silent as he pours another round of shots for us. Carefully replacing the cap on the bottle, he gestures to the book. "It will come in handy with your paper. Just give it a chance."

Is he trying to convert me or something? That doesn't have anything to do with my history paper. We drink our shots together. The path from the table to our mouths and back again is one fluid motion. Neither of us speaks. Warmth blooms in my stomach, spreading through me until there's a light tingling in my fingertips and at the sides of my tongue.

I slide my hands under my legs to ward away a subconscious chill. I try to catch his gaze, but he's looking past me, unfocused. When he speaks, his voice sounds distant. "My parents and Marc and I went on vacation once to the North Sea." His eyes shift to the window. "The sand was so white, and the beach stretched for miles. Marc and I spent the whole afternoon there on the beach one day, just lying back and watching the endless waves roll in.

"That trip was one of the last times we really got to hang out together, just the two of us," he says. "It was at the end of the summer just before I moved to Freiburg. The last day of our trip, we were on the beach again. A storm was coming, rolling across the sea toward us." Daniel's voice fades. His eyes are somewhere far away. On the North Sea, I guess.

He pours us another round of the apple schnapps and downs his quickly. Taking a sip, I set mine unfinished on the table.

Eyes still unfocused and buried in memory, he says, "Marc took my hand tightly in his." For a moment he's back here with me and pulls my hand into his with an iron grip. His gaze stays on me this time. "He took my hand, and he said, 'Promise me we will always be there for each other. Promise me.'"

My fingers are turning white under Daniel's grip, but I ignore the discomfort.

Transfixed, he stares into my eyes while wetness wells up in his own. "And I told him I would. I promised him I would be there for him." His voice spilling over with sorrow, he fights to get each word out. "I failed him."

Carefully loosening his grip on my hand, I move to the bed and encircle him in my arms, feeling the warmth radiating through his shirt. Accepting my embrace, he pulls me closer, burying his face into my shoulder. He's bigger than me, so it's a bit awkward, but we fit together nonetheless.

His face pressed into my hoodie, the fabric grows hot from his breath. Sliding my hand across his back and up his neck, I hold him. Under my fingers, his short brown hair is soft and his neck is warm. It makes me feel terrible, but I don't want this moment to end. Providing comfort to him feels so right. I could hold him like this all night.

Finally he pulls away, leaving damp splotches on my hoodie from his tears. Lashes wet, he wipes his eyes, clearing away the traces of what just happened.

I don't trust myself to say anything. My undisclosed feelings seem like a betrayal of his trust.

He runs his fingers briefly over the wet spots on my hoodie, as if that will help dry it. "Sorry," he says with a flare of embarrassment in his cheeks.

"Don't worry about it."

He inhales deeply to clear his sinuses. "I'm sorry to put you in this position."

"What do you mean?"

"After the, uh, misunderstanding that night we hiked on the Schlossberg, I realize it might sometimes be difficult for you to spend time with me."

That's one way he could put it. "It's okay, I get it," I tell him, hating the truth of what I'm about to say. "You're straight, and we're friends and will only ever be friends."

That seems to put him at ease, which is what it was supposed to do. My jaw muscles tense in silent frustration. There's no doubt that he's straight, so why can't I just be satisfied with what we have?

"Our friendship means a lot to me, Ethan. I hope you know that."

I swallow, forcing back my own roiling emotions about what he really means to me. "I'm glad we're friends too." I'm afraid if I stay any longer, I won't be able to withhold my own tide, and it's going to become painfully obvious that the nature of my feelings for him haven't changed. He suspects, that much is clear, but if he knew for certain, he would put distance between us. He would have to.

Meticulously proofing my voice for any trace of hidden emotion, I tell him, "I better go."

There's concern in his expression that he's said something wrong, but he doesn't object to me leaving. "Alright. I'll see you tomorrow."

Before I close the door behind me, he says, "Ethan."

"Yeah?"

"Um," he says, a small smile appearing. "Have a good night."

"Thanks, you too."

I can't get to sleep for a long time. The scent of him lingers in my memory—along with the warmth of his closeness, the strength of his arms around me, and the patter of his heartbeat when we were pressed together. Clenching my teeth down on the comforter, my heartache erupts in a muffled cry. Being so close while knowing I'll never touch him the way I want is crushing me inside.

I shake my head, trying to clear away the errant thoughts. I shouldn't even be thinking about him. What is it about him that breaks down every ounce of my self-control? *He's straight for Christ's sake, Ethan, just get over him already.*

We could just be really close friends, right? Two guys who know and understand each other intimately, but not sexually? Or am I really destined to feel the agony of unfulfilled desire in every moment we're together? Will it someday become tolerable, even satisfying, to simply spend time with him? Deeper inside me though, a defiant truth is restless in the pit of my stomach. It's telling me that a friendship with him is ultimately impossible, fated to leave me forever wanting.

Chapter 22

Two stories of curved glass loom above me. The flagship branch of the Spar Bank in Freiburg keeps watch over *Bertoldsbrunnen*, the center square in the middle of the Altstadt through which every Strassenbahn line passes. Class just ended, and the sun is already low in the sky, even though it's only midafternoon. Backpack slung over my shoulder, I pass through the sliding glass doors, which part for me obediently.

Though I've passed this building a hundred times, I've never been inside. There are only ATM's on the first floor, so I take the stairs up to the second. Rubbing my thumb nervously up and down each key in my pocket, I survey the teller windows. I did consider asking Daniel to come along and step in if I had troubles communicating, but I need some space right now. The memory of the other night is still too fresh in my mind. It took me almost three hours to finally fall asleep that night. Another option would have been to bring Niko along for moral support, but since his German is worse than mine, that seemed a little pointless.

This morning when checking my bank account, it was a lot lower than it should have been. Scanning through the transactions, I noticed something odd. Right below the most recent large transaction—$273.61 for withdrawing two hundred euro a week earlier—there was another identical withdrawal at the same ATM at the same time. Then I remembered how the ATM had slowly accepted my card and the failed transaction. *Wonderful luck, huh?*

We've all heard horror stories about tourists in places like Hungary and the Czech Republic—you know, those sketchy eastern European countries—who put their cards into ATM's that had a little gadget over the card slot. It would copy the card as it entered the machine, or it could be a fake ATM altogether. That wouldn't happen here in Germany. The most disturbing thing any of us exchange students ever see are fat bums with rehearsed speeches about how they ended up on the street.

I've just finished explaining the situation to the woman behind the glass teller window. Her face is pudgy, and enough product is packed into her hair to fuel the Olympic torch on its world tour. Throughout my story, she made the German equivalent to sympathetic noises, and now she's on the phone with her manager. After nodding and saying "*ja*" several times, she hangs up. "Unfortunately, sir, it is not possible for us to give you the money, because it never reached our bank."

Before I can tell her how utterly useless that information is to me, she continues, "However, I was able to locate the information about your transaction." She gestures to her computer. After a moment, a page rolls out of the printer next to her. "It shows that the transaction was broken off before it was completed." She circles some words at the top of the page. Überweisung abgebrochen it says. "You may keep this as . . ." she adopts a patronizing tone, "*Beweis.*" I don't recognize the last word, but almost immediately I understand its meaning. *Evidence.*

My eyes narrow as I take the paper from her. "Yeah, okay, I'll keep it as 'evidence.'" She wishes me good luck trying to get the money back, but I can tell she doesn't care. I could fax the printout to my bank in the States, but of course there's no way anyone there can read German. There probably isn't anyone who speaks fluent German within a hundred miles of my hometown. I might as well send them a poem about daffodils and ginger snaps.

It's dark by the time the Strassenbahn lets me off. Starving, I slog straight to my dorm and into the kitchen, ditching my backpack in a chair beside the door. Daniel is at the stove frying up his staple of tiny bacon cubes, onions, and chopped up *Maultaschen*, those plump ravioli made with meat and spinach.

Generally they're made with soup, but they're actually quite versatile. They sizzle in oil along with fat from the bacon. The smell is irresistible, but I'm determined to reestablish a more appropriate distance between us, so I don't ask him for a few bites.

"You're home rather late," he says.

I tell him briefly about the phantom ATM withdrawal while rummaging through my cupboard for something to eat. I have Spätzle—German egg noodles—that could be cooked up with Swiss cheese and onions, but it wouldn't be ready for a good half hour. I shut the cupboard harder than necessary. Maybe I should just make a sandwich.

Daniel is just sitting down to eat. "That's weird with the ATM. I've never heard of that happening to anyone." About a third of the fried Maultaschen are left in the frying pan. I catch myself staring and look away, but not before Daniel notices. "Do you want the rest?" he asks. "I can give you some of mine too. I can't eat this much anyway," he waves his fork over the plate.

"No, I'm fine." My stomach growls loudly as if on cue. Goddamn it. He must have heard it too, because he jumps up from the table before I can say otherwise. Grabbing another plate, he dishes up the rest of the Maultaschen. As if he hasn't been generous enough already, he pushes some of the food from his plate over to mine so we have equal portions.

I get myself a fork and sit down. "You didn't have to do that."

He smiles. "You're welcome."

I power through the food, not just because my stomach has turned into a ravenous beast, but also because it's so good. Ever since he introduced me to it earlier in the year, he's known I have a weakness for Maultaschen. I finish before him but wait since he's still eating.

"Will you be going anywhere over Christmas?" he asks.

My fingers fidget with the zipper on my hoodie underneath the table. I haven't thought much about this yet. Actually, I've been putting it off, because I don't have anywhere to go. "Um, I guess I'm not really sure what I'm doing yet." The words sound wrong and don't go well together. In German, it's hard to speak while actually saying nothing.

His head slants to the side like he's trying to figure me out. "What do you mean? You must either have plans or you don't."

"I suppose I don't."

"You suppose?"

"I don't have plans, alright?" I snap at him.

"Okay, okay," he raises a hand as if to calm me Jedi-style. "I was just thinking maybe . . ."

"Maybe what?" I prompt, the remnants of a hard edge lingering in my voice.

"I was thinking you could spend the holidays with me at my parents' home," he says. "If you want, that is."

I stare down at the tiled tabletop. It's not that I don't want to spend winter break with him. On the contrary, I would love it. But I shouldn't go. The more time we spend together, the harder it is to stop feeling the way I do. And when this comes crashing down, when he decides that I'm not interesting anymore or whatever it is that keeps him around, it's going to hurt. Bad. "I'll have to think about it."

He looks upset that I didn't accept his offer right away. "Alright, just let me know," he says, looking away as he clears his place.

I'm still at the table as he turns to leave the kitchen. Before he closes the door, we lock eyes for a long second. Then the latch clicks into place and I'm alone.

It was kind of rude of me to put him off like that. He was just being thoughtful to invite me. Besides, what else am I going to do over winter break? A few of the exchange students from the Sprachkurs might be staying in town, so I wouldn't be completely alone, but still. Niko isn't staying, and Corinne and Bastien are definitely going back to France. So who does that really leave?

I conjure up an image of Daniel with his family while I stubbornly remain in Freiburg by myself. A faint bitterness blossoms in the back of my mouth and swallowing doesn't make it go away. Who am I kidding? I can't turn him down any more than I can decide not to piss for the next three days. It's absolutely impossible.

I knock on his door and wait, tapping my foot against the concrete floor. When he answers, he's still wearing that expression with the mostly hidden disappointment. The tug on my heart is so strong, I'm convinced it's going to break free and jump through my throat. God I want to touch him so badly, to take him in my arms, pull him close, and tell him how much I care. Tell him I can't live without him.

But I can't. I can never tell him what I really feel. Our friendship would end that very minute and be gone forever. Instead I do what's all too quickly becoming normal. I conceal what I'm really thinking, what I really want.

"Hi," I begin, glancing down at my feet. "I, uh . . . I was upset earlier, about . . ." I'm making this up on the fly. "About the problem with the bank. And I was really hungry, so I wasn't thinking straight." That last part is true at least. "I would love to spend the holidays with you."

His face progressively brightening all along, he's now smiling like I just invited him to my birthday party. Jesus, our friendship is messed up.

"You'll have a great time," he promises me.

"Yeah, no doubt." I allow myself a smirk and turn to leave.

"I couldn't have left you alone on Christmas, you know," he calls after me.

Chapter 23

December brings with it a bitter cold that creeps relentlessly into everything. Daniel insists it's never this bad in Freiburg, especially so early in the season. To make it worse, I wasn't expecting a cold winter, so I left most of my heavier clothes back in Minnesota. Even in my room with the radiator on high, the chill permeates the air. Outside it's worse, of course. It's a constant race to get from the warmth in a building to the warmth in the Strassenbahn—if possible in a seat far from any doors and their blasts of arctic air. The only place that isn't quite so cold is Daniel's room, where I've been spending more time lately because of an upcoming test for my political science course.

As long as my mind stays busy while we're together, it isn't so hard to be around him. And he's an excellent resource, not only for helping me practice the language and formulating complex ideas for essay questions, but also for insights into the German political system.

"So any political party will get the percentage of seats in the Bundestag, the German parliament, equal to the percentage of votes they received?"

"Yeah," he nods, "As long as they received at least five percent of the vote. That's to keep out the crazy parties that only get a few votes."

"That's so weird."

"You Americans are the ones with the weird system. There is no hope that anyone but Republicans or . . ." he pauses.

"Democrats," I fill in for him.

"Right. It's impossible for any party but the Republicans or Democrats to win the election, so many people are forced to vote for a party whose views poorly reflect their own."

It's odd to be discussing American politics with a German, but he seems to have a pretty good idea of what an election feels like: voting for the guy you dislike the least. "I suppose you're right." Staring at my laptop, I consider my country's election system in a new light. It strikes me there's something I've never asked him before. "Have you ever been to the United States?"

"What makes you ask?"

"When we first met and you said you didn't speak any English, I just assumed that you'd never gone there. I mean, it's pretty hard to get around without it."

He grins, the tips of his ears glowing red. "I may have exaggerated my lack of English."

"I knew it." I shake my finger at him. "Why didn't you tell me to begin with?"

The muscles around his eyebrows tense like he's not sure how to answer. I stare expectantly until he finally speaks. "I was afraid you would want to speak English all the time. I've seen other American exchange students do it before. They make a bunch of English-speaking friends and never learn German. I wanted to give you a chance to use your German without feeling self-conscious and switching into English."

Now it's my turn to feel embarrassed. He cared enough when we first met that he considered how his ability to speak English might hinder me from learning German.

As an afterthought, I wonder, *why?* When I first moved in, he seemed decidedly uninterested in getting to know me. "I didn't realize you'd thought about it that much."

Glancing away, he says, "I would have done that for anyone." He's still looking away, so his expression is hidden.

I wonder if he isn't telling me the truth. He had no reservations about concealing his ability to speak a whole language we have in common. Has he been dishonest about other things too? I quickly banish the thought that he lied about being straight before it can take me for a ride into fantasyland. It's not even worth the time to think about, because it would be so atrociously stupid. But it does make me wonder if he has other secrets.

"So you *have* been to the States then?"

"A few times."

"Where have you been?

"Different places. Chicago. Seattle."

There's a subtle depression near his lip. He's biting the inside of his cheek. It's weird I know that, but he does it often enough that I recognize the look. It's from staring at him so much.

"And . . ." he continues hesitantly, "New York. Boston. DC. I spent some time in California, too."

"I don't fricking believe it," I explode. "You've been to more places than I have." It's true, and a pang of actual jealousy jets through me. If only Mom could have afforded it, I would have loved to go on trips all over the United States, and I wouldn't have waited until college to study abroad. Only a few years older than me and he's seen more of my country than I have. All of a sudden I'm pissed. I'm pissed that he lied to me about speaking English, pissed that he has the means to travel wherever he likes, pissed that I can't stop myself falling for him.

My head involuntarily jerks to the side in frustration. "I have to go," I tell him, standing up.

"Is something wrong?" He's gotten more direct about asking this kind of thing when I do something unexpected. It makes it harder to get out of situations without having to explain myself.

"No, I'm fine," I lie, grabbing my laptop and leaving him sitting alone. In the hall just outside his room, I lean back against the wall, clutching my laptop to me, my chest rising and falling beneath it. *Get a grip, Ethan. Get over him.*

This is tearing me apart. I can hardly spend an hour with him before it gets to be too much. How am I going to make it through a week at his house? I've already committed to going, so there's no backing out now. Not that I could ever say those words to him, anyway. Some part of me would prevent that.

Chapter 24

Snow is falling all around. The temperature isn't as cold as it's been, though, so I don't mind being outside. "What do you think of this?" Niko is under the awning of the nearest booth, holding a mug with a Christmas tree painted on the side.

"Uh, it's nice." Actually it's hideous.

"You're right, it looks like crap, doesn't it?" He sets it back down.

"Kind of, yeah."

We're at Freiburg's Christmas market. Vendors, mostly family operations and small gift shops, have set up booths along the pedestrian street and adjoining square just north of the center of the Altstadt. We just finished our last class before the winter holidays, but instead of heading straight to the bar like a good number of our fellow students, we're checking out the Christmas market instead. It's already dark out, but most of the awnings are wrapped in multicolored string lights. Between those and the green-painted streetlamps adorned with wreaths and other holiday decorations, the resulting atmosphere is well lit and cozy despite the temperature.

"So you're still hung up on Daniel," Niko states as we move on to the next booth, which is filled with stuffed bears and reindeer.

"Why do you think so?"

"You've hardly said anything since we got here, and you've got this sort of hopeless puppy look."

I look away from Niko, eyeing a brown bear with a gold bow tie. He sticks out from his brothers that all have blue and silver ones. Would Daniel like one of the bears? "I just don't know what to do about him. I think . . . I might be—"

"Don't say you think you're in love with him," he interrupts. His voice is kind but the words hurt.

"Is that so hard to believe?"

"No, not hard to believe." He levels his gaze to mine and puts his hand on my shoulder. "But Ethan, it's not worth it."

I turn so his hand falls.

He glances down, exasperation threaded through his voice as he speaks. "You're going after someone who can't return your feelings. At some point, it's going to come back to bite you, and when it does, it will hurt."

I don't have the strength to argue with him, mostly because he's right. In a lot of ways it already hurts. Taking my silence as a cue, he adds, "You're my friend, and I don't want to see that happen." His blue eyes are bright underneath his nest of blond curls, and he's wearing a green and red scarf tied around his neck, one end draped halfway down the front of his jacket. He's watching me so intently that I turn away, pretending to be interested in a carving of an elf. It strikes me again how perfect Niko and I would be for each other in so many ways. Except my heart is somewhere else completely.

At the *Glühwein* cart, we each get a steaming mug of the hot, mulled wine. I only have to blow over the surface a few times before it's cool enough to sip. The sweet spicy taste fills my mouth and warms my throat.

"You know what you need," Niko continues now that we've gotten our wine, apparently content to give me more unsolicited advice.

"I could think of one thing that would make my evening better," I mumble, giving him a glare that's only half joking.

"Shut up," he elbows me, his touch lighter than when Daniel playfully punches me in the shoulder or arm. "What you need is a guy in your life. Like a real guy, not some straight one."

My thoughts have been so tied up with Daniel lately that the idea of dating feels completely foreign. The mere thought makes my stomach twist uncomfortably. There's no commitment to him, but I can't shake the conviction that being with another guy would be a betrayal, at the very least of my own feelings. "I'm not ready for that."

Obviously ignoring what I've just said, Niko suggests, "How about him?" He points inconspicuously across the square to a cute guy with a goatee in a brown leather jacket standing with some girls.

"Not interested."

"I don't know how you do it, Ethan. I would go crazy lusting after a guy I could never touch."

"I don't *lust* after him."

"If you say so. I just think you should at least keep your options open for available guys. You know, the ones that like other guys."

If only I could just turn off what I feel for him, I'd do it in a second. "It's not that easy, alright? I can't snap my fingers and have everything change."

He sighs, meeting my eyes. "You have to do *something*, Ethan. It can't end any other way, you know that."

"I want to, but I just . . . can't." I take a deep breath, feeling my chest expand. "Can we drop it please?"

"Sure, whatever." Niko takes a long sip of his mulled wine and, jumping on the opportunity presented by a woman holding an umbrella, dutifully changes the topic. "I don't get why anyone needs an umbrella for the snow," he says, lifting his hands in confusion.

Laden with our purchases from the market and joking about tourists and foreigners with their snow umbrellas, we browse the last few shops, passing time until the crowd starts to thin. In three days, I'll leave with Daniel to spend Christmas with his family, so when it's time to go home, I give Niko a tight hug. It's only two weeks that we won't see each other, but I'm going to miss him. As we start to pull apart, he tightens his grip on the back of my neck, preventing us from fully separating. "Take care of yourself, Ethan, okay?"

I nod and promise I will. His concern makes me feel warm inside. It's good to know I have at least one good friend here. Other than Daniel, that is.

The next evening I call Mom on Skype. While it rings, my attention drifts to the clock. I quickly do the math in my head, subtracting seven hours from 7:30 P.M. There might have been a better time to call than during lunch. It rings again and again. Just when I'm sure she isn't going to pick up, the "bloop" sound chimes through the speakers, signaling the call has been answered. Not having showered, I'm reluctant to turn on the webcam, but I do anyway.

"What are your plans for Christmas?" she asks. "In your last email you said you might be staying in Freiburg."

"Actually, I'm spending most of winter break with a friend. He invited me to his family's place."

"Well, I'm glad you found someplace to be. Which friend is it?"

"Um," I stall, rolling a pen between my fingers. "Daniel invited me."

"Oh," she says, a knowing note in her voice. No doubt she's remembering our previous conversation about him and the tandem meetings.

"So what will you boys be doing?" It sounds like a loaded question.

I tell her what I know, which isn't very much other than that I'll be there for Christmas. New Years too, I suppose.

"Hmm," she says. I can see the gears turning in her head. No matter how much I look forward to talking with Mom before I call, after a few minutes there's never anything on my mind except how much I want our conversation to end.

"Ethan," she begins, picking her words intentionally, "is Daniel a, uh . . . special friend?"

The pen I've been twirling over my knuckles comes to a stop, and I give her an incredulous look, "Do you mean is he my boyfriend or something? Jesus, Mom, no he's not." *If only he were*, my mind readily supplies.

"Oh," she looks relieved for a second, then strikes again. "Is he also homosexual?"

"For fuck's sake, Mom." This is getting a little ridiculous. I can tell she's taken aback, because she doesn't say anything else. Sighing, I answer her question. "First of all, no one says 'homosexual' anymore unless you're Catholic or a scientist. You're neither, so don't use it. And no, he's not. If that changes, I'll make sure to let you know right away." I let the sarcasm soak in.

She gives me a helpless look that's supposed to make me believe she's trying. "I didn't mean to upset you."

"Whatever."

"Ethan, don't be like this. It's not easy for me like it is for you."

The nerve the woman has. "It was never easy for me. Don't pretend like it was."

She chuckles darkly. "It looked like it was going pretty easy when you and that boy Casey visited for the weekend."

"Corey," I snap, correcting her. "And that's not what I'm talking about at all. Why even bring that up? It was your own damn fault for walking in on us. The door was shut for a reason." At the memory of Corey's visit to my hometown, irritation rears up inside me, prickling all over my skin like lightning waiting to strike the first thing that comes too close. The next words out of her mouth after she saw us screwing were: "I thought you were past this."

Aside from mild embarrassment at being caught, Corey didn't even care. His parents were way worse I guess, which is why I'd never met them. That, and I didn't really want to.

Instead of backing off into my own thoughts, I lay into her again. "Did you ever wonder why I almost never came home from school last year? Goddamn, Mom, you need to think about what you say, because sometimes it makes me feel like shit."

"I suppose you're right. I'm sorry." Her voice sounds defeated.

The pen slips out of my fingers and bounces across the table. "I've got to go. I have homework to do."

She still seems upset by my earlier outburst but agrees to let me go. When she hangs up, I slump back in my chair. I'm pissed off by all her questions about Daniel. That's so like her. She always knows how I'm going to react when she asks crap like that, but she keeps on asking. No matter how much I deny it, she seems convinced that something more is going on between us. In a way, she's right, but how the hell can she know that?

Chapter 25

Lying down to sleep, my mind refuses to relax. Tomorrow at 10 A.M. we leave for Daniel's home. His family lives near Stuttgart, and on the map it looks like it might take about four hours. Daniel and I rarely spend that much time together. *What will it be like to be in the same car for half a day? Or in the same house for two weeks?* My thoughts alternate between curious, anxious, and terrified.

I toss my backpack into the trunk of Daniel's M3 and close it with a solid thunk. "Ready to go?" he asks, waiting at the driver's side door.

The sun hits my eyes, and I have to squint to see him. "Sure am." The adventure is about to begin. The leather of the passenger seat is soft, and it pulls me in. I exhale a controlled breath, fighting to rein in my anticipation of what the next two weeks will bring. I think back to the first time I was in his car when he drove me to the hospital. That was the day when everything changed, when his reticence first melted, paving the way for our friendship.

He hasn't started the car yet. Turning, he gives me a quick up down glance. If I didn't know him better, I'd swear he was checking me out. I've more or less given up trying to understand his occasional odd actions. "Let's drive," I say.

The engine rumbles into life, and we drive through narrow, snow-covered streets until we reach the main road. There are hardly any other cars out, even though the sun is shining and the temperature is a moderate negative five Celsius. Businesses and apartment buildings fly past as we move through the outskirts of the city. It's easy to guess this entire area was leveled during the war, because every building is stucco or simply concrete, never any of the older constructions Europe is famous for.

In just a few minutes, we've reached the onramp to the Autobahn. "Interested in seeing what this machine can do?" Daniel asks.

"Definitely." I tug on my seatbelt to make sure it's taut.

We pull onto the onramp, and I'm excited to see it's clear, as are the two lanes of the Autobahn ahead. Daniel presses the gas pedal to the floor, and the sudden acceleration locks me against the seat. The engine's gentle thrum through the small streets of Freiburg transforms into an aggressive growl, increasing in pitch as we accelerate. I glance at the speedometer, hastily doing the kilometer to mile conversions in my head. It isn't until sixty miles per hour that he shifts with catlike speed into third gear and the needle on the tachometer backs off from the redline. At the shift, the engine drops in pitch but immediately starts to increase again.

Thankfully the highway is pretty dead because of the time of day. As we pass one hundred miles per hour, he slips the transmission into fourth. The growl turns into a roar as we hit one forty. Daniel slides the vehicle deftly into the left lane as we approach another car from behind. At this speed, everything moves so quickly, and we overtake the car as fast as you'd pass a pedestrian alongside a normal highway. At one fifty, he finally slacks off on the gas and moves back to the right lane, speedometer drifting down as we decelerate.

When we've slowed down to ninety-five and the engine noise has diminished to a contented purr, he sets the cruise control. "What do you think?" He's smiling but keeps his gaze fixed on the road.

"Impressive." And it is. For all my drooling over the expensive cars that passed our trailer park, I never imagined I would actually get to *ride* in one of them. I refrain from asking who paid for this car.

My eyes aren't on the road anymore, because the sun streaming through the window is silhouetting his jawline. His hair has grown from its cropped style at the beginning of the semester to a bit thicker all around, but still short enough that it doesn't jut out to the sides where it touches his ears. A day or two of stubble covers his chin and cheeks. I wonder what it would feel like to run my fingers over it . . . or my lips. He flicks his eyes toward me, and I taste their liquid twilight color before looking away, embarrassed.

He doesn't say anything, so after a minute, I venture another look at him. He's wearing a knowing smirk, not exactly pleased but not upset either. It's not that uncommon for him to catch me staring at him, but he's never confronted me about it. He probably has a good idea what's going through my head, even. Does it just not bother him, or is there something else making him put up with me? He's made it clear there are physical boundaries that can't be crossed, but stealing glances in silence doesn't seem to rub him the wrong way.

There must be some reason why he doesn't mind it, especially since he seems to suspect how I still feel about him. I want to ask what he's thinking when he gives me those strange looks, the ones that I can never quite place or understand. The ones I've caught on his face so many times, ever since that first night we met. Sometimes I wonder if they're the reason I'm drawn to him so fiercely. He's attractive without a doubt, but it goes deeper than that.

"Have you ever had a boyfriend?" he asks.

Where the hell did that come from? Other than the night a week after the motorcycle ride to the Schlossberg, we've never discussed this part of my life. Not directly anyway. I might as well tell him. "Um, yeah."

"I thought so. Did you date a lot?"

"Why do you say that? And no, I was only ever with one guy."

He lowers the dial for his seat heater down one notch. "You're a good looking guy, I figured you probably weren't single unless you wanted to be."

Good looking guy, huh? I shift in my seat and the leather groans. "Like I said, I only ever dated one guy."

"When was that?"

"We met at the beginning of last summer. His name was Corey."

He glances over at me, then drops his eyes to the shifter before returning them to the road. "It didn't work out?"

"No, we weren't really a good fit. We broke up right before I left for Germany." I pause, biting my lip. "Well, I broke up with him."

"You're the one who broke it off?"

"That so hard to believe?"

"No, I didn't mean it like that," he says quickly.

I don't believe him. He still thinks I'm hung up on him, and he's right. But he probably thinks it's because I always fall for guys hard, which isn't true. The problem is, it's impossible for me to tell him he's the only one I've ever felt this way about. It wouldn't change anything anyway.

Neither of us says anything more. The minutes roll past like the hills outside until the sunlight and the rhythmic hum of the engine make me tired, and the soft leather welcomes me into it as my eyes close.

The light filtering through my eyelids gives my dream world a pinkish glow, but I would recognize that face anywhere. He's standing close, facing me, gazing at me with that expression that's always the same. His eyes don't waver but focus on me with a singular intensity. What does he see? My hand reaches up toward his face. I run my fingertips along his cheekbone, just below his eye, but he doesn't flinch or back away. His skin is soft like I always imagine. My fingers slide down to touch his lips, but ever so slightly he turns away. My hand drops to my side.

His eyes no longer meet mine, so I follow his gaze downward, watching as he reaches across the space between us and slips his hand into mine. The touch is warm and his grip is reassuring, but it's different from my desire. It's supportive, caring, even intimate, but not passionate.

As soon as it began, it's already ending. There's no time to savor the contact, because his fingers are withdrawing. I try to hold on, but he's slipping away. Then he disappears completely.

My eyes flutter open, blinking to adjust to the light. The sun is higher in the sky now and isn't bathing me in warmth, but Daniel must have turned up the heat, because it's still cozy. Yawning, I ask, "How long did I sleep?"

"Almost two hours."

"You're kidding me. Why did you let me sleep so long? You must be bored to death."

"I don't mind driving. It's nice to have the quiet time to think." Pausing, he adds, "Besides, you looked like you were out pretty good, dreaming about something exciting." He's sporting a sly smile.

Instantly my cheeks are burning hot. Oh God, what if I said his name out loud? Or worse? "I, uh . . . wasn't talking in my sleep, was I?"

"No, not really." *Son of a bitch. What isn't he saying?* A few moments pass, but it isn't until it looks like the silence is killing him that he finally spills it. "You might have grabbed my hand off the armrest though," he says, amusement dominating his expression.

Christ, I knew it was something horrible. I'm not sure it's possible, but my face reddens even more. "Sorry," I mumble. *Way to fucking go, Ethan, you didn't even make it three hours without crossing the line.*

Apparently he notices I'm upset. "Hey, it's fine. You were asleep, it's no big deal."

"Yeah okay, sure." It's bad enough I'm practically tripping over myself whenever I see him. The least I could do is try to not make it so obvious.

"No, really," he says. "Don't be so hard on yourself."

Silence is the only response he's going to get. I'm bored from the car ride, but closing my eyes again seems like a bad idea, so the time passes with me staring out the window at the passing countryside. I'm not sure if Daniel is unhappy about the end of our conversation, but he's silent as we drive. Occupied by my own thoughts, I don't try to strike up a new conversation either. It's probably bad to start the holidays by tacitly not speaking to each other, but I don't feel like talking.

It's mid-afternoon when we take an exit from the Autobahn onto smaller roads that wind their way through tiny villages, cropland filling the space between them. Despite the rural terrain, I know from the map in the glove compartment that we're close to the outskirts of Stuttgart, probably less than thirty minutes drive even.

The farms and villages fall away as wooded land appears around us. I'm staring at a herd of white cows when the metronomic *click click* of the turn signal sounds, and we turn off the main road onto a narrow paved lane that cuts through the trees. The driving surface is narrow with barely any shoulder, but Daniel drives fast, seeming to know every turn. One last bend and the road widens into a large clearing, dominated by a small mansion, its gray slate roof reflecting the afternoon sun.

"Holy shit." It shouldn't be a big surprise after this car and his motorcycle, but seeing the house just makes it so real.

"That's home," he says, releasing a sigh of what sounds like resignation. He pulls right up to the front door and turns off the engine. "Are you ready?" he asks warily.

"Ready for what?"

"To meet my parents."

"I guess that hadn't crossed my mind." I swallow, trying to quell my growing anxiety as we get out of the car. It occurred to some part of me early on that meeting his parents would have to happen, but until this moment it was never a realistic possibility. It's like hearing about those sinkholes on the news that appear in people's backyards. Sure, it could happen to anyone, but until a gaping hole in the ground is trying to engulf the garage, it doesn't seem like a real thing.

Daniel gives me a moment to take in the impressive structure. "Ready?" he prompts again.

"Yeah, I guess."

He taps the doorbell but lets us in without waiting for a response. The foyer is spacious with ornate, dark stained woodwork and contrasting hardwood floors. A staircase covered in lush burgundy carpet rises up to the second floor, while a hallway with several doorways leading off it continues toward what must be the kitchen. The doorbell's chimes continue to sound for a few seconds longer, echoing through the rooms.

He takes off his shoes and stows them in a cubby underneath a long bench at the side of the entryway. Following his lead, I slip my shoes in next to his.

From the end of the hall, a woman appears, a smile on her face. She must be Daniel's mother, because she looks quite a bit like him. Or rather, he looks like her. They have the same eyes, and her bright smile is the same, even though Daniel is often reluctant to let his out.

"I've missed you," she says, taking him in her arms and giving him a quick kiss on each cheek. "It's been so long since you were home." She says it with a touch of sadness in her voice.

He pulls back from her hug. "It's good to be home."

She turns to me, smiling and switching into almost accent free English, "And you must be Ethan. I'm Eva." She reaches out to shake my hand. As she does, the shadow of another expression flickers across her features. Just as quickly, she recovers her initial friendly bearing. I'm caught between being impressed by her near perfect English and curiosity at that look, even though it lasted less than a second.

Daniel cuts in, "Mother, you should speak German with him. He speaks it quite well."

"*Also dann reden wir Deutsch,*"—*Well then we'll speak German,* she says warmly.

Moisture gathers on my palms. My German is always worse when

I'm put on the spot. "Yes, of course," I tell her. "I try to use it whenever I can. Otherwise it would never get any better."

She nods with approval. "That's smart of you. And Daniel is right, your German is very good. You should be proud." Before I'm forced to feign humility, she continues, "How about we talk in the sitting room?"

Almost an hour later, I throw myself onto Daniel's bed, sinking into the down comforter. I love German beds, especially the covers. "By all means, make yourself at home," he says with lighthearted sarcasm.

Talking with his mom was nice, actually. She asked a lot of questions about home and Mom and my time in Germany and my studies. She told me that this was my home too during my stay, and to let her or their maid Maria (seriously?) know if there was anything I needed.

Apparently Daniel's father is still at work dealing with some problem that came up last minute. They didn't really explain where he works other than "at the airport." Eva assured me he would be home by the evening.

Daniel's bedroom is about twice the size of Mom's living room back in the States, and easily three times the size of our dorm rooms in Freiburg. With its high ceiling, four poster bed, and full-length curtained windows, the space possesses an elegance that would feel stiffly formal if not for the posters and decorations that clearly declare it a teenager's bedroom. Daniel might have grown up, but this room doesn't appear to have changed. To top it all off, a giant flat screen television is mounted on the opposite wall from his bed.

Daniel must notice me visually examining every square inch of his room. "What do you think?"

At first I don't respond, wanting to assess every poster on the walls and every trophy on top of the dresser. The posters are mostly for action movies, but there are some comedies as well. Their bright scenes make the walls pop with color, bringing them to life.

Walking along the dresser, I trace my finger down the line of track and field trophies. This place feels so much more lived in than his room in Freiburg, but there's something else too. I don't know if I can imagine the guy standing across from me being as outgoing and involved as he'd need to be to get all these trophies. Daniel watches me expectantly as I take a seat back on his bed.

"I like it. It feels like you, but . . ."

"But?"

I want to pick my words carefully so they don't hurt him, but I can't think of any other way to describe my thoughts. So I say it anyway. "It's you, but happier." Before living in Germany, I would never have been so blunt with someone.

He sighs and drops himself onto the bed a foot away from me. "Things changed. After Marc."

"I'm sorry."

"Don't be. It's probably good for me to be here again and remember the things I used to like."

I want to change the subject before he dwells on his brother too long. I scoot up on the bed a little farther and lie back. "You were pretty good at sports in high school it looks like."

"I wasn't too bad."

If the row of first place trophies on his dresser is any indication, he's being really modest. "Did you do anything besides, uh," I have to pause. "How do you say *track and field*?" I ask, supplying the English words where my German knowledge is lacking.

"*Leichtathletik*, and no, that was my main sport." He's wearing an intrigued smile.

"What?"

"It's just been a while since I've had to translate anything for you, that's all."

Warmth fills my chest, spreading through my face. A compliment from him means more than from other people, if for no other reason than he rarely gives them. A sidelong glance from him reminds me of something from earlier. "Your mom gave me a look when we first arrived. Why was that?"

"Huh?"

"When she shook my hand, she got this weird look her face for a second."

His hands slide into his pockets. "We just don't have people over much. Don't worry, she likes you. She thinks it's great you want to speak German with us."

I'm getting that familiar feeling he's concealing something again. "Why wouldn't I speak German with your family?"

"We had an exchange student for three weeks during the summer when I was in high school, and she just spoke English with us most of the time," he says, finally lying back on the bed beside me.

"That's stupid. Why would she come to Germany and not bother to speak the language?"

"No idea, but it didn't endear her to my parents very much. They can be kind of traditional."

Traditional. Is there deeper context to what he's just said? "Do they know that I'm, you know . . ."

"Gay?" he asks rhetorically. "No, I didn't tell them." He shifts, sliding a hand behind his head. "Do you think I should have?"

"I'm not sure." My eyes drift over the gold-painted patterns in the ceiling. I wonder if it's gold leaf. It can't be. I hope it isn't. "I usually don't tell someone until I know they won't react negatively."

"I would have preferred if you'd used that approach with me, too."

My cheeks are instantly hot, but before I can sputter an embarrassed apology, he waves his hand at me dismissively. "Kidding. Anyway, my parents, they have some hang ups about it, I think. It might be easier not to mention it, but it's up to you."

The idea of having to hop back in the closet for a week or so isn't appealing, but when it comes down to it, it's not that big a deal. "No, that's fine. I'm good at pretending to be straight."

He shakes his head. "You're really something, Ethan." Getting up and making toward the door, he says, "So you want to see your room?"

"I thought we were both sleeping in here." I bite my tongue, wishing I hadn't just admitted that.

The beginning of a frown forms around the edges of his mouth. "You'll have your own room," he says. I try to look glad, but he must notice my disappointment, because he adds, "It's just down the hall."

It turns out my room is a lot like his except not as personal, since it's decorated with the sparse and neutral art of a guest bedroom. The backpack with all my stuff is already on the floor, leaning against the foot of the bed. "How did that get here?"

"Maria brought it up," Daniel answers, leaning nonchalantly against the doorframe. I try not to think it, but I can't help admiring how great he looks. He always seems to wear his clothes a size too small, and right now his long sleeved shirt is stretching around his biceps and pecs. His hair is messy but in a good way, and that all too familiar feeling stirs inside me. I turn my wistful gaze out the window, so he doesn't get uncomfortable.

"Is it weird having a maid?" I ask. Facing away from him, I stare decidedly out at the yard. It wouldn't be best for him to get a frontal view of me right now. I'm starting to get set off way too easily around him.

"We've always had one," he explains. When I don't respond right away, he says, "Take some time to unpack. I'll be in my room." Still facing out the window, I don't hear him leave. Checking over my shoulder to make sure he's gone, I adjust myself and start pulling clothes and toiletries out of my bag.

Normally I wouldn't bother, but I decide to hang up my shirts. It feels important that at least something in my life is in order and under my control. Everything else gets stuffed into the chest of drawers next to the closet. Once all my clothes are put away, I find myself staring through the window's small rectangular panes again.

I'm determined to give Daniel some time to himself, so I dig out my laptop and the leather-bound Bible he assured me would come in handy. If only he had found the goodness in himself to explain how it would be helpful, my history paper might be further along. It isn't due until February when the winter semester ends, but besides the vague reference to Magdalena Ernst's connection with the White Rose resistance in Munich, I don't really have anything.

Sifting through search results on the laptop, I only find more dead ends in regard to Magdalena. The Maria-Magdalena Church keeps popping up, no matter how I phrase the keywords. After fifteen minutes of searching, I toss my laptop across the bed in frustration, holding back my strength just enough so it doesn't sail over the edge and onto the floor.

Maybe the Bible Daniel gave me will prove more useful. I stifle the irritation threatening to awaken at the thought of his "gift" and pluck it from the nightstand. The binding is worn and weak from age, so I hold the spine in my hand while flipping through, reading passages here and there. The pages are razor thin and make a crinkling sound when I turn them.

This isn't helping. If he thinks a religious awakening will help me with this paper, he's mistaken. And an asshole. I continue to flip through the pages.

Sprawled out on the bed, I've just exiled the book to a spot beside the laptop when Daniel appears in the doorway, softly rapping his knuckles on the wood to announce his presence. "Dinner will be ready soon."

"Do we have plans afterward?"

"Not really. Mind if we just stay in tonight?"

That's fine with me, and I tell him so. Despite napping for half the drive, I'm a bit worn out and still processing that his family lives in a mansion.

"Great. I'm sure we can find something fun to do."

Jaw pressed tightly shut, I nod in agreement. I'll enjoy whatever he wants as long as we can do it together, but I'm sure as hell not going to tell him that.

With just the two of us, dinner is swathed in a morose silence. "I thought your parents were going to eat with us."

Daniel's fork stops halfway to his mouth. "My dad is working late again I think, and my mom went out." He says it with a finality that makes me suspect he doesn't want to talk about it.

Maria has made us *Käsespätzle*—German egg noodles with cheese and onions. It's far better Käsespätzle than I've had anywhere else, but since we're alone in an expansive dining room at a table built for ten, both the room and the food feel empty. The only source of light is the chandelier, which must be on a dimmer switch, because it's barely bright enough to see our plates. My eyes keep trying to adjust to the murky dimness that sticks to every corner and surface, but they just end up hurting.

Daniel might be upset that his parents are nowhere to be found, but it's always so hard to tell with him. In either case, he doesn't say hardly anything while we eat. I try to catch his eye but his head stays down, fixed on his plate. Sliding my elbows off the polished mahogany, I finally give up and lower my gaze.

I'm relieved when we're both finished. This room is so empty and lonely it borders on creepy. Perfect for a state dinner, but absolutely abysmal for grabbing a meal with your friend. Or your brother—the thought pops into my head. How often did Daniel eat meals with Marc like this, the two of them alone and surrounded by silence?

He starts to clear our places. Feeling useless, I make to grab the serving dishes.

"I've got it," he says. "I'll be up in a bit."

I stare at him for a minute as he continues clearing. He won't make eye contact with me, so I leave the room.

It makes me a little uneasy being up in his room by myself, and my skin ripples with a phantom chill. With him here, the space feels warm and inviting. Without, it's just a big room with posters and expensive curtains.

When he comes up, I'm gazing out the window at the moonlight reflecting off the untouched snow in the backyard. "Hey," he says, joining me at the window.

"The snow is so perfect." The moon and stars cut through the darkness, turning the landscape into a cake covered by endless silver frosting.

"Do you want to go out?" He brightens with sudden inspiration.

I point out the window. "You mean like walk around out there?" Growing up in the Midwest, I'm not afraid of cold and snow, but for winter clothes all I have are a pair of sneakers and a jacket.

Reading my thoughts, he says, "Don't worry, we've got extra boots and everything."

It takes a minute for me to acclimate to the idea, but a night adventure into the cold is starting to sound like fun. "Yeah okay, let's go."

There's a small room in the basement with a walkout exit to the backyard. Every manner of winter clothing is hung on the walls or stuffed into organizers. Before outfitting himself, Daniel starts by handing me pairs of boots, instructing me to "try this" and when they're too big or too tight, snatching them back.

After trying on a third pair of boots, I say, "My shoe size is nine and a half. Can't you just look for that?"

"These are a size forty-eight." He takes the boots from me. "Do you know your Euro size?"

"No, I guess not," I reply lamely, feeling stupid.

He massages his jaw in thought, staring down into the tub of boots. Once more he plunges his hand into the mountain of footwear. His goal must be near the bottom, because he's really fighting to extract a pair from the pile.

Finally they come free, and he hands them to me. They're made of light colored leather that's soft and supple. The insides are fur lined, and a quick touch confirms it's real. Scuffs on the outside and wear on the fur show the boots have been worn many times, but they're well taken care of. At least they were before being relegated to the bin of spare footwear. The fur around the top is flattened and matted with bits of dirt.

Daniel watches as I slide my feet in and tie the laces. They fit pretty well.

"Might as well try this too, then." He hands me a matching light brown fur-lined parka from a hook in the corner of the room. I put it on and feel instantly warm. Once it's zipped and the clasps that seal the zipper are all fastened, I can't wait to step outside. And if I don't in the next minute or two, I'm going to be standing in a puddle of my own sweat.

"That fits too, huh?" He hands me gloves and a hat to complete my winter outfit.

I roll my shoulders inside the parka. "Yeah, it's good."

The walkout door to the outside is snowed in, so Daniel has to put some shoulder into it. Under his weight, the door plows the drift out of the way, and we're outside and free. The air is crisp and cold as we traipse under the lunar glow through the backyard and toward the trees. Before us, the snow is completely unbroken, so at first it feels like we're desecrating something special. As I settle into the gentle rhythm of following his steps though, my regret at disrupting the pristine winter night transforms into an appreciation of the quiet solitude that has been prepared just for us.

Eventually his lead brings us through the woods and to the frozen shore of a small pond. Taking a few tentative steps onto the ice, he carefully lowers himself until he's lying face up to the sky. Taking the space next to him, I let my eyes drift upward in amazement. While most of Germany is overwhelmed by light pollution, this secluded spot in the wilderness must be just far enough from Stuttgart to be largely unaffected. The sky is filled with a million pinpricks of the clearest starlight. Eclipsed only in a corner of the sky by the moon's bright silver, the stars otherwise dominate the sky.

"It's beautiful," I say, turning my head to look at Daniel. He's still staring up into the night, his breath rising in a pillar of water vapor. I wish he would look at me. The only thing I would rather be gazing at right now than the glowing sky are the dark wells of his eyes.

Distinctly aware that his gloved hand is just inches from mine, it's all I can do to keep from reaching out and taking it. I force my gaze back to the sky. Its vastness puts my problem with Daniel into perspective. As insignificant as I am in comparison, somehow it makes me feel less alone. Maybe someone out there like me is staring back, giving up their own worries to the night sky.

I don't know if I really believe in God, but when staring up into something so vast and incomprehensible, it makes you wonder if it really did just come into existence all by itself. It's certainly a more comforting thought that some omniscient being out there cares about each of us and our petty worries.

"Marc and I used to come here," Daniel breaks the silence. "He loved to be outside, especially when it was cold like this."

The synthetic material of his coat makes a scraping sound over the ice as he shifts position. Afraid the moment will dissipate just as quickly as our breath in the air, I weigh my words carefully. "Were you always with him?"

Daniel sighs audibly, another plume of white rising in the frigid night. "No, not always. Marc stuck to himself a lot, so he didn't have a lot of friends. I tried to be there for him whenever I could." As he finishes, it's abundantly clear why Marc's death must have been so hard on him. For the first time, Daniel wasn't there. He was away at university, probably buried up to his neck in term papers.

As quickly as it came, his willingness to share fades into the darkness. The wind racing over the ice blows snow into our hoods, and the cold starts to seep through the layers I'm wearing. Hoping that he might say more about Marc, I let the minutes slip by.

Finally, I can't hold it in any longer. "After my dad left, I kept thinking that he'd come back, that one day he'd be there, and everything would go back to the way it was."

Daniel's voice is hushed. "Except he never did."

"No, he never did." It's hard to tell between the cold in the air and the chill inside. "I hated him so much for it, but eventually I realized I'd spent years hating someone I didn't even know." I draw in a breath, and when I release it, it feels like a small burden has been lifted.

"If he wanted to come home, to be a part of your life now, would you let him?"

I've thought about that very question a lot over the years, but I always come to same conclusion. "No. Some things shouldn't be forgiven." Above us, the sky is so vast.

"You think so? Even if it meant having him back in your life?"

His answer makes me pause. When I first met Daniel, he struck me as being tough on mistakes, with forgiveness conspicuously missing from his toolkit. His question makes me reconsider that assumption. And I shouldn't forget his good humor regarding the incident on top of the Schlossberg.

It doesn't change what I think about my dad though. "No, I definitely don't want to see him again. After you lose someone, I think you eventually just get used to the fact they're gone." The second the words spill from my mouth, my throat constricts. A bolt of fear cuts through me. How could I have been so insensitive? "I'm sorry," I mumble, turning to see his reaction. "I didn't mean it like that."

He's still staring up at the sky, silent. "It took a few weeks for it to really sink in, for me to realize I'd never see him again. No matter how long I wait, I'll never again hear him laugh or tell a joke or sneeze. Marc always sneezed so loud. It was like he was getting attacked by his own sneezes." Daniel laughs for just a second, but there's no happiness in it. "And we'll never run through these woods in the summer. We'll never go swimming or complain about our parents or start stuff on fire."

A deep current in my chest stirs at his words. I can't imagine how hard it was on him. How hard it still is. I can barely hear him over the wind as he whispers, "The day I got the call from my mom, I didn't realize what it meant. I had no idea how much I would miss him."

Not trusting myself to respond verbally, I stretch my hand across the six-inch gap between our gloved hands and take his in mine. He squeezes back. His voice is strained, on the verge of breaking, and comes out as a whisper, "He's been gone a year, but I still think every day how I . . . I never got to say goodbye. There's so much I wish I could tell him."

"What about the funeral?"

Discordant threads of regret and guilt tug at his voice. "I left before the service even ended. I couldn't bear to hear it."

Time stands frozen like the ice beneath us. His hurt is as easy to feel as the hand still squeezing mine. Does it help to share our pain with others? Does it lessen the ache inside or at least make it more bearable? I've never talked to anyone about my dad before tonight, not even Mom and definitely never Corey. Even though I didn't say much, it still felt good to let it out. Sometimes things get stuck inside you like cancer, and there's no fix but to drag them out.

At last when I'm afraid I might freeze to the ice, I ask if we can go back.

"Yeah, we can go," he says, reluctance clawing at his words. Joints stiff with cold, I push myself to my feet and help him up as well.

Slogging back to the house isn't nearly as enjoyable as the trip out. I've been cold for so long that an empty, gnawing feeling fills my stomach, and my muscles and bones all ache. Concentrating on keeping up with Daniel, I order my feet to keep moving.

After what feels like forever, we emerge from the trees onto the front lawn, and he leads us through the front door of the house, possibly just to spare us the extra steps through the wintry darkness to the rear entry.

Unable to move even a step further, we stand side by side in the entryway, the chandelier above casting golden light over us as we slowly thaw. At first I could swear the warmth is actually pushing the cold in deeper, but my shivering soon subsides, shooed away by the smell of freshly baked goodies.

The soft, sweet sound of a woman humming drifts into the entryway. Still bundled up, I walk down the hall toward it. The sounds of Daniel's footsteps follow me. Standing at the doorway to the kitchen, I identify Daniel's mother Eva as the source of the humming. Her back to us, she's transferring cookies from a baking tray to a glass platter.

Lifting the tray, she turns toward us. The second her eyes flit over us she gasps, stopping mid-step. As if in slow motion, the dish slips from her slackened fingers and sinks toward the floor, the red and green cookies lifting off in free fall before the glass shatters on the hardwood. Broken cookies and broken glass burst outward from the point of impact, intermingling as they bounce across the kitchen floor.

Eva's piercing eyes remain locked on us, but her gripping expression immediately fades to embarrassment. Straightening her posture and smoothing the front of her apron, she closes her open mouth. "I am so sorry about that. You boys startled me is all." Cheeks bright red, she looks around the room as if trying to find an explanation stuffed into a cupboard or resting on the countertop. When none is forthcoming, she says, "Be careful of the glass. I'll have Maria clean this up."

I glance at Daniel. His expression is hard, but it isn't directed at me as he speaks. "Come on, Ethan, let's get changed."

Pulling my gaze away from Eva and the chaos of glass and cookies on the floor, I follow him downstairs.

Daniel is silent on the shattered glass incident as we put away our winter clothes. After we finish, I tell him I'll be in my room if he wants to do anything. He nods but doesn't say anything, so I leave him, considerably less than optimistic that he'll be making another appearance tonight.

Leaning against the headboard of the guest bed, I stuff some pillows behind my back to make the position more comfortable. As I grab my laptop from where I tossed it earlier, Daniel's worn Bible, which was still perched on the corner of the computer, flops off the edge of the bed. A muffled thud sounds up from the floor.

I grunt in irritation. I'm feeling lazy, but it can't just stay down there. Daniel would be offended if he saw me treating a book old enough to be a family heirloom so carelessly. So I roll over onto my stomach and reach down to pick it up. It landed on the spine and now lies splayed on the floor, open to the book of Psalms. My hand is an inch from the featherweight paper when I freeze. A tingle climbs my back, and the hairs on my neck rise into the air.

Lifting the Bible gingerly, I place it on the nightstand, swinging my legs over the edge of bed. Under the bright light of the bedside lamp, I press the pages of the open book until they're flat against the table, exposing the threads of the binding and the surface of the paper closest to the spine. *I'll be damned*—there's miniscule handwriting in the margin, written right along the binding.

I rotate the book, squinting to make out the words, my face hovering only inches above the writing. With the Bible on its side, there are words written above the horizon where the pages disappear into the binding, and more words just below it. It's German written in the old style, and it's difficult to make out. Word by word, I work my way through the sentence.

October 2, 1942. When I stepped into the street tonight, I could not help but shiver. Hakenkreuz banners hung from every lamppost.

Blinking to clear my vision after focusing on the tiny words, my eyes narrow in concentration. *Hakenkreuz.* It sounds familiar but I can't place it. *Kreuz* means cross, but I can't remember what *haken* means. I pull my laptop over and tap the word into the search engine.

Instantly recognizing the image that comes up, a shiver grips me, and I snap the laptop shut. It was only up for a second, but the icon is burned into my memory: a red square behind a white circle, a black symbol in the middle. It's then that I remember haken means "hooked," as in "hooked cross," the German word for the Swastika.

Straining to make out the words, I turn the page and read the next sentence hidden near the binding. *Curfew was an hour past, so I moved in the shadows only, knowing that the documents in my possession meant certain death for me if discovered.*

I push the Bible away. What the hell do I have here? And how did Daniel get this? I take a deep breath, letting air fill my chest. I'm overreacting. There must be a perfectly reasonable explanation for the book lying on the nightstand.

I allow myself another glance at it and the hidden writing along its center. Biting my lip, I hesitate before pulling the book back toward me. The two sentences I read are clearly part of something bigger. I flip back a few pages until I reach the book of Job. Fingers tingling, I again press the pages flat against the table and examine the binding. The muscles in my jaw grow tense. The same tiny handwriting is here as well.

This time I skip back a hundred pages to Deuteronomy, and I'm not disappointed. The writing makes its appearance here too. The entire Bible must be filled, or at least a substantial portion. The revelation sinks in. If this is real, my hands are holding a piece of history. A story, a journal, or *something* straight out of Nazi Germany. I close the Bible, appreciating the smoothness of the leather, the kind of texture that can only be created by frequent handling and passing years. The binding feels pliable, weaker than it really should, but that's no surprise. It must have been spread apart hundreds of times by the author of the miniature lines.

With a newfound respect, I open the cover, turning each page carefully until I discover where the penned lines begin at the first page of Genesis. The words are packed tightly together, written so small that it's a struggle to make them out. Their meaning comes slowly at first as my eyes and mind are forced to adjust to the cramped, old blackletter script used for written German well into the twentieth century. But as I continue, I begin to give myself over to the story being told, letting it fill me until nothing exists in the world except for the scrawled words before me.

August 14, 1942. I had a visit with Uncle today. We discussed something most unusual. When at first he broached the subject, I feared that his words were intended to test the depth of my loyalty. However, as his queries progressed, I became convinced of his sincerity. Indeed, if his thoughts on this particular subject are as he says—and I am certain they are, for he has never before given me cause to doubt the veracity of his words—he then has undertaken the gravest of risks. Yet despite my fear for his safety, I could not help but be moved by his passion and his bravery, and above all his conviction. I cannot bring myself to make mention of his beliefs here yet, so I shall simply say: there is hope that we are not all as blind as they believe. ~In regard to the book in which I pen these lines, I felt it prudent to take certain precautions and make record of this occurrence in a location more secure than my daily journal.~

Concentrating on such small writing has left black shapes rolling across my vision. Releasing the pressure on the pages of the Bible, they return to their normal position, rendering the tiny writing invisible in the curve of the binding.

I sit up, blinking rapidly to restore my vision, and release the shallow breath I was holding. Who was the author of this? And what was he getting himself into?

Beside the Bible is my German-English dictionary. The older style of the writing and vocabulary had me needing it on the second sentence. I glance at the clock on the nightstand. Twenty-five minutes have passed since I began reading. It was painfully slow going, churning through those sentences.

A tightness in the muscles over the bridge of my nose is threatening to become a headache, but I can't just stop reading, not now. Massaging first my temples and then above my eyebrows, I shake my head to clear the discomfort.

August 24, 1942. Uncle had business in the city again today and came by after it was concluded. Firstly he complimented my new dress, and I believed that he would not make mention of the topic we had previously discussed, for his words made me feel much like a child again.

Already suspecting who the anonymous storyteller might have been, this confirms at least that she was a woman. I let my gaze wander across the room before pulling it back.

Yet after exchanging the usual pleasantries, he once more made reference to our discussion of the previous visit. "How helpful it would be," he said, *"if the Albert-Ludwigs-Universität had also such a daring group of students as does the Ludwig-Maximilians-Universität."*

Albert-Ludwigs-Universität is the official title of the university in Freiburg, but I have no idea about the Ludwig-Maximilians-Universität. Could the student group referred to be the student resistance group that Daniel mentioned, the White Rose? If so, Ludwig-Maximilians might be the formal name for the . . . I wrack my memory until it comes to me. The university in Munich, that's where the White Rose was based. I forge on to the next page.

When I indicated that I agreed with his assertion, he pulled me close and whispered in my ear. He said, "Will you be ready?" Trepida-

tion gripped me tightly, but I refused to allow Uncle to see my weakness.
"Yes," I told him.

Another half hour has passed, and my head is throbbing. Tiredness and pain are preventing me from processing what I've just translated. Wishing I could sink into the covers this very moment, I force myself up to brush my teeth and pee. Passing Daniel's room, I notice his light is already off. He could have at least stopped by to say goodnight, though I shouldn't have expected much more.

I consider the alternative, that if I were at home in Freiburg right now, I would be bored and, worse yet, alone. Unbidden, the thought leaps into my mind that at this particular moment, I'm probably just as alone as I would be in an empty dorm.

Chapter 26

The down comforter and silk sheets hold me in their embrace until almost noon. The previous night wasn't a terribly late one, but since Daniel went to bed without saying anything, it can't hurt to give him some space. It's not his job to entertain me, after all.

The memory of reading the hidden lines in the leather-clad Bible comes bounding back. A shiver creeps down my back, and I'm thankful to be wrapped in blankets. My mind skips from one possible scenario to another. From the references to the university, it must be Freiburg where it all took place, which makes it feel so much closer.

I'm still mulling over what "Uncle" and the nameless author were up to and whether it really had anything to do with the White Rose movement in Munich when Daniel appears at the door. "Hungry?"

After lunch, which is actually just a very late breakfast, he suggests we watch some TV. "Sure," I agree, pushing myself up to sitting position. I'm lounging on his bed. "What do you want to watch?"

"Do you like the OC?"

Sounds familiar, but I've never seen an episode. "Isn't it about rich kids hanging out at the beach?"

His face flushes. "Yeah, pretty much." He nibbles pensively on the inside of his cheek. "So do you, uh, want to watch it?"

"If you want." It would be a truthful answer for just about any question he could ask.

He fetches a DVD case from underneath the TV stand across from the bed and pops the disc into the player. Scooping up the remote from atop the entertainment center, he heads back to the bed where I'm still sprawled out diagonally.

"Scoot over, man."

"You've got plenty of room, right there," I tease, pointing to the small triangle of space not being occupied by some part of me.

He grabs my ankles and tosses the lower half of me onto the far side of the bed. "That's better," he says, settling himself onto a stack of pillows.

We're a few minutes into the first episode when he says, "You know what would make this better?"

"What's that?"

"A few beers."

I'm lying on my stomach, propping myself up on my elbows to see the TV, so I have to look over my shoulder to see if he's serious. He's smiling mischievously. Yeah, he's serious. "It's barely afternoon."

"You're in Germany, remember?" Hopping up from the bed, he's almost out the door when he calls back, "Don't you dare take my spot again."

We finish the first episode as we finish our beers. My fingers already have that familiar tingle, and there's warmth in my stomach. My attention drifts, allowing my gaze to slide down his arm. His fingers are curled around the bottom of his empty glass. He's still tan, even though it's been months since we saw the summer sun.

"How about another?" he asks. It doesn't really sound like a question.

It's unclear if he means another episode or another beer, but when he comes back from the kitchen with our glasses refilled and clicks on to episode two, I see he meant both.

"Prost," we say in unison, clinking the tops of our glasses together.

The show is alright, but I end up watching him out of the corner of my eye just as often as I'm watching the TV. I steal an extra glance every time he takes a pull from his beer, mostly because he's less likely to catch me when he's distracted.

The story in the Bible has been gnawing on me since this morning. My inhibitions curbed by the beers, I try to sound casual. "Hey, do you know the official name of the University of Munich?"

He pauses the episode and gives me a look. "Why do you ask?"

"No reason. Just wondering if it was named after someone like the University of Freiburg is."

He's still eyeing me like he suspects a deeper reason for my question, but he answers anyway. "It's the Ludwig-Maximilians-Universität."

I knew it. "Ah okay. Good to know." I turn my focus back to the TV show, pretending to be interested in the keg party and drama with the water polo team that's going down. Daniel's attention lingers on me at first but eventually he turns back to the show as well.

His beer is about half gone when he accidentally tips the glass a little too far back. A pair of beer rivulets spontaneously form and slide down both sides of his mouth. Sputtering out a cough, he sits up, causing the streams of beer to slide down under his chin, navigating their way through a day's worth of stubble. The liquid continues, forging wet trails down his neck, past where his Adam's apple sticks out. He wipes away the wetness with his fingers, and then his tongue makes an appearance, darting out to lick them clean.

"Gross," I say, pretending to be revolted and giving his shoulder a shove.

He's still mid-recovery from the coughing spell, and his beer sloshes back and forth in the glass. "Careful, punk," he shoots back, but it's clear from his barely concealed grin that he isn't mad.

I push his shoulder again, harder than before. This time, a slurp's worth of beer jumps out of the glass and lands on his jeans just above the knee.

"Alright, you're asking for it." There's a playful glint in his eye as he slams his glass down on the nightstand. I barely have time to set down my own before he grabs my ankles and starts to pull me off the bed. I grab onto whatever is in reach: the covers, pillows, the bedpost.

But he's too strong and soon he's dragged me to the floor. He almost pins me down using just his arms, but at the last moment I manage to wriggle free. "Hah!" I shout as I sneak out of his grip.

My courageous escape is short lived, however, because he locks me down for good a second later, practically sitting on my hips and holding my shoulders down with outstretched arms. He's a hell of a lot stronger than I am, and I can't move more than an inch or two, even when I really push. He must know it too, because his enjoyment seems to increase when I give up exhausted.

"Yield?" he asks, brimming with winner's arrogance.

"Never," I grit my teeth and put up another futile effort to budge him off me.

We catch our breath for a few seconds, unmoving from our position. Daniel has never let himself be this physical with me before. It doesn't bother me, though. On the contrary, it makes me feel like we're just a couple of brothers roughhousing. The intimacy feels natural, but I don't like thinking about him in a brotherly sense.

I've been working to keep myself under control, but lying on the floor with him pinning me down like this is causing a stirring in my jeans despite my efforts. Maybe it's for the best that we don't normally wrestle like this. He's not actually sitting on my crotch, but he's pretty close. "Okay, I yield."

He doesn't respond or move. Things aren't settling down. My voice is panicked. "Get off me, man."

"Nah," he laughs, leaning over to make a grab for his beer. It's unclear whether he's going for a victor's drink or to get revenge for making him spill on himself, but I don't have time to find out.

Taking advantage of him only having one arm pinning me down, I shove him away with all my strength and scoot myself out from underneath him. Thankfully he lets me go, and I sit up, exhaling in relief.

I stay like that, pretending to catch my breath, knees pulled up toward my chest for a full minute until it's safe to get up. When I do finally move, Daniel watches me carefully. I hope he doesn't suspect what just happened.

After the third episode ends, we grab a snack downstairs, taking our seats on bar stools around the kitchen island. While I'm digging into a chocolate croissant, he says, "My mom told me they want to have dinner with us tonight. Christmas dinner."

Oh, right. I forgot that today was the twenty-fourth already. "It will be nice to meet your dad finally."

"Yeah, maybe."

"What do you mean?" I ask between bites.

He glances away, his foot tapping repetitively on the lowest rung of his stool. "We just don't really get along that well."

The minutes of silence stretch out like saltwater taffy, punctuated only by chewing. When we're done, I tell him I'm going to lie down for a while. I would gladly spend the day with him, but we still have over a week to spend time together.

* * *

After an hour or so, Daniel stops by my room to let me know that dinner will be ready soon. Curled up on the bed, I stifle a yawn. "Are we doing anything afterward?"

One hand resting on the opposite forearm, his fingers and thumb gently work together to massage the tendons. "I thought maybe we could just stay home and play a game or something."

He's leaning against the doorframe in what's becoming a familiar seductive pose. Damn him. "That sounds perfect," I say, knowing full well that telling him no would have been physically impossible.

Daniel is sitting next to me and his mother is across from us. The dining room is actually impressive when there are more than two people eating. The crystal chandelier hovers near the ceiling in the center of the room, much brighter this time. Under its full light, new details pop out to me that were previously invisible. The woodwork here is exquisite, far more elaborate than in the rest of the house.

A clinking of pots and pans from the kitchen around the corner indicates that Maria hasn't quite finished preparing the meal. Beside me, Daniel's hands are folded across where his belt buckle would be if he were wearing one. Bluish veins run through his hands like miniature subways, crisscrossing in an unpredictable pattern. The light brown hair on his arms ends abruptly at his wrists, as if stopped by an invisible barrier. What would it feel like to run my fingers over his arm? His skin looks soft, a taut velvet covering for the muscles beneath.

"So Ethan, what do you like best about Freiburg?" Eva asks.

Her question pulls my eyes upward. "Its history."

She nods, acting interested. "What do you find most interesting about it?" I guarantee she doesn't want to hear anything about this, but it would be rude to drop the topic so soon.

"I think it's cool to know what happened in a street or a shop in the past, or why a bridge was built and when. I think it's good to learn something about the places that I visit, to know that something important happened there."

Smiling politely, she says, "That sounds very interesting." She thinks I'm a clueless American.

Daniel saves me before it gets any worse. "Where is Father?" It's as though he were simply asking whether the trash needed to be taken out, but it's easy to see through his fragile pretense of disinterest.

Eva meets his eyes, pursing her lips. The sound of wheels rolling over the hardwood floor announces the arrival of Christmas dinner. With a wide smile belying the fact that she's here serving us instead of being somewhere else on Christmas Eve, Maria empties her serving cart of half a dozen dishes: glazed ham, red cabbage, halved potatoes, gravy, and a cheese fondue fountain with all the fixings on a tray around it.

Daniel and his mother are still locked in a staring contest, which is good, because my mouth is hanging open. When I did good in high school for a semester, sometimes Mom would take me out to Perkins. This is on a whole other level.

"Guten Appetit," Maria says, withdrawing her hands from the last pair of dishes.

Silence. Apparently I'm the only one paying attention. "Danke, Maria."

With a nod, she retreats soundlessly to the kitchen, leaving the serving cart in the corner.

"He isn't coming, is he?" Daniel says, working to free an invisible speck of dirt from under his thumbnail.

The tongs beside the ham stare at me expectantly. There's no reason to let the food get cold, right?

"He'll be home shortly, I'm sure," Eva says, unfurling the napkin from her plate.

"Why don't we wait then? It wouldn't be polite to start without him." Daniel cocks his head to the side as if issuing a challenge, never taking his eyes off his mother. "Ethan, put that down, we're waiting for my father." I freeze, tongs holding a piece of ham midair halfway to my plate, honeyed glaze beading along the edge.

"Don't be ridiculous," Eva glares back at him. "Ethan, please feel free to begin."

My arm unmoving, a drop of glaze falls onto the tablecloth. My eyes shift from Eva to Daniel. I place the ham back on the pile. At the end of this, things need to be straight between me and Daniel, not his mom.

"You're making Ethan uncomfortable," she says to Daniel. *That's for damn sure.* My eyes stay fixed on my plate.

"Don't change the subject. He's not coming, is he? If we waited for him, we would never eat."

"He provides for us, sacrifices so that we have what we need."

Daniel's façade of calm changes in an instant. Kicking his chair back from the table, he tosses his napkin onto his plate as he stands. "You think this is necessary?" he shouts, gesturing at the room. "This house? The cars in the driveway? It's nothing but a waste, and it's disgusting." His face is full of derision as he turns to leave, but before he's gone even three steps, he stops and levels his gaze against his mother. "We don't need this. *He* didn't need this. He needed you, and he needed a father." His voice catches, and he's starting to tear up, the water in his eyes poised and threatening to drip at any moment. Then he turns and is gone.

I flick my eyes between the glazed ham and Eva, staring dumbstruck after her son. Dinner is over, I guess. In case the slightest sound might alert her to my presence, I carefully slide my chair away from the table and back out of the room until I'm through the door.

Safely in the hallway, I sprint up the stairs two at a time, hoping to God that Daniel is upstairs and didn't just up and disappear. When I reach his room, he's already pulling on his coat. Seeing me, he hastily wipes the moisture from his face. He's staring at his feet and won't meet my eyes, but that can't hide his pain. "I'm really sorry, Ethan, that you had to see that."

"Don't worry about it." There's only one appropriate response. Crossing the space between us, I pull him into my arms. At first he only reluctantly accepts my embrace, but after a moment he relaxes into it. I push myself up on the tips of my toes for us to fit together properly, and when I do, his cheek presses against mine. His face is hot in contrast to the cool wetness where his tears streaked down.

My romantic feelings for him are forgotten for the moment, leaving me with the sole desire to comfort his hurt however I can. "It's going to be okay," I whisper, holding him tightly to me.

After what feels like forever, he finally pulls away. Wiping his eyes again to eliminate any trace of sadness, he inhales deeply as if to restore his composure. "Let's get out of here and find something to eat."

Picking up my coat as we pass my room, he leads us down a spiral staircase that emerges far from the dining room. A rear door tucked away behind the main rooms of the first floor grants us access to the outside. Cold, refreshing air filling our lungs, we break a path around the house to his car through the inches of snow covering the lawn.

I know the exhaust system on his car is stock, so it isn't any louder than it should be, but the rumble of a four hundred horsepower engine waking up isn't exactly quiet. The last of my hopes that Eva can't hear us leaving are squashed when Daniel guns it down the driveway.

It isn't until we turn off the long, winding driveway onto the main road that he exhales with a modicum of relief and finally speaks. "I'm really sorry that happened."

"It's okay." The heat from the engine is just starting to reach us through the vents. The allure of warmth draws my hands out from their hiding place inside my coat and into the stream of warm air. My stomach rolls over noisily, displeased with the dinner that never happened.

"You were talking about your brother back there, weren't you?"

His voice comes out hoarse. "Yeah." He's quiet so long I think he just isn't going to elaborate. Eventually he speaks, carefully picking each word. "I don't think I can talk about it right now."

Reluctant to give up so easily, I try a different tack. "What does your dad do for work?"

He glances at me, looking irritated. Apparently he doesn't buy that I'm actually trying to change the topic, but he answers anyway. "He works at the Stuttgart airport, I've told you that before."

"I know you have, but what does he actually *do*?"

"*Er ist der Direktor.*"

The meaning catches me by surprise. *He's the boss.* Is he saying what I think he's saying? "The boss? Of which department?"

Daniel looks toward the side of the road where the headlights' swath of illumination abruptly fades to darkness. "Of the airport."

"The entire airport?"

"Yeah." His voice is sad. "The whole goddamn thing. That's why he's never home and never has time for his family."

Daniel has never sworn in front of me before, not once. He slows down and pulls the car over to the shoulder.

I glance in the rearview mirror. The road is empty, no headlights in either direction. "Why are we stopping?"

"I don't feel like driving anymore." He turns off the engine and kills the lights with a twist of his wrist.

"I'm sorry about your dad."

He taps a button on his door and his window slides open an inch. Cold air invites itself in, at once both chilling and sobering. From the center console, he retrieves a cigarette and a lighter.

Tonight must really be a night for firsts, since I've never seen him smoke before either, not even when we're drinking. As he lights it, I fight the urge to say something. Even if I did, I'm not sure if the question would be why he's smoking, or why he's choosing to do it in a new sports car.

His first drag is long and deep, and his chest puffs out to draw it in. I've always thought smoking is gross, and I could definitely never be with a guy who does. As I watch him exhale though, blowing the stream of smoke out the window and relaxing back into the seat with an air of appeasement, I can't help but be turned on. The thought that he has buried desires left secretly unfulfilled makes him irresistible. Lips parted slightly and tongue restless in my mouth, a different kind of hunger swells inside me.

Eyes adjusting to the dark, I can just make out his right hand resting on the steering wheel. I reach out toward him, my outstretched hand camouflaged by the darkness. I should stop myself before this turns into something I regret. But I don't want to.

Our skin touches, and an invisible connection is made, like a current flowing between us. I run my fingers across his, over his knuckles, gently along the veins in his hand. His skin is soft and warm, and there's even a distant pulse.

His hand tenses, his grip tightening on the wheel. There is a warning note in his voice as he slowly says, "Ethan."

I withdraw my hand. Gritting my teeth, I fight to pacify the wave of desire rising in me like a tsunami, terrible and unstoppable. It needs a release, an escape, an outlet for its despicable power.

Frozen in the moment, neither of us moves. My eyes are buried in the darkness ahead while the cigarette's glow slides inexorably toward his fingers. I'm not sure why I touched him. Of course I wanted to, but I want to do a lot of things that I can't just act on. What made me ignore all boundaries and do it anyway?

Maybe it's because I'm fed up being frustrated by him, stuck on a merry-go-round of never being satisfied. Our friendship has come to a point that we cannot pass, not without crossing a line. Sharing drinks and roughhousing can only take you so far. Something has to change in our relationship, or I'm going to go mad.

Pushing him like this might ruin what we have, but what if that's secretly what I want? Would I rather lose him completely than be just friends? With an involuntarily shudder, I try to erase the thought of losing him.

Daniel's voice touches the silence, pulling me out of my thoughts. "You just can't *do* that, Ethan."

I refuse to face him. "I know," I whisper.

Flicking his unfinished cigarette out the window, he asks, "Then why do it?" The curiosity in his voice is genuine. He must actually want to understand.

Inside me, a voice shouts, *tell him*! That's absolutely crazy, of course. But if I can't have him, can't even be honest with him, then what's the point of this?

Before I can change my mind, the words force their way out, choosing English as their method of delivery. "I love you, Daniel." The syllables hang in the air like bubbles, so fragile that they might burst at any moment, leaving no evidence other than a shower of glistening droplets that they were ever there.

He exhales slowly and brings his hands to his face, rubbing his eyes as if to awaken from an unpleasant dream. He mumbles something, but I can't make it out.

"What was that?" My heart pounds against the inside of my chest.

Dropping his hands, he repeats himself, still speaking softly. "I know, Ethan."

"You do?"

He gives a tentative, half nod. "I wasn't completely certain, but after the night on the Schlossberg and the way you've acted since, it wasn't hard to guess that you weren't moving on."

"Why ask me to spend Christmas with you then?" Before he can answer, I add, "I get that you're straight, but if you thought I had feelings for you, why ask me to spend two weeks with you?" It's strange to talk about this openly with him, after hiding it for so long. Somehow though, I'm relieved to have finally told him.

He sighs and his shoulders droop. "I don't know. I suppose I hoped you would get over it or at least that it wouldn't come up."

"Except I haven't gotten over it, and it did come up." Speaking my feelings for him aloud so matter-of-factly makes them easier to understand, and it also makes it easier for me to see how irrational they are.

Daniel gives me an annoyed look. "Yeah, I can see that."

With a growing sense of panic, I ask, "Do you want me to leave? Take a train back to Freiburg?"

He levels his gaze on me like he's trying to read my face in the darkness. Finally he says, "No, I don't." He swallows, tracing a finger around the top of the steering wheel. "Not unless that's what you want."

Exhaling with cautious relief, I look away from him and out the window. If I do stay, how am I going to make it through the next week? Being around him is already unbearable at times.

"But Ethan, this can't happen again."

I suppress my embarrassment and concede, "I know."

"If you decide later that you can't handle spending time together, then it's probably best if you do return to Freiburg without me." His tone doesn't imply that he hopes I end up leaving, but the rebuke stings nonetheless. I nod but keep my mouth shut. If I speak now, my voice might catch.

Making no move to start the engine, he gives his words some time to sink in before announcing, "I'm starving." The topic must be closed as far as he's concerned.

I should resign myself to shutting up and being repentant for just having made another pass at him, but an idea pops into my head that I simply can't ignore. After all, if he's going to smoke in this car, he can't be *that* protective of it. "Can I drive?" I blurt out.

Shifting in the dark, his attention locks onto me. He's probably trying to gauge whether I'm serious or not. He doesn't say anything, but after a full minute he sighs and gets out, leaving the door open. My pulse doubles. He's actually going to let me drive! Jumping out and passing him as I round the front bumper, I nearly slip in the snow in my haste.

"Easy there," Daniel warns tightly as I drop into the driver's seat, sounding like he already regrets agreeing to this.

The seat is too far back for me to properly reach the pedals, but before I have to waste any time searching for the controls, Daniel pushes on a small switch between my seat and center console, and I slide forward. "Thanks."

"No problem, Shorty."

I'm not *that* short. I'm just shorter than he is. But he's like six foot, so that's not hard to do. I let the affront slide, but only because he's letting me drive his car. That's likely why he figured he could get away with it in the first place.

Switching on the dome light, he quickly explains where the controls are.

"Yeah, yeah, I've got it. Now where's the key?"

An irritated noise comes from the back of his throat. "You do know how to drive a *Gangschaltung*, right?"

"Don't worry," I say, grinning and switching into English for just four words, "I can drive stick."

"Oh God," he mutters. "Just don't kill us, okay?"

"I won't. I promise. So what about that key?"

"There is no key." He reaches over and taps the engine start button on the dash and the motor purrs to life. "Don't forget this thing is rear wheel drive, so be careful in the snow."

Now to remember how to drive a manual, I think to myself. It's not something I could ever really forget, but it's been almost six months since I've driven *anything*, manual or otherwise. Tentatively testing the clutch's resistance, I press it to the floor and release it several times until I'm comfortable with it. It's surprisingly smooth and fluid throughout its range of movement. Leaving the car in neutral, I press down next on the gas pedal to get a feel for the power of the engine. First I rev it up to four thousand RPM's, let it drop to idle, then back up to six thousand. The front of the car rocks with the motion of the engine.

I take a deep breath. So many times I've thought of this moment, the first time I would drive a *nice* car. Daniel's M3 definitely qualifies. My fingers tightening around the steering wheel, I ease the car into gear. It's a rocky start so I open up the clutch a bit and give it some more gas. The transmission whines and I feel Daniel's disapproving eyes on me, but we start to move. Steering us from the shoulder back onto the road, second gear goes more smoothly, and this time I let the engine do what it really wants. Even if I didn't know that this car was built to be driven fast, I could feel it in the way the engine behaves and responds. This isn't a Corolla or a Civic. It doesn't want to be shifted right away at three thousand on the tachometer; it wants to move at five or higher. Lower than that and it feels like it's fighting its own nature, trying to be something it isn't. It wants to be set loose. So that's what I do.

Pumping through the gears, we hit sixty miles per hour in short order. Daniel fidgets in the passenger seat. But he can't complain, at least not about the shifting anymore. This transmission is like an old friend of mine who's become famous—all at once I feel like we've known each other for years but I'm still not worthy of the company I'm in.

Open stretches of road fly past and roundabouts are a blur until we pull up to a little restaurant per Daniel's directions. It seems like the only one open in whatever village it is we've driven to. Exhaling carefully, I loosen my grip on the steering wheel and press the black button on the dash to make the engine stop. The last few minutes were everything I always imagined them to be. One day I might own a car like this myself. If I can graduate and get a good job, save up for a long time, I could have one all my own.

"I told you we wouldn't die."

Reluctantly Daniel admits, "You're actually pretty good." He nods to reinforce his approval and my chest glows with pride.

I'm not sure what makes me want to ask, but I suddenly wonder if Daniel ever let his brother do this too. "Did Marc ever get to drive this car?"

Only a trace of sadness skirts around the edges of his voice when he answers. "A few times, yeah. He didn't really have a knack for it like you, though."

Balancing the somber tone of talking about Marc with the lingering pleasure of getting another compliment from Daniel, I hold my tongue for a few seconds. "What do you mean? Did he get in an accident with your car or something?"

He looks away from me out the passenger's window. The whispered words are heavy between us. "No, never. He was only ever in one crash."

Oh God, that was it, wasn't it? It has to be. Why the hell did I even ask that? The lights of the restaurant cast an orange glow on the side of Daniel's face, leaving the rest wrapped in darkness. Whatever emotions are coursing through him right now are hidden by an inscrutable expression. "Come on," he says, "Lets go eat."

Chapter 27

The following morning doesn't begin for me until long after light first begins to fill the room. Glancing at the date on my phone, I remember today is Christmas. I think that it's tradition for Germans to exchange gifts the night before, but since we left during dinner and didn't get home until late, that obviously didn't happen.

His mom wasn't around last night when we got back, and it wouldn't bother me in the slightest if she steered clear of us for the rest of the break. To me she was friendly enough, but I don't ever want to find myself in another one of their nice family talks. I bet it would have been even worse if Daniel's dad had been there.

I'm still in bed when Daniel appears in the doorway. "It's Christmas," I tell him.

He nods. "I kind of forgot about it too after what happened last night."

I'm not sure if he's talking about the fight at dinner or when I came on to him in the car. I sit up, adjusting my pillow behind me. "Are things better with your mom?" It hasn't escaped my attention that I still haven't actually met his dad.

"Um," he says, "my parents both left actually. There was a note on the fridge. They decided last minute to visit their Spanish villa for a couple weeks."

This family is messed up. "Are you okay?"

"I'm fine. It's my own fault for thinking it could work to come home over the holidays."

"What do you mean?"

He takes a seat on the edge of my bed. "Things never really got sorted out after Marc passed. It was still a mess the last time I left, and nothing has changed."

"I'm sorry if I made things worse."

He shakes his head vigorously. "Not your fault at all. My mom even mentioned specifically that she likes you."

We're both quiet for a minute. "I got something for you," I finally say, crossing my legs under the covers.

"I thought we agreed not to get anything for each other."

"I ignored that. And you're hosting me at your house anyway, so that's already a gift."

"Well, I got you something too."

"That's not fair." But I'm secretly glad he did. In high school, I used to give a Christmas present every year to my best guy friend, but I never got anything back. I never made enough from my after school job at the grocery store to get him anything cool anyway, but every Christmas when I showed up with a wrapped box, he'd give me this clueless look like he had no idea what was happening.

"Do you want to exchange them now?" Daniel asks.

"Sure."

He disappears while I get dressed and grab his gift from my backpack.

When he returns, he takes a seat cross-legged next to me on the bed. "Who starts?" he asks.

I hand him the package. "You first," I say, pleased at the curiosity in his expression.

It's about the size of a textbook, wrapped with blue and green wrapping paper with silver stars that isn't exactly Christmas issue. I had to get the paper from Paula, because I wasn't going to buy a whole roll just for this one thing.

I think it's stupid when people try to save the wrapping paper by meticulously removing every piece of tape, so it's with a certain satisfaction that I watch him tear into it with abandon. From the jagged husk of wrapping paper, he withdraws a cherry wood picture frame with a photo of the two of us, Daniel's arm slung over my shoulder. Florian took the picture in our dorm's kitchen one of the first weeks of us being Tandempartners. It's my favorite photo, the one that I always stop to look at when flipping through the pictures of us on Facebook.

"This is awesome," Daniel exclaims. "I barely remember him taking this picture."

"Glad you like it." I hope he puts it somewhere he'll see it often.

"I love it." He pulls me into a brief hug and squeezes my shoulder when we separate. "Alright, now yours." He hands me a small package.

I tear apart the paper and carefully open the fancy box inside. It's a watch. A *nice* watch. The band has alternating silver and black links, while the dial is black with white chronograph subdials set into it. The bezel around the edge of the face is engraved with the brand "BVL-GARI."

"Wow." It's all I can say. I'm quite sure that this is a very expensive watch. But it's also amazingly stylish. It's impossible to take my eyes off it.

"Do you like it?" he asks hopefully.

"Oh, yeah! Are you kidding me? This is the nicest thing anyone has ever given me." It also makes my gift seem inadequate, but I don't bother continuing that line of thinking. There's no way I could have afforded something like this for him, so there's no point worrying about it.

He exhales in relief. "When you first saw it, I was afraid you didn't like it."

"Oh no, I was just surprised," I say. "It's perfect. Really." I slip it on my arm. It's a couple of links too long and dangles case down.

"We'll have to get it sized of course."

My awe at his gift is starting to fade into a genuine appreciation. It's a very nice watch, maybe even the exact one I would have picked for myself—if money were no object, that is. He must have spent a long time looking for the right one. I'm not sure what that means, but it's probably best not to read into it too much.

"Merry Christmas, Mom," I say into the gaudy phone. Ornate might be a fairer description of it. It's one of those ostentatious vintage phones with the giant receiver and the rotary dial. It took me three tries to get the number right. Honestly it's a surprise it even works to call internationally on a phone this old. I'm in a small room on the main floor that Daniel referred to as "the sitting room."

Mom's voice sounds scratchy. "Oh, it's you. Why are you calling so early?"

"It's like 10 A.M. there. That's not early."

"It is if you didn't get home until three in the morning."

I adjust my grip on the receiver. "Jesus, Mom."

"Don't give me that. I was out with Uncle Billy." She means *my* uncle, her brother. She continues, "I haven't heard from you in over a week. Are you having fun with your friend David? Or is it Daniel?"

"Daniel. We're fine. Better than fine actually."

"Oh really?" Her voice assumes a slightly higher note. "Why is that?"

Somehow I always end up saying too much. She'll sink her teeth into even the slightest bit of information. "I think we're starting to understand each other better, that's all."

"Does he know you're homose—" she stops and corrects herself, "gay?"

"Yeah, he knows." *That* seems like an understatement.

"Hmm."

There it is again, the dreaded "hmm." I hate it when she does that. "Alright, Mom, I have to go. It's expensive to call like this." There's no need to mention that the owners of this line probably won't give a second thought to the bill, even if I spent an hour on the phone with the space shuttle.

"Just don't wait so long to call again."

"Sure. Bye, Mom." I set the receiver down on the cradle above the rotary dial. Earlier this morning I was complaining about Skype's notoriously flaky connection in Germany, so Daniel directed me here. He told me to talk as long as I wanted, which is exactly what I did.

With Daniel's parents gone, and Maria sent home on paid vacation, we have the house to ourselves as the days tick past. Not forgetting his warning from Christmas Eve about keeping myself under control, I use the time as a chance to dig deeper into the idea that friendship alone might be a reality. It's an appealing thought if it could actually work over the long haul. Spending time with him is fun, even if we're just watching dumb TV shows or shopping for the afternoon in Stuttgart. It's been months since there was any trace of hostility in his words or actions, and he seems to genuinely appreciate being around me, which is an accomplishment considering the rocky points over the course of our friendship.

Straight friends are nothing new. I had them all through high school. In fact, the majority of my friends were always straight guys. We were close, too. So many sleepovers and backyard campouts brought us together, with nights spent around the fire talking about who would be the next to make it with a girl. That last part was something I had a hard time relating to, but in a strict sense of physical intimacy, the friendships with those guys weren't so different. We'd share drinks (especially anything with alcohol in it), ignore the rule about leaving one urinal between us when taking a piss, and once during a winter campout we even did a naked run through the snow.

There's something fundamentally different about Daniel though. He knows who I am and what goes on inside me, even when I'm fighting to bury it. Those other guys never knew, and they probably would have been disgusted if they did. Nothing against them—that's just how most high school guys are.

Daniel's seemingly boundless faith in our friendship, despite everything that's happened, is a testament to him as a person and whatever it is that makes him stick around. He's a good guy and a great friend, but I can't shake the feeling that there's more at work than just that. He's always been so tolerant, accepting even, not just of me but of everything I've said and done that would ruin any normal friendship. And those wistful, searching looks he's given me since the beginning of the year? They don't happen as often anymore, but I haven't forgotten.

Chapter 28

When I awake, my head is pounding, and the light filtering through my tightly closed eyelids is already too much. Inhaling shallowly, I pull warm, stuffy air into my lungs. My mouth is dry and tastes like booze and bile. Scattered images from last night break through the surface of my hangover. We went to a bar in Stuttgart for New Years and met a bunch of Daniel's friends. Once the drinks and shots began to flow, they didn't stop. It didn't help that Daniel opened a tab on his credit card for the two of us. Groaning, I roll onto my back and force open my eyes.

At first it doesn't make sense what I'm seeing. The bed in my room doesn't have a four-poster frame, but this one does. With a sinking feeling, I realize it's Daniel's bed. Quiet breathing beside me confirms his presence. This is the exact opposite of what needs to happen. The space between us needs to increase if I'm ever going to feel comfortable being "just friends" with him. The last few days since Christmas were going so well. It was actually getting easier to maintain a proper distance. I glance over my right shoulder at his sleeping form. The six inches between us now doesn't qualify as proper distance.

As carefully as possible, I lift the covers off myself and gingerly swing my legs over the side of the bed. *Goddamn it, where are my pants?* I'm just sliding my top half out of bed when Daniel rolls onto his side, his eyes flickering open. I flinch, afraid of what he'll say.

After letting him process for a good ten seconds what he's seeing, he still doesn't look angry or even surprised. "Morning," he mumbles.

"Uh . . . morning." Half my body is still in the bed with him, while everything waist down is dangling awkwardly over the edge, my feet hovering above the floor. I finish extricating myself from the covers and stand up. I'm only wearing boxers, but I don't want him to think I feel the need to cover myself, so I let my arms hang at my side.

"Sorry, for um, being here," I sputter. Then worrying that he might think I mean spending the holidays with him in general, I quickly add, "In your room, in bed with you." I need to cut my tongue out right now before it buries me in a hole. My cheeks burn, but he still hasn't said anything. His face is mostly obscured by the puffy down comforter. "I'm going to go now." I turn toward the door. "To my room, that is."

As I round the end of the bed, I notice too late that my clothes are in a heap on the floor. Before I can stop myself, my feet get tangled, and with a yelp, I fall over with all the grace of a soaked cat, arms flailing.

I want to keep falling, through the floor and the ground level and then through the basement, farther and farther until eventually popping out somewhere in China. Actually, being in Germany, I would probably bob up in the middle of the Pacific.

I might have lain there forever, rendered comatose by embarrassment, but the sound of Daniel's hoarse laughter pulls me back to the moment. When I finally get back to my feet, he's sitting up. The comforter sits across his waist, exposing the smooth muscles of his chest and stomach.

"You aren't mad?" I ask.

"It's fine." When I give him a confused look, he asks, "Do you remember anything after we got home last night?"

Images surface of meeting his friends at the bar and later the countdown to midnight and the New Year. The bar was so loud when they started the countdown; everyone was shouting out the numbers except Daniel. I remember giving him a jab in the ribs, and then he was counting down too. Lights of every color flashed through the darkness. *Fünf, vier, drei, zwo, eins!* Through the noise and chaos, a pair of eyes locked onto mine as the cheering and embracing and kissing ensued. I didn't give it a second thought, instead slamming back a waiting shot. It was the start of 2010!

Everything after midnight is kind of hazy in my mind. I don't even recall leaving the bar. I shake my head. "Nope, I definitely don't remember getting home, but hey, we made it here safe."

"Come on, Ethan." He's trying to sound stern, but his resolve is melting. "You got pretty drunk, and I didn't know what to do with you."

"You took advantage of me, didn't you?" I feign indignation.

Daniel rolls his eyes. "Yeah, right. Anyway, I got you to drink as much water as you'd take, and then you promptly passed out on the floor." He gestures to a spot near the window.

That's a relief at least. However I got pantsless into bed with him, it couldn't have been entirely my doing. Daniel must be able to see the gears turning, because he explains, "You seemed okay, but I didn't want to leave you alone in case you'd really had too much, so . . . I let you sleep here."

"And my pants?" It's funny that we had this same conversation months earlier, except last time things were the other way around.

"I figured you'd be more comfortable." He looks away. Was that embarrassment in his tone?

"I'm sure I was. Thanks." Actually I'm irritated. All joking aside, he's not making this easy at all. It's almost like he wants the extra attention and the closeness that extends beyond friendship. He just doesn't want to deal with what comes with it. I've never really understood him, but this morning he has me at a particular loss. Grabbing my jeans, I leave him sitting up in bed.

I head straight to the bathroom and toss my jeans into the corner. They land with a clink when my belt, still held in the loops, strikes the tile. Hands on the sink, I stare into the mirror. My hair is a mess, and I have dark areas under my eyes that make me look like a raccoon.

My appearance might as well be indicative of how I'm handling the situation with Daniel. As desperately as I'm fighting the urges of attraction, it's by far easiest when I'm pissed at him. For the moment actually, with aggravation coursing through me, it's easy to imagine us just being friends. The thought of spending time with him long term while not being romantically involved seems for the first time not only entirely possible but palatable.

Letting the hot water of the shower run over me, I hold the perception of us only being friends in the forefront of my mind. The longer I do, the more it seems like a realistic outcome. Instead of experiencing regret that he will never fulfill my desires, I begin to fill with satisfaction at what we do share. Now if I could only make myself feel like this all the time. It's a start, in either case.

A knocking on the door snaps me out of my thoughts. "Ethan, you almost done?"

The room is so steamy I can barely see from the glass shower to the door, and my fingertips are wrinkled from being wet so long. "I'll be right out."

Wearing a towel, I emerge with a cloud of steam from the bathroom. "Damn dude," he says. "You were in there for a half hour."

My shower meditation must have put me more at ease with him, because I don't hesitate to shoot back, "I wanted to thoroughly decontaminate after being in your bed." The words roll off my tongue as fast as I can speak them, and I have the feeling that my German has again reached a new level of proficiency.

"Whatever," he laughs and gives my bare back a playful push toward my room.

I watch him enter the bathroom, tugging off his shirt as he shuts the door. Waiting a minute to make sure he isn't coming back out anytime soon, I drop the towel and pull on a pair of boxers, followed by pants and a shirt. After inspecting my hair in the mirror, I withdraw the Bible from its hiding place in my bag.

September 9, 1942. In the weeks following Uncle's last visit, I found myself ever more considering the temperament of the university student body. The Party is strong, that cannot be denied. Yet there are whisperings of dissent that the war might not be going our way, at least not so much as the Party would like us to believe. Perhaps the time is upon us to create our own change.

It was with these thoughts gripping me that I received word from Uncle yesterday by post that he was making another visit to Freiburg. In his letter, he bade me prepare a picnic lunch, just for the two of us. We are to meet at Bismarck's Turm on the Schlossberg to enjoy the "wonderful natural beauty as can be found only in the deutschen Reich."

As Uncle is never one to describe Germany in such a patriotic way, I suspected immediately his words were chosen to avoid arousing the slightest suspicion, were his letter to be intercepted. Moreover, that he even suspected his letter might be read by the postal censors displays the depth of distrust that Uncle bears toward the Party.

For all the times having been up on the Schlossberg, I've never seen any Bismarck's Turm. An observation tower overlooks Freiburg from the very top of the Schlossberg, but it can't be more than twenty years old, and certainly not seventy or more. Quite a ways below that are some ruins, but no one would call them a tower. So where is Bismarck's Turm? Was it destroyed before the end of the war?

September 23, 1942. The day of our meeting having arrived, I prepared a lunch just as he had asked and met him at the indicated spot, although he arrived a significant period of time after our agreed upon hour. When I inquired as to the reason for his tardiness, he explained only that he had had to take certain precautions.

After taking our midday meal, Uncle opened his suitcase to reveal hundreds of copies of the first leaflet of the White Rose! Transferring them into the basket I had carried the lunch in, I was able to bring them home with me after Uncle took his leave and returned to Stuttgart.

So Magdalena *was* involved with the White Rose, at least indirectly through her uncle. If the White Rose had a presence in Freiburg though, why haven't I ever heard of it? The student resistance was famous in Munich, and surely I would have found something in my web searches if there was a mirror movement in Freiburg. The obvious answer is that no one knows. Coldness creeps down my fingers, disappearing into the book held between my palms.

Chapter 29

I suggest we go for another walk outside, this time in daylight, but Daniel is still worn out from last night and opts to take a nap. I didn't get the best sleep either, but I'm too restless to lie down.

Since Daniel's parents are still on their vacation of self-imposed exile, I start to explore the house. The ground floor doesn't have much exciting to offer. The only new room I discover there is for laundry. Back on the second floor, however, I venture for the first time past the bathroom that Daniel and I share. The door is shut to the master bedroom, and I don't dare enter. I know his parents aren't home, but the mere thought of any sort of confrontation with them scares me shitless.

Around the corner at the very end of the hallway is another closed door. I try the handle. It turns, but when I push, the door doesn't budge. Disappointment descends over me, but as I turn to leave, the metal glint of a key inserted into an old style lock below the handle catches my eye. Holding my breath, I take hold of the metal and turn. The lock slides back with a click, and this time the door swings open.

The room is dark and the air still. There are windows that stretch from the floor to the ceiling, but heavy drapes are drawn. I step inside, closing the door silently behind me. The hairs on the back of my neck lift in trepidation, and I suppress an involuntary shiver. Standing still on the soft carpet, I give my eyes time to adjust to the dimness.

When my vision improves, I cross the room to the drapes, tugging them open to bring light into the space. Sunlight pours in, revealing a bed against the wall and a desk between the two windows. It's not a guest bedroom like mine, because there are movie posters all over the walls and the colors are too opinionated. Where not covered, the walls are painted dark blue with silver accents near the ceiling.

Several of the posters are for movies I haven't seen, but some like *Avatar* and *Sommersturm*—a German movie—I do recognize. Pulling out the chair at the desk, I sit down, resting my arms on the wooden surface. It's unsettling, being in Marc's room. To know that someone my age once lived here, spent his hours worrying like the typical teenager about school and his future and maybe a special someone. A life that abruptly winked out of existence, leaving behind only painful memories in those closest to him. Taking in the space around me, I correct myself: he left behind this room too. Tidied up perhaps, but appearing more or less untouched since he lived here.

"Marc," I whisper. "I'm sorry." Sadness wells up within me. Somehow it's like I've gotten to know him, and being here sitting at this desk makes me feel a part of the loss that his family experienced. A picture frame stands on the corner of the desk. It's a photo of him and Daniel.

It's strange that I've never seen a picture of Marc before. The photo is similar to the one I gave Daniel for Christmas, in that his arm is slung around Marc's shoulder just as it was around mine. The only difference is that this picture was taken outside on a sunny day with big oak trees in the background. Glancing out the window, I conclude that the trees in the picture aren't present in the yard. The photo must have been taken somewhere else.

It's actually unnerving how much the photo looks like the one I gave Daniel. I pick up the frame to get a better look at their faces, an undercurrent of apprehension running through me. Daniel looks pretty much the same, so it couldn't have been taken more than a year or two ago. Reluctantly I shift my eyes away from smiling Daniel to see Marc for the first time.

My chest tightens. I slowly shake my head, not wanting to accept what's in front of me. A rock in my stomach, I grimace and set the photo down. It can't be.

Taking a deep breath, I take the frame in my hand once more. Nothing has changed. Marc still looks the same. He still looks like *me*. A lot. Our hair and cheekbones are similar, and we have the same build. He might be an inch taller or maybe Daniel just grew in the last year, but it's impossible not to see that we look pretty damn similar. No one would ever think we were identical twins or anything, but if we stood next to each other, it would be natural to assume we were brothers.

I carefully place the frame back where I found it, forcing myself to take regular breaths as the meaning sets in. All those odd looks I got from Daniel when we were getting to know each other. His sudden change in behavior toward me. His tolerance for things that would have made any normal guy send me the hell away.

I stand and move away from the desk. The aching in my chest grows in intensity as I reconsider the many aspects of Daniel's behavior over the last five months that have been hard to understand. It can't be true, can it? That all along, his interest in me was driven by this ulterior motive?

Around me a muffling silence descends, and the light and color in the room dim as I slump onto Marc's bed. My heart thuds, alternatively poised to flee or explode out of my chest. The sound of its beat echoes in my ears as the seconds slow. Throat constricting, my mouth gulps air to keep me breathing.

I take Marc's pillow in my arms and bury my face in it, wanting to hide from the whole world. The remnant of what must be his scent lingers in the fabric. A shiver ripples over my skin as I inhale. It smells almost like Daniel, but more woodsy.

What would the past months have been like if Marc hadn't passed away a year ago? Would Daniel and I have still become friends, or would we be nothing more than acquaintances living in the same building? In the back of my mind is a brooding answer. Its low voice cuts through my emotion, through my protestations, through my hope that I've made something out of nothing. The voice murmurs that it was never about me at all.

Searching for a rescue, a diversion, anything really, I realize that the circumstances of Marc's death are still largely a mystery to me, other than it was probably a car accident. Early on I assumed, quite rightly, that it would have been entirely inappropriate to ask what had happened. In this moment of closeness to him—in his room, curled up on his bed, smothering his pillow in search of answers—I wish I knew what happened. Where was he when he was taking his last breaths? Was he in pain? Was he alone, or did he have someone to hold his hand at the end?

Across from me on the nightstand is a book. Actually it's a journal. My stomach prickles with unease as my fingers close around it. Pages flipping beneath my thumb, the scent of ink and new paper caresses the still air. Almost every page is filled with Marc's loping handwriting. The last entry is near the end, dated sixteen months ago from next week. On the opposite page are a handful of words arranged into stanzas, printed in block letters that contrast with his flowing script in the rest of the journal.

Something about the lines makes me want to say them aloud, so I read softly. *"Rings ein Verstummen, ein Entfärben . . ."*

ALL AROUND, SILENCE FALLS, COLOR FADES;
HOW SOFTLY THE BREEZES CARESS THE FOREST,
COAXING IT TO GIVE UP ITS WITHERED FOLIAGE:
I LOVE THIS GENTLE DYING.

FROM HERE BEGINS A QUIET JOURNEY,
THE TIME FOR LOVE HAS PASSED AWAY,
THE BIRDS HAVE SUNG THEIR LAST SONGS,
AND DRY LEAVES SINK SOFTLY.

IN THE GENTLE RUSTLING OF THIS FOREST
I SEEM TO HEAR IT SOFTLY SAYING
THAT ALL DYING AND PERISHING
IS MERELY A QUIET, CONTENTED EXCHANGING.

—Nikolaus Lenau

I've never heard of the author, but the words are touching in their own melancholy way. The meaning of the lines tiptoes through me, threatening to confirm a terrible suspicion. There are just a few sentences in Marc's own hand beyond the end of the poem. I want to search them for an answer to why his entries end there instead of filling the entire journal, but a part of me is so afraid that my hands are trembling.

So often these days, I'm convinced it's not even worth it anymore. Not worth it to pretend, to convince anyone, to try and prove that my days and hours and minutes and every second are anything but a waste.

I can hardly remember the way it used to be. It was always tough going, but nothing like this. I want it to end so badly. I want it to be over. It will be so easy, so quick.

I swallow and allow my eyes to blink. There's just a little bit left. Jaw clenched, I read the last words before blankness fills the page.

I am so sorry, Daniel. If it weren't for you, I would have done this long ago. You were always the best part of my life. Don't blame yourself.

It feels like the wind has been knocked out of me and a vise is closing around my chest. I close the journal, struggling to breathe normally. As strong as any intuition, a new clarity forces itself over me. It shouldn't matter as much as it does, because either way he isn't here anymore, but there's no longer a question about what happened. Marc took his own life.

When I finally emerge from the room, I close the door softly behind me and turn the key in the lock. The latch clicks with a decisive finality, and somehow I know I'll never enter that place again.

Back in my own room and lying on the bed, my eyes slowly bore a pair of holes in the ceiling. The new information eats away at me like a corrosive acid. I don't understand exactly what it means yet, but it changes everything. Every moment Daniel and I ever spent together is now suspect. All along I thought it was me who was harboring the secret, but now it's clear I wasn't alone. At least mine was an honest one.

Daniel wanders into my room yawning, a little unsteady on his feet. I stare at him. At least on the outside, he's the same guy he's always been. "Did you sleep?" he asks.

"No." What else can I say? *So Daniel, I just found out I resemble your dead brother. You weren't planning on telling me, were you?*

"I was thinking we could go to a movie tonight. Sound fun?"

I don't even know what to think. "Okay."

"You alright?"

"What do you mean?"

Stretching his arms high over his head, he says, "You're kind of quiet, that's all."

"I'm fine." Considering what I've just discovered, I don't feel the least bit bad about lying to him.

The drive to the theater is quiet except for the sound of the wind and the engine, but not even its throaty purr can draw me out of my own head. The image of Marc's face is etched into my memory. What if it stays there forever? None of this is his fault, but I want to forget him, forget I ever saw the photo. Living a lie would be better than feeling like this.

The glittering lights of the theater shine across the parking lot as we walk inside. The place is practically deserted. Daniel peruses the films currently showing. "What do you want to see?"

"Doesn't matter." I stare at my feet.

His gaze lingers on me, and it feels like he's about to ask me something. His eyebrows bunch up, and there's frustration in his voice when he speaks. "Alright, I'll just pick something then." He pays for both of us, but I don't bother to look which movie he bought tickets for.

"How about we get some popcorn?" He tilts his head down slightly so he's looking directly into my eyes. We're standing just a few inches apart. He gives me a smile and touches my forearm lightly with his knuckles. My heart inevitably jumps at the touch, but the reaction is all but involuntarily. He's trying to cheer me up, but every second in his presence is just making me feel worse. What he's doing doesn't have a chance in hell of working.

"Get whatever you want. I'm going to the bathroom." I stalk away from him toward the black plastic sign with the formulaic outline of a man.

I'm alone at the urinals. It felt like I really had to piss, but now that I'm here I've got nothing. Zipping up, I flush the toilet even though there's no reason to. I stare at myself in the mirror in front of the sink. There are faint shadows under my eyes and creases across my forehead that I'm not used to seeing. I splash water over my face. The aching inside is getting worse. It's like a host of termites is eating away at the supports that hold me together. Too soon it's all going to collapse and take me along with it.

Daniel is waiting for me at the entrance to screen six. He's got a bag of popcorn and a large soda. He's smiling and trying to make it look like he's having a good time. If I didn't know him as well, I wouldn't see the worry he's concealing.

He lets me go ahead of him into the dark, so I can choose where we sit. The theater is mostly empty, but I head toward one of the side wings that's clear of any people. It's because the view is horrible from here. He makes a disgruntled sound when he realizes where I'm going, but he doesn't say anything else. In the middle of the row, he plops down. Instead of sitting next to him, I move down to leave a seat between us. In the dim light, it's hard to make out his expression, but he seems puzzled. He gets up and sits next to me. Setting the soda in the armrest cup holder between us, he offers me the popcorn, but I ignore him. After a few seconds of holding out the bag, he sets it wordlessly between his legs.

It's a relief when the movie begins, because I don't have to push away his attention anymore. Anger festers inside me as the scenes flit across the screen. How could I have been so stupid? All along I thought I'd found a true best friend, a guy who wasn't afraid to share a beer or sit right next to me on the couch. Instead I've been used. The worst part is that it's just as much my fault for being so naïve.

On the screen, Keanu Reeves is telling a government agent to let him go. He's an alien or something, supposed to deliver a message to Earth's governments. Daniel offers me the popcorn again. "Come on, Ethan, you must be hungry, we didn't eat dinner." He sneaks his hand under the armrest and tickles my stomach.

I scoot away in my seat. "Don't you *fucking* touch me."

Beneath the white glow of the screen, his face contorts in confusion. "What the hell is wrong with you tonight?" he demands, withdrawing his hand.

Instead of answering him, I get up and storm out of the theater. Crossing the red carpet of the empty lobby, I'm just opening the door to the outside when I hear him running up behind me. "Ethan, wait." His hand catches me around the arm as a wave of cold air hits us. I yank my arm away and turn to face him. "What's with you?" he says, out of breath. "You've been pissy all night. If you didn't want to see a movie, you should have just said so."

"It's not about the stupid movie." Golden light from the lobby spills out of the glass doors and onto the sidewalk where we're facing off.

"What is it then? You've been horrible to me all night."

I let out a mocking laugh composed of a single note. "Yeah, it's always about you, isn't it?"

"What's that supposed to mean? Damn it, Ethan, what's your problem?"

I meet his eyes, hoping he sees the fire in my own. "I know."

"Know what?" His tone hasn't changed. He doesn't get it yet.

"Daniel, I *know*." I pause, watching a plodding progression of emotion move across his face. Finally I detect fear. Fear about what I might be referring to. I confirm what he's dreading. "About me and Marc." Our breath is white in the air of the winter night.

His expression remains paralyzed for a moment. Then it softens, and he sighs, his shoulders dropping. "Ethan, I . . . I didn't know what to think at first. I wanted to tell you."

"Except you didn't, and even if you had, it wouldn't have made it any better."

"I'm sorry. I should have told you, but it's not what you think."

"Bullshit it's not. You lost your brother, and then you found a way to replace him."

There's pain in his face. It even looks real. "It's not like that," he says quietly.

It's ballsy of him to lie to me right now. "Oh yeah?"

He sighs again as though he's already given up. "Can we sit down?" He moves toward a bench outside of the glowing rays of light. "I'm afraid you're going to run away from here, and I'm never going to see you again."

I do want to run, just run away like after I kissed him on the Schlossberg. Except something inside compels me to stay, like I owe it to him to hear him out. It might be the countless hours we've spent together, or the softness in his voice, or maybe just that I'm so hopelessly bound by his spell that my will has finally failed me. I acquiesce but sit at the far end of the bench, leaving several feet between us.

Running his hand over the wooden slat beside his leg, he struggles to find words. "At first," he says, "I was really struck by how much you looked like him."

"Yeah, I get that," I hiss. It was a mistake to stay and listen to this.

"Ethan, give me a chance to get this out." He waits for me to say something, like he's issuing a challenge. The muscles in my jaw are tense and pressing against my cheeks, and it's all I can do to keep my mouth shut. He must be satisfied that I'm not going to interrupt again, because he continues. "I saw the resemblance the moment we first met, when you walked into the kitchen. It brought back every bit of pain from when he died. It was like it had just happened all over again. I didn't want to see you, talk to you, even know that you were living there." He runs a hand through his hair before turning back to face me.

"But you were always there, trying to start conversations with me or get me to do things with you." He stares at his hands. "I almost succeeded in pushing you away. Except the moment you showed up covered in blood and limping back from the lake. You were so vulnerable, and you needed me. I just couldn't do it anymore."

He pauses to see if I'm going to respond. In answer to my silence, he goes on. "Then we became friends." Exhaling with reservation, his words are cautious. "Did you remind me of Marc? Well yeah, you did, and you still do, because you look and even act like him sometimes," he admits. "The truth is, though, it's not about that anymore, and it hasn't been for a long time. My brother is gone. I know that." He rubs his forehead with his hand. "Ethan, the reason that I spend time with you, the reason that I invited you here for Christmas . . . it isn't because you're some sort of replacement for Marc. It's because you've become my best friend."

I shake my head, wishing my glare could communicate at least a part of what I'm feeling. "I might have believed that earlier, but there's something that doesn't fit in all this. For as much as you act like it bothers you when I've made passes at you, I think you wanted it to be that way."

"That's not—"

"Screw you," I cut him off. "Ever since we met, I thought I was so lucky to have found a friend who was cool with the gay thing. I even felt like I owed you something." I jump up off the bench, unable to sit so close to him anymore. "But that's what you wanted, isn't it?" My voice catches on the words. "So I'd adore you like he did."

He gets up from the bench and takes tentative steps toward me. "Ethan," he starts again, his voice a whisper. He comes closer, his arm reaching out.

"And that day after I cut myself in the lake. It wasn't about me at all, was it? You helped me because I finally reminded you too much of Marc to ignore anymore." The anger inside threatens to tear me apart. My vision clouds for a moment.

His movement slows, but his hand is still about to make contact. I remember how soft his palms are, what it feels like to be touched by him. For an instant I almost give in, but another part of me knows it's time to stop being so naïve.

A half second before his fingers would meet my skin, my hands thrust forward into his chest and shove him backward. We've touched so many times before, but never in anger. I only manage to push him back six inches, but the effect is immediate. His arm drops, and he stares dumbly at me, his eyes descending into gray.

Fury burns inside me. "You're an asshole," I snarl.

My muscles galvanized by adrenaline-fed anger, I move without thinking, an action of pure emotion. My fist rockets forward, an implement of vengeance forged from resentment and betrayal. My knuckles strike the right side of his mouth with a strength foreign to me. Rolling his head away from the blow, he staggers back but stays on his feet.

Pain explodes across my knuckles, and blood begins to drip from my ring finger where it made contact with his teeth. It's unclear which one of us is more surprised at what just happened. I've never hit anyone like that before. A vertical slit in his lip oozes red. From his expression, it's evident I've hurt him deeply, although physically the wound is minor.

As we stare at each other, I see his spirit draining from him, just like the blood from my finger. Slumping back onto the bench, he looks at me a moment longer, silent tears dripping down his anguish-ridden expression. Tearing his gaze away, he drops his face into his hands. To see this young man who's bigger, stronger, more mature than me reduced to this is more than I can bear. Especially because it has nothing to do with how hard I hit him.

Darkness has covered the land like a thick comforter, and only the occasional light sails past my window. The white and red high-speed train glides through the night. The train is nearly empty, and there's not a single other person in my car. Sliding the sleeve of my pullover back, I examine my new watch glinting under the fluorescent lighting. The automatic movement rotates the hands smoothly inside the silver case. It hasn't been sized yet, so the band is still too big, but I can't bring myself to take it off.

The loneliness pressing down on me is completely different from when I first arrived in Germany. It felt horrible at the time, but this is definitely worse. Despite all my efforts to ignore the feeling, there's a throbbing in my chest that refuses to leave. Whether I'm thinking about him or not, it doesn't budge. I close my eyes, and I see his face, sporting that smile he never lets out as much as he should.

Despite his deception and the anger inside me, my stupid heart refuses to let go of him. Unable to endure it anymore, I force my eyes open and stare into the blackness beyond the cold glass. "I still love you," I breathe, giving my secret up to the cold winter night gliding past. I'm such a mess. Damn him. God fucking damn him.

Chapter 30

Back in my dorm, the coming days creep by, and I slowly churn through a book on post–World War II Freiburg. I learn a multitude of facts that I can't make myself care about. Not even the bits about buildings I've seen and visited can arouse my interest. By the fourth day, with my thoughts darting every few moments to the memory of the hurt in Daniel's eyes after I hit him, it's no longer possible to concentrate long enough to read. TV shows are a little more distracting, and everything on Netflix is fair game until I get tired of that too. Finally when the thought of being inside any longer begins to make me physically nauseous, I go out. Pacing the familiar path around the lake behind the dorm, I circle it for an hour before finally heading back.

At some point I might come to terms with the resemblance between Marc and myself, but I'm nowhere near ready yet. Every memory of the months getting to know Daniel has suddenly been tainted with doubt. Where do his feelings for Marc end, if at all? Was our entire friendship just simulating the relationship he had with his brother, or was at least part of it real?

I've burned through every other thing that can pass the time before I finally dig out the timeworn leather Bible, spreading the binding apart to pick up the story where I left off. The age-old scent of Bible paper wafts up from the pages.

September 29, 1942. Despite Uncle's unspoken warning not to mention the leaflets to anyone, I was compelled to confide in my dearest Thomas. My Thomas who is my partner in everything. He has not yet proposed marriage, but I know that this is his intent. If there was anyone who could bear this secret, it is him.

But what if the person closest to you isn't deserving of that trust? What if they abuse it? I sigh, pushing away my own thoughts to concentrate on Magdalena's story.

It was in the evening, less than a fortnight after Uncle delivered the papers to my possession. Thomas and I took a stroll around the Münsterplatz. As it was a Tuesday, there were only a few others out and about. Even the Catholic Church has felt heavily the weight of Nazi oppression, and visitors to the Münster have long since dwindled.

Across the square from the Münster, we seated ourselves on a bench. Thomas ran his fingers over my hand, and then he looked into my eyes. "Tell me why you are troubled," he said. To a certain extent he was correct, but he couldn't see that I was also exhilarated. I wanted very much to share this with him. And so I did.

At first he was angry, not for the betrayal of the Reich, for which he also bears no love, but because of the danger Uncle had placed me in. It took much consoling and explaining, but at last he became acquiescent to my plan. After his fashion, he did suggest a change, about which he was absolutely adamant. Instead of carrying the leaflets from my family's home on the day they are to be dispersed, he insisted that we move them first to his apartment. His suggestion made sense. His apartment is much closer to the university. In retrospect, however, I believe that the true motivation was that he fears I might be discovered. By keeping the leaflets in his possession, he wishes to shelter me from that danger.

My eyes are watering from reading the miniscule writing when there's a knock on the door. Slapping the book shut, I get up to check who it is, opening the door warily.

"Hey," Florian says. He's wearing a nice polo and jeans. "Paula and I and a few others are heading out for a drink. Interested?"

To be nice, I pretend like I'm considering it for a moment before I tell him, "No, thanks, you guys go on without me."

"No problem. See you around, Ethan." He scampers back down the hall to the kitchen. I can't deal with people right now, not even nice ones like Florian and Paula.

It's with dogged determination that I throw myself into my studies when classes resume the following Monday. With just four short weeks before the end of the winter semester, the threat of term papers and final exams is beginning to weigh on the student body. The mood on campus is tense, like an invisible but unavoidable net is descending around everyone.

Just having made a stop at the jewelry shop in the center of town, I make my way back through the university with my new watch comfortably around my wrist. I debated for several days whether I wanted to get it sized, but ultimately I decided to do it. As upset as I am with Daniel, there's still so much I want to say. In a weird way, I feel like not wearing his Christmas gift would be like saying that the conversation is over. When we do talk again, I want him to know that I'm willing to bring an open mind.

Crossing the square at the university's heart, an unexpected chill catches me off guard. For all my concern about passing my tests and completing my paper in time, there's something bothering me far more. I still haven't seen Daniel. Not once. When I asked Florian last night, he denied having seen or talked to him. His answers left me feeling empty though, and I wonder if he wasn't telling me everything.

The unease is persistent, even though all my classes are done for the day. The heavy feeling doesn't withdraw, not even as I pass beyond the outermost university buildings to wait at my Strassenbahn stop. Snowflakes drift down morosely, a tribute to the last weeks of winter. Waiting beside me, a woman in a long wool coat pulls her young daughter closer, clutching her with gloved hands.

When I get home, I head straight to the kitchen to get dinner going. I chop half an onion and toss it in the pan with some olive oil. The stove is electric and slow to heat up, so there's time yet to get everything else cut up. Small squares of raw bacon and cubed pieces of Maultaschen go into the pan along with the onions, just as the oil is starting to sputter.

Someone must have forgotten to turn the TV off, because the local news has been on since I got home. It's only now though that I'm able to divert attention to what they're saying. A reporter is talking fast in front of the university square I walked through an hour ago. He's squished on the edge of the frame, so it's obvious they were trying to get one of the yellow brain shopping cart banners into the shot.

With that as a hint, I'm able to piece together just about everything as he describes increasing tensions between students and administration over the five hundred euro student fee introduced at the beginning of the year. "A protest is planned for the week before final exams, which university and city officials worry could escalate due to the depth of student anger against the new fee," the reporter warns before adding, "Heavy police presence is expected."

Germans don't have a tendency to exaggerate, but it's difficult to imagine a protest turning violent. The occasional demonstrations, always held in other parts of Germany, appear on the news as mild, sign-holding affairs. To be fair, Germans do have a history of making matters physical in order to get what they want, but university students? Docile Florian and cleaning-phobic Paula spring to mind. No, a university protest here could never get out of hand.

I've just finished frying the Maultaschen when the sound of movement in the hall attracts my ear. I freeze, partway through transferring my dinner from the frying pan onto a plate. Muffled voices carry through the closed door to the hallway, and I hold my breath. Daniel's room is right across from the kitchen, and I'm absolutely certain that it's his door opening when I hear the jingle of keys.

Setting the pan down as quietly as possible, I tiptoe to the door and press my ear against it. There are two voices, an older male and a young woman. The man I can hardly understand, but his speech strikes me as oddly familiar. "Real nice room you got here, sixteen square meters. Comes with that there bed and writing desk."

"How much is this one?" the woman asks. I don't recognize her voice.

In a moment of cruel comprehension, I grasp what's happening. The man is the Hausmeister with his rural accented German that seemed so difficult to understand at the beginning of the year. He's showing the woman the room. Which means Daniel moved out.

He's gone. Just like that. When or how he was able to move out so no one noticed doesn't matter, because he's gone. My throat contracts involuntarily from the bitterness on the back of my tongue. He left because of me. I slide to the floor and clutch my knees to my chest, but the tightness inside doesn't relent. I might never see him again. A hundred different scenarios flash through my mind about what made him leave, but at the heart of every one is the biting truth that it was easier to leave than to continue to live so close to me. For all the times I pushed him and he forgave me and moved on, this last time must have been too much. The knowledge makes me ache all over.

Only when the soreness in my back from leaning against the door so long exceeds the pain inside do I push myself to my feet. I can't eat right now, so I dump the food into the trash.

Sitting at my desk, I can't even find the will to move. How could he just leave? Daniel dragged me down a path of wanting something I could never have. Whether he was conscious of what he was doing, I'm not really sure, but despite everything I feel for him, the emotion overcoming everything else is anger. How could he think it was okay to use me like that?

Part of me still feels guilty about hitting him, but another is glad I took the chance when I had it. Slipping off the watch he gave me, I throw it across the desk. It hits the wall and falls to the floor.

I need to get out of here. I've spent far too much time alone. Instead of making me feel better, it's just given Daniel's deception more of a chance to gnaw away at my insides. *Fuck him.* He'll regret treating me like garbage. Or maybe not. It doesn't matter anymore.

In less than two minutes, I've pulled on a zip-up sweater and changed into my nicest pair of jeans, the ones with the pattern over the back pockets. Slipping on my shoes and jacket, I set out for town. There isn't exactly a clear plan in my head, but I know what I want.

The Strassenbahn ride is quiet, but inside I'm on fire. There's still anger, but something else burns there too. The thrill of the hunt. I get off one stop past Bertoldsbrunnen, the central square in the Altstadt. In contrast to the earlier cold, a warm front has swept into the city, and it lends an extra lightness to my steps. I was meant to be out tonight.

Freiburg has terrible street lighting, so the walk is mostly in the dark, but I've grown to know this city well. My goal is somewhere I've seen only in passing, never up close. That's going to change tonight. Up ahead a neon sign confirms I'm in the right place. There's no bouncer waiting to check me or collect a cover, instead just a shirtless guy with an overly defined chest working behind the bar. The music playing is some kind of off-brand pop, but at least it's not too loud. There are maybe ten other guys in here, but most of them are a lot older than me. Taking a seat at the bar, I order a beer.

"Coming right up," the bartender says to me. God his muscles are big. Way bigger than Daniel's. *Damn it, Ethan, get him out of your head. It only makes it worse.* And besides, he doesn't deserve my thoughts.

The muscled guy sets the beer in front of me, and I take a long drink from it, powering through the foamy head. "You must be thirsty," he says with a wink.

I nod and take another long drink. The only other person sitting at the bar is three seats down from me. He's older though, like fifty, and he probably hasn't shaved in a couple weeks. And not like he's intentionally growing out his facial hair, it just looks like he stopped shaving. I turn around in my chair and quickly scan the tables. The only two guys my age are sitting close and holding hands on the table, staring into each other's eyes. *Jesus Christ, take it somewhere else.*

I order another beer. It's only three euro thirty for a half-liter, but with the familiar warmness stretching its fingers through me, I slide a five across the counter and tell the bartender, "*Stimmt so.*" That means he can keep the change.

Raising his eyebrows, he takes the bill and slips it into his money pouch. I start in on the second glass, drinking it slower than the first for no other reason than that wheat beer is really filling. It's not possible to put down more than a liter or so an hour. It's just too thick. I set the beer down on the bar. Sliding my index finger down the contour of the glass, I'm able to collect a bead of condensation at the tip of my finger. I wipe it on the edge of the bar and take another drink.

For good or for bad, there's no clock in here. The level of beer in my glass gradually sinks, counting out a distorted measure of passing time like a clogged hourglass. The rational side of me has no idea what I'm doing here. But that's not what brought me out tonight, and it's not what's keeping me here.

The bartender has just gotten done pouring the older guy another beer when he comes back to me. "Lonely evening?"

My eyes wander up from the dark stained wood of the bar. "You could say that."

He sets a shot glass on the counter, fills it with vodka, and slides it over to me. "On the house."

I take the shot, wincing as the alcoholic burn sweeps down my throat. I don't usually mix vodka and beer. Frequent nights out with exchange students have taught me numerous drinking rules and sayings, even though I know most of them are bullshit. Germans have one: "Beer after wine, let that be; Wine after beer, that I recommend." The translation is a little unsatisfying, since it doesn't rhyme in English like the British one does: "Beer before wine, you'll feel fine, wine before beer, you'll feel queer." Not that I'm entirely concerned about the second part. In either case, I'm pretty sure neither nationality has any saying about mixing shots in there, since that's bound to get anyone messed up.

A guy in a woolen pea coat leans over the bar a few feet down from me. He looks about thirty. His hair is cut short on the sides, but it's a little longer and messier on top. The shirtless hunk of a bartender pours him a beer. They exchange a few words as he pays, but the music is louder now and drowns out their voices. As the guy takes his first drink, he glances over and catches me staring.

I shift my gaze away and take another drink of my own, keeping my attention decidedly fixed on the bar.

"Hey, I haven't seen you here before." He takes the seat beside me. The skin on the back of my neck prickles with anticipation.

I raise my eyes to meet his. "It's my first time." It feels stupid to admit that, but I've got nothing else.

"I thought maybe that was the case." He smiles, but it's not creepy like I'm expecting. I study him a minute before deciding what to say. His hair is receding just a little, and his face is slightly out of proportion, but overall he's actually kind of good looking. "I'm Karsten," he introduces himself.

"Hi." I don't know if I really want to talk to him, but why shouldn't I? "So what do you do?"

"I work for an architecture company." He's still smiling. "And you, a student?"

"Yeah." I squeeze the base of my glass between my thumb and forefinger and rotate it in place. "I'm studying history."

"Fun," he says, adding, "I don't know much about that." At least he's honest. He's giving me a look like he's trying to figure something out. "You're not from here, are you?"

"From Freiburg?" I ask.

"No, from Germany. You've got an accent. And you still haven't told me your name," he points out, looking me up and down.

"I'm Ethan."

"Ah, American," he gives a small nod as if to confirm his thought. "Your German is really good for an American."

I'm pretty sure that's a compliment, at least enough to feel myself blush just a little. "Thanks."

"Where did you learn to speak so well?"

"I took it in high school and then in college. Other than that, it's just what I've learned here." Endless hours spent talking with a certain someone no doubt helped.

He finishes his beer and orders another for both of us, even though there's still an inch left in the bottom of my glass. The bartender looks smug as he sets the beers in front of us, like he feels personally responsible that Karsten and I are getting along.

This is how it's supposed to work when meeting someone. They're not supposed to treat you like crap for weeks, only to send mixed messages once they finally warm up.

"Prost," Karsten announces, and I lock onto his dark brown eyes as we clink our glasses together. This time we drink more slowly. He tells me about his work. He's a draftsman for a company that designs solar installations. As he talks, the itch that drove me out here tonight becomes more agitated.

I let him talk for a few more minutes before I suggest, "Do you want to get out of here?"

"Sure," he says, pointing a glance at our half finished beers. Taking the hint, I tip back my glass and put down the rest of it. I do have to swallow mid-drink, but I don't lower the glass. Stifling a burp as I finish, I push the air out through my nose. It burns a bit from the carbonation, but the feeling isn't a new one.

Karsten raises his eyebrows. "You even drink like a German." He finishes his beer too and we get up from the bar. The room sways as I get up. The eyes of the two younger guys are on us as we leave. This isn't anything they haven't seen before.

I feel his hand on my lower back as we step through the door into the street. "You want to go to another bar?" He falls into step beside me, zipping up his jacket about two-thirds of the way.

I shake my head. A liter and a half of beer and a shot of vodka are about all that I can handle for the moment. "You live near here?"

He studies me, eyes whisking from my waist up to my face. "Just on the other side of Bertoldsbrunnen."

We don't actually discuss going there. It's just understood. He leads me down a narrow alley right off Freiburg's central square. "I didn't know there were apartments in this part of town."

He gestures at the buildings stretching up four or five stories. "Of course. Everything above the shops." He lets us in an arched stone doorway. By the light of a single incandescent bulb, we ascend the stairs. They're wooden, polished smooth and worn down in the center from decades of use.

The moment Karsten unlocks his apartment, I announce, "I have to piss."

"Bathroom is on the right."

Pushing past him, I slip into the room and relieve myself. Outside the door, I hear him taking his shoes off. Zipping up, I turn on the water and let it run over my hands. I stare at my reflection in the mirror. *What are you doing?* The guy in the mirror doesn't respond.

The apartment is dark except for the weak rays of a distant street lamp filtering in the window. Karsten is sitting on a couch in the living room. I sit down beside him, barely a foot separating us. Reaching over, he traces a finger down the side of my cheek. My heart flutters in my chest. This is the moment to turn back. The finger trails down my neck. Except I don't want this to stop. Months of frustrated jerking off have finally caught up to me. Is it so bad to want to be touched by another person?

At my shirt collar, his hand closes around the fabric and pulls me gently toward him. His lips are on mine, slowly drawing me out of my shell. His tongue catches me by surprise at first, but it's smooth and cautious as it touches mine. His hands pull my jacket off my shoulders, sliding it down.

The coolness of the night hasn't left his hands, so as he slips them under my shirt, I shrink back. A wave of goose bumps spreads across my skin only to disappear a moment later. His mouth is still on mine, the abrasive stubble slowly grinding away at my defenses. *Why am I holding back? Isn't this what I want?*

He shifts from his sitting position and lays me back on the couch, tugging off my shirt. Now my hands are the ones grappling with his sweater. I'm not having much success. Sitting back on his heels, he removes it himself, taking his t-shirt with it.

My hands slide over his chest, over his abs and his pecs, along his biceps. He has a good body. I hope he's not disappointed with mine. My stomach is flat and my muscles are toned, but I'm self-conscious anyway. He kisses me again, starting on my lips and traveling across my cheek and down my jawline.

A low groan escapes me as his mouth reaches my chest, continuing its journey downward. His hands are fumbling at my belt, then at the top button of my jeans. I'm straining upward against the fabric of my boxers until he slides his hand inside and resolves that problem. My tongue is listless in my mouth as his hand moves up and down.

It feels good what he's doing, but we're sinking progressively deeper into the couch. "Damn, you're hot," he breathes. I freeze for a moment at the sound of his voice. "What's wrong?" he asks, halting the movement of his hand.

"Nothing," I whisper. "Just . . . let's not talk."

"Fine by me." From the way he says it I can tell he's amused, even though I can't actually see him. He gets up off the couch and, grabbing my hand, leads me through the dark to his bedroom. Pulling me up onto the bed, he lays me down on my back and starts kissing me again. His hands are likewise occupied, tugging on my jeans until they slide down over my butt. He breaks contact for a moment to take them all the way off.

My boxers stick with my jeans, so other than my socks, I'm not wearing a thing. He undoes his belt and unzips his jeans, guiding my hand to the opening in the front. I wrap my fingers around him, feeling his firmness, his heat.

While I touch him, he reaches over to the nightstand for something. There's a sound of a cap opening in the dark and then I feel his touch, slippery and wet. I wasn't sure that was where this was going, but now there's no question and a voice inside me is screaming for him to stop.

Pushing my hand away, he lubes himself up too. He's dutiful about my request to keep his mouth shut, because he doesn't say a word as he slowly enters me. It hurts at first, but I close my eyes and imagine that it's someone else. Someone younger with blue-gray eyes. And somehow it doesn't hurt as much anymore. Meanwhile, his hand returns to what it was doing earlier, up and down, unrelenting.

His hips are moving faster now, and so is his hand. Daniel is here with me, he's here, he is. This is our moment. My eyes are squeezed shut. The rush is building inside, an unstoppable force rolling through me like a wave. What he's doing with his hand feels so good. Daniel and I, so close now. My stomach tensing, I clench my teeth and come on my chest.

He expels a low, satisfied grunt as he finishes just after me. For a full minute the only sound is his panting breath.

After withdrawing, he wordlessly excuses himself to the bathroom. By the time he comes out, I'm fully dressed and putting on my shoes.

"You don't have to go," he says. I flinch at the sound of not-Daniel's voice.

I stare at him like he's just offered me a nice glass of bleach. "Yeah, okay, thanks, but I'm going."

"Suit yourself."

Outside, the night air hasn't fully cooled yet, and its freshness drags me reluctantly back toward sobriety. *What have I done?* There's no choice but to walk home now, since the last Strassenbahn must have left hours ago. I make to check my watch for the time but remember it's sitting on the floor of my dorm room, probably somewhere near my forgotten phone.

I don't know what to feel worse about—that I just had sex with some random guy, that he was way older than he should have been, or that the only reason it was good was because I was imagining it was Daniel, which is probably why it didn't register as an issue that he didn't use a condom.

I stop dead in the middle of the pedestrian bridge that arches over the main train station. My heart thuds in my chest. "FUCK!" I scream into the night. I feel like I'm about to puke, and it doesn't have a thing to do with what I drank.

There's no one around to hear me, since it has to be past one in the morning. Not that it matters anyway. My feet carry me homeward without any direction from upstairs. A breeze picks up behind me as the path swings away from the Strassenbahn tracks. The spot where Daniel and I stopped for me to throw up after our night at the KGB bar is just up ahead.

Something cold and small lands on my head. I reach up to feel what it is. It's wet. Birds don't fly at night. Another splatting impact sounds up from the paved path. Now there are more all around. I get hit with another.

The raindrops are huge. How the hell am I getting caught in a freak rainstorm in *February*? I'm still at least twenty minutes from home, and the rain is coming down harder. This night is such a mess. *My life is such a mess.* And I don't have the energy to take another step.

Feeling like the piece of shit I am, I drop to my knees in the middle of the path and bury my face in my hands. Cold droplets beat onto the path, soaking me along with everything else. Marc's way out doesn't sound so crazy now. Like he said, it would be so easy. I could just step in front of a train.

As the warm salt of my tears mingles with the cold freshness of the rain, I begin to understand how someone might give up hope that things will ever get better. Shivering and soaked, I push myself to my feet and continue through the downpour toward home.

Chapter 31

By Saturday, I've carved out a special place inside where I retreat to in every spare moment. It's a place where the story of Daniel plays out over and over again. The moment when our eyes met after I'd cut my foot and how it changed everything. The kiss that sent me sprinting away from him. The nearly disastrous time when he wrestled me to the floor. Every close moment we shared. And then, the crushing realization that nothing was as I'd thought. Mostly I dwell on the last part of our story, the part where I drove him away.

Then I spiral into what happened after he moved out. What was I thinking, hooking up with that guy? Was I trying to get back at Daniel? Because that's possibly the stupidest thing I've ever done. The only person I ended up hurting was myself, maybe in more ways than one. If only I could forget that night ever happened.

I can't stay like this forever, curled up in bed waiting for things to change. I dig out my phone and call Niko. As it rings, a blade of guilt stabs my stomach for not calling him sooner. It's been two weeks since classes started again, and I haven't made any effort to return his calls.

"Hey, Ethan," Niko answers. "Haven't heard from you in a while."

"Yeah, sorry about that . . ." My throat is scratchy and I try to clear it.

I hear a small sigh from the other side. "It's fine," he says. "You sound like hell."

Niko's honesty is one of the things I love about him. "I feel like it too." Now it's my turn to sigh.

He's quiet for a moment. "Why don't you come over?"

"I'd like that."

"Have you eaten yet?"

I glance at the clock. It's eleven-thirty in the morning, so he must be referring to lunch. I don't bother to tell him that I still haven't gotten out of bed. "No, not yet."

"Alright, I'll make something. See you soon."

I shower and brush my teeth and head to catch the Strassenbahn. It snowed last night, but it's too warm for it to stay long. The path is covered with saturated slush that's strong enough to hold its shape but splashes out from under my feet when I step on it. It's strangely gratifying to clomp through the heaps of it at the edge of the path, watching it explode from beneath my shoes.

Half an hour later I step off the Strassenbahn just down the street from Niko's building. A mom and her two kids are walking toward me, bundled up more than they need to be for the weather. The two boys are laughing and pushing each other. I let them pass without making eye contact.

The front door of his apartment building must not have been pulled shut well enough by the last person to leave, because it's slightly ajar. I let myself in, making sure to close the door firmly behind me. Satisfied when I hear the click of the mechanism, I climb the stairs to Niko's apartment.

He opens the door tentatively after I knock. "Oh, it is you. How did you get in?"

Seeing Niko forces me to acknowledge that I haven't spoken to anyone about everything that's happened. My eyes instantly turn red and my bottom lip begins to quiver. Before I can say anything, he wraps his arms around me and pulls me close. "You're going to be fine, Ethan," he whispers. "Everything is going to be fine." I need him so much right now that I squeeze until my arms are sore. I'm afraid I might be squeezing the life out of him, but he doesn't complain.

We hold each other without any move to pull away until I've absorbed every bit of his presence that I can contain within me. When we break our embrace, I take a seat at the kitchen table. He's in the middle of making something I don't recognize, probably some Polish dish, apparently containing sausage and noodles.

"So what happened?"

I open my mouth to begin, but then close it immediately. I can't possibly imagine where to start. He watches me but remains quiet. After a minute of silence between us, I decide to begin with the drive from Freiburg to Daniel's home. For the most part, Niko just listens, though occasionally he asks for clarification on this detail or that. He takes a particular interest when I describe Eva's reaction to Daniel and me after our walk.

"She dropped the platter of cookies just like that?"

"Boom, shattered all over."

His eyes widen just a little, like he's starting to piece things together already, but he lets me continue. When I get to the part about the watch Daniel gave me for Christmas, he asks to see it.

Sliding my shirtsleeve up, I hold my arm out for him as the watch's alternating black and silver links catch the overheard kitchen light. He pulls my wrist toward him, inspecting it before letting out a low whistle. "Do you know what that's worth?"

I shrug. "I figured it was expensive. Maybe four or five hundred euro?"

Niko chuckles. "Yeah it's expensive, except you're off by a bit. Try four or five *thousand* euro. At least."

"You're kidding."

Shaking his head, he jumps up to check on the noodles. "Nope, no joke. That's a Bulgari Diagono chronograph, and I promise it set your friend back a pretty penny."

My heart flutters, and my face gets hot. Could that really be true? Rotating my wrist slowly, I see the watch for the first time. Its gleaming band of silver and black and the meticulous artistry of the chronograph subdials seem that much more special.

What does it mean, him giving me something like this? He could have picked other watches. His family is well off, sure, but it seems like a princely gift even by those standards. It's hard to comprehend that the metal object wrapped around my wrist is the most valuable thing I've ever owned.

"Does it change how you feel, knowing its worth?" Niko asks, pulling me out of my thoughts.

"No," I say quickly, running a finger around the case and along the band. I wish I understood *why*. Was he trying to impress me? Or did he just have to get the perfect watch for me, regardless of the price?

"And yes."

Nodding, he says, "I thought maybe it would."

"Is that bad?"

"I don't think so, no. Anyway, so what happened after that?"

I struggle to remember where to pick up the story because of his revelation about the watch. It feels like lead around my wrist, and I tug my sleeve down to cover it up. There are just a few last things to tell him before my tale comes to an end, and they're the ones that I really don't want to say. I would hide them from myself if I could.

I tell him about Marc's room and the photo on his desk. Niko drops down into the chair next to me. "Wow. I'm so sorry, Ethan." His face is blank and he's staring off at the wall. Finally he looks back at me. "What did you do then?"

"I didn't tell him what I'd found out, so we ended up going to a movie. Things sort of went to shit real fast. Before it was over I ran out of the theater."

"I bet you did. Did he follow you?"

I nod. "I confronted him and he tried to explain that it wasn't like I thought. He said that it wasn't about Marc."

"Did you believe him?"

"Not for a second." I look up at Niko. "Should I have given him more of a chance?"

His lips pull together in thought. "I think you were right to do what you did."

Lowering my eyes to the place setting in front of me, I turn my spoon over between my fingers. "I wouldn't go that far."

"What do you mean? Did something else happen?"

"You could say that."

He gives me a curious look. "Well?"

"After I told him I didn't believe him, he tried to touch me, comfort me I guess, and I kind of . . . " My voice trails.

"Come on, it can't be that bad."

Putting off saying it isn't going to make it any better. "I hit him, alright?"

"Damn, Ethan." Niko massages his jaw. "Did you hurt him?"

"Physically? Not really, just cut his lip. I probably hurt my hand more than his face." My shoulders slump forward. It was so hard to leave him that night. I doubt I would have done it had I known how upset he was. "I haven't seen him since," I admit.

"It's been two weeks, and you live with him. How can you not have seen him?"

This is the other part I've been dreading to admit. "He moved out. He just . . . *left*," I breathe the words, my voice catching in my throat.

"Oh." He doesn't say anything else.

"Do you think he ever felt anything for me? As a friend, I mean. Was any of it real?"

Niko is quiet for several moments before speaking carefully. "I think, that unless he's a complete sociopath, at least some of your friendship was real." Boiling water gurgles in the background, steam rising out of the pot with the noodles. "What do *you* think?"

I've considered this a thousand times already. Most often, it's the spot to where my infinite circle of thought returns. "I want to think that he was telling the truth. Except I can never know for sure, and I'm so scared of finding out I'm wrong."

He nods, giving me an apologetic look. "I think that's fair. So what did you do after you found out he left?"

Niko is my best friend in the world right now, but I can't tell him about that night. I already know what he'd say. It's the riskiest thing I could have done. I need to get tested. I need to promise him I'll never do it again.

But I don't need that conversation right now. Not with everything else. I glance back to the stove. "You should check that."

He eyes me for a moment before getting up to grab a colander. He's straining the noodles over the sink when we hear the sound of a handle turning, and Niko's bedroom door opens.

A guy about our age with decent definition steps out. His hair is a mess and it looks like he just got out of bed. These observations take place in less than a second and are all peripheral, because he is also completely naked. Seated and already staring toward the door, I get a serious eyeful.

The moment the guy notices me—about a half second after I've seen everything—he yelps and jumps back into the bedroom, slamming the door behind him. My eyes are wide, but I regain my composure and glance over to Niko. He's staring at the now-closed door, still holding the colander filled with pasta. Steam billows up from the sink.

"Who was that?" I venture. So often it's Niko who pokes friendly fun at the situations I get myself into with Daniel. It feels kind of good to have the tables turned.

He's bright red. "That was Alex. From the KGB bar, you remember?"

"Oh, yeah." With a hint of smugness, I add, "I didn't really get a chance to see his face."

I didn't think it was possible, but Niko flushes even more. "He was asleep when you called, and I didn't want to wake him up just to tell him you were coming over."

"Would you like me to tell him you have company?"

Niko doesn't dignify the question with an answer but instead begins chopping up the sausage, mixing it with the gravy he's made. After putting the noodles and sausage gravy into large bowls on the table, he disappears into the bedroom. Even though I haven't had breakfast yet, the savory gravy smells really good, and my stomach rumbles loudly.

Muffled voices drift from the bedroom before the door opens again and Niko emerges with Alex in tow. This time he's upgraded his wardrobe to light yellow basketball shorts and a t-shirt. "Hey," Alex says nervously.

"Hey." I'm not sure what else to say. Taking seats around the table, we dig into Niko's creation. The taste is just as good as the aroma, and soon I'm stuffed. I try to make polite small talk with Alex, asking him if he still works at the KGB bar, which he does.

"Have you heard about the protest next Thursday?" Niko asks both of us.

Alex looks to me to answer first, so I nod. "I saw something about it on TV. I felt like they were trying to make it out to be more than it is."

"I wouldn't be so sure," Alex says. "Students are really upset about this."

I'm skeptical. "There are always protests for some reason or another, how is this is any different? It's just five hundred euro. That's nothing." Niko's eyes flick between Alex and me.

Alex speaks before Niko can say anything. "It's different to most Germans. In the United States, tuition fees are exorbitant and education is already a luxury. What's worse, the quality of that education is determined solely by how much you are able to pay for it. Your best universities are naturally the most expensive, and to attend them is a privilege of the elite," he says bluntly. Alex is German, so his ability to formulate arguments in the language far exceeds my own. "To introduce tuition fees in Germany isn't like raising taxes. It means that something that was considered a fundamental human right, like access to the fire department or healthcare, is no longer available to everyone."

"That's not really the same thi—"

"No, it's exactly the same. Imagine if you were getting robbed but the police wouldn't help unless you could afford to pay them. That's how your healthcare works already." His words hang in the air. His arguments are decisive, and I'm at a loss as to what to say. Niko is staring at his plate. The topic seems to be at an end.

I excuse myself as soon as I can after we finish cleaning up. "Let's hang out sometime this week," I tell Niko.

"For sure."

I wave to Alex on my way out, and he nods back. Once I'm in the hallway, I let myself release the breath I was holding inside. Out of nowhere, the image comes to mind of Alex bursting out of the bedroom bare ass naked, and I burst out laughing. The sound echoes up and down the stairs. Even though it's my own laugh, it still sounds rich and wholesome.

Chapter 32

Once again flipping through the pages of Daniel's Bible, my fingers come to a stop at the point where I left off last time. Pressing down on the wisps of paper, the words lining the binding are revealed.

October 2, 1942. When I stepped into the street tonight, I could not help but shiver. Hakenkreuz banners hung from every lamppost. Curfew was an hour past, so I moved in the shadows only, knowing that the documents in my possession meant certain death for me if discovered. There was great risk in moving the leaflets by cover of night, but greater danger still lay in being observed carrying such a large parcel in daylight to the apartment of my beloved Thomas. It was his thought, not only to move the leaflets to his apartment, located very close to the university on the Adolf-Hitler Strasse, but to do so by night.

Apparently Niko was right about Kaiser-Joseph Street once being called by a more sinister name. The war and its aftermath usually seem so far away. Reading this puts it in chilling perspective. All of this happened just decades ago, in streets hardly changed in the intervening years.

Thomas took the bundle from me. Then, placing his hand on my cheek, gave me a kiss that was too brief, fleeting for fear of discovery, and bade me a swift journey home. Though I did not know at the time, that was the last we would ever touch.

I waited at the end of the street, watching him. He was just fifty pac-

es from the door to his apartment when rays of portable lanterns were cast on him and the command uttered that stopped my heart. "Stehen bleiben!"

Concealed in the shadows some distance away, I watched as the Gestapo searched him. They found the parcel containing the leaflets, and they tore at the brown paper until the package burst open. Papers fluttered into the street, and at that moment I knew that all was lost.

Chapter 33

I step into the late afternoon sun, my shoe scraping on a rough edge of the stone stairs that lead down to the university square. I've just handed in the paper that was supposed to be about the student resistance in Freiburg under the Third Reich. Instead I turned in a paper detailing the numerous historical remnants scattered throughout Freiburg from the time of the Nazis.

The handwritten lines in Daniel's Bible share a fascinating history, but they could never be used for any academic work. There's no way to cite it or prove its veracity, except to reveal the book. Aside from the obvious problem of doing this without Daniel's permission, which he would likely never give, it would have put me in an odd position. Questions about how a critical piece of Freiburg's history snuck into my possession would be sure to follow. Of course, the very same question should be asked of Daniel. *How did he get the book?*

The wind blowing through the square is cool, but the snow has mostly melted at least. In a month it might be warm enough for students to venture out and populate the benches, but we're not quite there yet. The only students outside are walking direct lines between building entrances.

Reaching the street, I hang a right toward the center of town. As I learn more of Magdalena's story, I can't help but wonder whether it was in this street or that alley where she conducted the secret meeting with her boyfriend, Thomas. Was it the one with the honey shop? Or the one with the vines overhead where Daniel and I poked along for our second tandem? She must have walked down these same streets for years. From pre-1945 pictures I've seen, they haven't changed much. How did she feel, carrying hundreds of copies of a document where even one could mean her imprisonment? Was she afraid or only exhilarated? And as she watched Thomas be captured by the secret police, was she hidden by a recessed entranceway or darkness alone?

I dig my hands into my pockets and veer around a gaggle of young girls. It's getting close to evening, and a deep fried something sounds like the perfect end to the semester. It definitely has to be better than ruminating on the lives of people who lived seventy years ago.

There's a little seafood joint called Nordsee at the center of Bertoldsbrunnen where the Stassenbahn lines cross that sells fried fish in numerous forms: sticks, squares, sandwiches. You name it, they probably have it made from fish.

Waiting for a Strassenbahn to glide past, I cut across the square, unable to avoid noticing how many people are here. It's often a busy square, but usually people are actually moving. Whether to change to another Strassenbahn or visit one of the many shops that line the square, people are generally trying to *get* somewhere. The thing is, most of the people gathered here aren't going anywhere. They're just standing around.

"What would you like?" the plump lady behind the counter asks. I drag my gaze away from the square.

"Fish and chips, please."

"Three or four piece?" She must ask that question hundreds of times a day.

"Four."

"With or without remoulade?"

Remoulade is two parts tartar sauce, one part heaven. "With, please." I drop a pair of two-euro coins into the plastic payment tray on the counter.

While she scoops potato wedges and four fish rectangles into a paper cone, I survey the people around Bertoldsbrunnen square. More of them are arriving by the minute. Something is definitely going on, because they're clumping up in the center around the statue of Bertold on his horse. It's an ugly statue, which is completely appalling, because I learned during the research for my term paper that it's actually an updated version of an older and far superior statue of a Roman soldier. I get that they were bitter about the whole Roman Empire thing, but why replace a historic statue with a horrid ugly one?

At last she slaps a dollop of remoulade on top of the cornucopia of fish and fries and hands me the paper cone. Taking one of the tiny wooden stickers from a box on the counter, I jab the top potato wedge, making sure to get an appropriate amount of the remoulade on it.

In the time that I was purchasing my heart healthy snack, two giant police vans have arrived and parked on either side of the square, and policemen in riot gear are now filing out of. White and green police cars are tucked alongside Kaiser-Joseph Street as well. The crowd at the center of the square is even larger now too, and it's starting to coalesce into a tight group. Extending my wrist beyond the length of my hoodie, I risk revealing my watch to check the time. It's a quarter to four. Then the realization strikes me. Today is Thursday. This is the protest against the student fee increase warned about on the news.

I should just steer clear of it completely and head home. Six months ago, I probably would have left without a second thought. But this is an important event for the university, and I want to be here to see how this all plays out. I even have a snack to enjoy in the meantime. Watching a blip about it on TV afterward just won't cut it. History is worn into every cobblestone in this town, and just because I'm only here for a year doesn't mean I shouldn't stick around to witness a very small part of that story.

I stab a fish rectangle and smear it in remoulade as I cross the square. The fish is hot and greasy and tastes amazing. A man at the center of the crowd is standing on a wooden box at the foot of Bertold's tasteless statue. It's the same guy I saw at the university a few months ago with the megaphone. He's just standing there and watching everyone, like he's trying to get a read on what kind of turnout there will be. No doubt there are plenty of students just like me who forgot this was happening today but got interested while walking past. Considering it's just after class at the end of the semester when attendance is highest, it was probably planned that way.

The police, batons at their sides and clear plastic riot shields in hand, form lines at the edges of the square. Some of them look young, in their early twenties, but every face is impassive and every pair of eyes stares straight ahead. It's unnerving, because their calm demeanor proclaims they know what's coming and we don't.

The streets leading into the square are open, but the Strassenbahn trams have stopped running. There are hundreds of us now standing over the tracks, making it impossible for the trams to pass. The cops remain at the edge of the square, exerting no effort to stop the flow of students and bystanders into the area. Some of the latecomers pass right by and take up watchful stances behind the police lines, but most join us in the middle. I pop the last piece of fried potato into my mouth, but since I'm wedged in by the statue, there's no place to throw the paper cone and wooden sticker. I drop them on the ground, trying to be discrete about it, but a short girl with dimples and long blond hair notices and glares disapprovingly. With a shrug, I look away.

When at last the mass of students has swelled to fill almost the entire square and only a narrow gap is left between those at the edge and the lines of police, the young man on the box picks up his megaphone and begins to speak. "Welcome everyone!" He sweeps his arm across the crowd assembled around him. "Students, professors, citizens," he pauses, a touch of a smile appearing as he gives a pointed look to the police ringing the square, "and officials." His hair is dark and lays a few inches past his ears, and his clothes are unimpressive—jeans and a dark jacket. It's his voice that takes us. It's clear and confident, but subtly imploring.

"We are at a crossroads," his words echo around the square. A quiet settles over everyone that belies the great number of us assembled here. Even the police seem to be baited by his words. "There is a question before us. Whether we will allow education to be sold as a commodity as many other countries have begun to do, or whether we will stand up against class warfare, against a system that empowers the rich, against a government that once again dares to curtail human rights."

Cheers and shouts break the silence, and the girl who caught me littering throws her arm in the air, yelling fiercely, "*Freie Bildung für Alle!*" It takes me a second to backtrack and translate, because I wasn't really paying attention to her. *Free education for all.* In German though, "freie" more closely means available than having no cost. I hear the phrase yelled again, a few feet away. "Freie Bildung für Alle!" This time it's a tall guy with acne and a deep voice. The call is repeated across the crowd until the entire square shouts with one voice.

Box Guy's words are rapid but gilded with passion as the megaphone cuts through the chanting. "Show the university and the government that we will not allow this to happen! We march to the university to confront the administration!" He jumps off the box, and raising the megaphone into the air, he begins to lead the protest up the street.

A warning tingles in my fingers and is reiterated when I see nervous glances exchanged between the cops on the far side of the square. At the order of an officer, two full lines of policemen break rank and pack themselves into one of the massive vans. The moment the doors shut, the van tears down the street, tires squealing over the cobblestone.

Chanting "Freie Bildung," the several hundred strong horde forges on down the street normally reserved for the Strassenbahn. We turn onto a wide pedestrian street that serves as one of the main arteries to the university. The other half of the police force that didn't zoom away in one of the vans is following us at a cautious distance.

I'm still stuck in the middle of everything, and I've even started chanting along just to fit in. These people are more serious than I anticipated. I'm trying to work my way out of the throng, but everyone is shoulder to shoulder, directly in front of and behind me. It's an unstoppable current of bodies sweeping me along. For a moment, I could swear I catch sight of Daniel several rows away but when I turn to get a better look, he's nowhere to be seen.

We're less than half a block from the university when the police van that peeled away from Bertoldsbrunnen screeches to a halt beside the administration building. Men storm out, forming a solid line at the top of the stairs leading into it.

Unfazed, Box Guy leads the protest right up to the edge of the steps. Another quiet settles over the mob, though this time it's an uneasy one, punctuated by hushed voices. Without the aid of the megaphone, the young man yells, "If the president of the university will not appear, we will demand entry to the building." Even without the electronic amplification, his voice carries across the square. My chest feels tense, fearful but ready to flee.

No one speaks, and the police stand impassive. From a second floor window, at the edge of a curtain, I can just barely see a woman peeking out. She looks scared. I wipe my sweaty palms on my jeans.

Box Guy places one foot on the first step, then places his other next to it. Across the front line of protesters, each one does the same thing until they're all standing on equal footing. The crowd-packed square shifts forward a foot to fill the space. Someone pokes me in the small of my back when I don't move, so I shuffle forward to fill the tiny gap in front of me. Again the students at the base of the stairs take another step, and the hundreds of us behind them press forward to fill the gap.

They move up one more step, and then another. Inch by inch they advance, until the ten of them, shoulder to shoulder, are standing on a level just below the line of police in riot gear. Less than a foot remains between the protestors and the police, who are standing in such a way that it's impossible for the students to ascend onto the landing.

The officer in the middle begins speaking rapidly to Box Guy, but it's far enough away that there's no chance of hearing their exchange. He finishes and resumes his stoic position at the top of the stairs. Box Guy looks over his shoulder, scanning the crowd gathered behind him. Every person in the square is silent, waiting to see what he's going to do. Turning his head back to the officer in front of him, he steps forward.

In the split second before the officer can react, I think, *no!* With their riot shields, every cop on the landing simultaneously pushes outward and the row of protesters flails backwards, unable to catch their balance on anything. Angry shouts from all across the square erupt as the row behind the first is likewise unable to stop the fall and loses their balance as well. We're helpless to watch as the hundred or so students packed onto the stairs fall backward like human dominoes.

I almost start to believe it's going to end there in a pile of bruised university students when something that looks like a brick or rock flies out from the mob near the base of the stairs and hits one of the cops in the side of the head. He stumbles as the object ricochets off his helmet and rolls to a stop on the landing behind him. I squint, trying to make out what it is. It's too small and rough to be brick. Then I realize it's a cobblestone.

"*Pflastersteine!*" someone yells over the growing commotion. As if on command, a dozen heads nearest to the building disappear from view as their owners begin scrabbling at cobblestones. A moment later, a barrage of the squareish stones erupts from the crowd. Some find their targets on the police, while others shatter windows on the first and second floor of the administration building. Several bounce harmlessly off the stone façade. Agitated shouts and enthusiastic whoops both fill the air. With a sickening realization, it finally registers that a handful of the protesters *wanted* this to turn violent.

216

It's time to get the hell out of here. I'm stuck in the middle still, but I can see that the police at the back and sides of the square are pushing in with shields, swinging their batons. Trying to disperse us, no doubt. Someone pushes me, and I try to grab the guy next to me to keep from losing my balance. It's not enough to halt my momentum though, and I tumble forward. I fight to get my hands in front of me to break the fall, but in the mass of moving bodies, my left wrist gets pinned under my knee as I make contact with the ground. A sinking feeling fills my chest as I hear the grating sound of metal striking stone, confirming that my watch, caught between my knee and the ground, bore at least some of the impact.

There's no time to inspect it for damage though, so I jump back to my feet to avoid getting trampled. Sliding my hand ahead of me like a fish fighting its way out of a net, I push through the agitated mob. As I advance, the gaps between the bodies grow wider, and it becomes easier to move.

I'm halfway to the edge of the crowd when several low bangs echo across the square. A second later, gray objects whizz overhead, one striking a girl in the shoulder just in front of me. She screams and falls, but oily gray smoke is erupting from the canister. Instinct taking over, it tells me I don't have time to see if she's alright. Before I can get away, the gas hits my eyes.

Like everyone else in the vicinity, I stagger away from the chemical contagion, coughing with painful spasms. Eyes blurry and watering, I continue to push my way through the fleeing mass of students. I can barely see, but when I glimpse another gray cloud of tear gas ahead, I veer away, stumbling over an uprooted cobblestone that never had a chance to take flight. My throat is raw from fighting to expel every molecule of the burning smoke from my lungs, but my feet keep moving forward.

Finally, the spaces between bodies increase dramatically, and the edge of the square is just ahead. Squinting and pressing my nose and mouth into the crook of my elbow, I sprint through the clouds of gas that are quickly spreading over the entire square. I'm just rounding the last clump of noxious fog when a cop grabs me roughly by my hoodie. My legs continue forward and slip from underneath me, but his grip holds me aloft. From the corner of my eye, I see several cops farther away, likewise subduing protesters escaping from the edge of the amoebic expansion of tear gas. Handcuffed, they're being packed into the back of one of the police vans.

At the fear of arrest, a new surge of adrenaline courses through me as I regain my footing. I drive my shoulder as hard as I can into the cop's body-armored chest, and his grip loosens. I push off to sprint away, but his iron grip closes again on my shirt collar. Before I can think, his billy club whips through the air, making contact with the back of my head. A surreal mixture of lights and blackness explodes across my vision and my knees buckle beneath me. As I crumple, I see an image of someone racing toward me, a black bandana tied over his face just below his eyes. *I know those eyes.*

I've just rolled over onto my back when the masked man leaps over me, fist cocked back, and smashes the cop's temple with the combined force of his momentum and the muscles propelling his arm forward. Somehow the officer is on the ground beside me. I'm still trying to understand what just happened when a pair of strong arms are abruptly pulling me to my feet. "Ethan," a voice says. A hand slaps my cheek. "Ethan, look at me. We have to go. Now."

The cop who grabbed me was some distance from his buddies, but what just happened hasn't escaped their notice. "*Stehen bleiben!*"

"Ethan!" he says again, dragging me back toward the billows of tear gas. "We have to move!" All around us, students are still fleeing, zigzagging to evade the cops and the gas.

My brain is processing everything in slow motion as he drags me along with him. Then in an instant, some switch flips inside me, and everything returns to normal speed. Blinking rapidly, my vision clears enough to see where we're going. Daniel's arm around my back and his hand tucked under my armpit, he guides us back through the center of the square, back toward the toxic gas.

"Deep breath," he commands a moment before he pulls me into the foggy eddies. My legs pumping mechanically, we cross the majority of the square without breathing. My lungs scream in pain, now more from oxygen starvation than the gas exposure. I close my burning eyes and lean more heavily into his body, relying on him completely to guide us safely through. I'm marginally aware of the piercing ache in the back of my skull, but numerous other discomforts override it for the moment.

I chance further pain by opening my eyes for a brief second. Clear air is just a little farther ahead. The moment we burst through, we both gulp down mouthfuls of fresh air. As we do, my foot catches on something, and I start to pitch forward. "Oh no you don't," Daniel says gruffly, and his arm tightens around me, lifting and supporting as he stops my fall enough for me to regain my balance.

This side of the square is devoid of anyone except a few wheezing protestors. Most importantly, there aren't any police. Staggering to a rest against the smooth stone of a building, I double over panting. For the first time, I see the damage to my watch. Across the crystal face is a deep scratch from where it struck the cobblestone. My heart sinks, and it feels like I've downed another gulp of tear gas.

My head is pounding, and I feel queasy. Lifting my gaze, I glance at Daniel. His eyes are bright red and watering, but his breathing is less ragged than mine thanks to the bandana covering his face. He pulls it down so it hangs around his neck.

"How did you find me?" I cough out the words.

He glances away. "Just happened to be nearby."

I don't believe him. "You were following me."

His exhaling breath turns into a rattling cough. "We can't stay here, Ethan."

I spit a caustic wad of saliva onto the cobblestones. "*You* can do whatever you want, just don't follow me anymore." My stomach roils between the throbbing at the back of my head and the acrid burn in my throat.

"They'll be looking for everyone they can find. You saw how they were arresting everyone."

I think back to the group of handcuffed students being loaded into the back of the vans. "But it's all over, why would they arrest us now?"

I can see the weariness from the day in him. Not just because of his bloodshot eyes and labored breathing, but in the way his shoulders fall and his gaze grinds into the cobblestones. "Because Ethan, you tried to flee. And now because I hit that cop." He shakes his head. "They'll be looking for us. They'll know you took a blow to the back of the head, so if you go to a hospital or get stopped on your way home, they'll arrest you."

My head and my stomach are threatening to defeat my grip on consciousness, but I force myself to concentrate a few minutes more. "So what do we do?"

"They'll be watching the Strassenbahn lines out of the city and the major streets for stragglers," he says in a low voice, as if he's mostly talking to himself. "We're actually quite close to the edge of the

Schlossberg."

"You want to hide on the Schlossberg?" At first it sounds crazy, but even with my waning grip on reason, it starts to make sense. I hate his logic, and I hate that he's here with me. It doesn't seem like I have a choice, though.

He nods cautiously, reaching a conclusion. "We'll wait it out, return to the city when it's dark. Come on, Ethan."

As close as we are to the edge of the valley where Freiburg makes its home, it doesn't take long to get out of the city. Magdalena's account, having always seemed so dated and removed from my reality, now feels frighteningly close at hand. After sprinting across a single major street with Strassenbahn tracks running its length, we confine our movements to alleys until reaching a wooden bridge that carries us over one of the River Dreisam's tributary streams and into the forested foot of the Schlossberg.

The pain in my head has receded to a dull ache, but the ground is swaying beneath me, and the feeling of bile rising in my stomach can't be ignored any longer. A few hundred feet past the tree line, I drop to my knees at the edge of the path. My breathing comes in short, clipped bursts.

"Are you alright?"

"I'm fine," I manage to say. I hock up a wad of spit, but it does nothing to diminish the pressure on the back of my throat. Seconds pass, and I know exactly what's coming.

For the second time this year, I throw up in front of Daniel. This time it's not the smooth vomiting of liquid, the discomfort suppressed by alcohol. Instead, it's everything terrible that it can be, only exacerbated by the fish and fried potatoes I had before the protest.

When I finish, I clear my throat and spit until my mouth is dry. I'm determined to hawk up every miserable bit of slime and acid from my throat, which now hurts more than before. Who would have thought an acid coating over tear gas burns would do that?

I feel a hand on my shoulder, but I pull away. "Just leave me alone, okay?"

"Don't feel bad that you got sick. That tear gas was horrible."

I stand and put a few feet between me and the spot where I was sick. "I wish you would have just left me with that cop." Daniel stares at me, the muscles in his brow weaving themselves together. I should be thankful he just saved me, but I'm embarrassed for throwing up in front of him and hurt that this is the first time I've seen him in weeks. Before he can work out a response, I question him. "So your plan is just to hang out here in the woods for God knows how many hours? I feel like shit and I'm thirsty and I'm cold."

He shifts his weight from one foot to the other, looking at the ground. "I'm sorry."

"You should have thought about that before you committed a felony and dragged us out here," I say angrily. Even though I know that if it weren't for him I might be in jail right now, I'm determined to make him feel as horrible as I do.

He doesn't try to defend himself. "There's a place we can go while we wait," he says.

I look at him with skepticism. "Where?"

We're at the foot of an odd little enclosed tower, about thirty feet tall and built of the same reddish stone as the university and the Münster cathedral. An imposing metal door stands in front of us, but the structure has no other openings except an observation deck on the upper level. Above the door is a plaque, affixed to the stone, that reads: BUILT BY THE STUDENT BODY OF THE ALBERT-LUDWIGS-UNIVERSITY FREIBURG 1900.

"What is this place?" I ask as Daniel dials in a combination on a lockbox attached to a corner of the structure. Cracking it open, he withdraws a key. "And how do you know how to unlock that?"

"I used to be part of a student group that had access," he says. "It's one of a couple hundred towers built throughout Germany honoring Otto von Bismarck. He's the Kaiser who unified the German states into a single nation." He slips the key into the metal door and turns the mechanism. "It's not as good a view as the newer watchtower at the top of the Schlossberg, but it's impressive enough."

An eerie realization creeps through me. A tower dedicated to Otto von Bismarck. Bismarck's Turm. This must be where Magdalena met her uncle for lunch the day they exchanged the stacks of leaflets. In the dwindling light, I quickly scan the area around the base of the tower, wondering where they might have sat. Nothing strikes me as a probable location, so I follow Daniel as he heads inside.

Because it's evening already, barely any light filters down from above. It's difficult to see anything until the blazing white glow of Daniel's cell phone illuminates the area around us. "We also used this place to store supplies for our day trips into the Black Forest." He swings the beam of white light around to the back corner of the tower floor, revealing a full case of bottled water and a plastic tub full of individually wrapped snacks like peanuts and granola bars.

"Thank God," I breathe in relief as I snap the seal on one of the bottles and take a pull. My mouth still tastes like stale vomit and tear gas, so I swish the water around before spitting it onto the stone floor. Despite everything that's happened between us, some things still haven't changed, because I feel Daniel's disapproving gaze on me. The water is no substitute for mouthwash, and my teeth still feel gritty, but at least I'm no longer questioning whether something actually died inside my mouth.

We each grab a handful of the snack packs and climb the stairs. Following the glowing light of Daniel's phone, we take our seats on the stone across from each other on the observation deck. I don't expect to have an appetite, but I only have to stare at the granola bar for a minute before my stomach turns over, demanding to be fed. My fingers tear at the wrapping. How did I end up in this situation? Two hours ago I was enjoying a leisurely stroll through the Altstadt.

Eating in the fading light, I finally take a minute to study the young man across from me. He hasn't touched anything yet except for the water. I can tell he hasn't shaved in several days, and it looks like there are dark circles under his eyes, but it might just be the shadows.

"Why did you do it?"

He levels his gaze on me. He knows I'm talking about getting me away from the cop. He makes me wait before he responds. "I don't know why, I just did."

His voice gains an inflection as he says it, and I know he's lying. "Bullshit. Try again."

He sighs, and just like earlier, I see that his weary sadness, usually confined to just his eyes, has reached deeper inside him. "I don't want to talk about it." His voice isn't angry, it's just . . . forlorn, as though he's already resigned himself to a certain fate.

"Don't give me that, Daniel. There's a reason we're here right now, and I want to know what it is."

Bringing his doleful eyes up to meet mine, he bites his lower lip. "I saw that cop grab you." He breathes in, and then out. "But I was busy finding a way out for myself. I was just going to let them arrest you."

"Why didn't you?"

A laugh devoid of any humor escapes him, as though this should be obvious. He stares out the opening in the top of the tower and into the night. When he speaks, his voice is quiet. "Because it was you." He says it as if this explains everything. "When he took his nightstick to you, I couldn't stop myself."

I reach around the back of my head and probe the bump gingerly. The cold air seems to be helping, but it's still swollen and painful. When I pull my fingers away, there are smears of partly dried blood on them. I stare at it, considering the implications of what he's said. "Why did you move out?"

"After you—" He wrings his hands together. "After you hit me at the theater, I realized that all of it was my fault. I deserved to get hit."

As much as I want to agree with him, I know it's not true. "You didn't deserve it. I was being an ass."

Smiling weakly, he says, "Maybe, but you were right. I owed it to you to stop screwing up your year abroad. That's why I left."

"Didn't do a very good job at staying away, did you?" I say, shivering from the cold stone beneath me. He gives me a sad look. He's really making it hard to stay angry with him. More softly this time, I venture an olive branch. "You didn't screw up my year."

He looks up, a flicker of hope kindling in the darkness. He stares at me for a full minute, as though he can divine the truth if only he observes me long enough. "How . . . how have you been the last few weeks?"

"It's been okay." I glance away. "Kind of rough, actually." After everything, it's still so hard for me to show him any weakness.

"I'm sorry," he says. "Do you want to talk about it?"

"I'm going to the doctor tomorrow." Wetness fills my eyes. Seems these days I can't hardly make it a week without crying.

"The doctor? What for?"

"I had unprotected sex with some guy. I'm going in to see if I can get tested for anything I might have gotten." My tone is flat, but in a messed up way I've been looking forward to telling him. To make him feel like it's his fault. Because it sort of is. At least, that's what I want to think. It's stupid, but it makes me feel better to blame it on him.

Daniel is silent for several seconds. His voice is guarded when he replies. "Did you know this guy?"

"We talked for about twenty minutes at the bar. Does that count?"

The low sound of a long exhaling breath bridges the distance be-tween us. "Ethan," he whispers. "Oh, Ethan."

Neither of us speaks for several minutes, but the cold is taking its toll on me. "How much longer should we stay?"

My question pulls him out of his pensive silence. "Another hour or so at least."

"That long?"

"To be safe, yeah." He waits for me to respond but when I don't, he asks, "Are you doing alright?"

I nod, but then concede, "I should have worn a jacket."

Fifteen minutes pass in silence, and the chill bores deeper into me, my teeth beginning to chatter of their own accord.

Daniel's voice glides through the darkness. "Is that your teeth?"

"Yeah-h-h," I say. "I'm fi-i-i-ne."

"Come over here."

I shake my head, causing my teeth to break their pattern like an irregular heart beat.

"Don't be stubborn, you're obviously freezing."

I wait another minute before I surrender to his logic and my cold-ness. I make as though to sit next to him, but he spreads his legs out and says, "No, right here."

If I weren't so cold, I wouldn't do it, but I know it will keep me that much warmer. "Okay." I set myself down between his legs, my back to him, with just a couple inches between us.

He unzips his jacket and wraps his arms around me, pulling me closer until my back is pressed firmly against his chest. The heat from him pours through his sweatshirt and into me. Letting myself relax, I lean my head back on his shoulder. From this angle, a smattering of stars is visible through the tower's opening. Tilting his head to the side, he presses his cheek against mine. His skin feels so hot that I pull away in surprise at first, only to melt back into him after a moment.

Even after my confession about hooking up with that guy, he's still here for me, holding me tight. I don't believe the love is really for me, but it's love he's showing me nonetheless.

I could use his support so much right now, but I want this night to be done with. I would gladly spend every minute of my year abroad with him, but I know it's going to end all too soon. Something changed between us that night at the theater, and it can never be the same. In another half hour, Daniel will decide it's safe to go back, and then he'll disappear from my life again. It's not a question; it's just the way it is.

The minutes tick past. Dreading that which I have no power to change is agonizing in the worst way. I wish it could be over right now, even if that means leaving Daniel's warm embrace. Even if it means this is the last time we see each other.

When he unwraps his arms from me, I know it's time. The moon has risen high into the sky, and the sounds of the city, initially distant but certainly present, have all but ceased. Leaning forward, I pull my knees up to my chest, feeling the cold rush in to steal the warmth from where our bodies made contact. The sound of his jacket zipper is the only noise besides the breeze. We aren't touching, but I'm still sitting between his outstretched legs.

He touches my shoulder. "Ethan."

"I know," I say. The vapor of my breath is barely visible in the darkness. It hurts, but I tell him what I know he's already thinking. "It's time to go, but we shouldn't be seen together, just in case. Probably best if we stay apart for a few weeks, maybe more. Am I right?" I wish I could keep him from hearing the bitterness in my words.

"It's not like that."

"Sure." It probably is wise to put some distance between us for a while because of what happened with the cop, but I know it's not the only reason he thinks it should happen.

"Come on, don't be like that."

"You disappeared, and now you're about to disappear again." I release a long, controlled breath. "It's best if you just get it over with. Go on, I'll make it home fine."

"Are you sure?"

"Yes," I whisper. "I'm sure." My head resting on my knees, a soft scraping on the stone is the only indication that he's moved. My eyes stay shut as he descends the stairs.

From the bottom, his voice echoes up off the sandstone. "Goodbye, Ethan."

After a while I start to get cold again, so I pick myself up, wipe away the moisture from my eyes and traipse down the stairs and outside. I press the metal door into the frame until the locking mechanism snaps into place, and I begin the walk home.

Chapter 34

It's afternoon, two days since the protest, and I've just gotten back from my second visit to the clinic. Everything they could test for came back negative, but they told me to get checked again in three months for the big question, which they can't test for right now, at least not reliably.

I'm not worried as much as I probably should be, considering the situation, but with everything else going on, it's too hard to focus on that. Which is a blessing, really.

I'm allowing myself a breath of relief when a harsh knocking on my door echoes around the room. *Jesus, what now?* I freeze and, for a moment, wildly consider not answering. Heart thundering in my chest, I open the door. A dark green uniformed police officer stands next to a man with suit pants and a woolen pea coat. The man's face is angular with a mustache, and his hair is dark and thick. He flashes his identification from a folding wallet with a badge and begins speaking rapid German. "I am Detective Kohler. Are you Ethan Matthew West, nineteen years old, American citizen?" He pronounces my last name like *vest*.

I stare dumbly at the two men, aware on some level that my identity has been reduced to a single sentence. My vision blurs momentarily like it does sometimes when my concentration in class starts to fade. "*Antworten Sie mir,*" Detective Kohler demands. *Answer me.* Everything snaps back into focus.

"Yeah, that's me."

The beat cop grabs my shoulder and turns me around roughly, snapping my wrists into handcuffs.

"You are under arrest for suspicion of inciting civil disobedience and resisting arrest." The detective recites this like an automaton, almost as if he's bored. "You have the right to remain silent. You have the right to consult an attorney. You have the right to name evidence in your favor. As a foreign citizen, you also have the right to consular assistance and translation assistance."

Now securely handcuffed, they lead me into the hallway, wearing only jeans and a white cotton undershirt. I stare at Kohler, resisting the urge to tell him what I think about his monologue of my rights. Behind him at the end of the hall, Florian's door is open an inch, just enough for him to see what's happening. "Have you understood everything that I have told you, or do you need translation assistance?"

"That won't be necessary," I say defiantly.

He raises his thin eyebrows. "Very well, then."

Before they have a chance to pull me away, I ask, "Can I put on my shoes at least?" The cop with his hand clamped around my arm glances at my bare feet and then to Kohler, who nods his assent. I'm led back to my room to slip on my shoes. "And my coat?"

"You won't be needing it," Kohler says brusquely, indicating with a tilt of his head that it's time to go.

Outside, they shove me in the back of their green and white police Volkswagen. A hard plastic bench takes the place of where the backseat should be. We pull away from building 52, but I refuse to look up at the balcony where I know at least two of my roommates are gathered.

I'm in a holding cell by myself. None of the other cells are filled. If they're out arresting everyone from the protest, why isn't there anyone else here? I cross my arms to fend off the chill. It doesn't help that I'm only wearing a t-shirt.

The second I recognize Detective Kohler coming around the corner, I unfold my arms. "Ethan West," he says from the other side of the bars. "Come with me."

The officer with him swings open the door and handcuffs me, giving me a toothy smile that isn't friendly at all. They lead me to a small room at the end of a hall around the corner. A rectangular privacy window near the ceiling lets in a modicum of natural light, while a panel of fluorescents supplies the rest.

The uniformed cop opens my handcuffs and exits the room, leaving me alone with Detective Kohler. Setting a folder carefully in front of himself, he takes a seat. "Ethan Matthew West, nineteen years old, American citizen, studying at the Albert-Ludwigs-Universität," he repeats his earlier sentence that he must think sums up who I am. "Do you know why you're here?"

If there was any doubt before, I'm now completely convinced this guy is a dick. A wall mounted camera stares at me from the corner of the room. Setting my hands palm down in front of me on the stainless steel table, I look him in the eye and repeat his sentence word for word from this morning. "For suspicion of inciting civil disobedience and resisting arrest." It's cold in here too, but a bead of sweat trickles under my arm. I don't smell that great anyway, because I hadn't showered before they showed up to arrest me.

Kohler gives me a tight smile. "Mr. West, let us speak frankly. I know you participated in the riot." He pulls a photo from his folder. It's a black and white still frame from a video surveillance camera. From the look of it, it's from a camera mounted on one of the police vans. It's when the cop first grabbed me, but my face is turned away from the camera. Having experienced the struggle as it happened, it's strange to look at a picture from this angle.

"Why do you think that's me?" I hold my voice steady.

The sickly sweet smile returns to his face as he pulls another photo from the folder. This one was taken a moment later when I shoved the cop to get away. My face is clearly visible, even at the distance from the vans. "That's not me."

"No?" he asks, his smile disappearing. "I quite think it is you, and I'm certain a judge would agree."

"So what do you want?"

"Very perceptive of you. As a matter of fact, I do want something." Kohler leans back. "We could drop these charges, let you finish the rest of your year here."

I refuse to take his bait, so I keep my mouth shut, pretending to be interested in a rogue hangnail on the side of my thumb.

He pulls out a third photo. "Tell us who this is, and I'll let you go." My fingers freeze mid-movement on my thumb. It's a picture of Daniel rushing out of the smoke before he struck the cop holding me.

In reality, it's a perfect shot of his face, but the cloth covering his nose and mouth to protect himself from the tear gas makes it impossible to identify him.

"I have no idea who that is. He just ran out of the crowd." I try to sound unconcerned. My lies need to be convincing. "Lucky for me that he did, but I suppose I'm here anyway. Sorry I can't help you."

The detective shifts position to cross his legs under the table. With a smug look still smeared across his face, he opens the folder and reveals one last photo. My heart sinks like an anchor slicing through frigid water.

The image is from after we ran across the square and stopped to catch our breath. The video camera that took this one wasn't as high quality, but it was a lot closer to us. Daniel's bandana is off here, but the camera is facing from behind us, so it could never have caught his face. It would make this photo useless, except that in this still shot, he's leaning over me as I'm doubled over. His hand is resting on my shoulder as he examines the wound on the back of my head. Any idiot could guess from our proximity and the intimacy of his touch that we know each other well.

Desperation and rage rise inside me simultaneously. For the first time I speak to the detective in English, "Did you fucking pull the footage from every camera at the university?"

Following me into English, his voice is smooth and metallic. "Almost the entire city in fact, but these are the only shots we have of either of you."

I force myself to breathe and regulate my anger. "Why do you even care? There were hundreds of students there for you to get convictions or whatever bullshit quota it is you're trying to fill."

"He struck one of my men." His tone cold and unfeeling, he abandons all pretense now. "Your violent friend put him in the hospital, and I'm going to make sure he's punished."

I stare at my hands. There's nothing I can do. It was hopeless from the beginning. This man is out for blood. Daniel's blood.

Scooping the photos up, Kohler deposits them back into the folder. When he speaks again, he's switched back to German. "Now you know my position, Mr. West. Give me the name of this man, and you will go free. Otherwise . . ." He trails, making his warning all the more ominous.

The threat to Daniel has lent me a steely composure. Glancing at the camera in the corner, I bring my gaze to bear against his, but I stay silent. His eyes narrow when I don't respond.

"You'll be prosecuted and deported. Are you really willing to give up your year abroad?" He taps each finger one at a time on the table. "I don't think that's what you want."

I clench my fists. "You have no idea what I want."

He chuckles mirthlessly. "No? I think I do, and I can tell you that a night here will do you good."

I force myself to ignore him and direct my gaze to the video camera in the corner. "I wish to exercise my right to consular assistance," I state clearly. Kohler snorts in derision and leaves the room, jerking his thumb in my direction on the way out. Not wasting any time, the waiting uniformed cop outside scuttles in to put my handcuffs back on.

I'm lying on the bed in my solitary holding cell when I hear a woman say my name. "Ethan?" I know she's American, because her English is perfect and clear.

My eyes flip open and are met by bright fluorescent lights and the gray tiled ceiling. She's wearing a conservative pantsuit and carrying a small briefcase, her blond hair pulled back into a bun. In fact, everything about her is innocuous and plain, except that she's beautiful. And there's a tiny American flag pin on her lapel.

"You're from the consulate?"

"That's right," she says. "My name is Jenna Carlson, consular officer, Frankfurt Consulate General."

Swinging my legs onto the floor, I sit up. "Thanks for coming."

"No problem. It's my job."

"Long drive, huh?" *Stupid question.*

She nods and gives me a brief smile. "Yes, we're the closest consulate I'm afraid, but I do like seeing Freiburg now and again." We stare at each other for a moment. "Are you comfortable?"

"Kind of cold, they wouldn't let me bring anything but this t-shirt."

She frowns. The expression of disapproval draws a new element into her appearance. There's a fierceness to her gaze that makes me believe someone will get an earful about my complaint. "I'll make sure that's taken care of. Anything else?"

"I have a few questions, I guess." We're still talking through the bars of the cell, our voices low even though no one else is here.

"I can't give you any legal advice," she warns.

"Yeah I figured, but just in general, what usually happens?"

Indecision plays across her lips, apparently over whether or not she should engage in this gray area. My eyes gazing up at her must push her to answer, because she lowers her voice until it's barely audible. "It isn't terribly bad what they are charging you with, but I've seen Americans deported for less. Unfortunately, they won't appoint you a court defender, because the crime isn't serious enough."

Looking nervously toward the door where the officer is stationed, she motions for me to come closer to the bars. In a way that can only be a result of working in a profession dealing daily with classified information, her voice becomes even quieter. "I would be careful and get a lawyer if you can afford it. They won't be lenient with your case because the officer involved was hurt badly." Jenna inhales swiftly, restoring the lost breath from her rapid talking, and smoothes the front of her suit. Resuming a conversational volume, she informs me that I won't be released until the following morning. "Unfortunately, you have no choice but to spend the night here."

Hands wrapped around the bars, I drop my head down. "That's it then, I suppose."

Jenna smiles weakly. "It's the best I can do. I'll see that you get something to stay warmer in here."

"Thanks," I murmur as she turns to go.

"Good luck, Ethan."

Her retreating form disappears behind the security door at the end of the row of cells. The watch from Daniel is still wrapped around my wrist. It's a comforting thought that he's somehow here with me. Then I remember the scratch. I run my finger along the rough line. It's more like a gouge than a scratch; it's deep and crosses the bottom third of the glass.

I'm sure the crystal face is replaceable, probably an easy fix even. It would be as simple as taking it in to a jewelry shop, but something deeper is bothering me about it than the fact that it's damaged.

Just because it *could* be repaired, does that mean it should be? What if there is a reason it got scratched? More than just an unlikely push and an unluckier landing. Maybe fate is simply needling me, reminding me that even though this gift came from Daniel, it was really meant for Marc. If he hadn't died, would Daniel have gotten the watch for him instead? In a way, the timepiece is like our friendship—similarly invaluable but ultimately ruined by an inherent flaw.

* * *

My back and neck are stiff from sleeping overnight in the holding cell bed, and the bump on my head is still sore. At least I wasn't cold last night. One of the cops brought me a blanket after Jenna left, and surprisingly he wasn't a complete asshole about it. I imagine calm and composed Jenna bringing out the claws and tearing those idiot cops a new one. Probably didn't happen like that though.

I feel like hell, but I wait without complaint, knowing they can't keep me in here forever. Eventually Kohler strides down the row of cells, a mug of coffee in hand. Steam rises from the surface of the black liquid.

He taps his fingers one at a time along the cell bars just like he did on the table yesterday. Leaning in, he says, "I'm going to let you out. Take a few days to think about whether you're willing to throw away the second half of your year abroad to protect someone who attacked a police officer." He produces a key and unlocks the door. Holding it open for me, he adds, "Don't try to travel before you make up your mind."

I walk past him and down the hall toward the exit. I've almost reached the door when he calls down the row of cells. "If you don't help us, you *will* be deported. I promise."

Clenching my teeth, I ignore him and pass through the door into the lobby.

"Ethan!" Niko jumps up from a bench against the opposite wall and throws his arms around me. "Thank God you're alright."

Despite everything, his concern puts a smile on my face. "Yeah, I'm okay. How did you know I was here?"

He releases me and backs off a bit. "You don't smell so good." He makes a face. "I stopped by your building when you wouldn't return my calls yesterday, and Florian told me you'd been arrested. What happened?"

I shake my head and exhale a drawn-out breath, from which Niko backs away. "Long story. Let's get out of here so I can explain."

"Okay, sure." Letting me go ahead of him, I notice him glare at the pair of officers at the front desk as we pass.

"How long have you been waiting here?"

"Almost two hours, but they wouldn't let me see you." Niko kicks the toe of his shoe at the rug in front of the entry. "It wasn't until I started threatening to report them to the EU for abusive process that they took me seriously. I don't think they would have let you out so soon otherwise."

Still only wearing my white t-shirt, I hold the door for him with a preemptive shiver as we pass into the cold but sunny morning. I have to admit that I'm impressed with his persistence, and I tell him so.

"I'm Polish," he says, as though that explains everything.

I frown, not understanding what he means.

He shrugs. "In Poland, sometimes you have to push to get things done."

I get the feeling he's making a huge understatement.

We wait for the Strassenbahn in silence, and when it comes we take seats next to each other in the back. I explain everything that happened since the night of the riot, which I already told him about the day after.

I finish, but Niko remains quiet. The Strassenbahn rumbles to a stop that isn't either of ours, each of the cars shuddering as they cross an uneven section of track. Finally, he says, "I don't know what to tell you."

"I need to get a lawyer."

He looks at me hopefully, like maybe it's possible to fight this. "Where are you going to get the money for one?"

My watch is heavy around my wrist, exposed as it is on my bare arm. "I think I have an idea, but I also need your help to get a hold of someone." I give him a meaningful look.

Chapter 35

Whenever I imagined myself finally exploring the interior of Freiburg's impressively massive Münster cathedral, Niko was always with me. Now entering the square surrounding the edifice, I find myself missing him. At the very least, he would undoubtedly have plenty of obscure facts to share. I could have asked him to come along, and I'm sure he would have, but this is something I need to do alone.

The spire stretches far above my peripheral vision as I approach, mingling with the twilight of early evening. Once again I'm impressed by the exquisite stonework latent in every facet of the structure. Multi-layered channels forming a pointed archway at the entrance, I draw open the reinforced wooden door that's twice my height and step inside for the first time.

The interior is crafted with an equal attention to detail that has weathered the centuries gracefully. Rows of pews stretch toward the front, their pattern periodically disrupted by the colossal columns that support the roof. At this time in the evening on a Tuesday, tourists are few. The scent of old stone and unmitigated silence mingle as I take slow steps toward the front, finally seating myself on the smooth dark wood of a pew.

Closing my eyes, I let go of what feels like the most difficult breath of my life. The lawyer's words echo in my mind. "If you don't give up your friend, there's nothing I can do to stop your deportation." He didn't understand why I wouldn't do it. I didn't bother trying to explain that I couldn't do that to Daniel any more than I could cut off my own hand. It would be unthinkable.

I can't believe this is how it's going to end. The year abroad I always dreamed about—the joy and the sadness and everything in between, the drunken nights and hours of studying, the sensation of German words rolling off my tongue as fast as I can speak them—all of it was leading up to . . . *this*?

At the beginning of the year I had all the time in the world, or at least it felt that way. There was no reason to appreciate every individual moment, because there was always the promise of hundreds more. No pressure at the back of my mind, telling me to remember every minute with the people dear to me and to be thankful for each of them. And after Daniel and I got close, time only moved faster, fusing into a collection of months and weeks and evenings and disappearing seconds.

At the far end of the pew, a girl about my age sits down. Our eyes meet briefly, allowing a second of silent communication to pass between us before we both look away. I wonder what she's going through that drew her into the Münster. Whatever it is, I'm certain it's completely unlike my problems.

Why did I have to fall in love with him? Why couldn't we just have been friends? Everything could have been so much easier. Yet I wonder if I had the chance to go back and change everything, would I?

Pushing past my anger, which is still very much alive, I try to remember all the hours we spent together. Riding on the back of his motorcycle, creating a beer rainforest on the stairs, or hearing about Marc over half a bottle of apple schnapps—the more I think about the friendship we built, a single emotion begins to block out all the rest. Thankfulness. And as much as I resent it, I can't deny its existence. At least until I come to the memory of discovering the photo of Marc.

Bringing a hand to my face, I massage my temples with my thumb and ring finger. Will my feelings about Daniel ever be anything but a tangled mess? Taking a deep breath, I look around to make sure no one is paying attention to me. It's so empty in here, barely anyone is even close enough to see me withdraw a book from my backpack. Just one journal section remains in the leather-bound Bible, and in it the resolution to Magdalena's efforts and what might be the true story of the student resistance in Freiburg, a resistance lost to history.

October 15, 1942. The trial took place at ten o'clock in the morning.

The evidence was damning, but not once did Thomas mention my name, nor where the leaflets had been printed. I considered coming forward, in hopes of helping reduce his sentence. In the end, I said nothing. Yet it was not out of cowardice that I did not join my beloved Thomas on the stand today. He would not have wanted that, because he knew as I did that the Nazis do not give, they only take. They would have gladly sent us both to our deaths.

If our positions had been reversed, and in fact I do very much wish they were, I would have wanted for him to do the same, to protect himself and survive.

The trial concluded speedily in the afternoon with a guilty verdict. They took Thomas to the university square where he was summarily executed by guillotine. There are no words that can describe my pain as his blood spattered on the stone.

December 5, 1942. My hatred for the Reich is nothing compared to the love I will always have for you, my Thomas. Today I leave Freiburg, perhaps never to return, as I cannot bear the thought of ever again walking these streets without you. We will never again walk hand in hand, but you will always be in my heart. —Magdalena Ernst

I slowly close the book. *Holy shit.* I almost wish I hadn't read the end.

Were her efforts a waste? What about Thomas? Is his sacrifice to be simply forgotten, the only record of it buried in the binding of an aging Bible? I'd like to believe that a greater importance lies in what we do, an importance that extends beyond being recognized by others for our deeds. But if they're ultimately forgotten anyway, how much can they really matter? The thought that the history of Magdalena and Thomas might one day disappear completely strikes me as tragic.

Avoiding the main streets that carve through the Altstadt, I let my feet carry me away from the Münster. The dismal end to Magdalena's account weighs on my shoulders along with everything else that has happened, threatening to crush me. My plodding steps through the empty alleys lead me toward the university. Passing the buildings on the periphery, I cross into the sprawling courtyard at its heart.

Coming to a stop in the very center, I close my eyes and call forward the memories of all the times I've been here over the last six months. So much has happened in this square. Beyond the countless occasions I came here after class or to meet with Daniel or Niko, this was where the protest against the student fee was finally put down.

And now I know it's also where Thomas was executed. My stomach twists uncomfortably.

Taking a deep breath, I open my eyes. I want to go home, but whatever has drawn me to this spot tonight isn't quite ready to let me leave yet. What else can there be here? The square is deserted.

Circling along the outer edge, I finally come to the spot where Daniel and I rested after escaping from the riot. The memory is still so fresh in my mind. Leaning up against the reddish, flat stone in the same place I did that day, I reach out a hand and touch it to the cool surface. It's the spot where Daniel stood beside me. My throat and chest feel tight.

Across the alley, a metallic gleaming attracts my attention. A metal plate or something is mounted about eight feet up, catching the illumination of a solitary streetlight. Moving closer, I can tell it's a plaque. How have I never noticed it before? Angling my perspective so the bronze reflects the light, I read the four words engraved into it: PLATZ DER WEISSEN ROSE.

I'm taken by a sudden flare of realization. Freiburg's university courtyard is named the *Square of the White Rose*. Can it really be? Despite the tragic end to their story, I manage to smile. However the dedication and naming of this place were accomplished doesn't matter, because it's confirmation enough that the story of Thomas and Magdalena hasn't been lost. It might not be common knowledge, it might not even be officially recorded anywhere, but *someone* has made the point that what happened here seventy years ago must not be forgotten.

Chapter 36

Under my coat is a thick sweater, but my feet are cold. The ice on the lake at the heart of the Seepark has receded to a jagged frosting around the edges, but tonight is unusually chilly. When the wind picks up, it steals my warmth from between the slats of the bench. Pulling down my hood to clear my peripheral vision, I take in the sight of the stars' wavering reflections on the lake's surface.

I've waited too long. I should leave before it gets any colder. No light shines down from the new moon, so it's just me and the stars out tonight. Around a bend in the lake, movement catches my eye. A shifting in the darkness confirms someone is coming down the path. The hairs on the back of my neck bristle, and the wind manages to work its way between them, too.

Daniel emerges from the cloak of night, the bench creaking as he takes a seat next to me.

"I was starting to think you wouldn't come," I say.

Neither of us looks at the other, our gaze fixed firmly on the lake. "I wasn't sure I was going to."

"I'm glad you did."

"Your trip to the doctor?"

"Negative for everything they can test for right now." The rest of my sentence doesn't need to be said.

"I'm glad." He sounds relieved. "But then why did you ask me here? Niko said it was urgent."

"He told you what happened?"

"Said you were arrested, something about security footage from the university square, that was about it." He pauses, then breathes, "I'm really sorry." Our conversational tones contrast with what we're discussing. Only a hint of tension that neither of us can hide intertwines itself with our words.

"I'm being deported," I say after a moment of hesitation, wishing so much that it weren't true.

"What?" Daniel exclaims, abandoning his calm demeanor. "Just for being at the protest? You can fight it, Ethan. Of course you can fight it." He's speaking fast, like he's explaining the plan of action more to himself than me. "We'll get you a lawyer, a really good lawyer. We'll get this fixed, don't worry."

It would be so easy to believe him if I hadn't already spent the last week making absolutely certain that what he's describing is impossible. "I already have a lawyer." My hand sneaks to my left wrist, massaging the bare skin there.

"You do? Then why are you being deported?"

The wind picks up again, distorting the image of the stars glistening on the surface of the water. Tugging my hood back over my head, I say quietly, "The lawyer worked out a deal that would have made it so all the charges against me would be dropped, but—" I hesitate, unsure how to say this. "I declined."

"Why didn't you take it?" Daniel almost shouts in exasperation.

I look away, scanning the curve of the winding path around the tip of the lake. "They wanted something I couldn't give."

"What did they want? My God, Ethan, don't be stupid. Do whatever they want but don't let them send you away." I wince when he calls me stupid.

Shifting to face him, I wait until he turns to meet my gaze. In the absence of light, the deep tempest blue of his eyes that I love so much blends with the night. His hair is longer now. It's starting to curl even, and a handful of the wavy strands catch the wind. "They wanted you," I whisper.

"Ethan, I . . ." his voice fades as the revelation sinks in. If we weren't mere inches apart, I would never have seen the cascade of shifting emotions pour through him in the intervening seconds. At last he says, "I'll turn myself in tomorrow morning."

It's strange how quickly he came to that conclusion. It was almost faster than when I decided I could never give him up. I place my hand on top of his. "I've made my decision. I told the prosecutor I wouldn't do it. I've already rebooked my ticket home."

His voice is colored by shades of disbelief. "You'd sacrifice all of this? Your year abroad, just to protect me? Why did you come to Germany, Ethan? Because it wasn't so you could get sent home like this."

His words bite, but he has a point. Why am I doing it, really? I've made it clear I don't believe him, at least not entirely, that our friendship hasn't been heavily influenced by my resemblance to this brother. So why stick by him at all? I think it's because as angry as I am, I still don't want to see any harm come to him. Whether I get deported or he gets sent to jail, I'm still going to lose him. The only choice I have now is to protect him or not.

It makes me feel immature to admit this, but I decide to answer his question anyway. "I always dreamed of studying here, ever since my first day in high school German class. Our teacher made Germany sound so exotic and wonderful. For some reason I always thought there was something special waiting for me here." I pause, allowing myself a moment of regret at my decision to leave. "But that obviously wasn't true." I curl my fingers into fists to stave off the cold.

His voice is thoughtful. "Are you so sure?"

I don't know if it's a real question, but I'm afraid to respond. Instead, I pull out the Bible from the cavernous inside pocket of my coat. Setting it on the bench between us, I slide it over a few inches until it touches his jeans. Now it's my turn to pose a question. "You've read the story hidden inside, I assume?"

"Yes," his tone is cautious. "I've read it. I wasn't sure you'd discovered it."

My nod is lost in the darkness. "You remember Thomas, the one who got caught and beheaded? He never gave her up, even though it might have saved his life."

He exhales slowly. "Their story isn't our story. And this situation is completely different."

"Is it really so different?" When he doesn't answer, I press on, "Where did you get that Bible anyway?"

I can barely see it, but I know well the sheepish look he's wearing. Even so, his voice echoes a reluctance to change topics. "*Uncle* in Magdalena's story was my great-uncle Eugen. He was the Stuttgart businessman who financially supported the White Rose in Munich until they were discovered and executed. But unlike his support of the movement in Munich, his involvement in Freiburg was never public knowledge. My family found the history hidden in the Bible long after the war. We can only guess why he never mentioned his connection with Magdalena."

Any doubt regarding the veracity and authenticity of the account in the Bible is obliterated by his explanation. "Maybe he felt guilty over Thomas' death."

"Yes, that's possible," he says quickly. "Can we please talk about the present? There must be something I can do."

"Daniel, I told that prosecutor to go to hell. There's nothing more you can do. Coming forward won't do anything now except land you in jail. I'll probably still get sent home either way."

He looks at me helplessly. "I could get my dad to use his government contacts to intervene."

"No, you can't," I say in exasperation. "Don't you see that? It would be too easy for them to figure out you're the one they're looking for if you get involved at all, especially if your dad starts pulling strings."

"I don't know what to do."

It takes all my effort not to be overcome by his willingness to sacrifice himself just so I can stay in Germany. I have to remind myself that in some strange way he must still be trying to protect his brother—or the idea of him. It's almost like he's seeking atonement for being missing when he was needed most. Why else would he risk so much?

I stand up to go. "You do nothing. That's all you can do."

"Don't leave," he manages to say before his voice breaks.

It hurts to see him in pain, so I sit down again. As I do, the same question I've asked myself time and again for weeks whispers itself in my mind. Who is he really afraid to lose? "I have to."

"I could come with you," he pleads. "I could enroll at a university in America, we could make it work. Please, Ethan." His expression betrays how much he wants me to say yes. There's hope there, and that rare vulnerability that's uniquely his. "I don't want to lose you." In his last utterance, I find the confirmation to my fear.

I want to agree and tell him yes, yes! But I can't. There is a driving force in him just like in me, but he isn't motivated by passion. His need is different than mine. As much as I want to go along with what he's saying, a certain part of me knows I will never be happy if I do, spending my days so close to him yet never being truly satisfied. I need to stop this before he does something he regrets.

Tentatively reaching out, I place my hand on his chest over his heart. I can feel its beat, his pectoral muscles contoured under my fingers. He doesn't pull away or try to move my hand. In his beating heart, I find my answer. "You don't know what I would do to keep you in my life, Daniel, but it would never work," I say quietly.

The words slip from his mouth. "I can't live without you, Ethan." I wince and drop my hand from his chest, but his words keep coming. "I don't know how or why, but I can't. It's different than what you feel for me, but it's real."

I shake my head, refusing what he's telling me. "No, Daniel, it's not."

Now it's his turn to be taken aback. The hurt apparent on his face almost stops me from saying what I'm about to. Almost. "Everything that you've done for me, everything that you've said—" I stop abruptly, holding my breath, but I have to say it.

"Daniel, the way you treat me, I might as well *be* Marc. Except I'm not. You say you care about me, but whatever you feel, it's really just for him. I know it whenever you look at me, whenever you speak to me. It's like he's standing in the background, and you're seeing right through me. I'm stuck between you two. At first I didn't understand, but now it's so clear. All the time we've spent together, everything that's happened—it's all been for him."

I sigh, dropping my gaze to the ground before recovering. "I just don't believe that any of this has ever been about anyone other than you and Marc."

In a strangely childish gesture, he slides his hands underneath his thighs and looks up at me. When he speaks, it's with a decided resignation, as though he knows he could never convince me otherwise. "You're not being fair." He holds my eyes like I'm the only person he's ever known. Slowly and softly, he says, "Sometimes it's hard to separate my feelings for you and Marc, but they *are* different. You're the most important person in the world to me."

I want to believe him. It would be so easy, so comforting. But it would be all wrong. I could never forgive myself for giving in right now. My tone hardens. "I know you're not into guys, so the only other possibility is that I've been filling the gap your brother left."

The look in his eyes defies the logic I've thrown at him. There's no convincing him. My voice is harsh as it lashes out, "If it's true what you say, then prove that what you feel is for *me* and couldn't possibly be for Marc."

Stung and staring into his lap, he says, "I don't think I can."

"I know," I whisper. Standing, I turn and walk away, leaving him alone in the dark.

Chapter 37

Wind whipping as I wait on the platform for the express train, I zip up my jacket a little farther and adjust my backpack, remembering uncomfortably how cold I was on top of the Schlossberg a month ago. Perfectly on schedule, the behemoth machine glides to a stop, spanning the entire length of the platform normally long enough for two trains.

Immediately after I board, the doors slide shut with a definitive thud. This train won't stop again until it's far from Freiburg. As it gains speed, I find an empty cabin and take the seat by the window. We're going faster, still accelerating, and the trees fly past as flashes of color.

My last trip to the police station, accompanied by my lawyer, was mostly painless. Detective Kohler wasn't even there. In exchange for voluntarily leaving the country, I was only charged with promoting public disturbance, whatever that means. I had to fork over two hundred euro and my visa was revoked, but I wasn't banned from returning to Germany in the future.

It happened so quickly and then it was done. The cold and methodical way the cops processed everything belied the gravity—at least to me—of what was happening. It might have been routine for them, but the whole affair turned my life to shambles. Mom doesn't even know I'm coming home.

Saying goodbye to Niko was almost harder than my last conversation with Daniel. He held me for a full minute, and his eyes were wet when we separated. When I told him how much I'd miss him, he said he knew we'd see each other again. I want to believe him.

Clutching my bag, I let the sadness spill into me. I'm leaving for real. After all the work to get here, my year of studying abroad has to end like this. Thankfully I'm alone in the cabin, so I can release what's held inside. Regret and sorrow pour through me as the shining Inter-city Express crosses Germany at one hundred fifty miles per hour.

My eyes are no longer red by the time the train arrives at the Frankfurt Airport, but it's with forced determination that I sling the bag over my shoulder and alight onto the platform. Everyone rushes off the train, scurrying like mice to get to their flights on time. I can barely find the strength to move forward, but I have to. It takes all my effort to make it to the escalator connecting the high-speed rail plat-form to the terminal. The rising staircase pulls me toward something I can't bear to do.

My steps are labored after I make it to the top. Then I see him. He's right there, standing in the crowd. I do a double take, making sure my mind isn't starting to deceive me as well.

He's scanning the crowd, looking for someone. For me. Our gazes meet, and from those eyes I know so well, a rush of silent words pours out. His regret for what happened, his wish for it all to be different, his fondness for our friendship and for . . . me.

He breaks our connection to cut his way through the crowd, final-ly coming to stop in front of me.

"Why are you here?" My voice is tired. I can't do this anymore.

Reaching into his pocket, he withdraws an envelope and holds it out to me.

"What is that?" Still no answer.

Our fingers make the briefest contact as I take it. Inside is a return ticket to Minneapolis, much like the one already in my possession, but with one small change. It's dated for five months from now. There's no use asking another question that won't be answered, so I wait.

"I'm going to turn myself in," he says, glancing down at my hands still holding the envelope. "My family keeps a lawyer on retainer. He's good. He got the local prosecutor to agree to drop the charges and de-portation proceedings in exchange for whoever actually hit that cop."

Could it really be that he'd do that for me? After all the effort to protect him, he somehow managed to turn it around. He's willing to go to jail for me. Or for Marc. It's the old question, the same one I've had to ask myself during our every interaction since seeing the photograph.

"Daniel," I sigh, my shoulders slumping under the weight of my backpack. "You have to stop this. It's not fair to me, or to him. Or to you, even. You'll be sent to jail if you do this."

"I *want* to do this. For you."

My voice is almost lost in the noise of the train station. "I get it." And I do. His eyes rise to mine, as if to see if I really mean it. I pause, holding myself together while I say what I need to. "It's not right the way you treated me these last months, but if I'd lost someone the way you did, I might have done the same thing."

"I'm so sorry, Ethan." Regret taints his expression. "But don't go."

He doesn't understand. It would never work for me to stay. Not because of the German government's vendetta against me, but because my love for him is one that will never fade to friendship. I step a little closer, reach down, and give his hand a squeeze. His eyes are hopeful. The thrum of energy between us is stronger than I've ever felt it. I swallow hard.

"Daniel, I can't be what you need me to be." And he can't be what I need either.

From his hurt expression, I can tell he's not letting me go that easily. He knows that I'm attracted to him, probably even believes I love him, so why doesn't he see that's all I'm ever going to want? Anything less would be living a lie, and it would be wrong. "How is it that you still don't understand?"

"I want to." His voice is husky.

"It's been right in front of you all along, but you always pushed me away when I tried to show you."

His eyes gaze deep into mine. "Show me now," he whispers.

Is he really saying what I think he is? I swallow, and my lower lip trembles. "Do you know what you're asking?"

"I know," he says softly.

After everything that's happened, I don't know if I can do this. Does he actually need this to understand why I can't stay? Or is this his way of giving me the chance to finally show him how much he really means to me? Maybe it doesn't really matter.

"I'm going to do this just once and then never again," I breathe.

He blinks once slowly, and in that action I can feel his acceptance for whatever comes next.

Despite the noise and chaos all around, the air between us is still, poised in anticipation. He steps closer, and my hands rise to touch him, my palms pressing against his neck and jaw. He leans in as I pull him toward me and part his lips with mine.

His touch is warm and firm against my face. I venture an exploratory nip of my tongue against his, then again, more audacious this time, drawing him deeper in. Not resisting or holding back, he gives of himself just as he's giving me this minute, letting it be mine and only mine. Not his, and not Marc's.

My mind empties of every conscious thought, consumed completely by what's happening. For the very first time, my actions aren't rushed or colored by shame. They simply *are*. There's no need for concessions or apologies.

This is the kiss that ended prematurely in the forested hills of the Schlossberg, and it's a hundred others that never happened. Into it I channel every atom of my love for him, for every second that we were together and for a million more when we weren't.

He mirrors my advance without the slightest hint of hesitation or withholding any of himself. Yet at a certain level, his touch isn't filled with the same chords of ardor and passion that I've stopped trying to hold in check. Like a swelling tide, I let everything I feel for him flow through me. For these brief seconds, he's mine, the way I used to want him.

Used to. The realization catches me by surprise.

Reigning myself in, I'm the one to finally break the contact, and I slide my hands down his neck and onto his shoulders. He gives me a shy smile, flicking his eyes to the side before resting them back on me, as if to ask if he did okay.

In that moment, all the anger and hurt still bottled inside me since discovering the photo of his brother drain away. For the first time, I can see the whole picture. One where there's room inside him for both Marc and me.

It's clear to me now that he didn't need me to show him anything. He knew all along. I drop my hands from his shoulders with a rush of sadness—not for the fleeting taste of the romance that could never be, but because this really is goodbye.

"You're not going to stay, are you?" His melancholy expression deepens with each passing second.

If the intensity of the kiss proved anything to either of us, it was that I could never be his Marc, and I would regret taking his offer to stay from the minute I agreed. There's so much to say, but I can't find the words. "Daniel . . . Marc's not coming back." I exhale slowly. "And neither can I."

I'm not sure what I expected from him, but the heartache in his expression is so complete I'm afraid it might swallow him whole. At first I wonder where his sadness is coming from, but the eyes that I know so well betray him. The kiss a minute ago, that was for me. But this look is for Marc. From the depth of his distress, it's almost like Daniel is losing his brother for a second time. That I'm the cause of his pain is almost too much to bear. He never got closure the first time, and now it's happening all over again. I can see the tumultuous waves of emotion crashing against the shores of his self-control.

I can't leave him like this. What would I do? Just walk away, check myself through security, and get on my flight? I might have been that selfish once, but I could never do that to him now.

He opened himself up to give me what I needed, probably violating every ounce of reason in the process. But I couldn't do the same for him, could I? The moment the idea surfaces, every part of me rebels against it, but somehow it still feels *right*. An unsettled feeling grips my stomach. I can do this. For him, I can do this. Is this how Daniel felt when he asked me to kiss him?

Unbuckling the strap across my chest, I let the backpack slide off my shoulders and fall to the ground. Confusion joins the aching sadness in his face.

I step closer to him once more, my voice quiet. "None of it was ever your fault, Daniel." I give him a moment to realize what I'm talking about. "It's okay to let him go. He'll still be with you always. In here," I say, picking up his hand and placing it over his chest. "But you have to let him go."

His eyes search mine, delving so deep I'm convinced he's going to brush up against my soul. "I don't know how," he murmurs, his words fragile.

"Say goodbye," I tell him, not looking away. I let my expression fill with the innocence that was once mine and the youth that still is.

A shadow of uncertainty across his face lasts only a second before being replaced by understanding and recognition. His mouth opens slightly, a flood of words so close to the surface. Without further hesitation he wraps his arms around me, pulling me into a grip so tight it's hard to breathe.

Our cheeks touching, he begins a steady stream of German in his native dialect he never uses with me. His voice dips lower as he continues, getting throatier as he releases everything that's been stuck inside him for the last eighteen months. Between the speed and the dialect, it's hard to understand what he's saying, but mostly I'm not trying to. I know his words aren't for me.

Finally, the flow of his sentences slows, and he whispers one last thing in my ear before letting me go. *"Ich liebe dich, mein Brüderle."* This I understand perfectly. *I love you, little brother.*

His face is red and filled with tears, but the storm of hurt inside him just a few minutes ago is gone. Wiping at his eyes with his sleeve, he takes a deep breath, regaining some of his composure. I'm sure he still has a long way to go, but the dam has finally broken.

He glances at the floor. Embarrassment and gratitude mingle together in a combination I've never heard before. "Ethan, I—"

I give my head a small shake to stop his words. He doesn't need to explain anything.

An hour ago I was convinced we would never see each other again. Now I'm not so sure. So many things didn't turn out the way I expected.

Clearing his throat, he says, "I almost forgot. There's one more thing." From his pocket, he pulls out the watch he gave me for Christmas, holding it out to me. Niko must have told him where we pawned it.

Face smoldering, my fingers are hesitant to reach for it. Pawning the watch was something I've regretted every single day, but there wasn't any other choice, at least not at the time. As if he can hear my thoughts, he smiles almost imperceptibly.

I take the clinking metal band from him and press the clasp together around my wrist. It still fits perfectly, not that it wouldn't, since it was only out of my possession for two weeks. The scratch across the face hasn't changed a bit, but it doesn't bother me as much anymore.

Daniel looks thankful that I've accepted it. "Hold on to it this time, okay?"

My gaze travels from the face of the watch to meet his eyes. It must just be the rays of sun falling in from the skylights, but their distant grayish blue color, always reminiscent of an impending storm, seems lighter than before.

A familiar feeling tugs at the back of my throat, and a part of me wants to reach back out and touch him. Another, now wiser part knows that will never happen again. Some things are meant to happen just once and live on only in our memories. Others—I glance to the timepiece on my wrist—are meant to stay with us always, despite their flaws.

Did you enjoy this book?

If you did, please consider leaving a review at an online retailer, Goodreads, or even a forum or blog. Word of mouth is important to any book's success, but especially for Indie books that don't have the hefty resources of a publishing company behind them!

Chase Potter lives in St. Paul, Minnesota with his husband Mitchell and their dog Alex in an aging duplex they're slowly working to rehabilitate. Although he has felt driven to write from a young age, *The Race for Second* is his first novel. Growing up in rural Minnesota, Chase has also lived in Germany and Austria, and he has spent time in Switzerland and France. Both the feelings of isolation growing up in a small town and his struggles to adapt to foreign culture and language have served as inspiration in his writing. He loves biking, swimming, road trips, and of course, German beer. In addition to English, he speaks German and French.

Made in the USA
Lexington, KY
22 August 2016